FREEDOM OF THE SONG

FREEDOM OF THE SONG

PHYLLIS CLARK NICHOLS

THORNDIKE PRESS
A part of Gale, a Cengage Company

LIBRARY OF CONGRESS CIP DATA ON FILE.
CATALOGUING IN PUBLICATION FOR THIS BOOK
IS AVAILABLE FROM THE LIBRARY OF CONGRESS

ISBN-13: 978-1-4328-7810-8 (hardcover alk. paper)

Published in 2020 by arrangement with Gilead Publishing, LLC

Printed in Mexico
Print Number: 01   Print Year: 2020

*For my astonishingly gifted friends
Camille Simmons and Letha Crouch,
who have made music with their
lives, who have experienced with
me that indescribable joy of
making music together,
who have shared with me their hearts
and their remarkable songs of faith,
and who know the freedom not just of the
song but of the Singer.*

CHAPTER ONE:
EVIL NEVER SLEEPS

Gretchen knew there would be trouble with her drunken husband if she didn't get Bella out of the room. The smallest thing could set him off, and Bella didn't seem able to stop her humming. Gretchen's hands trembled as she nudged Bella into the bedroom and closed the door. She walked to the dresser for the hairbrush. "Sit on your bed, Bella, and I will brush your hair. Let's be quiet. Listen for the crickets and the owl."

With her back turned, Bella sat on the edge of the bed for their nightly ritual, and Gretchen sat beside her. The brush glided through her granddaughter's hair as easily as the October breezes came through the bedroom window. Gretchen's pulse began to slow as the sounds from the television were replaced by the night sounds of crickets and Bella's quieted breathing.

Before Gretchen could say a prayer of thanks for one more confrontation avoided,

Ernesto crashed through the door. "I told you and that crazy brat not to walk away from me."

Gretchen jumped, trying to shield Bella from what was to come . . . what always came.

His rough hand shot out and snatched a fist full of silken strands of Bella's platinum hair. He backhanded Gretchen as he yanked Bella from the bed.

Bella screamed and wrenched as he pulled her toward the bedroom door. Her hands covered her face and muffled her cries. "Mammá, Mammá!"

Gretchen, reeling from her husband's strike, rose from the bed with the stealth of a large cat surveying her prey. Her face was still and resolute, her gaze on him intense. Greasy dark hair and three-day-old gray stubble could not mask the meanness in his face. His Anderson Trucking shirt, unchanged since Wednesday, was unbuttoned and exposed years of gluttony.

The stench of his cheap liquor infused Gretchen with rage. Her pulse raced again as she regained her balance. Mysterious strength, fueled from fear and anger, rose in her. Her granddaughter, Bella, was in the grasp of his grimy, hateful hands. *Not this time. Not my Bella.*

"Mammá!" Bella screamed.

"Shut up, you little blonde freak. Shut up, I said." He let go of Bella's hair, then backhanded her, knocking her against the bed. "If you had just shut up when I told you to, I wouldn't have to do this."

Bella fell to the floor. Eyes closed tightly, she curled into a fetal position on the hand-tied rug and whimpered. "Mammá."

Ernesto stumbled as he kicked the young girl in the face. Regaining his stance, he reached for his belt buckle.

Gretchen controlled her urge to pounce. Every movement of muscle as she inched toward the dresser was deliberate and calculated. With a voice as calm and determined as her movement, she called to her grandchild, "Bella. Get up, Bella, and run to Caroline's." The hand mirror on the dresser was almost within her reach. "Go, Bella. Caroline is playing the piano. Go now."

Ernesto glared at Gretchen and loosened his belt, staggering toward her as he clutched the metal buckle, one of dozens he had purchased as souvenirs at truck stops when he was on the road.

Gretchen shuddered at the memory of the wounds their sharp edges inflicted upon her. *This is the last time.* She clenched the cold handle of the ornate, silver-framed hand mirror. It was the only genteel thing left in her life, the last tangible tie to home, her Austrian birthplace, and to her own grand-mammá. With it firmly in her grasp, she screamed, "Bella, run to Caroline!"

Ernesto loomed between Bella and the bedroom door. Paying no heed to her bleeding face, the girl scrambled up and across the bed to the window on the other side. Gretchen had opened it earlier so that Bella could hear the hoot owl in the woods across the street and to let the October breezes freshen the room as they sat on the bed for their nightly hair brushing. Earlier in the spring, Bella had crawled out this window many times late at night, walking the short distance to sit secretly in the Meadows' garden while Caroline played the piano.

Drunk, but not too drunk to know that Bella was escaping, Ernesto lunged across the bed for her. His gruff hands reached for her adolescent body but caught only the lacy hem of her nightgown, a handmade Christmas present from her mammá. "Come back, you little embarrassing mis-fit . . ."

Bella heaved her body through the window opening and pulled her gown from his grasp with a rip. Gretchen bit her lip when she saw the protruding nail in the window casing cut Bella's leg. *Please, God, don't let the pain stop her.* But Bella froze. Her delicate fingers gripped the window ledge, and she hung suspended just above the straw-covered ground behind the bank of azaleas. The look of fear in Bella's face pierced Gretchen's heart. "Let go, Bella. Let go."

Ernesto was face down on the bed, his unsightly belly contaminating the quilt she and Bella had made at their safe place in the woods. Holding his belt in one hand and the torn piece of Bella's gown in the other, he struggled to turn over.

Gretchen stood behind him with her right arm raised. She caught sight of Bella's bloody face in the hand mirror she gripped and heard her Bella's whimpering. "Mammá. Mammá."

Ernesto's brutality had finally snuffed out Gretchen's gentle nature when he grabbed her granddaughter. She never thought of escaping through the unguarded door and running with Bella to Caroline's. The blood-stained quilt and the pleading, silvery-green eyes in the window — eyes like hers and her grandmammá's — kept her here to finish this.

"Go, Bella. Go. I will come for you."

Years of bridled fear and anger fueled

11

Gretchen's strike. The mirror came down hard across her husband's chest as he turned over. She lost her balance in the force of her thrust and came down on top of him.

"You're not going anywhere but straight to hell!" Grabbing her throat, he lifted her off him.

At the window, weak and frightened, Bella lost her grip on the window ledge and fell to the ground. "Mammá. Mammá."

Bella became aware of pain, not of her battered face, but of her tender, bare feet stepping on the sharp remains of cracked acorns along the sidewalk. *Mammá said, "Always put on your shoes, Bella."*

The owl moaned from his nearby perch in the edge of the woods. Bella stopped, her eyes surveying the limbs of nearby oak trees.

At the corner, Bella stood under the streetlight, looking toward the woods and then glancing down the street. *Go to the safe place? No, no. Mammá said, "Go to Caroline's."* Bella turned the corner and walked without hesitation down the street toward the iron gate that would creak when she opened it. Head bowed, long pale arms hanging limply at her sides, she plodded, paying no attention to the blood still oozing from her cheek and leg.

One more corner and one more block to the gate. *No music.* She lifted the latch and began to hum "David's Song" when the rusty gate creaked. Walking obediently to Caroline's door, she could see the piano through the bay window. Her hand, crusted with blood and peeling paint and splinters from the window ledge, reached for the bell.

Caroline rolled out of a peaceful sleep, wondering if she had really heard the doorbell. She brushed her hair from across her face to see the digital clock on her bedside table. Eleven forty. The second ring assured her she wasn't dreaming. In one motion she rose, grabbed her robe from the bedpost, and put it on as she walked through the great room to the terrace door. Her nights had been peaceful the last few months since her intruder had been identified as a young autistic girl. However, she still moved toward the door with caution. She turned on the outside light and peeped through the café curtains.

Outside, illuminated by the porch light, stood Bella, whose midnight secret visits to this studio had caused mystery and fear for weeks. In her shock, Caroline's hands fumbled to unlock the deadbolt and open the door. "Bella, Bella, what happened?" She wanted to embrace Bella, but she knew not to, not now. It would only upset the girl more.

"Mammá said, 'Go to Caroline's.' " In a shredded nightgown and bleeding, she could barely stand. Her arms hanging motionless by her sides, she stared at the pebbled terrace floor. "Mammá said, 'Go to Caroline's.' "

"Oh, Bella." Caroline took her arm and gently led her in and closed the door. Hearing Bella speak for the first time was almost as much of a shock as seeing her blood-spattered gown and silky, platinum hair plastered to her head. "Bella, where is Gretchen?"

"Mammá said, 'Go to Caroline's, Bella. I'll come to you.' "

Caroline cautiously pulled Bella's hair away from her eyes. The flesh around her right eye was already swelling, and blood seeped from an open wound on her cheek and trickled from her nostrils. Caroline seated her in the chair next to the piano, the chair where Gretchen always sat. Bella rocked back and forth.

Caroline rushed around the counter to the kitchen for a towel, picking up her cell phone on her way to the sink, and called

911. She communicated her assumptions deliberately and as if they were the truth. "This is Caroline Carlyle. There is an emergency at the home of Ernesto Silva. He has severely beaten his granddaughter, and I'm not certain about his wife. That address is 401 Third Street Northeast. The gray frame house on the corner. We need police and an ambulance. Please hurry before it's too late. I can't stay on the line, just get there." She dampened a towel, grabbed another dry one, and made her way back to where Bella sat quietly, rocking and humming "David's Song."

Oh, dear God, no. Please don't let this be happening. Oh, please not to Gretchen. She dialed Sam's number with shaking fingers and knelt in front of Bella while she waited for him to answer. Her left shoulder held the phone to her ear as she wiped blood with the damp towel.

Caroline hated to call Sam. He was eighty-six and didn't need this, but he was her guardian, her counsel, her friend, the one she always called. His home was just a quick walk through the garden to the big house at the front of the Twin Oaks property. Sam finally answered.

"Sam, it's Caroline. I'm okay, but I need your help. Bella just showed up at my door

15

covered in blood. She said that Gretchen had told her to come. I've already called 911, but call Caleb, Sam. Call Caleb." Caroline knew that the sheriff would respond immediately to Sam.

"What, Caroline? Say again. Are you okay?"

"I'm safe, Sam. It's Gretchen and Bella." Caroline repeated her story.

"That son of a . . . I'll call Caleb and be right there."

Caroline was unaccustomed to hearing such from Sam, the distinguished, retired judge and Moss Point's patriarch. She continued to wipe the blood from Bella's face. "You're safe, my precious one. I'm so glad you're here," Caroline gently whispered. She hummed with Bella as she tried to stop the bleeding. The music possessed Bella and kept Caroline from screaming and running down the street herself to give this wicked man what he deserved.

Sam's knock on the kitchen door was synchronous with the distant sound of a siren.

Caroline went to the kitchen door, removed the chain, and turned the deadbolt. There stood Sam and his wife, Angel. Caroline sagged against the door in relief. Longtime family friends, they had been her

16

safe haven, inviting her to come and live in their studio apartment after David's death six years ago.

Sam took one look at Caroline and hugged her to him. "Are you certain you're all right, child?"

She pulled away from him and looked down at her robe, now stained with Bella's blood. "Yes, Sam. I'm just trying to get Bella's face cleaned up and the bleeding stopped, but I'm scared to death about Gretchen. I don't know what happened, but in my heart, I know it must be . . ." Her voice cracked. "This is evil. This is Ernesto." Caroline motioned for them to follow her around the counter that separated the kitchen from the great room. "Right now, Bella's calm, calmer than I am. We need her to stay that way."

Sam and Angel, both in bathrobes, nodded silently in agreement.

"I just heard the siren when you knocked. I pray it's not too late."

Angel asked, "How do you know what happened? Bella doesn't talk, does she?"

"She's talking tonight, and I don't really know what happened. Bella's been hurt, and I know that Ernesto's been home for days." She shook her head. "This can only be bad." Caroline bit her lip, holding back her tears.

"Yeah, I spoke with the sheriff and he was already on the way. He'll call me here when he has word," Sam said.

Angel stepped over to Bella for a clearer look.

"I think we'd all feel better if we got Bella to the hospital. We don't know what other injuries she might have."

"You're right. Could you all take her? I need to check on Gretchen," Caroline said.

Angel put her used tissue in the pocket of her robe. "Now, think for just a minute. Gretchen sent Bella to you. She trusts you with this girl. Besides, don't you think it'll upset Bella if we take her to the hospital?"

Sam added, "Caleb and the medics will take good care of Gretchen, and he'll let us know what's happening. I'll make sure you stay informed."

Caroline reluctantly agreed. "I suppose you're right. Angel, could you please get more clean towels from the —"

The phone rang.

Sam answered. "Caleb, what'd you find?"

"Not good, Sam. Neither of them in good shape. Mrs. Silva's taken a bad beating. Bleedin' bad, and she's in and out. Keeps

18

sayin' 'Bella.' "

"What about him?"

"Silva's not so bad, but he's too drunk to be feeling much right now. We can't rule out an intruder 'cause the bedroom window's open. But it looks like all the meanness took place right here in this bedroom."

"Well, the girl's here with Caroline. She's had a beating too. She needs to go to the hospital. We can't tell how bad she's hurt."

"They're loading these two in the ambulance right now. I'll call for another one to pick up the girl."

"Could you ask them to tone down the siren? This girl's fragile. Sirens won't help a soul in Moss Point at midnight."

"Yeah, I'll take care of it, Judge. Will I see you at the hospital?"

"We'll follow the ambulance."

Not since the eighteen-wheeler jackknifed on the outskirts of town and killed four people several years ago had three been brought to the emergency room at one time. Moss Point Memorial's ER was more like an outdated army barrack, with a single row of hospital beds separated only by blue curtains. Caroline stayed in this makeshift room while Flo, the nurse, cleaned Bella's face and examined her.

19

"Well, she's going to need stitches above this eye, and her nose looks broken, but not much we can do about that." Flo reached for another clean gauze pad. "I'll get her face and hands and leg cleaned up. I think the doc will need to give her a little something to calm her down and help with the pain."

Caroline saw Bella flinch when Ernesto shouted his drunken obscenities from beyond the thin drape that separated them. She sensed Bella's agitation and asked Flo, "Is there any way Bella and Gretchen can be spared this further abuse? Can't you give him something? Make him quiet?"

"Get him out of here," Flo hollered to an orderly in the hallway.

Caroline noticed the orderly's face showed a hint of pleasure in his assignment. "Yes, ma'am. Any special place you want me to put him?"

"He doesn't appear to be hurt too bad. The street, the dumpster. I don't care. Just get him away from here." Flo gently cleaned Bella's punctured leg.

The orderly rolled Ernesto out of the area into an adjacent hallway.

Caroline smiled at the willingness of the small hospital to forget about protocol when a man had beaten his wife and granddaughter.

The doctor had been with Gretchen for what seemed like a very long time. All was quiet except for his occasional order to a nurse.

And then footsteps traced their way to Bella's curtain. Dr. Jacobs pulled the curtain back and asked Caroline to step outside. She hadn't spoken with him since last spring when Angel was hospitalized with her heart attack. "Caroline, I suppose you're the nearest thing to family to Mrs. Silva. All she has is that helpless young girl and that sorry piece of . . . excuse me. I mean that sorry excuse for a husband that put them in this mess."

Caroline stepped closer to Dr. Jacobs and lowered her voice. "You're right, I'm close to them."

"Well, then, since this is an emergency situation, I'll tell you. Mrs. Silva's in serious condition. She was barely able to nod her head to give us permission to treat the girl. She's lost a lot of blood. She has internal injuries and possibly some impairment of cognitive functions. Looks like he tried to choke her. I just can't be certain right now what blood loss and oxygen deprivation will mean. We're airlifting her to Atlanta. She'll get better care in their trauma unit, and she won't be near . . ."

"Do what you must do, Doctor, but what about Bella?"

"Flo says nothing serious. Only the gash on her cheek and possibly a broken nose, but I'll check her out and give her something for pain."

"Dr. Jacobs, I need to be with Bella. She won't go with anyone she doesn't know. But I don't want Gretchen to be alone either. Will you fix it so that Bella and I can fly to Atlanta with her? I'll be responsible for Bella."

"Done. Go home and get what you need for a few days. I'll make arrangements for you to fly with them. Be back in twenty minutes."

CHAPTER TWO:
TESTED

On Wednesday morning, room 602 at the hospital was as quiet as a recital hall an hour after the concert. Caroline squirmed in a fake leather chair that stuck to flesh and whose cracks she had memorized. It was no more comfortable than when she arrived four days ago, not even for her petite frame. Sitting up straight and stretching her arms high above her head gave some relief. She pulled the scrunchie from her ponytail and leaned over with her head between her knees, allowing her dark brown curls to almost touch the floor. The cracked linoleum had the look of a high school biology lab and had probably been doused with similar organic fluids and cleaning chemicals through the years.

Caroline massaged her scalp and brushed her hair with her fingers. Her unruly, wavy hair, inherited from her father, was the only undisciplined detail of her life. She sat up and tried taming it once again, pulling it severely to the top of her head and entrapping it with the scrunchie. Tendrils escaping along her temples were beyond coaxing. She coiled into the chair and wrapped the blanket tighter around her.

Gretchen, free now of the tubes that had sustained her since the surgery, rested in the bed next to Caroline's chair. The bruising on her face and neck was turning from a deep purplish-blue to green, and the swelling was subsiding. Prints of the brute's hands and fingers still encircled her neck — marks of evil — but she was beginning to look more like Gretchen. Her unblemished hand, like wax, rested on the white sheet. Caroline studied it, thinking of the gentle way Gretchen caressed Bella's hair. *How can one person's hand bring so much pleasure and another's so much pain?* Caroline could almost hear what Sam might say in his courtroom voice before pronouncing Ernesto's sentence: "Something wrong with a man who caresses his hound dog and kicks his wife in places where no living thing should be kicked."

The doctors did not know how long Gretchen's brain had been deprived of oxygen from the attempted strangulation and the amount of blood loss. They'd know more when she could talk. Her size, her delicate features and porcelain skin, left them all wondering how she had survived such a vile attack.

Caroline's phone rang. She unwrapped the blanket and reached for it in her bag beside the chair, hoping not to disturb Gretchen's sleep. Roderick's number appeared on the screen. She stepped into the bathroom and closed the door. Since meeting him in the summer and playing a recital in his Kentucky home, Caroline looked forward to his calls. "Good morning, Roderick. You can't know how good it is to see your name on my phone."

"Yours too, Blue Eyes. How are things this morning?"

"Improving slowly every day. The doctor removed the tubes last evening, and we'll see how Gretchen does today. I just hope she can talk."

"And Bella?"

"Oh, she's more resilient than I thought. Her little face is healing and no permanent damage to the eye. She's with your sister and Dr. Wyatt Spencer. Fortunately, or unfortunately, this situation has given him the opportunity he wanted to observe Bella."

"Dr. Spencer?"

25

"The professor from the University of Georgia."

Roderick interrupted her. "Yes, I remember Dr. Spencer."

"Well, he has permission to use the facilities here at the hospital. So he brought in a few colleagues from Athens to take a look at Bella. It seems his way of staking the university's claim on Bella. But I'm so grateful Sarah's here to monitor things."

"That's my sister, Sarah the child psychologist to the rescue."

"And to my rescue. It's amazing to watch her with Bella. They're really bonding."

"That's what she's trained to do, and she's good at it because it's her passion."

"Passion. Oh, that everyone's passion would lead to goodness." Caroline pulled the blanket tighter around her.

"So, you're philosophizing this morning?" Roderick asked.

"No, just thinking. Had plenty of time to do that the last few days. Since I've known Bella is a savant, I've had to honor Gretchen's need to keep it secret. If Ernesto knew Bella and Gretchen had been away from the house and up to the University of Georgia, I fear there would have been more than a beating."

"Do you suppose he found out?"

26

Caroline's right eyebrow automatically rose. "Don't think so. All the testing and observation have been done in secret, but there's no need to keep it quiet now."

"You're right. Bella's free, and so is Gretchen. With Ernesto behind bars, their lives will be quite different. And yours too, Caroline. Gretchen has lived with a controlling man. She will have difficulty maneuvering through these next few months alone, without someone telling her what to do. She trusts you, and that means that she will be relinquishing control to you."

She wasn't certain she was prepared for this much responsibility. "When are you coming home, Roderick?"

"I leave London tomorrow. Acer's meeting me at LaGuardia with the jet. He'll fly me straight back to Rockwater, and weather permitting, he'll fly me to Atlanta early Friday morning."

"You're coming here?" Her pulse quickened.

"Yes. You don't think I'd leave you alone with Dr. Wyatt Spencer too long, do you?"

Caroline grinned for the first time in days. "You're worried about Wyatt?"

"Of course. I have to make certain that Dr. Spencer's making his professional mark with a young musical savant and not his

27

personal mark in the life of the talented and beautiful pianist, Caroline Carlyle, who discovered her."

She hoped what she heard was a bit of honest jealousy. "I knew there was something more that I liked about you besides the fact that you like to fish. You're honest and straightforward."

"Oh really? I'd like to think my business associates would agree. Although they'd probably add that I'm cautious. But somehow with you, my caution heads downstream to wherever that big trout is waiting for your return to Rockwater."

She pictured Rockwater — the mansion, the gardens, the stream, and the view from the loggia windows. "Tell me, Roderick, what color is Kentucky bluegrass in October?"

"I won't tell you. If I do, perhaps you won't return to see for yourself, especially since your piano is now at home in your bay window instead of mine."

A bit of melancholy enshrouded her. She had met Roderick in July after discovering that he owned her beloved Hazelton Brothers 1902 piano, the instrument that had defined her and had been her place of joy and well-being during her childhood. Her parents sold the piano to pay for her college

28

education. Selling the piano away from her had been like separating conjoined twins, but playing this recital for Roderick's friends at his invitation had been like returning home after a long and solitary journey.

The trip to Rockwater, the Adair family estate outside of Lexington, had been magical. Roderick had stirred feelings in her that she was still sifting three months later, familiar feelings that had long been put away, the way you dispose of a dead woman's clothes.

For six years since David's death, her life had been on autopilot, void of any feelings other than her pride in being Moss Point's piano teacher and in charting the progress of her students. But meeting Roderick and then his covert piano swap had disconnected her autopilot button. Roderick had surprised her by delivering her antique piano and loading her studio grand onto a truck bound for Rockwater while she and Angel were on a day trip to Atlanta. He declared it on loan, like a painting or a museum piece.

She and Roderick had spoken several times since the stunning delivery, but they had not seen each other. She wished it had been something other than this tragedy that brought him back to Georgia. "I'll be so happy to see you, Roderick."

"I'm sorry. Just when I could have been of help to you, I was away. But I'll see you Friday. I must go for now. Take care, my . . ." Roderick paused. "Take care, Caroline."

Caroline didn't miss his caution. "You too, Mr. Adair."

Gretchen's stirring caught Caroline's eye. She dropped her book and rushed to the bedside. "Good morning. Finally, you're awake. Let me call the nurse." Caroline reached for the call button.

Gretchen stretched her eyelids and attempted to talk. "Bell . . . Bel-la?"

"Bella's just fine. There's so much to tell you. Do you remember anything I've been telling you?" Days of Gretchen's unconsciousness had not kept Caroline from talking to her as though she could hear.

Gretchen nodded her head and flinched in pain.

"You must still be sore." Caroline patted her hand. "Everything's fine now. You'll be back to normal in a few more days. Bella's great. She still has a sore nose, and they'll remove the stitches from her cheek Friday."

"Er . . . Ernes . . . ?"

Caroline took Gretchen's right hand. "Er-

30

nesto only had some bruises and minor lacerations. He's in jail where he's going to stay for a very long time." The bruised woman struggled to speak. "I hit . . . hit him . . . my mir . . . mirror." A single tear, maybe of relief or maybe of sadness, rolled down Gretchen's left cheek.

Caroline gently wiped it away with the corner of the sheet. She knew that Gretchen bore scars of other beatings. She also knew Gretchen had been longsuffering with Mr. Silva, forgiving him and making far too many excuses for him. She stayed with him out of gratitude for something in her past and because she was financially dependent on him. Perhaps soon Caroline would hear her story — the part of Gretchen's story that caused her to leave her family in Austria and marry an American soldier in Germany.

Caroline walked to the window and turned around to look at Gretchen. She could not conceal her excitement any longer. "I have a surprise for you. It's even a grand surprise for me too. Roderick's coming Friday. You'll finally get to meet him."

"He . . . he . . ." Gretchen's reach for her throat revealed the cast on her left arm.

Caroline walked back to the bedside and pulled her chair close. "It's okay, Gretchen,

31

it's okay. Don't try to talk. The doctor says talking will be easier when the swelling goes down. Your left arm was fractured, and you'll be in a cast for a few weeks. That's the only broken bone."

Gretchen became very still.

"Let me talk now that you're awake. Remember, I told you about Roderick's sister who is a child psychologist, Dr. Sarah McCollum. I met her when I went to Kentucky for the recital. You saw the letter from her I found in my suitcase when I got home. Well, she and her husband just moved from Boston to Raleigh-Durham. He's teaching medicine at Duke, and I think she's taking some time off because they want children. When Roderick found out what had happened to you and Bella, he called Sarah."

Gretchen tried to nod again.

"Apparently Sarah meant what she said in the letter — I mean about helping with Bella. She called me right after she talked to Roderick and was on a plane for Atlanta the next afternoon. I don't know what I would have done without her, and Bella's so comfortable with her."

"Bella . . . where?" Gretchen strained to formulate her words.

"She's with Sarah and Dr. Wyatt Spencer. Let me back up a bit. I called Dr. Martin over the weekend to cancel my piano lesson at the university on Monday. Do you remember her? I took you and Bella to meet her when I first suspected Bella is a musical savant. And she introduced us to Dr. Spencer, the professor and psychologist."

Gretchen nodded. Her acknowledgment meant she could remember. Surely that was a positive sign, and Caroline would report it to the doctor.

"I told Dr. Martin that you and Bella were here in the hospital. So ten minutes later, guess who calls? Dr. Wyatt Spencer, insisting on coming over. He's been here since Monday to work with Bella and review the test results. Lucky for us that Sarah arrived on Sunday afternoon. I filled her in on his interest in Bella. So now, she's Bella's self-appointed guardian — a professional one at that. Dr. Spencer has a group of experts observing Bella this morning. I suppose you remember Dr. Spencer from our trip to the university."

Not even the soreness and discomfort could keep Gretchen from smiling and nodding in agreement.

"I know, I know, Gretchen. Now they're all going to see what you and I already know. Bella has a rare gift."

"Sarah?" Gretchen struggled to speak.

33

"Yes, and Sarah's there to protect her. I can't wait for you to meet Sarah and see Bella with her. She'll never allow anyone, not even the ambitious Dr. Spencer, to upset or exploit Bella."

Gretchen drifted off to sleep again. Her faint smile hinted at a more peaceful rest.

"Okay, Bella, my name is Tom. Do you think you can lie very still for just a few moments? If you can lie really still, I have some candy for you when we finish." He covered her body with a thin sheet.

Mammá says, "No candy, Bella." Where is Mammá?

Bella lay on the metal table for the CT scan. Her body was still, her arms motionless at her sides, but her fingers played the song in her head. *I'll come for you. Go, Bella. Not to the hiding place. Not to the safe place. Mammá said, "Go to Caroline's." Play the piano. Where's Mammá?*

Sarah stood beside her, caressing her arm, while the tech in bright blue scrubs made preparations. Sarah spoke to him of Bella's hypersensitivity to music and suggested that he turn off the CD player. He complied and described the procedure to her.

Sarah explained to Bella that she would stay right there.

Bella lay quiet and still as she was in-structed. Lying still in the darkness was nothing strange to her. Only the cold table and the metal cylinder closing in around her were new. *Mammá says, "Go to your hiding place. Bella, be still and quiet so he will not hear you. Shhh, Bella. Be still. He will go away soon. You're safe here, Bella."*

The test took only a few moments, nothing like the hours she had spent on the floor in the back of the bedroom closet. Her mammá kept quilts there to cover her.

Mammá says, "Bella, you were good. Tomorrow, we can go to the safe place." Good and quiet. Where's Mammá? I want to go to the safe place.

Bella's petite twelve-year-old frame was lost in the hospital gown and robe. Her grandfather's clumsily aimed kick left her cheek and eye area deeply bruised, but not even the awkward patch over her eye kept her from playing the piano with perfection. This morning, she had been hustled from a second CT scan, through an ungainly interview, and to a university conference room where a studio piano had been rolled in. Six professors sat in a semicircle of folding chairs around the piano observing her. Despite some objections from the jury,

Sarah had pulled her chair within Bella's reach and sat down with her legs crossed casually. The other professionals would not bully her from her role as Bella's protector.

Bella played the last phrase of the Clementi sonatina. She hung her head and rhythmically rocked back and forth, rubbing the palms of her hands together. "Mammá said, 'Go to Caroline's.' Mammá said, 'Go to Caroline's.' "

In his uniform of khakis, a blue-striped shirt, and a yellow sweater draped over his back with its sleeves tied in a loose knot just below his Adam's apple, Dr. Spencer was parked in chair number one. He sat casually, long legs crossed, exposing his sockless, tan ankles and twirling his pen between his fingers before pointing it at the pianist in the sixth seat. "Do you have something a bit less structured, say something from the Impressionist period, that you could play for her? I'd like to see what she'd do with that."

The pianist rose from her chair and approached Bella. "May I play the piano now?"

Still rocking, Bella was statuesque and unmovable. "Mammá said . . ."

The pianist looked to Dr. Spencer. He gave her the go-ahead nod. She moved

36

behind Bella and placed her hands on Bella's shoulders, attempting to steer her from the piano.

Bella winced. Her rocking motion increased, and she rubbed her head near the bandage covering her stitches.

Sarah rose quickly from her chair. "I think this is enough for today. You seem to have forgotten this girl has been traumatized from a beating less than a week ago."

Dr. Spencer looked at his watch. "But it's only two thirty. Could we give her a break and maybe start again?"

"I think not. She seems tired and a bit agitated. Perhaps tomorrow you may see her again." Sarah put her clipboard in her bag and removed her reading glasses.

Dr. Spencer approached her but kept a respectable distance. "Do you know how important this is? We need this time while we have controlled access to her."

Sarah did not waver. "Yes, Dr. Spencer, I am aware of the value of knowing as much about Bella's abilities as we can discover, but this is bordering on something less than professional, and certainly has crossed the line of insensitivity, and I will not allow you to continue beyond what is best for this child."

Dr. Spencer nodded. "Of course, you're

right. I apologize for my . . . for my enthusiasm with this project."

"Might I remind you this project has a name? Her name is Bella."

"You're right again, Dr. McCollum. Please forgive me. Actually, this will give me time to talk with my colleagues about the test results and to send the data back to the university. I'd also like to review the recordings we've made today. Would you like to be a part of that?"

"Thank you for the invitation, but I, too, have had enough for one day. I do believe you will need signed releases before the videotapes can be used."

"Yes, that's true. I'll have my secretary fax that document over this afternoon. Do you suppose I could get Mrs. Silva's signature?" He made a note on his pad.

"That, I will discuss with Caroline and Mrs. Silva when it's appropriate. Mrs. Silva is improving but is still quite sedated. Until proper documents are signed, I'd like to have the recordings please."

She saw reluctance in Dr. Spencer's face, but she had him. He motioned for the technician to hand them over to her.

She dropped them in her bag. "And I'd like copies of any test results also."

"Certainly, I'll be sure you receive those,

and thank you for making today's work possible. I'm very grateful."

Sarah liked his more compliant attitude. Sincere or not? The future would tell. She took Bella's hand. "Let's go see Caroline. Maybe your mammá is awake. You haven't seen her in days. She misses you."

"Mammá said, 'I'll come to you.' "

"Yes, she did Bella, but let's surprise her and go to see her."

Bella looked at Sarah and smiled. Nothing Sarah had seen or heard all day delighted her more than that one simple expression. They walked hand in hand out the door and down the long corridor, leaving six stunned and energized professors perched like vultures around a silent piano.

Dr. Spencer pulled his chair in front of the five other chairs, sat down, and waited for the door to close and the sound of footsteps to fade before he spoke. "Well, ladies and gentlemen, there is no doubt about it. We have truly witnessed a savant — an autistic, musical savant, one of slightly less than one hundred in recorded history."

His colleagues agreed in unison. Dr. Purcell put his pen in his pocket. "So, what's the next step? I guess the real question is what do we do after we have discovered such a rare individual?"

"I have some very definite ideas." Elena Daniels, in a mocha-colored suit and brown alligator pumps, stood and walked to the piano. She adjusted her leopard print scarf, which had been flirting with her cleavage all morning, and tucked thick strands of auburn hair behind her right ear. "We need to move quickly to claim this moment. Think what it could mean for the university and for our own careers."

Wyatt Spencer sat straighter in his chair as if to reclaim his seat of power. "Need I remind you we didn't discover Bella? That honor belongs to one Miss Caroline Carlyle, who is the key to the next step. Presently, it would appear that Dr. McCollum has earned Caroline's trust. Our next step is to earn Dr. McCollum's trust. I believe what she says will determine what happens next."

Elena played with the gold chain around her neck. "Perhaps not."

"And what's that supposed to mean?" Wyatt bristled.

"What would happen if the press learned of Bella? Wouldn't that attention put this whole issue in an entirely different arena?"

Wyatt had no doubt Elena's beguiling smile had disarmed any number of men, including professionals, but he wasn't playing. "I suppose it would. But just explain to me how the press could learn of Bella when only a group of professionals who practice rules of confidentiality know about her."

"Oh, I can think of a number of ways. After all, her grandfather is in jail for beating her. That makes news, doesn't it, especially in a small town?"

Wyatt's palms were sweaty. The air in the room was heavy with ambition, and he was finding it stale and hard to breathe.

Wednesday morning had been quiet, but the afternoon was different. The corridor was abuzz with nurses and rolling carts. Caroline stood at the door of Gretchen's room. She saw Bella, in robotic gait with arms close to her body and her head slightly bowed, staying close to Sarah. As they approached the door of Gretchen's hospital room, Sarah stopped. "Bella, here's Caroline, and we're going in to see your mammá."

Bella responded with a piercing stare.

Caroline approached Bella and put her arm around her shoulders. "Hi, Bella. I hope you had fun today." She looked at Sarah. "How did it go?"

"Bella did great. The panel was a little . . . overly excited, I guess you'd say. But Dr. Spencer seemed to remember his place when reminded." Sarah grinned as though she'd very much enjoyed putting the experts in their place. "But more importantly, how's Gretchen?"

"Improved, and she's actually been able to talk today." Caroline stepped inside the door and took Bella's hand. "Bella, how would you like to see your mammá? She asked about you this morning."

"Mammá said, 'I'll come to you, Bella.' " Bella began her rocking motion.

"That's right, she did. And she's here. Let's go inside." Caroline led the way.

The knock and Bella's voice had awakened Gretchen. Unable to move, her eyes searched the room for Bella. Before the last few days, only the time spent in sleep had separated them since Bella's birth twelve years ago.

Caroline approached the bed and took Gretchen's hand. "Sarah and Bella are here." She moved aside. *Thank You, Father, for sending Sarah all the way from North Carolina to help with Bella, and thank You for providing a hotel just down the street so they could be near.*

"Bell . . . Bella." Gretchen struggled to speak. "My Bella." Gretchen extended her right arm.

Bella rushed around Sarah and straight to her mammá like water seeking its own level. "Mammá! Mammá!" Bella climbed onto

43

the bed and nuzzled her head in the crook of Gretchen's neck. Her body language was mechanical and her words sparse, but her convulsive sobs proved she could feel and feel deeply.

Gretchen's face winced in pain. Caroline knew Gretchen had borne a living hell for years and would bear her present pain to have Bella next to her heart. Pain and love so intertwined.

"I am here, Bella. No Bella? No music." Gretchen strained to speak and to kiss Bella's silken hair. They lay quietly, needing no words to express their joy of being together and safe again.

Sarah moved to Caroline's side and put her arm around her. "Oh, to know such pure love."

Caroline's bottom lip quivered. This reunion and remembering her love for David brought back a sudden and surprising tidal wave of grief and longing. The pain of losing him only weeks before their wedding washed over her like the Guatemalan floodwaters that took his life. "But you can't know great love without risking great pain."

Sam hung up the phone and walked to the back-porch door. Twin Oaks had been uncomfortably quiet the last few days with

Caroline gone. He missed her music. Normally at four o'clock in the afternoon, cars were coming and going with her piano students. The studio and the garden were both still this afternoon. Autumn cloaked the sycamore trees in brilliant gold and the Japanese maples in crimson. Sam was glad for the colorful signs of life, even the rust-colored chrysanthemums that reminded him of funerals, for he knew the gray of winter was approaching. At eighty-six, he treasured the seasons, knowing there couldn't be many more autumns.

Angel stepped into the kitchen and filled the teakettle. "Sam, want a cup of tea?"

"Is it tea time already?"

"I do believe it's tea time when we decide to have tea, and I'll not put one more brush-stroke of paint on that canvas until I have my brew."

Sam smiled at the thought of Angel painting again. A heart attack had come too close to snatching her from him last spring. For him, every day was a gift. "How's the portrait coming?"

"The sketch now has skin. You'll see. Who was that on the phone a while ago?"

"It was the sheriff. Seems like the possibility of doing prison time has suddenly stimulated Ernesto's interest in the condition of his wife and granddaughter."

Angel reached for the canister of tea bags and put three in the teapot. "They're not going to let that brute out on bond, are they?"

"Not if I can help it." Sam sat down at the glass-topped breakfast table. He pulled the crystal pitcher full of roses in the middle of the table to him and inhaled their fragrance deeply as if to rid himself of malodorous thoughts of Ernesto Silva. "Haven't seen my mama's tea pitcher in a while. Thought you were saving it for something special."

"I was, but I just couldn't figure out what that something special was, and besides, who will enjoy it when I'm dead and gone?" Angel leaned against the stove waiting for the teakettle to whistle. "Stop changing the subject. Now just what can a retired judge do about Ernesto? And what will happen if Gretchen doesn't press charges this time?"

"Oh, don't you worry about that. When Ernesto kicked Bella in the face, he had no idea he had given himself the boot into prison with or without his wife pressing charges. What Gretchen wants to do about it is immaterial now. He's going away for a long time."

"Till Gabriel blows?"

"Depends on when he blows, but let's just say Ernesto'll have plenty of time to think about what he's done."

Angel removed the teakettle at the first hint of a whistle, filled the teapot, and brought it to the table. "You know, I've been wondering. What'll happen to Bella and Gretchen when she's released from the hospital?" She sat down across from Sam.

"Been thinking about that myself. I suppose it's possible Ernesto could make bail, and then he's back home. Not good."

"Well, that lessens the options. Gretchen and Bella can't return home." Angel lifted the lid of the teapot and a whiff of steam escaped. "What would you think about having them come here for a few days?"

"Now, why is it that I think it doesn't matter what I think?" Remembering how many dogs and cats and even a possum Angel had rescued through the years, he figured she had a plan, and he loved her for it. But he wasn't about to tell her he had been thinking the same thing.

"The reason it doesn't matter is that after living with you for sixty years, we think just alike." She giggled and passed him his cup of tea, with one sugar and a few drops of milk, just like he liked it. "They could share the blue room or the bridal suite."

47

"And Caroline? She can't stay alone if Ernesto's out of jail." Sam's thick eyebrows always met in the middle when he was worried. Now that Ernesto knew Caroline was involved, she was in as much danger as Gretchen and Bella.

"Of course, she'll stay here too. But getting Miss Independent to agree will be the trick."

"I'll just tell her you need help with Gretchen and Bella. It'll be as easy as getting Ned and Fred to take a bag of Caroline's cookies."

Ned and Fred, twins who were sixtyish, had kept Twin Oaks and the gardens beautiful for decades. Fred didn't speak much, but Ned's words, though sparse and uneducated, showed integrity. They were simple-minded but honest men who had pledged themselves to protect Caroline when they discovered signs of an intruder last spring.

Angel poured the last few drops of tea into her cup. "Speaking of Ned and Fred, how long before they'll be finished clearing our land for the park?"

"Depends on the weather. They cleared the fence line next to Twin Oaks first. Oh, I forgot to tell you. They found the old shack Gretchen and Bella fixed up down in the thicket along the creek bank."

"Well, if we're to have a ribbon cutting on the new park next spring, they'd better get to clearing more than the fence line. We won't have eight acres of daffodils and irises and American Beauties in April if we don't get the bulbs and roses in the ground in the next few weeks."

They drank their tea.

"Angel, do you ever think about how all this started?" He didn't wait for her to swallow her tea to respond. "It was Caroline's piano playing."

She put down her teacup. "Surprise, you do have your own thoughts."

"Well, it was Caroline's piano teaching that brought her to Moss Point after David was killed. It's been her teaching and playing that have brought us and this whole town such beautiful music the last six years. It was her piano playing that lured the mysterious intruder through those woods to her studio window in the dark of night."

"Beautiful little Bella," Angel added.

Early Thursday morning shift changes in the hospital spelled activity. The day nurses checked vital signs and helped Gretchen to the bathroom. Caroline looked around at the mop bucket on wheels, a stack of fresh linens that still smelled of hospital, and the

49

breakfast tray with unsalted eggs and dry toast.

It was only nine o'clock, and Caroline had already heard from Angel. Caroline had agreed to stay at Twin Oaks to help with Bella for a few days when Dr. Jacobs released Gretchen on Monday, barring complications.

Caroline imagined Hattie, Angel's cook and housekeeper, dancing through Twin Oaks with dust rags, the sponge mop, and stacks of clean linens. And she knew Angel would create bouquets of fresh flowers, and Hattie would make her famous eight-layer chocolate cake. If she knew Sam, he was on the phone with the sheriff ensuring a peaceful and uneventful arrival for Gretchen and Bella at Twin Oaks — an arrival that would not include any sign of Ernesto Silva.

Perfect timing. The doctor's news meant they'd remain in Atlanta for the weekend. Sarah could make good on her promise to take Bella to the aquarium downtown Saturday. Since Roderick was somewhere over the Atlantic this morning and would arrive in Atlanta tomorrow, perhaps they would join Sarah and Bella on their excursion.

While Gretchen napped, Caroline made calls to cancel piano lessons next week.

Then she called Wyatt Spencer. She left a message when he didn't pick up. "Good morning, Wyatt. It's Caroline to let you know we'll be returning to Moss Point on Monday. Thought it might help your planning to know that tomorrow will be your last day with Bella for a while. We'll chat later."

With Gretchen resting, Bella and Sarah off with Wyatt, and Roderick in flight from London, Thursday dragged on like a month of Sundays. Sarah and Bella came by for a brief visit before heading off for dinner and the hotel. Thinking all was quiet for the evening, Caroline changed into her sweats and T-shirt, removed the last hint of makeup, grabbed *Chopin's Funeral,* and sat down on the cot to brush her hair before reading.

Wyatt didn't want to chance calling to ask if he could come by the hospital. Caroline might say no. After a long dinner with his colleagues, he untangled himself from the web Elena Daniels was spinning and drove to the hospital.

Wyatt peered through the glass window in the door of room 602. The room was dim, the only light being directly above the cot where Caroline sat brushing her hair. He'd

51

never seen her hair down and free of clamps or combs.

It had been a spring night in early May when he'd driven to Moss Point. It was their second meeting about Bella. Their conversation over dinner in her studio apartment was stimulating. And he had not forgotten the sunset stroll through the garden with their after-dinner tea. Jasmine laced the arbor covering the garden bench where they sat in front of the pond. She picked a jasmine blossom and twirled it between her fingers before sticking it in her hair.

For him, Caroline was a study in contrasts. Her face was like the one on his mother's cameo brooch, soft and the palest pink, but with dark, wavy, long hair. Her eyes were like blue topaz, still and intense. He feared they looked beyond him into places he might never see. Soft spoken and gentle she was, yet definite and unwavering. A feminine vulnerability that said "Touch me," and yet she turned her head when he bent to kiss her good night. Her silky cheek, the wisps of her hair catching the stubble on his chin, and the smell of jasmine would be forever wed in his mind.

He'd found it difficult to keep his professional distance with her and knew he must be cautious. The summer months had provided little opportunity to see her. He was forced to keep his knowledge of Bella a secret, but now with her grandfather in jail, that would change, and he didn't want Caroline caught off guard.

He could see Caroline through the glass pane on the hospital room door. He tapped lightly so as not to disturb Gretchen.

Caroline laid down the brush and looked for her shoes. She gave up and answered the door in her bare feet. "Good evening, Wyatt." She tugged at her T-shirt and brushed her hair back as she stepped into the hallway and closed the door. "I wasn't expecting you."

"I know. You think we could go somewhere and get a cup of coffee? I'm buying." He didn't suppose there was jasmine blooming anywhere in Atlanta in late October.

"Now?" She put her bare right foot atop the left one and balanced herself by holding the doorknob.

"That's what I was hoping. Something wrong with now?" Towering at least a foot above her, he'd forgotten how petite she was.

"Oh, but I really shouldn't leave." She looked back into the room to see if the noise had awakened Gretchen.

"Sarah said Mrs. Silva's doing much better. Surely you could leave for a while."

"But I'm dressed to stay in for the evening."

He liked the way she was dressed, casual and unfussy. "I must warn you, if you refuse, I might hedge my bets you wouldn't create a scene in a hospital hallway if I picked you up and carried you out."

He didn't miss the lifting of her right eyebrow before a smile forced the appearance of the dimple in her left cheek. She looked up at him and chuckled as she nodded her head in agreement. No polished veneer on her face, only soft, velvety skin that he couldn't resist touching. The back of his fingers lightly brushed wisps of curls away from her dimpled cheek.

Caroline turned away quickly. "Let me get my shoes."

Roderick stopped at the nurses' station to ask for directions to room 602.

The nurse looked up from the desk and pointed down the hallway to her left. "It's down that way — where the young couple is huddled at the door." The nurse returned to her charts.

Roderick watched as a younger man touched Caroline's cheek. Previously brimming with excitement at the thought of surprising her tonight, his spirit abruptly felt like a dank cellar. "Yes, I see. Thank you. It's a bit late. Perhaps I'll just come back tomorrow." He walked toward the elevator, his head bowed and his steps heavy.

Chapter Four:
A Professor, a Blonde,
and a Brunette

As the double glass doors to the hospital opened, the evening's chilly breeze slapped Caroline's face. She stepped onto the sidewalk with Wyatt at her side and paused to gaze at the Atlanta skyline against the night sky.

Caroline shivered, brushed her hair back, and folded her arms to keep warm. "I didn't know it would be so nippy. Could we just get something in the hospital coffee shop?"

Wyatt wore a sweater draped across his shoulders with the sleeves tied around his neck and resting on his chest. He loosened the knot. "Here." He pulled the sweater from his shoulders and placed it around Caroline. "Take my sweater. We'll just take a short walk and come back."

"Just a brief walk?" Caroline pulled the sweater tighter around her and brushed her hair back again.

"Yep. It'll do you good to breathe something besides hospital air. Have you been out of that hospital since you got here?"

"No. You want to know how many ceiling tiles are in the room?"

"Ceiling tiles?"

"Or maybe you'd rather know the entire contents of a bag of glucose?"

"I was right, you've been breathing too much hospital air."

They walked a few blocks in awkward silence before Wyatt took her arm and twirled her around. "Hospital coffee shop it is. I think you're getting cold." He never let go of her arm until they reached the hospitality room. They ordered at the counter and found a table.

The waitress brought his coffee and Caroline's chamomile tea. "Well, the coffee's only one step above branch water during the muddy season, as we'd say in Texas, but at least it's warm and quiet in here." Wyatt reached for more sugar.

"You could've had a cup of chamomile as I suggested." Caroline swirled the water in the metal teapot.

"You and your tea." Wyatt grinned and quit stirring his coffee. "I remember being in your studio apartment — your teacups, teapots, and endless supply of tea bags.

Where did you acquire this tea-drinking habit?"

"From my grandmother on my mom's side. Her parents were from England. My brothers didn't take to her tea parties, so I was the one who learned the art of tea from Grand Ma'am."

"I can imagine."

"So much for my tea-drinking heritage. I'd really like to hear more about your time with Bella."

Wyatt reached into his pocket for his notepad. "The time in this controlled environment has been invaluable. No question, Bella's a musical savant."

"So, we've known she was rare, and now we have a label."

"Yeah, she's rare, astonishingly so, and we haven't found her limits yet. She's rarer than rare because she's female, beautiful, and sighted."

"So how she looks makes her even more rare?"

"Odd, but true. Most musical savants are male and blind with physical characteristics suggesting mental limitations. But not so with Bella. Oh, we're aware she has limitations, and we'll do some more observation and testing to determine what they are. Tomorrow, I have her scheduled with an ophthalmologist. Need to check her vision."

"Good. I've wondered about how well she can see. Sarah told me you brought in a pianist from the university, and there was nothing she played that Bella couldn't reproduce."

"Better than that. The professor could play a cluster of notes, no melody, just a cluster of notes, and Bella reproduced them perfectly every time. Brain like a tape recorder."

"She's the same with me. Been doing that for months, but she doesn't speak much."

"Bella's somewhere on the autism spectrum, which might explain her silence. She seems to function though, takes commands, but you're right about her communication skills. They're still puzzling for us as well."

Caroline sipped her tea, propped both elbows on the table, and leaned forward. "That's interesting. You know, in all these months, I had never heard Bella speak until last Friday night when she showed up at my terrace door bleeding. But even then, she only repeated what Gretchen had told her. 'Go to Caroline's. I'll come for you.' " She sat back, cupping her tea in both hands to warm them.

"I've certainly heard that phrase a number of times the last couple of days. You know,

I'm going to need time with Bella in her environment. I don't really know about her life skills and how much Gretchen is required to do for her. How do they spend their time? How do they relate? Does she have other gifts? What could Bella learn with appropriate instruction?"

"So much we don't know, and I want to help."

Wyatt was grateful further observation would take him back to Moss Point. "You're already helping, but I'll learn much more when I can speak with her grandmother. I do know Bella hears and understands language."

"She's very creative and artistic. Next to my piano, my most prized possession is an unusual work of art Bella made for me. But right now, I'm more interested in her musical abilities. Do you think because she understands language that she can understand music?"

"Excellent question with no answer yet. A few prodigious savants have been documented though."

"You mean like a musical prodigy?"

"Absolutely. They're only classified as prodigious if their gifts are so elevated, they would rank among musical geniuses even without their limitations. They can also create, not just reproduce. Unfortunately, I don't know yet if Bella can create. Since she can't describe these processes to us, the big question emerges — the question no one has ever answered. How do you get into the mind of a savant?"

"Guess the next big step is to establish if she's a prodigious savant."

"Maybe, maybe not." Elena Daniels's comment about going public with this story was still unsettling to him. "Caroline, you need to be thinking about the immediate future and what will happen when Gretchen is released from the hospital."

"That's taken care of. Had a conversation with Sam today, and all three of us are moving into the big house at Twin Oaks for a few days. Sam thinks Gretchen and Bella will be safer, and Hattie will be there to take care of them."

"Who's Hattie?"

"Oh, Hattie's been with the Meadows for decades."

"You mean she's the housekeeper?"

"A housekeeper and cook who's more like family. Sam and Angel never had kids of their own, so they educated Hattie's son and daughter. Elijah's an architect in Chicago, and Dinah's a pediatrician in Augusta. Hattie lives to take care of folks, so it's worked both ways."

"Could be some problems arising that Hattie can't take care of though."

"What do you mean?"

"Problems like what happens when the public finds out about Bella." He watched Caroline sip the last of her tea and stare into the bottom of the empty cup.

She put her cup down. "I've known that will happen at some point, just hoped it would be later."

"Yeah, well, later may be sooner. With Ernesto in jail, at least we don't have to be so secretive about our work." Wyatt pushed away from the table and stretched, extending his legs.

"For now, he's behind bars, but there are such things as bail, you know."

"In Texas small towns, we have a way of taking care of bail when there's an Ernesto involved."

"I'm sure Sam and Caleb will do their best to see that he goes to prison for a long time."

"Okay, so that takes care of him for a few years, but what about Bella, and what about Gretchen? How will they make it?" He sat up straight in his chair and leaned forward with his elbows on the table.

"I've thought about it, but I don't have it

all figured out yet. I think I knew early on after I met them that they'd be new characters in my story."

"What story? You writing a book?"

Caroline laughed. "No, I'm not writing a book. I'm talking about a life story — how people enter and exit your life, sometimes even radically changing you."

"Life story. Interesting concept." Wyatt compartmentalized his life into work, play, and family. Bella was tucked away in the work category, hopefully a stepping-stone in his career.

"Some characters enter briefly, and then they're gone too soon." Caroline was looking into that place he feared he'd never see. "Others enter, and you just have the sense they're going to be around for a while, and they'll make a difference in your life. That's how I think of Gretchen and Bella."

"You're quite a woman, Caroline Carlyle. You really care about them, don't you?"

"I truly do. It's a long story, but they've helped me break through this glass cocoon I've lived in for six years."

Wyatt saw a glimmer of hope. "Glass cocoon? Explain that for me."

Caroline didn't answer right away. "Why don't we talk about Gretchen?"

"Gretchen it is. Would you like another

cup of tea?"

She declined. "It's just that Gretchen's been in a virtual prison of fear for at least twenty-five years. I think she had more freedom when she first moved to Moss Point. But after their daughter, Karina, gave birth to Bella illegitimately, and then ran away, well, Gretchen's had little freedom. Ernesto gives her grocery money and allows her to shop for food. Otherwise, she's at home, slipping out to their safe place in the woods or over to my studio, but only when he's driving his truck on a long run."

"So, Gretchen lives in a prison of fear, and Bella lives in the prison of her limitations?"

Caroline removed Wyatt's sweater from her shoulders and draped it over the chair next to her. "Perhaps, but I think Bella lives freely in the world she has found at the piano."

"Like you? Like the piano is for you? The one thing you can control?" Wyatt looked for any change in facial expression.

Caroline looked him directly in the eye. "That's how you see me?"

"Not completely, but what's more important is how you see yourself, glass cocoon and all."

She turned in her seat to get up. "Well,

we'll save that for another discussion. Right now, I see myself in need of sleep."

Wyatt pushed away from the table and put his notepad back in his pocket. "Fair enough, but one more question — did Ernesto's attack on Gretchen make the local newspapers?"

"I don't know. I haven't seen the local paper this week. Why do you ask?" She took the sweater from the back of the chair and handed it to him across the table.

"If it did, I'm just not certain we can contain what we know about Bella for very long. There'll be questions, lots of questions." He picked up the ticket off the table as he stood. "How you deal with those questions will change lives, Caroline."

Wyatt stopped at the counter to pay the bill, and Caroline walked out into the hallway. He put the change in his pocket and joined her. "Come on, I'll walk you back to Gretchen's room."

"You know, I remember a bench right outside the front door of the hospital. I think I'd like to sit there and breathe some fresh air for just a few minutes before I turn in." They walked through the hospital lobby and out the front door. "Thanks for the tea and the update, Wyatt."

"My pleasure. Here, put the sweater back

on, it's chilly." They stood face-to-face. He came closer and spread the sweater around her back and across her shoulders. Her eyes told him he was too close. "Would you like to sit?"

"Thank you, but I'd really like to be alone for just a bit." She removed the sweater and handed it to him.

"Are you sure? Do you think that's smart this late in downtown Atlanta?"

"I'll be fine. What time are you picking up Bella tomorrow?"

"Around nine."

"I'll have her ready. Sarah will be with her. Thanks again." She turned away from him and seated herself on the edge of the bench.

Wyatt walked down the street. The city lights against the black sky reminded him of cheap paintings on black velvet — the kind sold at street corner gas stations back home. He stopped at the end of the block and stood in the darkness where he could still see her lonely silhouette etched against the lights of the night.

She was a mystery to him, but she was noticeably comfortable in her own skin. Perhaps he'd been too bold and that was what had caused her to send him away. He mustn't push, but, he thought as he leaned against the shadowed wall, he wouldn't leave her alone in the dark.

The hour was late in the hotel room just a few blocks from the hospital. Bella was tucked away for the night alone in her bed. Just a few feet away, Sarah lay sleeping. The city lights made the room brighter than Bella's room at home, and she was having trouble sleeping. As she began to drift, another siren startled her.

I want to go to the hiding place. Where's Mammá? I'll be good. I'll be quiet. Mammá says if I'm quiet, he will not hear me. Bella whimpered.

Sarah's eyes opened, and she slipped out of bed to kneel on the floor next to Bella. "It's okay, Bella. Everything's okay." She took Bella's hand and held it to her cheek. "Shhh, Bella. Everything's okay. You're safe. Your mammá is safe."

"The hiding place." Still whimpering, Bella got the words out. "Mammá said to go to the hiding place."

"But there's no hiding place here. You don't need a hiding place, Bella."

"Go to the hiding place. Be still. Be quiet." Bella got out of bed, dragging the spread with her to the closet.

Sarah was quiet and did nothing to stop her.

Bella opened the closet doors, got down on the floor, and crawled into the farthest corner of the closet and covered herself with the spread. *I'll be good. I'll be quiet. He will not hear me.*

Roderick's night had been like patches of wakefulness held together by worn threads of sleep — jet lag and leftover images of a hospital hallway. Rising early on Friday morning didn't bother him. A quick walk from his hotel across the street and he was standing outside the hospital room, looking through the window at Caroline asleep on the cot beside Gretchen's bed.

He dialed her cell phone number and watched her reach for the phone in the seat of the chair beside her. "Good morning, Blue Eyes. Got your sweats on and want to walk down to the stream?" He saw the beginning of a smile on her face. Surely a shared love for the piano and a Kentucky trout stream would give him an advantage over a hip young psychologist.

"Oh, Roderick, please don't say that. Do you have any idea how much I'd enjoy a walk with you and sitting on that boulder, dangling my feet above that stream this morning? Your magical brook that washes away the dirt and grime of life. I can imagine the fall leaves floating downstream."

"Well, if you won't join me for a walk, would you consider joining me for breakfast?"

"Breakfast?" She looked at the clock. It was 6:15. "Oh yes, I'm so glad it's finally Friday. What time will you be here?"

"Would now be too soon? Look out your window. I'm standing at the door." He so wanted the look of delight on her face to be genuine.

"Roderick." She tossed the phone on her bed and ran to the door, opened it, and stood. When he took one step toward her, she moved into his arms as naturally as waves gently lap against the shoreline at sunrise. She was warm and soft from sleep, and he didn't want to let her go.

CHAPTER FIVE:
AN INVITATION
AND PHONE CALLS

Caroline dressed quickly. Roderick had convinced her to leave the hospital and have breakfast at the Ritz-Carlton where he had spent the night. He waited for her in the hospital lobby.

She woke Gretchen. "Gretchen, it's early, and I'm sorry to wake you up, but I couldn't just disappear without telling you."

Gretchen opened her eyes slowly. Trying to turn toward Caroline brought a grimace of pain to her face and made Caroline want to throttle the man responsible. "Caroline?"

"It's me, Gretchen. I got a surprise early this morning. Roderick showed up a few minutes ago to invite me to breakfast. He actually flew in last night. If you're feeling well enough, I'll go with him."

Gretchen cleared her throat and uttered a gravelly, "You mustn't linger with me. Go and take pleasure in your breakfast and the company." She breathed deeply and reached

70

for Caroline's hand. "You're smiling, my friend."

"I am?" Caroline paused. "I . . . why, I think I am. Anyway, we'll be back in a bit, and you'll get to meet him, and I'm sure Sarah will bring Bella by before their nine o'clock meeting with Dr. Spencer."

Gretchen tried hard to speak. "Today will be a lovely day, my sweet friend."

Caroline released Gretchen's hand and leaned to kiss her lightly on her cheek. "I think you're right. It will be a most lovely day."

A short cab ride and Roderick and Caroline were in the dining room of the Ritz-Carlton. He'd asked for a table for two at the window. As she sat across the table from Roderick, Caroline couldn't stop smiling. He was calm and confident, mysterious and transparent, all at the same time. The gray streaks near his temples hinted at the age difference that was of no concern to her. His eyes were brown and warm and still — not darting from place to place but fixed on her — so that it was easy to talk with him.

Roderick was the first man and the only man, since David's death, who made her feel like a woman again. Grief had tucked her sensuality away into a safe place like

Grand Ma'am had put away the good linens in the cedar chest. Six years of living in black and white — her life a flat, gray shadow. But thinking about Roderick brought vivid color and made her real again. Daydreaming, which had disappeared like the autumn leaves, reappeared like tender, green buds, but she kept her daydreams to herself. Caution scripted a role for each of them. She was unsure of the rhythm of this new movement or even its theme, but she was certain it would be a new melody with fresh lyrics.

She finished her last bite and put her napkin on the table. "The Belgian waffle was excellent, but not like the last breakfast we had at Rockwater."

"I cooked an omelet for you, didn't I?"

"You did, and a good one I might add. Haven't had one like that since July."

"Well, I haven't forgotten how to make them. What about a trip to Rockwater?"

She leaned forward, raised her right eyebrow, and pointed her finger at him. "You're really tempting me this morning. First, a teasing invitation to walk to the stream and now another invitation to Rockwater. You mustn't do that."

"I see that eyebrow, and I don't often have fingers pointed at me, at least not when I'm looking." He took her finger and held her hand briefly, sending a delicious shiver through Caroline. "Why mustn't I offer you an invitation?"

"Because it's too tempting and things are very complicated right now — with Bella and Gretchen, and who knows with Ernesto's trial?" Her speech slowed. "Then, there's my teaching and other responsibilities." She shook her head in disappointment.

"Okay, then let's negotiate."

"Negotiate? But you're the businessman and trained negotiator. Do you really think it fair to negotiate when you have so many advantages over a small-town pianist?"

Roderick couldn't conceal his smile. "Unfair advantage? Let's put that on the table and examine it. A concert pianist with blue eyes like Wedgwood saucers masquerading herself as a piano teacher? And I have an unfair advantage? Very disarming, madam, so why don't you see if blue eyes work?"

She pushed her chair slightly from the table, sat back, and crossed her arms. His comment forced the appearance of Caroline's dimple. "So . . . if you're saying the negotiating table isn't tilted, then what's your best offer?"

He continued with his business jargon. "That's more like it. I know it's late October, and it looks like courtroom battles, mergers, and restructuring will be going on in your life in the next couple of months. So, what do you say about a Christmas recital?"

"Christmas recital?"

"Well, yes, and if I have to make an exchange of pianos, then consider it done." He turned his head slightly, looked at her out of the corner of his eye, and strummed his fingers on the table.

She wasn't about to stop now when she seemed to have the advantage. "And what about snow? You know the whole white Christmas thing?"

"You want snow? I'll order snow."

She stood up and extended her right hand across the table. "Done deal."

He rose and shook her hand. "Well, that was easy enough. Today must be the day for deal making."

"Yes, today is a most lovely day, Roderick Adair." *And I have something to look forward to this Christmas. I wonder if it really snows in Kentucky in December.*

Even though Dr. Spencer and the other team members from the University of

Georgia accepted the hospital's invitation, Dr. Elena Daniels had refused to stay in the dorm-like facilities provided. Instead, she had insisted on the hotel down the street. After all, she was a professor, and she no longer accepted grad student treatment.

She looked at the time on her computer screen. Eight thirty. She was meeting Dr. Spencer at the hospital in half an hour. Her computer research had been unsuccessful. No online version of the *Moss Point Messenger,* and no mention of this Ernesto's beating Bella and her grandmother in any public records. Her hopes of communicating by email with someone at the local paper had gone farther south than Macon, so she resorted to a more direct approach. In her hand was the number for Delia Mullins, the *Messenger*'s news editor. She dialed the number.

"Delia Mullins speaking." No "Good morning, how may I help you?" Just a monotone "Delia Mullins speaking."

"Ah . . . good morning, Ms. Mullins. Are you the news editor?"

"Yep, you got news?"

Elena paused. Even she was bumped off balance with such a direct approach. "Ahh, no." She paused again. "Well, perhaps I do."

"So? Who is this, and what's the news?"

"I'm calling from the hospital in Atlanta where Gretchen and Bella Silva are being treated for wounds sustained in a brutal beating."

"Yep, I already know about that. Not news around here."

Elena's integrity and professional manner were a matter of convenience, especially when they stood in the gap between her and launching her career. "I was wondering if we could get a copy of this week's paper. Some of us at the hospital, who've been giving care to Gretchen and Bella, are very interested in the story."

"I can send you a copy for two bucks, but you won't find that story in the *Messenger.*"

"You didn't run a feature story about this beating?" Elena's original plan required the local feature story.

"Nope, no use. Already enough damage. So, what's your news?"

Elena was astute in the art of deflection. "Oh, I guess I'll check with some other papers. Perhaps the news editor at the *Atlanta Journal-Constitution* would be interested."

"Interested in what?" Delia was playing into Plan B.

"Well, it seems this young girl has some very rare gifts, and I thought someone

76

might have already run the story. I'm certain the AP will pick this one up."

"What kind of rare gifts? Psychic or something like that?" Silence. "You think the AP will really pick it up?"

Elena smiled as she slipped her feet into her stilettos. "Oh, yes. This girl has some really rare musical abilities — I think I heard the term *musical savant.* But Caroline Carlyle knows all about it. When this hits, it's going to be big. Television. CNN, who knows? Maybe even a book or movie rights." Elena walked in front of the mirror, unbuttoned the top button of her blouse, and reached for her bottle of spray cologne. She dampened her cleavage and fogged the room.

"Musical savant, you say?"

"That's what I heard." She tossed the cologne bottle into the top of her bag and adjusted her blouse for maximum exposure.

"I need the name of a source. What'd you say your name was?"

Click. Elena folded her cell phone shut, grabbed her computer bag, and sashayed out the hotel room door. She imagined Delia sitting there stewing over the possibilities of a big story right there in Moss Point.

Sam was about to walk out the door when

the phone rang. He waited at the porch door to see if Angel called him back. She did.

"Sam, it's Delia Mullins. Says it's important," Angel called from the sunroom.

Sam returned, walking cane in hand, and picked up the kitchen phone. "Well, hello, Delia. What's so all-fired important? Somebody sneaking cigarettes into the courthouse jail again?"

Undeterred, Delia's words were like machine-gun fire and their trajectory was Sam's ear. "Just got a call from an unnamed source with a long-distance number asking about the Silva case. Asking questions, Judge."

"What kind of questions?" Sam sat down on the stool Angel kept under the phone on the kitchen wall.

"Wanted to know if we had run the story yet. I told her it was no news as far as this paper was concerned. Said since we didn't carry the story, she'd call another newspaper — the *Atlanta Journal-Constitution,* she said."

Sam tried to minimize the potential fallout. "Now since when's the *Atlanta Journal-Constitution* interested in a family altercation in Moss Point?"

"Said something about the granddaughter having some kind of gift — musical savant, she said."

"Oh, did she now?" Sam tapped his walking stick on the floor.

"She did. Played me like Jimmy Gordon plays his fiddle. She thinks I live somewhere on the outskirts of stupid, but if there's a story here, Judge, it's mine. She said Caroline Carlyle knows all about it."

"I just wonder who this *she* is?"

"Don't worry, I got her number, Judge."

"I'll bet you do." The wrinkle between Sam's brows deepened.

"But Judge, I need Caroline's cell number."

"Well, now, Delia." Sam paused, figuring out how to handle this. "I tell you what, I think I'll give Caroline a call myself, and then I'll have her call you. Will you be in the office today?"

"I'm at the office every day unless I'm out on assignment. This is a big story. I'm on this like a chicken on a tumble bug. I'll be listening for Caroline. Later, Judge."

"Angel, where are you?" Sam hung up the phone and sat down at the breakfast table.

Angel returned from the sunroom with her palette in her hand. "Here I am."

"Can you get me Caroline's cell phone number? I need to talk to her now." Sam could smell trouble, and both his nostrils

79

were full this morning.

"You want to talk about it first?"

Sam clenched his teeth against the frustration brewing. There wasn't any use in taking it out on his wife.

"Just get the phone and dial her number, please. Can you sit here while I tell her what's going on?"

She laid her palette on the kitchen counter and went to the library for the cordless phone. Sitting down at the table, she dialed the number and handed him the phone.

It rang several times before Caroline answered. "Good morning, Sam. Was this supposed to be my wake-up call?"

"Hello, Caroline. No, I figured you to be awake. How are things?"

"Things are just wonderful. Guess where I am?" She smiled at Roderick as they crossed the street.

"Well, the hospital would have been my first answer. But then again, if you were at the hospital, you wouldn't have asked me to guess. So, I give up."

"Roderick arrived late last evening. He picked me up for breakfast, and we're on our way back to the hospital."

"Good. I'm glad he's there. Caroline, something's up and maybe this is a wake-up call for all of us. I think you'd better strap on your seat belt — the test rocket's on the launching pad. Got a call from Delia Mullins a few minutes ago. Seems some unidentified woman called her this morning asking about a news story — Gretchen and Bella."

"A news story?" Somber, tight lips replaced her smile.

Caroline was deeply engaged, but still felt Roderick take her arm and guide her across the street and to a quiet spot in the hospital lobby.

She listened intently as Sam told her what he knew of the unidentified caller and of Delia's intentions.

She put her phone away and looked at Roderick. "The word's out about Gretchen and Bella. We could be looking at major press. I'm so glad you're here. This is beyond my experience, and I want to do it right for Bella."

Roderick and Caroline made it back to the hospital in time for his reunion with his sister, Sarah, before she took Bella to their last day with Dr. Spencer. Caroline and Roderick spent the morning in the hospital room, whispering while Gretchen rested. When lunchtime came and Gretchen was still sleeping, Caroline didn't resist Roderick's suggestion of leaving the hospital for lunch.

Friday noon temperatures provided perfection for their lunch on the back terrace of a sidewalk café. The southern angle of autumn sunlight varnished their table. The hardwood trees, standing guard around the terrace, allowed the release of an occasional leaf of deep gold, which landed gently on their table and the surrounding chairs. Caroline captured a few of them for Gretchen and one for her journal — a tangible memory of this day.

She sat in disbelief that he would spend his first day back in the country with her. They chatted about his latest travels and business dealings and made plans for Saturday's visit to the Georgia Aquarium, then Roderick offered his plane to fly them all back to Moss Point on Monday. Their conversation slowed to quiet rest, but neither seemed to mind. In the lull, Caroline heard music, not audible to anyone else, but the music that filled her most of her life. Music that accompanied beauty and wonder and serenity and perfect contentment. A lovely day indeed.

Caroline could have waltzed through the rest of the day happy and content. But her plans were thwarted when her phone rang that afternoon. To avoid alarming Gretchen, she stepped into the hall to answer. It was Delia from the paper. Caroline answered the reporter's questions as truthfully as she dared, dodging as many details as she could. Her explanation of how this story could change the lives of Gretchen and Bella doused the flames of Delia's determination only briefly. Caroline sensed the embers were still smoldering, but at least there was another week before the next publication.

Delia Mullins salivated for this story the way Moss Point's residents' mouths watered at thoughts of the lemon-coconut cake Mabel served on Sunday at Café on the Square. Delia's only experience in newspaper publishing had been at the *Messenger.* Her twenty-seven years included weddings, obituaries, an occasional travel story, but no experience with the Associated Press. She'd think about that Monday, but testing the interest level with the *Atlanta Journal-Constitution* gave her somewhere to channel her enthusiasm in the meantime. It was late Friday afternoon, but she dialed the feature editor anyway.

Harry Newton answered his phone. He was interested but didn't need to resort to anything akin to interrogation tactics.

Instead, assuming a certain unwritten code of ethics existed among news editors, Delia gushed information like the fire hydrant at the corner of Peachtree and Pine. She had no way of knowing Harry's pencil was in motion, and that he'd be in his boss's office pitching the story for the *Journal-Constitution*'s Sunday edition before she turned the key in her vintage Ford Galaxy.

CHAPTER SIX:
SIGHT, SOUND, AND THE SECRET'S OUT

Bella had been amazingly calm and compliant during most of the week's testing. Sarah stayed within her reach even during the attempted MRI, which Sarah stopped due to Bella's agitation. Other tests requiring wires and leads to be attached to her head turned into play when Dr. Daniels put her big straw hat on Bella's head. The hat and the promise of seeing her mammá or playing the piano rendered her a virtual puppet in their hands for all other testing.

The team's observations of Bella raised questions regarding her vision. She had been able to see well enough at night to get from her house to Caroline's alone, even when she was injured. Her behavior at mealtimes indicated adequate vision. But anytime walking was involved, she held on to Sarah's arm and walked slightly behind her, assuming the position and gait of someone blind. She tended to get closer than normal to any object she wanted to see, and she always played the piano with her eyes closed. They assumed these were learned behaviors and were related to autism.

Dr. Ed Ferris, a leading ophthalmologist at the hospital, agreed to test Bella.

Sarah asked to observe the eye exam. "You know, Dr. Ferris, I am a child psychologist, and I'm more than mildly interested in how you will perform these visual tests on Bella. Don't they normally require verbal responses?"

"Insightful question. You're correct, but to prepare for this, I spent a few minutes on Wednesday watching Bella play the piano and was able to ascertain her gross visual capabilities by simple observation, but I recommended a more sophisticated test to check her visual acuity. I think we can get that done without a problem."

Dr. Ferris got reacquainted with Bella and began by asking her to walk across the room unaided. Sarah coaxed her, and Bella complied. He played a game with her, tossing a sponge ball for her to catch. She never missed and rarely lost eye contact with him when reaching to capture the ball in midair.

On his way out of his house that morning,

Dr. Ferris had grabbed one of his wife's music boxes, which he'd bought as a keepsake reminder of their trip to Austria. It was hand-painted porcelain — pale yellow with intricate coral-colored roses — and shaped like a grand piano. As a surprise for Bella, he pulled it from the brown grocery bag, unwrapped the nubby beach towel he'd used for padding, and held it in his hand. "Listen, Bella." He lifted the lid, revealing its delicate inner workings. It played "Pachelbel's Canon."

The tops of her knees became her imaginary keyboard as her fingers replayed the familiar melody, but her fingers stopped when he closed the lid, starting to play again only when he opened the music box a second time.

Bella stared at the music box but made immediate eye contact with Dr. Ferris when he closed the lid again. When he did not reopen it, she simply closed her eyes and hummed the melody, accompanying herself with the movement of her fingers.

Dr. Ferris was not getting the response he desired. "Bella, would you like to hold the music box?" Her eyes met his — silvery-green pools of color, perfectly still eyes with no hint of nystagmus, the involuntary eye movement usually seen in his patients who were visually impaired. That's what he wanted to see.

Bella took the miniature piano, held it close to her face, and opened its lid with care. Dr. Ferris noted her hand and eye coordination. He gave her a few minutes to open and close her newly found treasure while he explained the procedure to Sarah. "Normally with young children, we use the Allen figures, silhouettes of common objects like a rabbit, a car, or a cake — objects children could recognize and name. But Bella's somewhat nonverbal."

Sarah interrupted. "Thus far, she is nonverbal, but I have hopes that will change."

"I think we all have high hopes for Bella." He looked again at Bella, noting her enjoyment of the music box. "I've not seen any agitation this morning. Having her calm will make the testing easier."

"I agree. What is it you need me to do?"

"I'm going to use an electroretinogram to check the pathway from her eye to her occipital cortex. Will she tolerate electrodes around her eyes?"

Sarah reached for the straw hat on the table behind her. "She tolerated them very well earlier in the week. Of course, we used this to make a game of it. Will the hat be okay?"

"Oh yes, a hat's better than a mild sedative any day. You think you can get the music box?"

Sarah turned to Bella and asked to see the music box. Bella's hands gave it up, but her eyes held on tightly. Sarah let it play while the doctor prepared Bella for testing.

Dr. Ferris took great care in attaching the electrodes, especially to the bruised area around Bella's right eye. He reached for the hat. "Bella, would you like to wear your hat?"

Bella took the hat in both hands and seated it atop her head.

He continued his explanation to Sarah as he brought the equipment nearer. "I can check the pathway, but, Dr. McCollum, you understand that what I cannot determine is how Bella's brain interprets and integrates those impulses and information."

An hour later, Dr. Ferris announced that Bella's vision was well within the normal range and no corrective lenses were needed. Her mannerisms, which had suggested some visual impairment, could only be explained by her autistic tendencies. Dr. Ferris carefully removed the electrodes. Bella reached for the music box, held it near her face once again, and opened the lid.

He noticed her perfectly formed, slender

fingers cradling the piano. "Bella, you really like the music box, don't you?"

Her gaze shifted to him without the movement of any other muscle.

"Would you like to keep it?" Dr. Ferris reached for the brown paper bag and beach towel and handed them to Sarah. He whispered, "Wife doesn't know I took it this morning, and giving it to Bella may cost me another trip to Austria, but it would be worth it."

Sarah persuaded Bella to put the music box in the bag for safekeeping.

Friday came too soon for Wyatt Spencer, and he knew this would be the last day of its kind with Bella for the foreseeable future. Even with the autism and no structured education, Bella showed strong signs of intelligence, but there was so much yet to learn about her.

Dr. Spencer was pleased with the report of Dr. Ferris's findings, another item checked off his long list of things to be done. None of these neurologists, ophthalmologists, and psychologists had ever been in the presence of such a rare individual, let alone had four and a half days to observe her. They had learned that her vision was normal, that she could reproduce anything the pianist played on the piano, and that she never forgot what she had played.

Friday afternoon, they planned to observe her when she was left alone. Sarah seated Bella at a table in a room by herself where she sat with her hands in her lap, rocking back and forth for the next hour. Just before the doctors gave in to their boredom of staring through a one-way glass window, Bella began singing a beautiful melody.

Dr. Spencer reached into his briefcase for his personal tape recorder. For the next hour, they heard operatic arias in German and Italian sung by a child with perfect pitch. He explained, "Miss Carlyle told me that Bella's grandmother loves opera and told her all the stories and introduced her to opera." Bella's voice and her ability to mimic those she heard astounded them, yet she could not carry on a conversation.

Dr. Spencer's tape ran out before Bella did. "Listen, guys, we missed valuable stuff here today. We sent the video boys home too soon. This won't happen again. We mustn't take anything for granted with Bella."

At four o'clock, Dr. Spencer allowed Sarah to enter the room. Immediately, Bella became silent again. The crayons and drawing paper on the table in front of Bella had gone untouched for three hours. But when Sarah sat beside her and picked up a crayon and put it into Bella's hand, Bella drew pictures of pansy blossoms, hearts, and hands of all shapes and sizes. When one sheet was covered, Sarah passed her another. Her singing returned as she drew.

Dr. Spencer needed to earn points with Sarah, so at five, he called it a day before Sarah stopped the session and accused him again of being insensitive. The doctors and other University of Georgia staff on his team shut down their computers and reached for their bags.

Standing between the team and the window, Dr. Spencer said, "What we assumed was an isolated, doorless, music-filled room in Bella's brain may have a window or two, and it's up to us to find them." He lowered his head and clasped his hands together in front of him. "There's something about this experience with her that's almost sacred." He paused, and silence permeated the room. When the moment had passed, he continued. "I know you jumped through hoops to be here this week, getting substitutes to cover your classroom responsibilities for the last five days, but consider it an investment in science and the future of humanity. Let's say goodbye to Bella, and

I'll see all of you in my office on Monday at five o'clock. Anyone have a conflict?"

They all affirmed their availability except for Elena Daniels. A week with her, and it would have surprised him if she cooperated on any plan or idea that wasn't her own. "I don't know why we must wait until the afternoon. Let's get on this first thing Monday morning."

Dr. Spencer responded, "Elena, I think we'd all prefer that, but we have other responsibilities which have been neglected this week."

She picked up her computer bag and walked to the door. "Perhaps you all are too busy for this project. I'm perfectly capable and willing to take the lead on this."

All eyes were on Wyatt Spencer.

"Elena, let's talk outside." He picked up his bag with his left hand and grasped her arm with his right, practically pushing her into the hallway. When the door was closed, they faced each other. "Need I remind you that you're involved in this study simply because I invited you? I have the lead on this project, and that's not likely to change. If you're not on the team, perhaps you'd like to tell me now." Silence. "Will I see you Monday at five?"

"Why, I wouldn't miss it, Dr. Spencer!"

The sarcasm in her voice collided with her words and she stomped off without stopping to say goodbye to Bella.

Dr. Spencer stepped back into the conference room. "Let's speak to Bella before we all head back to Athens." Without another word, the team followed him in single file like penguins to the room next door. He knocked and went in. "Hello, Bella and Dr. McCollum. How about we call it a day?"

Bella continued singing and coloring, and Sarah rose from the table. "Good idea." She touched Bella lightly on the shoulder. "Bella, let's go see your mammá and Caroline, and you'll get to see my brother again." Bella's lyrics dissolved into humming as she put the crayon down and stood up.

Earlier in the week, Dr. Spencer had established the thumbs-up sign as their way of saying to Bella that she was doing great. Her lack of response gave them no reason to believe she understood the sign, but nonetheless, it had become ritual during their testing and interaction with her. Their previous experience with children with autism had taught them the importance of ritual. The team gathered around her in a semicircle, each speaking about their pleasure in meeting her. When each had spoken, their thumbs went up as if on cue from Dr.

Spencer.

Before they could turn and walk away, Bella picked up her hat from the chair next to her, put it on, and shocked them all with a smile, revealing white and perfectly straight teeth. She raised both arms high above her head and returned the thumbs-up sign — her first visible response to them all week.

The team received it as a diva welcomes a standing ovation. Dr. Spencer pointed to the door. "Way to go, Bella. Now let's get going. I'll walk with you and Dr. McCollum to see your mammá."

It was almost five o'clock. Harry Newton and Phil, his photographer, had made it to midtown Atlanta in record time during heavy traffic. As Phil pulled into a handicapped parking space, Harry called the front desk and made nice with the receptionist, who gave him Mrs. Silva's room number. He got out of the car and turned to Phil as they entered the building. "Receptionists are always forthcoming with information requested by the patients' pastors."

Phil readied his camera when they neared the elevator. "You got no scruples, Harry. I can't believe you'd impersonate a pastor. That's low."

95

"I've been in some churches where the pastor was impersonating a pastor," Harry retorted.

"You're dog meat, man. Now that's really low talking about men of the cloth that way." Phil pulled the lens cap from his camera and pretended to snap Harry.

"You mean lower than parking in a handi-capped parking space and hanging that fake parking permit on your rearview mirror?"

"It's not fake. It's real. It was my great aunt's. I kept it after she died."

"That's what I said — low." The elevator door opened to the sixth floor. "You get ready to capture anything that looks like a young girl with blonde hair. We'll get release forms later. Just make it look like you're taking a picture of something else if you can." Harry stepped in front of Phil as they exited the elevator. They stopped at the nurses' station near room 602. "Nurse, could you tell me, please — are Mrs. Silva and her granddaughter both in room 602 or is the granddaughter in a separate room?"

The nurse looked up from her computer screen. "Pardon me, are you family?"

At precisely that moment, Harry looked up to see, not more than thirty feet in front of him coming down the hall, a couple escorting an adolescent girl with long curly blonde hair and a bandage over the brow of her right eye. "Never mind, nurse, I see them now." Harry had an instinct about a story, and he was meeting one in the hallway.

"Come on, Phil. You know what to do," Harry said quietly as though he was the leader of a SWAT team engaging in a surprise assault. Phil followed Harry down the hall toward the girl, flashing photos of everything in sight to disguise the close-ups his camera allowed him to take of Bella as she came closer. Both parties were about to converge at the door to room 602.

Harry Newton wasn't the only one with instincts he followed.

Wyatt Spencer moved abruptly in front of Bella and pulled her behind him out of sight of the guy with the camera. "Hey, buddy, what do you think you're doing?" He stepped deliberately past room 602, pushing the door open as he went by it, and made sure Sarah and Bella moved inside. He closed the door. "Hey, I asked you what you're doing!"

The tall guy nodded to the cameraman, who backed down the hall and turned the corner out of sight, protecting his camera and photos. It looked like he'd done this drill before.

"So, who are you and why'd you get rid of your cameraman?" Wyatt was stepping into the man's personal space when Caroline and Roderick came through the door into the hallway. "Answer my question before we call security." By this time, Wyatt was in the man's face, and the man was fumbling for his wallet.

"My name is Harry Newton, and I'm a feature reporter for the *Atlanta Journal-Constitution.*"

"So that's who you are, now what are you doing here?" Wyatt pursued.

Harry turned to Caroline. "Are you Caroline Carlyle from Moss Point?"

At that point, Roderick stepped forward and joined Wyatt. "Sir, you're much more apt to get the cooperation you desire if you're more forthcoming about your purpose in being here."

"I'm here to get information about Gretchen Silva and her granddaughter. Feature story for the Sunday paper."

Wyatt fumbled for the pen and notepad in his shirt pocket. "So what makes you think there's a story here? And you can't print any of those photos without permission. Do you understand?"

"Got a call about an hour ago from a

Delia Mullins, editor down in Moss Point. Said Gretchen Silva and her granddaughter had been brutally beaten by the husband over the weekend and they were patients here. Is that true?"

Roderick looked resolute. "Since when does a domestic disturbance which occurred a week ago become a feature story? I would imagine that kind of thing happens daily all over the state, does it not?"

"It becomes a feature story when the granddaughter is a musical savant."

"How do you know that?" Wyatt thought he knew, but he asked anyway.

Caroline stepped forward and stood between Wyatt and Roderick. "It's okay, gentlemen." She looked at each of them. "I read Mr. Newton's columns and consider him to be factual, fair, knowledgeable, and we can only hope he'll be compassionate. If the story must be told, he is a fair one to tell it." Wyatt was surprised, and Harry Newton looked like he was as well. "Gretchen Silva has asked me to speak for her and for Bella. Shall we find a place to sit?"

Late Friday afternoon was quiet in the hospital hallways. The family waiting area was empty and provided a private place for this conversation. Caroline introduced

99

Wyatt and Roderick to each other and explained her role and Wyatt's involvement with the Silva family.

Though he was denied access to Gretchen or the granddaughter, Harry Newton got his story from the piano teacher who discovered Bella. Caroline begged him to spin the savant angle of the story and appealed to his benevolent sensitivity to minimize his coverage of the beating. Harry made no commitment.

Forty-five minutes and it was done — the story told to a major reporter who was now on his way to do his own research. Sunday was coming, and only God knew what would happen when the story broke. Control and concealment of the story would now turn to damage control. Left stunned and still sitting in the waiting area, they talked themselves into believing this storm would pass quickly, and life would return to normal. After all, who would really care? Though those present probably all had ideas about who might suddenly appear as interested parties now, names were never spoken.

Caroline explained to Wyatt about the anonymous call Delia Mullins had received that morning. Wyatt chose not to reveal to Caroline that Dr. Elena Daniels was the probable anonymous caller.

Wyatt had been completely engaged in the interview and in the debriefing afterward, but he did not miss the way Roderick naturally assumed his protective role of Caroline. He disliked the comfortable way she turned to Roderick and took his hand when she became uncomfortable with the reporter's questioning. He had no knowledge of who Roderick was or his relationship to Caroline, but his teenage years on the rodeo circuit back in Texas taught him to recognize a formidable opponent when he saw one.

CHAPTER SEVEN:
TEA AND PEARL BUTTONS

Caroline stood at the hospital window looking out on a lazy drizzle and colorless gray skies on this Saturday morning. She turned when she heard footsteps.

Gretchen, now untethered from tubes and walking unassisted on her eighth day in the hospital, stepped out of the bathroom in her hospital gown and Caroline's borrowed robe. "My first real shower in over a week, and the warm water was so soothing."

Gretchen's comment summoned Caroline from her place at the window. "All six hundred and eighty-two gallons of it? Must have faded your bruises; they're only slightly green now," Caroline teased her. "But you look like a prune."

Gretchen stopped towel-drying her hair. "A prune?" The confused expression on her face reminded Caroline that English was not Gretchen's first language.

She took Gretchen's hand and turned it

palm up, exposing the dimpled flesh of her fingers. "It's just an expression. See your hands, you know, like after you wash dishes for a while or go swimming. The water shrivels your flesh, and it looks like a prune."

Gretchen laughed for the first time since the incident, a gentle, restrained laugh, but it brought a smile to both their faces. "Does that mean in a few minutes, I will look like a plum again?"

Caroline hugged her. "It's so good to hear you laugh, and I've ordered something to put a real smile on your face. The nurse is bringing two cups of tea, and I went downstairs and picked up a couple of Danishes for our breakfast. Won't be as luscious as your pastry nor as good as my pot of tea, but what do you think?"

"I think it is a perfect morning to have a cup of tea with my friend. My imagination is too small to dream of having such a friend, one who puts her life on hold to take care of me." She kissed Caroline on each cheek. "And one who invites me to tea, even in a hospital room."

"Come, sit down. A real friend would dry your hair before the tea arrives. And a bit of makeup will make a new woman of you." As the dryer did its magic, Gretchen's platinum hair glided through Caroline's fingers like long threads of spun silk.

With her hair braided and coiled at the nape of her neck and a hint of manufactured color on her cheeks and lips, Gretchen joined Caroline in the two chairs across the room.

The nurse delivered two cups of tea, and Caroline reached for the bag of pastries.

"You sure you don't want to get back in bed for a while?"

"I think the bed must be tired of me. I shall give it a rest and have my breakfast with you." The friends enjoyed their breakfast as though they were sitting in the tearoom at the Ritz-Carlton and their pictures might appear in the society column tomorrow.

"Ah, my friend, your big heart is light this morning. Would it have anything to do with a certain Kentucky gentleman?"

Caroline's phone rang. She smiled when she recognized Roderick's cell number. "Gretchen, my friend, you speak of a gentleman from Kentucky, and he calls." She wiped apricot filling from the corner of her mouth.

Gretchen sipped her tea while Caroline took the call.

"He just phoned to say Sarah and Bella

104

have had their breakfast. They'll be here in about an hour. The aquarium doesn't open until ten, and they're stopping somewhere to buy a couple of umbrellas since it looks like the rain has set in for the day."

Gretchen looked out the window, partly because it reminded her of early winter days in Austria when she was a child and partly because she was hiding a tear. "Roderick is a very thoughtful man. I only wish Ernesto was a thinking man. His thoughtlessness has changed lives and cost so much, mostly to himself." She had only inquired once this week about Ernesto.

"Please don't worry, things will be fine. I'll see to it." Caroline patted Gretchen's knee.

"I am grateful for the gift you are to us, but, Caroline, you have a life. We are not your responsibility. I must find my own way now."

"But you don't have to do that alone. I know . . ." Caroline paused. "I've hidden myself in my studio and surrounded myself with work to numb my pain. I didn't want my family to know how much I was still grieving. Please don't do as I did. Please don't shut me out." Her voice trembled.

Gretchen's tears flowed. "How quickly our laughter condenses to tears. Would that our tears evaporated into laughter as quickly. Just a moment ago, we smiled at the day, and now we dry each other's tears."

"That's my point, Gretchen, we dry each other's tears and learn from each other. For years, I've bounced through the daily motions as if some puppeteer was pulling all the strings. But when I saw how you rose above your pain and cared so deeply for Bella, I realized I had been shielding myself from others out of fear of losing anyone again." She pointed her finger at Gretchen. "I watched you, my friend, and you taught me about purpose and relationships. I need you, and I know you need me too."

Gretchen wrapped the bathrobe more tightly over her knees. "I remember sitting on your garden bench telling you how I grew up in Austria and how I loved my grandmammá's piano playing. But there is so much more you do not understand."

"I want to understand, and I'm grateful you trust me with your story."

Gretchen told how her grandpappá died and her grandmammá came to live with them in their White Russian community in a little town in Austria. Her family had lived a genteel life, but war robbed them of their wealth and their status. Nevertheless, her mammá had insisted on spreading the fine linens on their primitive table, and they often dined in candlelight and remembered better days.

When Gretchen was nineteen, her parents arranged her marriage to Peter, the thirty-year-old son of a White Russian family who owned a grocery store a few blocks away. As the eldest children in each family, Peter and Gretchen abided by the wishes of their parents because it was expected of them. But Peter was a gentleman and Gretchen began to love him.

As Gretchen told her story, the strong accent of her mother tongue returned, the accent she had hidden, but not forgotten. "But then a thoughtless act changed my life and charted the course for two future generations." Gretchen gripped the teacup so tightly Caroline thought it might shatter.

"It was the beginning of December, and our parish looked like a Christmas card — candles glowing from inside frost-covered windows, boughs of cedar tied with red ribbon hung on front doors down every cobblestoned street.

"It was Friday evening, and Peter was to escort me to the church for a special evening of music. Ah, how I had looked forward to that evening. But Peter sent a message late in the day that a shipment of food had just arrived, and he must put it on the shelves in the market. It was impossible for him to finish his work and take me to church. I chose not to complain, as his busyness meant a better start for our marriage. But I could not bear to miss the music."

Caroline sat perfectly still, not wanting to break the rhythm of Gretchen's story.

"Elfi, my younger sister, had a fever, so she could not go with me, and my parents did not wish to leave her. So I went alone. When the evening was over, a light snow was falling and I had many blocks to walk to reach my home, but I did not mind. The music of Christmas had filled me with such joy, and I was humming the carols over and over again. In the next block, I saw Nicolai, Peter's younger brother, coming out of the tavern weaving and shouting in drunkenness.

"Peter was a dutiful son, but Nicolai was different. I crossed the street not wishing to deal with him. I had only walked a short distance into the thickening snow when I heard Nicolai's voice following me, taunting me, using language that no young man should use. I do not think he knew who I was."

Gretchen's gaze shifted from the window to Caroline's eyes. Her speech slowed. Well-aged pain buried deep inside surfaced as she continued. "Nicolai dragged me into the alley and . . . and . . ." Her eyes welled up with tears, and she dropped her chin, unable to look at Caroline. "The alley was dark and so quiet. I still remember the cold stone street and the taste of the wool scarf he stuffed into my mouth to muffle my cries. I heard the pearl buttons bounce on the stone and roll away as he ripped open my blouse. The weight of his body and the scent of his cologne were smothering. I struggled. I did. I struggled, but Nicolai was strong. His forearm across my neck as he held me down, and his heaviness, I can still feel. When he was finished, he walked away as though he had just stepped outside the tavern to dump a bag of garbage."

The two friends sat in silence as the reality of that horrible scene hovered around them like a dense, malodorous fog. Just above a whisper, Gretchen continued. "I got dressed and wrapped my coat tightly around me to conceal my torn clothes. I do believe an angel guided me home, for I have no recollection of how I got there. My parents met me at the door. I must have been later than they expected. Lines of worry etched their faces. I held my handkerchief to my bleeding lip and told them that

I had taken a bad fall on the icy street. If they did not believe me, they never told me."

Regaining her composure, Gretchen loosened her grasp on her teacup. "I was grateful Elfi was asleep. I undressed and sat in the darkness. It is very strange what one's mind can do to distract oneself. I still remember sitting on the edge of my bed thinking about the three pearl buttons on my blouse. It was my grandmammá's blouse, an old one, but a beautiful one, and she prized it for its buttons. Now they, along with my honor, lay somewhere in a frigid alley. By daylight, the snow would cover all evidence of what had happened to change my life."

Caroline remained quiet, even when Gretchen paused in her story.

"Only when I was certain my parents were asleep did I return downstairs to the bathroom. The ceiling light was dim, but bright enough to reveal the bruising on my back from the cold stones of the alley. I showered for as long as it was safe without waking my mother. I scrubbed my hair and my face and my neck to remove the stench of his cheap cologne. But I knew it didn't matter how long I tried to cleanse myself, no amount of soap and water would wash away my memories and shame.

"The holidays brought many gatherings with Peter's family. Nicolai's drunkenness left him with no memory of assaulting me, so he behaved normally. It was I who could not bear to be in his presence. I truly did not want to disappoint Peter, but I feigned illness at times when I knew Nicolai would be present. I did not have to pretend illness for long, for February brought confirmation that I was carrying a child, Nicolai's child.

"It was all too much. I could no longer bear being in the same room with Nicolai, and it was not in me to hide this from Peter and I could not tell him the truth. And how could I bring this grief on my parents? So, I left. I left before the winter snows melted. I had no money, so I took a few pieces of my grandmammá's jewelry and some money from the china teapot Mammá kept on the top shelf of the cupboard. I did not take it all, only enough to buy a train ticket.

"And you know the rest. The money took me to northern Germany where I got a job making pastries in a small café. My heart was broken into so many pieces. One piece for the things I had taken that were not mine. Another piece for the disgrace I brought to Peter, and a big piece for the great pain my disappearance caused my family." Gretchen's tears returned. "And

Elfi, my little sister." Her tears dropped into her lap. "I never told Elfi goodbye."

Caroline squeezed Gretchen's hand. The picture was clearer with missing pieces of the puzzle now in place. "Oh, Gretchen, I'm so sorry. I had no idea."

"How could you? I have never told anyone. Ernesto never asked questions, and I never lied to him. We were both alone and in pain, and he took care of me. He married me knowing that I was carrying the child of another man, and he has provided for me for the last twenty-eight years. We never spoke of it, but I think he was angry that I did not conceive another child."

"But nothing gave him the right to treat you the way he has."

"Caroline, I do not tell you this to make you angrier with Ernesto. I have had many years to think about this. We can never predict the outcome of our actions — even when they are thoughtful ones. Nicolai, intoxicated with alcohol mixed with the fearlessness of his youth, changed the course of many lives with one thoughtless act. But what I did also changed people's lives. It was all I could think to do at the time, but I have prayed for God to forgive me for the hurt I have caused. How can I ask Him to do that if I cannot forgive Nicolai and forgive myself? And now I must forgive Ernesto."

"I've never known anyone like you, Gretchen. You've experienced such pain, yet you're filled with gentleness and grace."

"Ah, how I wish it were so, my friend." Gretchen wiped her cheeks. "There is still pain, and I have anger. When Karina became pregnant at sixteen, Ernesto, in one of his rages, said horrible things to her. The names he called her pierced her heart. She thought her father hated her, and I could not make up for that. Then the young man, whom she loved, betrayed her and left her alone and so afraid.

"After Karina gave birth to Bella, Ernesto became worse. He was always so angry and so hard on Karina. When she could no longer bear the situation, she did as I did. She left. Neither Bella nor Karina were invited into this world through acts of love. Neither of them could help that, and I grieve for both of them. Karina's fear of her father drove her away, and Bella is all I have left, and I will not allow Bella to suffer any longer because of my actions or Ernesto's anger."

"Neither of you will suffer anymore, Gretchen. I truly believe good things are on the horizon."

113

"I would be so grateful if that is true, but what I want most is to see my Karina again and to make Bella's life better." They sat in silence for a moment. "When I left Austria, I took one other thing, the silver-framed hand mirror my grandmammá had given me on my twelfth birthday. I sold her jewelry to buy a train ticket, but I could never part with the mirror." She lowered her head. "I used this mirror to strike my husband. It is shattered. Now, there is nothing left of my past. I must look to the future."

A stillness filled the room that neither Caroline nor Gretchen chose to break. After a while, Caroline urged Gretchen to rest before Bella's arrival.

Caroline sat in the stillness while Gretchen napped. Scenes flashed through her memory — dropping her favorite teapot, Gretchen's asking her for the broken shards, and opening a box to find the figure of a delicate hand holding a heart all made from the broken pieces of her treasured vessel. Bella had made this for Caroline, and Gretchen had been so proud to return the shattered pieces now transformed into a work of art.

Caroline knew well that shattered treasures and defeated lives could be restored. She stepped into the hallway and phoned Sam. "Good morning."

"Top o' the morning to you, fidgety fingers," Sam answered.

"You haven't called me that in a while."

"Just figured since you haven't played your piano for over a week your fingers must be fidgeting by now. We'll be so glad to see you Monday."

"Me too. I guess Angel and Hattie are busy today."

"Busy? Why, you'd think the Queen of England was coming to Twin Oaks the way those two women have been cleaning and cooking. The meal plan for the next two weeks is posted on the refrigerator like a billboard, and Polly just delivered two buckets of fresh flowers for Angel to arrange. You know the only time Angel allows Polly to do the arranging of flowers she orders is when it's somebody's funeral. I could tell Polly's knickers were in a twist when she walked in the door. Can't figure this one out. Polly gets mad 'cause Angel arranges the flowers, even though she charges just as much to deliver 'em in a bucket as she does to arrange them. And Angel pays the full price, so I can't figure why she just won't let Polly arrange them.

That mess is in the same category as black holes — can't understand either one of 'em."

"It's a female thing, Sam, and some things just aren't meant to be understood." Caroline told him about Monday's travel plans before she announced the real reason for her call. "I need a favor."

"You got it. Anything you ask, and ol' Sam'll bust a gut to do it."

"This is really important. Gretchen's doing so much better, and this morning, we had our first real talk since the attack. She told me how she struck Ernesto with her silver-framed hand mirror. She knows it was shattered and assumes it's gone. But Sam, you gotta get it back. It's really important to get it back."

"Now, that may be a gut-buster. We're talking about a crime scene and a weapon and evidence here. I know I'm an old judge, but even an old judge might not be able to pull this one off. But don't you worry, ol' Sam's busted a gut before."

"Just keep this to yourself and Angel until I can explain. You're the best. See you Monday, and I'll call when I know our arrival time." Caroline closed her phone and smiled. Her plan was set in motion.

CHAPTER EIGHT:
THE FEEL OF WATER

Gretchen woke when she heard Caroline greeting Roderick, Sarah, and Bella. She moved to the edge of her hospital bed and sat up, extending her arms to her granddaughter. "Good morning, my Bella."

Bella let go of Sarah's hand and rushed to her mammá.

Gretchen hugged her gently, avoiding the brim of her straw hat, which now had become as customary for Bella as wearing underwear. "Oh, good morning, my beautiful gift. I am so glad to see you." She guided Bella to stand in front of her.

"Let me take a look at you. May I take off your hat?"

Bella removed the hat before Gretchen could reach it. Dressed in new jeans and an Atlanta Braves T-shirt Sarah had bought for her, Bella twirled around like a spinning top.

"That's better." Gretchen gently moved her fingers like a comb through Bella's hair.

117

"They have removed your bandages and now you only have Band-Aids to cover your wounds."

Sarah left Roderick standing just inside the door and eased over to the bed. "Yes, she's healing quickly, and she's been so good this week about the bandages and everything else. The doctor says she's his best patient ever, and I agree." She lifted Bella's hand and gently kissed her fingers.

"Oh, Dr. McCollum, how will I ever be able to thank you and Caroline for all you have done for Bella this week? And, Mr. Adair, you came all this way. Being here, taking her to the doctors, and look at her new clothes . . ." Gretchen's lip quivered as her eyes filled with tears. She took a deep breath. "What will I do to find a way to say thank you?"

"Your words and being near your Bella are all the thanks I need." Sarah turned to Caroline. "And I had time with the piano teacher over there."

Caroline piped in, "I don't know how I would have handled all this without you. I was so worried about how Bella would respond. The hospital setting, all the tests, all the strange people — doctors, nurses . . . But it's been amazing the way she has reacted. She has just taken to you. You're like

118

the Pied Piper."

Roderick broke his silence. "Now, let's not forget she *is* a trained professional, but I'll admit, they have become quite a pair."

"You give me far too much credit. I'm beginning to think Bella will be far more social if given the opportunity. She's adjusted to major changes quite well this week."

Gretchen had regained her composure. "You are another answer to my prayers of the last twelve years. God has brought you and Caroline to Bella at the perfect time."

"Oh, Gretchen, I don't know. No one's ever called me an answer to prayer. But perhaps Bella's calmness during this entire trauma has more to do with the spiritual realm than we know. So, don't stop praying."

"Oh, I will never stop praying. It would take me to the end of my days to express my gratitude for what is happening to my Bella. Now everyone will know how special she is. Her music will lighten the hearts of so many."

Caroline remembered the Sunday edition of the *Atlanta Journal-Constitution* coming out tomorrow — possibly the beginning of public awareness that could change Gretchen's life and Bella's future. "That's true. They have only to look at her and listen to her play to know how truly gifted she is."

Roderick stepped into the circle. "And just think how I feel! It's my privilege to take these three exceptional ladies to the Georgia Aquarium this rainy Saturday morning."

Caroline picked up her bag and eased toward Bella. "Oh, that's right. We have a really special treat today. You've worked so hard all week with all these doctors and tests; now it's time to play."

Bella surprised them and clapped her hands. "Play Caroline's piano, play Caroline's piano."

Astonishment washed their faces. Gretchen pulled Bella to her and hugged her. "No playing the piano today."

Caroline added, "But my piano's waiting for you. We'll be back at Twin Oaks in just two more days."

Roderick opened the door. "Well, if we only have two more days, then we should get going. Don't forget your umbrella; it's really coming down out there."

Caroline and Bella, hand in hand, led the way out the door, and Sarah and Roderick followed, guarding the rear in a supportive, protective way. Even with the makings of a happy day before her, Caroline's heart was somber with sadness remembering Gretchen's story.

Caroline grasped Bella's hand tightly as they dashed from the cab to the entrance of the Georgia Aquarium. Underneath the shelter, she shook the droplets from the umbrella, closed it, and looked back to see Roderick and Sarah closing the cab door and huddling to stay dry. Caroline approached the ticket booth and was reaching for her wallet when Roderick stepped ahead of her to the window.

He gently pushed her aside. "Four tickets, please."

"But this was to be my treat. You've already done so much." Caroline clutched her wallet.

"You must be kidding. Since when have I had the privilege of entertaining three stunningly beautiful ladies on a Saturday in Atlanta?" He pushed his money through the opening in the window, took the tickets from the red-haired, gum-chewing ticket agent, and stepped aside. "Besides, my mother would never have approved of such, would she, Sarah?"

"Rod's right. I'm just glad he still remembers."

"Enough said, sis." He returned his wallet

to his pocket and handed out the tickets. "Let's go, ladies." He stepped between Caroline and Bella, offering his left arm to Caroline and his right to Bella.

Caroline took his arm as though he had invited her onto the dance floor and watched to see what Bella would do. Bella, still wearing the hat Elena Daniels had given her, stood rigidly beside Roderick. She looked up at him, but not even the brim of the hat pulled tightly down on her forehead could hide the quizzical look on her face.

Caroline removed her hand from Roderick's arm and leaned forward. "Like this, Bella." She placed her hand in the bend of his arm, looked up at him, and smiled. "Thank you, Roderick."

Bella leaned forward, then straightened up, took Roderick's arm, looked up and smiled, and said, "Thank you, Roderick. Thank you, Roderick."

They laughed. Sarah smiled with satisfaction, and looking at her, Roderick said, "I think it's going to be a wonderful day."

"I think it's going to be a wonderful day, a wonderful day," Bella mimicked.

They entered the Georgia Aquarium, an ark-like building, with Sarah observing closely, hoping this would not be stimulation overload for Bella. After all, prior to a week ago, Bella's world existed in a modest frame house at the corner of Third Avenue and East Broad in Moss Point. An outing for her was a trip to the local grocery store or to the "safe place," the shack in the woods where she and her mammá went to do their needlework and to secretly hear Caroline play the piano.

Sarah suggested they walk first through the Ocean Voyager Exhibit, a hundred-foot underwater tunnel with viewing all around. Roderick led the way but allowed Bella to set the pace. It was like oozing through a glass cylinder into a well-lit, underwater ocean scene. The movements of the creatures were slow and fluid like the water, almost as if they were swaying to the enchanting, calming music seeping through the undetectable speakers all around.

Sarah watched Bella's head pivoting from side to side in order to see the schools of fish surrounding her. About twenty feet into the tunnel, she stopped. Unlike other children, who were squealing in delight, she stood in total stillness and silence. Her eyes followed the movements of the hammerhead sharks, oversized groupers, and schools of trevally jacks. A large manta ray passed overhead, creating a shadow like a lazy cloud creeping across the sun. Bella loosened her grip on Roderick's arm and turned to follow the giant ray's path. She remained fixated for several minutes.

Neither Roderick, Caroline, nor Sarah would disturb Bella's experience. As fascinating as the sea life was, Sarah was more interested in noting her observations of Bella in this setting. However, she did not miss how her brother studied Caroline.

Realizing they were stopping the traffic flow, Sarah took Bella's arm. "Would you like to hear the whales sing?"

Bella turned to Sarah without answer or change in facial expression.

"Do you know what a whale is?"

Still no response. Bella followed Sarah's lead through the last twenty feet of the underwater tube. As they came out of the tunnel, she pivoted for a final look.

"Come along, Bella, I want you to see the beluga whales. I think you'll like them." Sarah nodded to Caroline. "We've enjoyed the aviary at the north entrance to the hospital. Every morning when we came in, we stopped to visit the birds. In fact, Bella made a friend with one of the frosted peach canaries there, didn't you?"

Sarah took Bella's hand and led her away from the tunnel. "Do you remember how the canary sings?" Sarah whistled a couple of notes.

Bella grinned, pursed her lips, and whistled the song of the African canary.

"Did you know that it's the male canary who sings? And he won't sing if his mate is around." Sarah glared at Roderick. "Fancy that!"

"How sad. He has a beautiful song but won't sing to his mate?" Caroline asked.

"Odd, isn't it?" By this time, Sarah was following Bella as she quickly passed the sea lions and the African black-footed penguins, not slowing to look at either. "It is rather sad. Such a beautiful song, and he sings it to himself."

Bella, still whistling the canary's song, pulled her hand from Sarah's and ran down the dark sloping aisle as if she instinctively knew where she was going. Sarah, Caroline, and Roderick could hardly keep up. Their walk down the gray-carpeted ramp afforded their eyes time to adjust to the near darkness. Reaching the landing, Sarah saw Bella, statuesque in front of a thirty-foot-high wall of acrylic windows and whistling to the beluga whales.

"You found them, didn't you? The sea canaries. These are the singing fish I wanted you to see." Sarah thumbed through the

125

brochure. "Fishermen called them canaries because they could hear their songs from miles away, and these fishermen could actually feel the sound's vibrations through the hulls of their fishing boats." She pointed to the smaller whale near the glass. "And look, they have no dorsal fin. That's so they can swim under the ice."

"Well, sis, you're just a walking encyclopedia today. An expert in African canaries and Arctic whales. So how did you become so knowledgeable?"

"If you really must know, I've been reading the plaques at the aviary, and I just read the booklet they gave us with our aquarium tickets."

"Oh, so that's what you're supposed to do with this material?" Roderick teased his sister.

"It is if you're interested. Apparently, you're interested in other subjects this morning."

Sarah joined Roderick and Caroline on the benches provided for whale watching while Bella stood as close as she could get to the glass. The belugas put on quite a show — creamy white, twenty-five-hundred-pound creatures with rounded foreheads like giant melons — looking as though they were suspended in gray, fluid space. When they occasionally moved their heads from side to side, Bella mirrored their movement.

Caroline stood up. "Look at her." She approached Bella, took her hand, and stood beside her with their backs turned to Sarah and Roderick. The smallest of the whales returned to the glass where they stood. "Look, Bella, she's like you. She's just the color of your hair."

Peaceful environmental sounds of the deep surrounded them. Bella mimicked the sounds of the whale as they stood face-to-face.

"Quite a sight, isn't it, Rod?" Sarah asked.

"It certainly is." Roderick never took his eyes off Caroline.

"The whales, I mean."

"Of course, the whales."

"I can't really explain it, but Bella has this otherworldliness about her — her beauty, her rare gifts." Sarah paused. "And . . . and I wonder if maybe she's sensitive to things we might not see or hear."

"You're right. She's far too beautiful and good for this world."

"Rod, are we talking about Bella?"

He turned to his sister and smiled. The look in his eyes answered her question.

Sarah asked, "So when does this male canary sing his song?"

He gave no response. They sat silently for a while, engulfed by thoughts, and hypnotized by the music and the sea canaries' ballet.

Bella was mesmerized by the sights and sounds of the water and the fish. Although she tried to duplicate the songs of the whales, her adolescent voice could not reproduce the deep, haunting sounds of the belugas. *Sarah says "sea canaries." Real canaries make happy songs. Sea canaries sing sad songs. Bella likes sad songs. Mammá says, "Bella, please sing a happy song with me."*

Bella's body was as still as a life-size statue. On occasion, she rocked back and forth with the pulse of the music in her world. Even then, her body was stiff and her arms hung at her sides and her feet showed no signs of rhythmic sensation.

Make a happy song, whale. I'll make a happy song for you. Bella makes happy songs.

Caroline's eyes were set on the beluga whales as she and Bella stood hand in hand in front of the glass, but her mind had floated back to Rockwater. It was a steamy July afternoon in Kentucky. After walking about a mile from the house to the trout stream, she and Roderick had climbed Beckoning Boulder to sit and rest, their feet dangling ten or twelve feet above the natural spring his family called Blue Hole. He told her how three generations of Adair men had learned to swim in this pool, shaded by tall hardwoods and guarded by stones worn smooth over the centuries. As they perched in silence, absorbing the moment, she had yearned to slip off her clothes and dive deeply into the spring without so much as the splash of one drop to disturb the cool water's peacefulness. In her fantasy, Roderick joined her as they swam into the pool's depths to find the spring's source.

Dangling between daydreams and beluga whales, she glanced over her right shoulder. His gaze was penetrating and his smile perfect. Thoughts of a July afternoon caused her to look at him too long, and even though neither of them moved, she was teetering too close to the edge of losing her balance. *I can't do this. One minute I think I'm ready to move on with my life, but if I allow myself to think of him this way, I could be setting myself up for more pain. I've already come close to drowning in my sorrow, and I won't do it again.* She turned to Bella and gasped as though she had just broken the surface of the deep blue pool for air.

"Bella . . . Bella, have you ever been swimming?"

Bella was mesmerized and offered no response to Caroline's question.

She knelt and took Bella's hand. "Have you ever been swimming? I mean in the water like the whales swim?"

"Bath time. Bath time. Mammá says, 'It's bath time.' "

"Bath time?" She heard Roderick's baritone chuckle and turned to see the "that's Bella" look on Sarah's face. "So that's the extent of your swimming. Mine too," she said sadly before standing up again.

Roderick was moved to think that Bella didn't know what it was like to swim. As a young boy, he'd spent most of his summer afternoons in Blue Hole until his skin was shriveled and his mother accused him of growing fins and gills. Then he remembered that July afternoon at Blue Hole with Caroline, sitting atop the boulder, listening to her musical voice and thinking that God had fashioned her blue eyes at the same time He made Blue Hole. Desiring to know how she and the cool water would feel against his skin, he restrained himself from removing his shirt and diving in, begging her to join him. He was fascinated with

130

Caroline Carlyle. Like this pool, she was refreshing and deep.

When the Atlanta dealer had notified him of this pianist's interest in his grand piano, he asked Liz, his secretary, to do some research. The photo of Caroline in the University of Georgia's recital hall, a list of her accomplishments, and the intrigue of why she wanted to know about this particular piano had hooked him. His recital invitation had been to assuage his own curiosity.

After his father's death and the post-college termination of his engagement to Julia Crownover, whose commitment to his money was far deeper than her desire to build a life with him, he was singularly focused on building Adair Enterprises — acquiring companies, dismantling, reassembling, and selling them — all the while demonstrating his Midas touch. He took pride in his reputation for being ruthless, but occasionally he felt shame for his addiction to power. His justification became that creating more wealth provided him and Sarah more money to give away.

Nimble and smart, jetting across continents with vapor trails marking his path and sailing in and out of boardrooms with a wake of changes to fill his tracks, he had kept the wedding hounds at bay for the last fifteen years. Florists up and down the East Coast delivered parting bouquets to the women he dated, women whom he knew would be setting a trap for some new fellow before the blossoms had wilted. He trusted no one but his sister Sarah.

But for Caroline, no parting roses. He had filled Rockwater with her favorite white irises — strong emerald stems supporting delicate, pure white petals with velvety curves arranged in such a way that the depth of the blossom was entirely visible. Standing regal in crystal vases, the irises had a grace he'd never seen in a rose. For the last three months, Lilah, his housekeeper who had raised him, had deliberately kept fresh irises on the breakfast table, because she wanted them as a reminder of Caroline. He needed no reminder, and Lilah understood it better than he did.

The turn of Caroline's head and her smile summoned him back to real time. Here he was on a cool, rainy October morning in the Georgia Aquarium staring at her. She was like the iris — delicate, but not fragile; strong, but with a softness that showed no hard edges; transparent, but not without mystery and depth. Perhaps it was the ethereal, aquatic sounds around them, or perhaps it was because she was only a few steps away, but for this moment, he was at peace.

"Excuse me, sis, I'll be back in a moment." He left the viewing area quietly.

Sarah scrawled her thoughts in her notebook until he returned a few moments later with a scowl replacing his smile. "What happened? Did a deal just go south?"

He sat down on the bench next to his sister. "You might say that."

"A big one?" she pressed.

"Yep, and I lost it entirely, and I don't like losing."

"I'm sorry. Another one'll come along."

"Not like this one." He leaned to whisper to her. "Manager won't allow us to swim with the belugas."

Sarah's back straightened as she moved to the edge of her seat. "What?"

"I went to see the manager to arrange for us to swim in the tank with the whales. His answer just reminded me of how much I hate being told no."

"Are you serious, Rod? Swimming with those whales could be dangerous."

"The manager said the same thing because Bella can't swim and we're not certified divers."

"I can understand the manager's position."

He tried to keep his voice down so that Caroline and Bella wouldn't hear of his failure. "Okay, the guy has a point, but so do I. I thought Bella would love swimming with the whales."

"Maybe it would be a better idea to teach her to swim before you put her in a tank with several two-thousand-pound creatures."

He smiled at her. "Sarah, why is it that you're always the practical one?"

"I'm the oldest, and I just am, and I'm practical about Caroline too, little brother. And I think you're wasting time not telling her how you feel. She's smart and sensitive, but she's cautious and unassuming. She'll never make a move toward you the way other women do. So if anyone's going to make a move, you're it, Rod. Now tell me, what are you afraid of?"

He was about to tell Sarah that he'd made special dinner reservations when sounds of a Rachmaninoff concerto came from Caroline's purse. He watched her step away from Bella to answer the phone. "Oh, hello, Wyatt." Pause. "We're avoiding the rain and enjoying the Georgia Aquarium this morning."

With Thursday night's picture of Caroline and Wyatt Spencer in the hospital hallway still in his mind, Roderick leaned over to Sarah. "Need I answer your question now?" They joined Bella while Caroline finished her conversation with the doctor.

She put her phone away and approached them. "The feature editor has sent Wyatt a preview of the Sunday article. Wyatt says we'd better buckle up because it's going to be a . . . I think he said, 'a tumultuous ride.' "

After an hour with the whales and two hours of taking in all the sights and sounds of the enclosed sea, they stopped for lunch. Bella looked longingly at an ice cream sundae being delivered to the next table.

"Well then, it's ice cream sundaes for lunch. Why not a sundae on Saturday?" Roderick ordered four.

While the girls scraped the last bit of chocolate from the bottoms of their bowls and chatted between bites, Roderick slipped into the gift shop and returned with a CD of whale songs and a poster of a beluga whale for Bella. He would have purchased a life-size poster if they'd had one. He wanted Bella to remember this day.

He was about to tell Caroline he'd arranged an eight o'clock seating for a rooftop dinner at the Sun Dial when sounds of the C minor concerto returned. She apologized and stepped away from the table. Although he could not hear the conversation, he read her lips and the tension in her face. She promised someone she'd get there as soon as possible. He feared it was Angel or Gretchen.

A composed Caroline had left the table, but an agitated and excited one returned. "That was Mason. I must get to Ferngrove. Betsy's going into labor, and I promised her I'd be there. I can't miss the birth of my godchild."

CHAPTER NINE:
WELCOME AND GOOD NIGHT

An hour later, Roderick was in the cockpit with Acer checking the weather one last time before takeoff. Although it would be sundown before the weather cleared, the cloudiness and drizzle posed no threat for flying.

In the passenger cabin, Caroline checked her seat belt as she held the phone to her ear. It was difficult to even hear Sam's voice above the noise of the jet engine. "You tell Betsy ol' Sam can't wait to see that little baby girl. And tell her I'm sure glad she won't be born on Halloween."

"Okay, Sam. I'll tell her. We're about to take off, so I gotta go. I'll stay in touch."

She had already called her parents to explain that Roderick was flying her to Ferngrove in his private plane. Her dad would pick them up at the local airport and get her to the hospital.

The landing gear caused a slight jolt when

137

it returned to its flying position. Her three-to four-hour drive was now reduced to a forty-five-minute flight, thanks to Roderick.

Sarah was taking care of Gretchen and Bella until she could return. Surely the baby would be born within the next twenty-four hours so she could get back to Atlanta for Gretchen's hospital release and trip home to Twin Oaks on Monday.

Roderick came through the cockpit door and took the seat facing her. "I apologize. The flight's too short to make coffee or a cup of tea."

"Oh, I'll be fine. If I need caffeine, I'll get a cup at the hospital. I just can't figure why I'm so excited." She twisted the pearl ring she always wore on her right hand.

"Could it be that you've just been through a trauma that nearly cost a good friend her life and now you're headed home for the birth of your godchild? This last week hasn't been exactly an adagio movement for you."

She smiled. "Do you always know what to say?"

Confidently, he replied, "Yes."

She raised her right eyebrow. "Must be so reassuring to always say the right thing."

"Didn't tell you that I always say it. You asked if I always know what to say. But sometimes, it's best not to say anything, not even if it's the right thing."

"Sounds like the beginning of a philosophical discussion."

"And one we don't have time for right now. So, tell me about Betsy — the condensed version, please. I have about five minutes before Acer will need me in the cockpit."

"Condensed version? Well, first, I must say thank you for working out the details to get me to Ferngrove so quickly. I can't tell you how important it is that I get there."

"It is my unexpected pleasure, Miss Carlyle. I'll get to meet your parents and your best friend."

"That's right. They've wanted to meet you. Al-tho-ugh," she said in her most Southern drawl. "Betsy probably won't be at her best."

"Understandable."

"Oh, but she'll be at her happiest. Let's see, the condensed version. We've been conjoined at the heart since we were four years old. Betsy Ann Bradley, my best friend since preschool, married to Mason Dixon Harris III, the closest thing I have to another brother. And just how Southern can you get? Mason Dixon Harris. We were neighbors and like the Three Musketeers growing up, but it wasn't until college they realized they loved each other." She looked out the window of the plane into gray nothingness. "Their falling in love surprised them and me. Imagine falling in love with your best friend. What could be better? It was just right, you know. We all knew it."

She looked back at Roderick. "Mason introduced me to David at their wedding rehearsal dinner, and you know the end of that story. And because David had taken me to Guatemala with him on a few trips and I knew a few people, Mason and Betsy have little Josefina, my first godchild."

"Josefina? This baby on the way isn't their first?"

"No. The doctor told them it was highly unlikely Betsy would ever conceive. After three trips to Guatemala, Josefina has parents, and Mason and Betsy have a beautiful, brown-eyed Mayan daughter."

Roderick moved to the edge of his seat and reached for Caroline's hand. "Now, life has emerged out of David's death."

"I guess you could say that. Anyway, when Josefina was two years old, Betsy comes up pregnant. Surprised even her doctor. And then she surprised me by asking me to attend a couple of Lamaze classes with her when I was visiting Ferngrove this summer.

She wants me in the delivery room with her."

"Such wonderful surprises, and it would seem they have a tried and true friend in you." He squeezed her hand.

"Betsy and Mason are very important to me, the kind of friends I'll grow old with. We know too much about each other, and we've shared so many of life's hitching-post experiences — all the school stuff, championship games, piano competitions, proms, graduations, a wedding, an adoption, and a funeral. This birth I can't miss." She pointed her finger at him as though giving instructions. "Can you believe Mason called this little one 'Booger' until the ultrasound indicated it was a girl? I wonder what they'll name her. Knowing him, it'll be something like Masonette."

"You ponder that while I make sure they don't have this baby without you." Roderick rose, leaned forward, kissed her on the forehead, and walked toward the cockpit.

He was reaching for the door handle when he heard, "Roderick?" He pivoted in the aisle.

Her words wouldn't come. "Never mind." She touched her fingers to her lips. As she turned her palm toward him as if to send him a kiss, she stopped halfway through the motion.

He stood waiting.

"Thank you for knowing what to say." Blue eyes met brown eyes as she dropped her hands to her lap.

Roderick waited a moment, smiled, and disappeared through the cockpit door.

The digital clock above the door read five fifteen. Caroline moved like a woman on a mission through the hospital waiting room, waving at her mother and apologizing for not introducing Roderick properly. She was approaching the double doors when she thought of Josefina. She dropped her bag, walked over to Mrs. Bradley, and picked up the toddler from her grandmother's lap. Three-year-old Josefina giggled and placed her palms on Caroline's cheeks. "CC, my candy kisses?"

"No, sweet pea, CC didn't have time to get to the candy shop. I promise to bring a really, really big bag next time, okay?" She hugged her and whirled her around. "Now, I have to go see your mom, and when I come out, you're going to have a new baby sister."

She put Josefina back in Mrs. Bradley's lap and hastily slipped through the wooden double doors into the delivery room, no doubt the same double doors her mother had entered nearly thirty years ago when Caroline was born.

Mason met her with a hospital gown. "Here, put this on. Doc says it won't be long. She's already dilated to eight and a half centimeters, and her contractions are about two minutes apart." He held the gown while Caroline stuck her arms through and tied it at the nape of her neck.

"You're perspiring as though you're the one having the contractions. Where's Betsy?" At that moment, from behind the blue curtain, Caroline heard a distressed voice crying, "Ma-son." "Never mind, I think I figured it out." She raised her right eyebrow to Mason and flew around the blue curtain.

"Betsy, I'm here. I made it." She took Betsy's hand.

Betsy's face looked like it did after their last visit to Daytona Beach eight years ago — skin the color of a boiled beet and eyes donut-puffy. Her blonde hair was plastered to her head from perspiration.

"Hey, friend, if I have to sweat like you and Mason to be a part of this delivery, then I'm outta here." Like her father, Caroline used humor to lighten tense moments.

Betsy, the former basketball player, smiled. "Oh, that's right, CC. I forgot. You never did like sweating and breathing hard."

Always ready with a redneck wisecrack, Mason rolled his eyes and said, "You're going to miss out on some of life's greatest joys and pleasures if you're not willing to sweat or breathe hard, CC."

He got Caroline's raised right eyebrow again. In fact, he had probably gotten more of those in the last twenty-five years than any other person in her life. He just seemed to evoke them.

Another contraction. "Ohhhh . . . sh . . . shut up, Mason, and give me your hand."

Between contractions, Betsy told her of the names she had picked out. "We thought about Sarah Elizabeth or Briana Elizabeth, and Grace Elizabeth, or maybe Eva Marie for her grandmothers. We'll just decide when we meet her."

"Sounds like you never got over your mother naming you Betsy instead of Elizabeth." She wiped Betsy's brow with a cold cloth. "You remember when you insisted your real name was Elizabeth and you made me call you Elizabeth?"

"I remember. When you wouldn't do it, I called you CC because I knew you hated it." Betsy tensed, her face contorted in pain, and the bed railings rattled under her pulsating grip. "Oh, oh, I think it's time. Get the doctor. And Mason, do you see that aluminum pole holding the bag of medicine? If you tell me to push or to breathe, I will make it your permanent bow tie. Now, just get the doctor."

Twenty more minutes of hopeful agony, another pint of sweat, and Dr. Handley was holding a squalling bundle. Caroline and Mason, on opposite sides of the bed, stared at the baby. Mason, eyes bulging, looked across Betsy's knees at both of Caroline's raised eyebrows. "Is that what I think it is?"

The doctor grinned like Mason did when he put the whoopee cushion in their biology teacher's chair in the ninth grade. "Here, Mason, let's introduce little mama here to Mason Dixon Harris IV."

"What? Betsy, we have a son! And I promise you this, Betsy, no son of mine is going to sleep in a nursery with mocha brown and pale pink striped walls and pink polkadotted curtains." He turned to the doctor. "And he won't be the fourth. That business stops with me. He's a first."

The doctor grinned. "Guess this little one was a surprise from the get-go. But he's got all his fingers and toes and a healthy set of lungs, I'd say."

Betsy and Mason laughed and cried for a few minutes. He whispered something in her ear, which triggered a smile and a simultaneous tear. She nodded in agreement.

The nurse interrupted by slapping an instrument in Mason's hand. "Here, Papa, this is your job. It's time to cut the cord."

Mason performed his duty. The doctor passed the baby to the nurse as he returned to his position between the stirrups at the foot of the bed. "Okay, nurse, let's get this quarterback cleaned up and checked out. And, Mason, why don't you go let the family in on the big surprise while I finish here with Betsy?"

"Come with me, Caroline." Mason strutted through the double doors to the waiting room for his announcement. "At exactly seven fourteen this lovely Saturday evening in October, Betsy gave birth to an eight-pound, five-ounce, twenty-one-inch-long, strong, handsome, and brilliant David Mason Harris, named for the best friend a man could ever have." He turned to Caroline. "And Betsy and I promise to raise him to be every bit of the man that David Summers was."

No raised eyebrow this time. Instead there was a deep crease in her brow and a tremor in her chin. When she could no longer suffocate her urge to cry, Caroline, without words, buried her face in Mason's chest and her arms went around his neck. They held each other, squeezing gladness and sadness together, until their tears turned to laughter.

Betsy could hear the mixture of gasps, squeals, and laughter coming from the waiting room. She surmised what naming their son David would mean to her dearest friend.

Caroline returned to the delivery room to take advantage of a few quiet moments with Betsy while the baby was being checked and before the parade of family started. "Oh, Betsy, are you sure about the name? I mean, anybody with a pink and mocha nursery and chests of pink and white baby clothes hasn't been thinking about names for a boy."

"Of course I'm sure. You know how Mason loved David. They had a bond like ours. He was like a brother to Mason — like you're a sister to me." She winced in pain. "Are you all right with this, CC? Will it make you too sad?"

The smile in Caroline's teary eyes answered Betsy's question. "You've given me such a gift. Naming him David and being here for the birth, which may be the only birth I ever experience." She looked away briefly before the humor returned. "That is, unless Sarah Elizabeth surprises us in a year or two."

"You have to be kidding. No. No way. Josefina was the engine and little David will be the perfect caboose. And don't count yourself out, friend. You're not using a walker yet, and didn't I hear you arrived in a private plane?"

Caroline's face flushed. "I was always the one with the imagination, reading and dreaming while you were running track, so what's happening here?"

"I figured it out. You have to imagine it, Caroline. There's something between you two, isn't there? He came to Atlanta to be with you and brought you here. Something's going on." She waited for Caroline to respond.

"Oh, who knows? Would you like some ice chips?"

"If in God's providence something is happening between you two, then you'll get a head start by dreaming about it. And if there isn't, you still had some sweet moments imagining. After all, it's imagination, not love, that makes the world go round."

"Imagination? Not love? What books have you been reading?" She handed Betsy a cup of ice chips. "So, do you want to meet this man who's larger than my imagination?"

"Now?" Betsy instinctively ran her hand through her damp blonde hair.

"Uh-huh. It's now or maybe never, at least until I've done some imagining."

"But I'm a mess."

"Yeah, you are. But you're a beautiful mess, and besides, don't talk about the mother of my godson like that." Caroline bent to kiss Betsy's cheek.

The nurse brought the swaddled baby and laid him on Betsy's breast. "Your family can come in for a few minutes now."

"I'll get your parents and Josefina, then Roderick can come in. Do you mind if my folks come in too?"

"No, let's have a party. We have a son." Betsy glowed, and not just from perspiration.

"Okay, a party." She hesitated. "Betsy, I can't stay. I have to get back to Atlanta tonight. There's a big story about Bella coming out in tomorrow's *Atlanta Journal-Constitution,* and I need to be there for the fallout. Then I'm bringing Bella and her grandmother back to Twin Oaks Monday."

"You're still a do-gooder, friend. I understand. You were here for the important part."

"I wish I could stay, but from the sounds coming from the waiting room, I think you

149

may have more help than you really want over the next few days. I'll be back in a few weeks."

The plane's engine was humming twenty-two thousand feet over Middle Georgia. They would be back in Atlanta by eleven o'clock. The afternoon drizzle and fog had disappeared with the daylight and left a crystal-clear October evening. The full moon was lovely. Hurtling through this vast night sky in a metal engine-powered tube, Caroline stretched out across the seat to watch the stars flitter by.

The dark sky was so big, immeasurable, untouchable, and little David was so small, but he had been weighed, measured, and deemed completely huggable. Now a new person with a unique fingerprint and personality and potential, David had his beginning in a shared, pleasurable act of love. In this union, two microscopic particles found each other and started a divide-and-multiply process that nine months later resulted in his birth. It was a miracle of created intelligence that instructed the cells to divide to make eyes and ears and fingers and lungs. And after a prescribed time for cell multiplication, he burst forth into the world. How did he know when he could survive outside his mother's body? And was birth as painful to him?

She bowed her head in gratitude for his safe delivery, for the love that created him, and for the way Mason and Betsy welcomed him into the world. She prayed for this little one, who would grow up and start the cycle over again.

As she pondered, she thought of Gretchen and how an act of violence also produced a child; and how that child, in starting the cycle again, had produced Bella. Tears appeared when she thought that Bella was not invited into the world nor welcomed by the two who created her. Instead, when she burst into a world she couldn't understand, her parents abandoned her long before they knew how unique she was. Caroline gave thanks for Gretchen, who had been violated and continually abused, yet had never lost her faith nor her ability to imagine something better in this world for Bella.

Perhaps Betsy's right. Maybe it is imagination that makes the world go round. She closed her eyes and rested her head. Her thoughts bounced and rolled like a broken strand of pearls until they settled in one spot. She imagined. She imagined a Christmas recital at Rockwater. She imagined the smells of the Scotch pine Christmas tree

151

and Lilah's gingersnaps baking, and the sparkle of lighted candles on the mantle, and the taste of mulled cider while the snow was falling. She imagined the sounds of a crackling fire in the library and cuddling in the evening with Roderick on the paisley sofa that hugged its occupants. She dreamed of how his cashmere sweater would feel against her cheek when she rested her head on his shoulder, and she imagined how he would look at her when they were alone and when they were in a crowded room.

"Miss Carlyle, pick up the phone, please."

Caroline sat up straight, feeling like her teacher had just caught her daydreaming during the spelling bee. She reached in the arm of her seat for the phone.

"Remember, mash the button so that I can hear you."

She fumbled with the phone and finally found the red button. "Yes, I'm here."

"We'll be landing in about ten minutes. Are you strapped in?"

"Yes. I mean I will be momentarily."

"What about a late supper? You've had nothing to eat since your ice cream sundae at the aquarium today. You've flown a few hundred miles and delivered a baby since then."

"I have, haven't I?" She stretched and

152

rolled her shoulders.

"I was dreaming about a grilled three-cheese sandwich and a glass of red wine. Sound good to you?"

"Umm. Sounds perfect, maybe with a cup of chamomile to top it off."

"Chamomile it is. Sit tight for the landing."

Why must you have that edgy baritone voice that would melt me even if I had never seen your sculpted face or your brown eyes that see to my soul, Mr. Adair? Her magic-carpet imagination had taken her to Rockwater for Christmas, but the lateness of the evening and her bone-tiredness returned her to reality.

"Thanks for the ride, Acer. I'll call you when I know the departure time. You can make the flight plan then." Roderick closed the car door, waved goodbye, and ushered Caroline through the revolving front door of the Ritz-Carlton. "Let's see if the kitchen is still open or what I might have to do to get it open." He left her to enjoy the massive floral arrangement on the table at the entrance while he spoke with someone at the concierge desk.

He returned with a card in his hand. "They're closed for service, but the cook is still here and has agreed to stay late to prepare us something as long as we keep it simple."

"Simple it is."

"I've taken care of your room here for the night. I phoned Sarah earlier and asked her to get your things, so here's your room key."

"Thank you, Roderick. You have anticipated my every need today. I'm sincerely grateful. I do need a night's rest. Your generosity seems unending, but I'd be more comfortable paying for my room."

Roderick liked that about her. She was not intimidated by him, and she did not assume that because he was wealthy, he should pay.

The chef, an older Bahamian man with a broad smile who smelled of grilled onions, greeted them at the closed door of the restaurant and allowed them to take the table of their choice. He followed them as Roderick led Caroline to the table for two by the window overlooking the pool.

"We'd just like a grilled cheese sandwich and a glass of wine. And if it's not too much trouble, I'd prefer maybe two or three kinds of shredded cheese on buttered and grilled French bread if you have it. The house red wine is fine." Roderick was exact about most things.

"Yes sir, I have Gruyere, Swiss, and a white cheddar that would make a fine grilled cheese sandwich. And maybe I'll throw in a bit of American cheddar for color. In fact, if you like it, I may add it to the menu. I'll bring some strawberry preserves just in case." The chef put their water glasses on the table and disappeared into the kitchen.

"Sounds really good. Was this another way your Francophile mother spoiled you?"

He pulled his chair closer to the table. "Ah, you remembered. Yes. She had a way about her, a way of making even the simplest things special. Mother always said, 'It's not enough to eat. We must dine.' "

"She made sweet memories for you. Wish I had known her."

"She would have loved you, Caroline, and she would have quickly won your heart too. You're really like her in many ways, especially with your music and your appreciation of beautiful things. When you come at Christmas, I'll show you her room."

"You mean for the holiday recital?"

"Yes, of course, when you come for the recital." He wanted a Rockwater Christmas with Caroline, but it wasn't time to invite her for Christmas. "By the way, you have your mother's charm and sensibility and your father's eyes and wit."

"Oh, that's right, you've had no time to report." She twirled the tendril of hair at her temple. "Well, you've driven through Ferngrove on a fall afternoon. You've met my parents and Betsy. You've seen the hospital where I was born, and you've probably heard more Betsy and Caroline stories than you cared about, so what do you think?"

"Well, I'm still thinking. And by the way, your parents' pastor had more tales about you than your mother did."

"Oops. Please tell me my brothers didn't show up."

"No, but I'll bet they're as real as your mom and dad. They made you who you are, so what's not to like?"

"You truly do always know what to say. Thanks for getting me there and putting up with all my kin."

The chef brought out two glasses and the bottle of wine. "Your grilled cheese sandwiches are coming out shortly." He poured the wine for Roderick's approval.

They recalled the day's activities while they sipped their wine. He wanted to taste the wine that touched her lips. He wanted to tell her of his Christmas dreams and that he woke every morning with thoughts of her, but it was too soon.

He remembered how she stood on the stairway, calling it an evening after her July Rockwater recital. He had never asked to kiss a woman before, but that time he'd asked. She had said, "Yes, when you don't feel the need to ask." He recalled how, not coyly, but sweetly, she had kissed his cheek and climbed the stairs to her suite. He was now beyond asking, but he would be more imaginative. After all, he was the son of a creative woman who instinctively made life more — more beautiful, more fun, more delicious, and more memorable.

They ate their sandwiches and drank the wine. The chef appeared to check on them. "How's the grilled four-cheese sandwich?"

Roderick put down his napkin. "At the risk of being presumptive, I'll expect to see the menus reprinted before tomorrow evening."

"That good, you say?" The chef nodded. "Sir, I tried one myself, and I must say with an array of fresh berries and peaches, this deserves its own line on the menu once I come up with a proper name for it. How did you like it that I crusted the bread with grated parmesan in my panini press?"

"That crisp was a tasty idea. You could name this for my mother. Her name was

Angeleah."

"Oh, sir, that name is far too elegant for a grilled cheese sandwich."

"If you won't name this sandwich for my mother, could I ask for one more thing?"

"Certainly, Mr. Adair. What could I get you?"

"Two cups of chamomile tea, and we'll have it on the patio by the pool. That way, you can lock up and go home."

"I'll bring your cups of tea to the patio." He put the ticket on the table.

"Wait, I'll sign it now." Roderick signed the check. Unseen to Caroline, he wrote a note asking that one yellow iris from the flowers in the foyer accompany their tea and added a hundred-dollar tip to the check.

He stood and offered Caroline his arm. "Shall we, Miss Carlyle?"

"I could never refuse you, Mr. Adair."

He wished it were so.

They brushed the leaves out of the chairs before sitting. Caroline curled her feet under her in her chair. "Who would have thought so much could happen since our breakfast yesterday on this patio? I mean a pushy reporter featuring Bella in a story tomorrow, a trip to the aquarium, the birth of my godson, and the best grilled-cheese

158

sandwich ever. Seems the fall breezes were whirling more than red and gold leaves the past thirty-six hours."

"I certainly wouldn't have imagined it."

He said "imagine." I wonder what he would imagine. She pulled up the collar of her denim jacket.

"Are you too cool?"

"I'm cool, but not so cool as to miss the harvest moon." She pointed through the tallest tree limbs. "You see a moon like this only in October, and it's full tonight, looking like one of Grand Ma'am's china plates on a deep blue tablecloth. Maybe that's why little David was born this evening. The moon's full."

"I can tell you it was quite beautiful from the cockpit on the flight up. Looks so different at that altitude and away from the city lights."

"Lots of things are more beautiful away from the lights of the city." She remembered the view from her suite at Rockwater and the full moon over rolling Kentucky hills.

The chef appeared with two cups of tea, one yellow iris, and the smile of one who was planning a surprise party. "Here's your tea, and here's your gentleman's request for you, lovely lady." He handed the iris to Caroline and smiled even more broadly.

"And I can see why you wanted to drink your tea out here in the light of that big old harvest moon. Don't get to see that but once a year, and looking at it with a lady this beautiful is something most men never get to do. Enjoy."

Roderick stood to thank him. "I would agree, and thank you for your service. We'll just leave our teacups on the table here."

The chef walked away humming "Moon Over Miami."

The air was cool and humid enough to produce steam from the teacup. She twirled the iris between her fingers and brushed it to her chin. "Thank you again, Roderick. You've found many ways to make this a day I'll long remember." *If you kissed me, it would be a day I'd not likely forget.*

"I'm glad. That means it'll be a while before I'm forgotten." He sipped his tea.

"Oh, I'd say a few days at least." The leaves swirled around them. "You have a way of making certain you're remembered. Inherited that from your mother, I suppose."

"One of many traits she passed down to me." He continued looking at the moon.

She held the steaming cup near her face. "Today seems to be a day of thinking about mothers. With Betsy's baby coming, and

I've been thinking about Gretchen and her daughter, and then Bella. And of all things, this day brought your unexpected introduction to my mother, and here we sit talking about yours."

"Well, we all have mothers."

She giggled. "Can't argue with that. You know, I think we're getting punchy. Long day and who knows what tomorrow will bring once the article hits."

"You're right. You must be very tired, and I should get you upstairs. Not every day you get to deliver a baby."

Roderick rose from his chair and put his cup on the table. He extended his hand to Caroline. She shivered as she rose from her cushioned seat. They stood facing each other in silence except for the late-night noises of the city and the rustle of leaves on the patio. The moonlight's play on the surface of the pool gave enough light for her to see his eyes. He was looking at her the way she had imagined earlier. The night breezes had ruffled his hair, and she imagined touching the dark curl resting on his forehead.

Roderick ran his finger along the crease in her collar. His hand brushed her neck as he pulled her jacket tighter around her.

She shivered again, but not from an

October night's chill. Stepping closer to him, her hands rested instinctively on his chest, the iris in her left hand. Her heart was beating rapidly like the wings of a moth circling the light. She felt his arms as they encircled her, embracing her gently and securely, but not tightly, the stubble of his beard against her temple.

He brushed the tendrils of hair from her cheek and kissed it softly. "It's been a wonderful day, Caroline Carlyle." He released her, took her hand, and turned for one last look at the October moon.

You really didn't have to ask, Roderick. Even in her late-night wonderings about Roderick, she couldn't have imagined a more perfect setting for their first kiss. She ached to know what it would be like. But her yearnings went unanswered.

The dried Japanese maple leaves crunched under their feet as they walked across the patio to the back entrance of the hotel. Neither spoke, but the silence was not awkward, not even during the elevator ride to the eleventh floor or the walk down the hallway.

He took her key and opened her door. "Sarah brought your things over from the hospital, so they should be in your room. I'll knock on your door at eight for breakfast." He took her hand and pressed it to his lips, and then he handed her the key. "Good night and rest well, Blue Eyes."

"You too, Roderick."

She closed the door as he walked away, and with her back to the door, she sluggishly slid to the floor and pulled her knees to her chin and wrapped her arms around them. Her body drained of energy and her heart weary with questions, she sat in the darkness. *Are you not feeling what I'm feeling? Am I not allowing you to see that you really don't have to ask? You really don't have to ask.*

Chapter Ten:
When the Caterpillar
Crawls on the Rosebud

Roderick handed Caroline the Sunday morning newspaper when he knocked on her door at eight o'clock. He had already read the article, but neither his face nor words gave hint to his evaluation of the story. They walked to the restaurant and took their seat at the table next to the window — the same table where they ate their midnight sandwich the night before.

Caroline ate her muffin before reading the article. "Now I understand what Wyatt meant yesterday when he warned me about a tumultuous ride. How much more sensational can an article be?" Caroline slapped the newspaper down on the table for the second time and picked up her cup of coffee.

"Unfortunately, that's what sells papers."

"Yes, but why not tell the readers how beautiful she is and how rare her abilities are? He used practically none of the research

Wyatt gave him. Instead, he gives the story the tone of a circus sideshow and makes Bella sound as though she's been purposefully hidden away from the world for years by a brutal man."

Roderick took the paper and put it next to his briefcase on the floor. "Well, there is a bit of truth here, Caroline. Bella and Gretchen have been imprisoned in a way, and besides, Newton is setting the stage for follow-up articles. He won't give it all away in one story."

"Oh." She sighed. "But I just can't bear to think how this will affect Gretchen when she reads it. As much as he's put her through, it will hurt her that Ernesto has been depicted this way."

Roderick noticed her fingers moving on the table as though she were playing the piano.

"As cruel as he's been, she still recognizes him as her husband, and showing her face in Moss Point will be so difficult now. You can't get lost in a small town like you can in the city." She sipped the freshly squeezed orange juice just delivered to their table.

"I think you underestimate her. There's a resilience about Gretchen, and she has a forgiving and understanding nature."

"Oh, if you only knew her story, then

165

you'd know how resilient she truly is. She didn't swear me to her confidence, but it is so tragic and deeply personal, I just need her to say it's okay before I tell anyone."

"I understand. I don't need to know. I think I know enough about Gretchen to know she'll weather this."

"You really think so?"

"Of course I do. What's the most important thing in the world to Gretchen?" He paused. "It's Bella. That's kept her going for years, putting up with an abusive husband and even surviving this beating. What makes you think one insensitive article is going to make such a difference in her life? She's a survivor, and she'll do what's best for Bella."

"A cup of coffee and one conversation with you, and my world seems a better place."

He longed to be the one to make her world a better place. He knew that with her his world would be complete, but he couldn't reveal that yet.

She cleared her throat. "I mean, I feel better about this situation. You make it seem not quite so dubious. And besides, what worse could happen to her?"

"Now you're more on track." He looked at his watch. "The one who could cause her the most pain is in jail, and he'll stay there for a while. That'll give Gretchen time to build a new life without him, and we'll make certain that life is one where Bella can thrive."

"So, now our job is just to get through the next few weeks of dealing with the mysterious unknowns."

"What possible unknowns could put that crease in your pretty brow this morning?" He leaned forward and propped his elbows on the table. He studied her darting eyes and the movement of her hands, stretched with tension, as she talked.

"Like, will there be a trial? Will Gretchen have to face Ernesto? And what if Karina comes home? And will the media be hounding Gretchen and Bella?"

Roderick reached across the table and took her hand in midair and held it. "Yes."

Caroline looked at him. "Yes? Yes, what?"

"Yes, there will be a trial unless he confesses. And, yes, either way, Gretchen will have some part in the procedure." He pressed her hands to the table and held them securely. "And no, I cannot imagine the media not making the most of this story. Too many interesting and potentially sensational elements. But we'll deal with one reporter at a time."

"You shoot straight, don't you?"

"I won't play games with you. I'm telling you what I honestly think, Caroline." *That is, except how I feel about you. I fear if I told you, you might disappear, and I couldn't bear that, not after I found you.* "And this business about Karina? What if she does come home? Won't that make Gretchen happy? Doesn't she want to see her daughter?"

"Oh yes, seeing Karina again would mean the world to Gretchen. But Karina is Bella's mother and still legally the one responsible for her, and who knows what she might do? We have no idea what kind of life she's living now or where she is. Honestly, Gretchen doesn't even know if Karina's still alive."

"Well, we'll just deal with that caterpillar when he crawls on the rosebud."

Caroline laughed heartily. "What? We'll deal with the caterpillar when he crawls on the rosebud? Where did that one come from?"

"My mother again. Glad I remembered it." He released her hands and relaxed back in his chair. "You know, I learned to read faces, muscle movements, and nervous eyes in the boardroom, and frankly, I was getting worried about you. First time I've seen your cheek muscles tighten with a smile instead of frustration this morning."

"Oh, it's the caterpillars. They make me smile because I know they'll be butterflies very soon. Right?"

"Right, and it's about time to meet Sarah and Bella in the lobby. Glad they had breakfast in their room this morning." Roderick looked at his watch again. "One more thing we need to talk about before we leave for the hospital."

"Just one?"

He wished they had a million things to talk about this morning and that court trials and the media were not on the list.

"Yes, just one more this morning. How are you planning to get Gretchen and Bella back to Moss Point and Twin Oaks?"

"Good question." Her facial muscles tensed again. "First, I think Gretchen's doing well enough that we don't need an ambulance. I was planning to rent a car and drive home as soon as the doctor releases her in the morning."

"Are you comfortable doing that alone, or would you prefer that I drive you down?"

"Oh, we'll do just fine. Besides, it'll only take an hour. Sam offered to come and get us, but I think my plan is the easiest for everyone." She paused. "I assumed that you and Sarah would fly out tomorrow. Acer's still here with the plane, isn't he?"

"Yes, he stayed last night after the trip from Ferngrove. But I could get the car in the morning and drive you to Moss Point and be back in Atlanta by early afternoon, then back to Rockwater before sundown."

"I can't impose upon your good nature any longer. After all, you just returned from England, spent one night at Rockwater, and then flew straight here. You must have things to do and business to take care of."

He chose not to tell her that he had flown directly from LaGuardia to Atlanta Thursday night to surprise her, only to find her with Wyatt Spencer. Keeping this from her made him uncomfortable, but he knew explaining it now would be going against the grain, and he hated splinters.

"If you're certain you're comfortable, then I'll give Acer a call this morning so he can make his flight plan."

After finishing breakfast, they walked to the lobby of the hotel where Sarah and Bella were waiting for them. Roderick pulled the *Atlanta Journal-Constitution* from his briefcase and handed it to Sarah. She read the article in the cab on the way to the hospital.

"Sarah, why don't you and Bella stop to see the canaries when we get to the hospital?" He gave her his there's-a-good-reason-

170

I'm-saying-this look. "We'll take the paper up to Gretchen while you visit the aviary." He knew his sister would understand that Gretchen needed a few minutes to read the article and process it.

Bella went straight to see the birds when she and Sarah entered the hospital. "Sing with the canary. We sing happy songs."

"Just for a moment, Bella. Your mammá is waiting for you."

"I'll see Mammá. I'll make happy music for Mammá."

"She would enjoy that so much, and so would I. Yesterday, we heard the sea canaries. Do you remember?"

"Sea canaries make sad songs." Bella closed her eyes, swayed to the left and right like a nimble young tree being blown by a late afternoon breeze. With her eyes and mouth closed, she moaned. *I like happy songs. Mammá likes happy songs.* She opened her eyes, stopped swaying, and became silent. The canary had begun his song.

Bella approached the glass for a closer look. Her eyes searched for the lone canary whose song was more beautiful than the rest. She whistled his song with him.

Sarah observed and made notes for several

minutes before disturbing Bella. "Come, my little canary, let's go see your mammá."

Sarah says, "My little canary." I sing canary songs. Mammá likes happy canary songs.

Looking especially fresh, Gretchen was obviously ready to greet Roderick and Caroline when they entered her hospital room. The mint green robe, a gift from Sarah, was pulled discreetly around her and tied loosely at her waist, still tender from injury, surgery, and tubes. Her platinum, shoulder-length hair was secured at the nape of her neck. Only a woman with porcelain skin and a perfectly shaped oval face could wear her hair so simply and still be so beautiful. The swelling around her left eye and right cheekbone had almost subsided, the deep purple bruising fading to a yellowish green. She still moved cautiously as she hugged Caroline but never winced when Roderick kissed her on her left cheek.

Roderick excused himself to make some calls, giving them privacy.

When Gretchen had returned to her chair, Caroline handed her the paper, then slipped to the window to look out on what Grand Ma'am would have called a buttermilk sky, churning, clabbery clouds attempting to clear after the cool showers and mist from the day before.

Before Gretchen could finish the article, Caroline's phone rang. Harry Newton was checking to see if they had read the article. He reported the story had been picked up on the wire service and would be in dozens of papers in the next couple of days. He would be publishing a series of articles on Bella and savant syndrome over the coming weeks.

Caroline stifled her desire to tell him what she thought of his journalism, realizing her antagonism would never produce positive results. "Goodbye" didn't come soon enough.

Before she could zip her purse, her phone rang again. "Oh, good morning, Sam."

"How's my blue-eyed beauty this morning?"

"Fair to partly cloudy."

"Guess you've seen the article then?"

"Oh yes, and you?" Caroline watched Gretchen's eyes move slowly from side to side across the newspaper page.

"Soured my stomach before breakfast, and Delia's already called madder than an old, wet, settin' hen, claiming Harry Newton stole her story. She's ready to skin and stuff him and hang him on Caleb's wall next to the antelope."

173

"Well, tell her she'd have to stand in line." She didn't miss the tear rolling off Gretchen's cheek and bleeding through the newsprint.

"And Caleb called. He's had to listen to Delia's whining, and seems he's already had two calls at the sheriff's office this morning. A couple of reporters from some cable news networks."

"What did they want?" Her mind was spinning now like a funnel web spider weaving its web over her nandina bush.

"Information about Ernesto and the coming trial and wanting to know if the wife and granddaughter were back in Moss Point yet."

"Oh, I see." She hoped Sam could understand her cryptic responses.

"Can't talk freely, can you, little one?"

"You are so right, Sam. We'll be home tomorrow. Don't know what time yet. It'll depend on what time the doctor releases her."

"We can't wait to see you, and more than ever, we know you did the right thing in bringing them here to Twin Oaks. Their house is still a crime scene, and we can shield them from the media storm and from Ernesto if he makes bail. With all this media attention, he may decide it's safer in a jail cell for another few days. I know you can't talk, but something else good may come out of this press business."

"That would be incredibly wonderful right now."

"This may motivate Ernesto to do some thinking. This much attention may encourage him to plead guilty and get through this without a trial."

"That's lovely, Sam. Can't wait to see you." Thoughts of not having a trial put the hint of a smile across Caroline's face. "Bye, now. I'll call you in the morning." She returned her phone to her purse.

She grabbed a tissue, handed it to Gretchen, and sat down in the chair in front of her. Choosing not to break the silence when Gretchen folded the paper, she stared into Gretchen's blank face.

Roderick walked back into the room, but Gretchen did not acknowledge him. "Were we really hidden away? And I never came close to death, did I?" She squeezed her eyes shut. "Why would this man write such things?"

"I'm sorry, so sorry." Caroline felt Roderick's hand on her shoulder and looked up at him. "Unfortunately, Roderick was right. It's the sensational stuff, not always the truth, that sells papers."

"But how can they print what is not the truth?" Gretchen continually rubbed her hands together.

Roderick stepped closer. "Because they are very good at using words and skilled at walking on the edge of the truth. I understand why you're so upset about this, but remember, Monday will bring new headlines for a new story. This one will soon be forgotten."

"I know you are right, Mr. Adair. I am at peace that Bella will likely never understand what has happened, but what I do not know is what this means for Ernesto." She wiped the tear that found its way to the corner of her eye.

Sunday passed quickly in room 602. Roderick ordered a pizza for their lunch and proclaimed it a going home party. Conversation, *I Love Lucy* reruns, and frequent interruptions by nurses filled the hours.

Late in the day Caroline approached Gretchen's chair. "We really should go. You're looking like a little rest would do you good." Bella hugged her mammá and took Sarah's hand instinctively. Roderick and Sarah said their goodbyes to Gretchen before leaving for the hotel. The Atlanta streets were quiet on this autumn Sunday afternoon; only an occasional car and the rustle of leaves in the brisk breeze disturbed the silence. The four-some chose to walk several blocks before hailing a cab. The air smelled good.

A "weekend's over" melancholy settled around Roderick as he said good night to Caroline. He set the alarm clock, turned out the light, and stretched out the full length of his bed. He thought of Monday and of going home to Rockwater. Lilah would leave his dinner in the oven, and Liz, his administrative assistant, would be there to go over his messages, hand him his stack of mail, and prioritize the week. The Stanton deal would close before Friday, and a six-inch stack of third-quarter projections would materialize on his desk.

But business wasn't on his mind. His mother was. Rockwater, his family's French country house in the middle of horse country, was the grand house his father had built for his mother, Angeleah. She filled the house with music and the grounds with rose gardens, prize-winning daylilies, and mazes of wildflowers and herbs for the cooking garden. As children, he and Sarah had spent countless autumn afternoons planting tulip and daffodil bulbs in the meadows surrounding the house.

Since the death of his mother when he

was an adolescent, Rockwater had never been the same. Her tragic death took life and music from the house and from his father, who died a year after Roderick's college graduation. It was as though his father lived to see Sarah married and Roderick securely running the business, and then he willed himself to die.

Called the Lone Wolf by his associates, Roderick ran Adair Enterprises, headquartered in Lexington. He chose to have his office at home in the quarters he built for himself off the back courtyard — smaller quarters that did not echo with emptiness.

Lilah ran the house and managed the gardener and housekeeper just as she had done for his mother. She knew to keep the massive pillows fluffed up in the library and not to bother the books spilling over from once-ample shelving to the window seat and the red carpet under tables and the large desk.

He grabbed the extra pillow and stuffed it under his head. *It's late October, and Caroline has committed to a Christmas recital. That'll keep Lilah happy and busy — planning the guest list, dressing the house for Christmas, meeting with the caterer, and planning holiday meals. But mostly, she'll be happy to know Caroline's returning. I'll figure a way to keep her here for Christmas. A Rockwater Christmas with Caroline.* With Caroline under the roof, the fragrance of fresh flowers and melodies would float again through the loggia. A dream come true for Lilah . . . and, he had to admit, for himself.

He sensed that Liz, on the other hand, viewed Caroline as a threat. He hadn't missed how she accentuated her assets, trying to gain his attention. Her slightly overgrown bosom was indiscreetly visible in low-cut silk blouses of every color, and toned, shapely legs reached long and far from beneath abbreviated skirts. Though Roderick never shifted his stance about their professional relationship during the five years of her employment, she still had some intoxicated notion of being Mrs. Roderick Adair, according to Lilah. He valued Liz's experience and her corporate knowledge; otherwise, he would have helped her find another position in one of his companies, explaining she had far more assets than were being used in her present position. Her flaunting and flirting kept Lilah's eyes rolling and him laughing. He figured the cleavage would rise along with the skirt hems when Liz learned Caroline was returning for another performance in December.

No more thoughts of Rockwater. *I'll be*

home tomorrow, and I know what I'm return-
ing to, but not Caroline and her friends. They
will have to deal with the media, the trial,
financial questions for Gretchen, . . . and
what'll happen if Karina shows up trying to
exploit Bella? Caroline must be waiting for the
caterpillar to crawl on the rosebud, whatever
that means.

Roderick rolled to his side and pulled a pillow to his chest, wishing it were Caroline and he had the right to do something to help.

CHAPTER ELEVEN:
COMING HOME TO TWIN OAKS

Gretchen was far too grateful that she was going home to complain of a bit of nausea due to the car's motion and her weakness. She spoke to Caroline sporadically on the hour's drive while Bella sat in the back seat listening to her new iPod, a gift from Roderick. "Mr. Adair is such a generous man. I think it a mystery how he was able to purchase this new little plastic box of music before we departed Atlanta this morning. Bella loves it." She glanced over her shoulder to see Bella's head swaying and her fingers moving gingerly across her knees, playing what she was hearing.

"I do think Roderick is a man who is accustomed to making things happen, and besides, Roderick has Acer." Caroline adjusted the visor to shield her eyes from the sun's glare.

Gretchen thought she recalled the name

but could not remember. "Acer? Who is this Acer?"

"He's Roderick's pilot, and he was in Atlanta overnight awaiting their departure today. I'm sure all Roderick has to do to get things done is to pick up his phone."

"It is lovely of him to pick up the phone to do things for others. I know he is wealthy, but he does not seem to spoil himself. And Sarah . . . she was so generous to buy such fine new clothes for Bella and this beautiful green robe and slippers for me."

"They are both generous, and not just with their money. By the way, I think Sarah had something to do with the music loaded on Bella's iPod. She advised just a few tunes at first because Bella likes to listen to the same piece repeatedly. We can add more later. And Roderick suggested loading the CD that he bought for Bella at the Georgia Aquarium." Caroline looked at the rearview mirror as if to check on Bella. "I don't know what we would have done without Sarah and Roderick this past week."

"That is so true." Gretchen paused for a moment. "Caroline, they came because of you. I know that Dr. McCollum came for Bella as well because she thought her experience as a child psychologist might be helpful. But Mr. Adair? There is no doubt why he came. His eyes answered that question every time he looked at you."

"Do you really think so? I mean, really?"

"My eyes have not seen it for a long time, but one does not forget the look of love."

"Why, Gretchen, I think that bump on your head has rattled your brain!" They both giggled like sophomores. "We're almost to Moss Point."

"Oh, then I must speak with Bella." Gretchen was a bit embarrassed at coming home in her robe and slippers, but she was determined they would use their best manners in greeting the Meadows. Getting the straw hat and earphones off Bella would be more difficult than removing the stickiest pastry dough from between her fingers. Once Sarah had shown Bella that she could put on the earphones and her straw hat, they became like appendages. "Bella? Bella!" No answer. Gretchen winced as she turned to reach into the back seat. Her surgery wound was still healing, and her broken ribs would be tender for several weeks. She tapped Bella on the knee to get her attention.

"Bella, please turn off the music."

Bella surprised her by complying with the first request.

"Please put your music box away. Put it in your backpack."

She took off her hat, removed the ear-phones, and handed them and the new music box to her mammá.

"No, Bella, put this in your backpack with the music box Dr. Ferris gave you."

Bella did not budge but sat quietly for a few moments while her mammá spoke to her, reminding her about her manners. But Gretchen knew the look in those silvery-green eyes. The new magic music box might go in the backpack, but the music would still be reverberating in Bella's head.

In the middle of her mammá's instructions to stand up straight and to say thank you, Bella began to make an unusual sound. Gretchen strained again to turn and see Bella's face. It was an unfamiliar sound. "Bella, please stop making those . . ." She paused to listen again. "Those sounds."

Caroline laughed. "Uh-oh, songs of the sea canary." She whispered to Gretchen, "The whale sounds. She really loved them."

Bella said, "Sea canary, sea canary," and started making the mournful sound again.

Gretchen laughed with Caroline. "Oh my, a new song, and one that's loud and not so lovely. Bella, could you please stop singing?"

"I can sing. No more Mr. Silva. I can sing. No more Mr. Silva." Bella smiled.

The pain had never been more transparent in Gretchen's face, a bittersweet sadness. Her Bella now had freedom to sing, but at such a price. Bella had breathed freedom, and her music would be like the breezes now, and who can contain the wind?

Gretchen felt a bit anxious when Caroline called Sam and Angel to give them a heads-up as they approached the city limits. As they pulled onto the property, Gretchen saw Sam, Angel, and Hattie standing in the driveway. The wide driveway, normally covered in sycamore leaves in October, was swept clean, as was the yard. She imagined Ned and Fred had already worked their magic this morning.

Sam, assisted by his walking cane, was the first one to reach the car. Angel followed in one of her colorful muumuus, and Hattie, in a flowered apron that did nothing to camouflage her wide girth, was right behind Angel. Sam opened the car door for Gretchen and extended his arm. "Why, good morning, Mrs. Silva! I cannot begin to tell you how glad we are to see you. You and little Bella will bring some life to this big old house."

Gretchen carefully turned herself around in the seat to accept his arm. No gentleman had extended his arm to her since the last

185

Sunday morning Peter escorted her to church before she ran away from her family to hide her pregnancy. "Mr. Meadows, I'll never be able to thank you enough for inviting us into your home. I promise we'll be as little trouble as possible, and I promise to get better very quickly. We would never want to take advantage of your kindness."

Angel stepped forward and kissed Gretchen on each cheek. "Kindness? Do you know how tired we are of listening to each other's stories? It'll be like a vacation to have you with us, won't it, Sam?"

"Of course, it will, and I'd never disagree with this little lady of the house." Sam extended his other arm to Angel, and the three walked toward the porch. Hattie made over Bella while Caroline was getting the last bag. "And Bella, we're especially glad you'll be here. You will play the piano for us, won't you?" he asked.

Bella began her excited rocking motion. "Play piano, play piano. Caroline, play piano?"

Caroline took Bella's hand. "Yes, Bella, you can play my piano. Let's get you settled first." They followed Hattie to the door.

Bella fidgeted with Caroline's grasp of her hand until Caroline released it. She clapped both hands as she walked. "Play Caroline's piano. Play Caroline's piano."

"Why, she's just as excited as that speckled puppy I brought home about forty years ago." Sam led Gretchen through the porch and into the kitchen.

"Yes, she is indeed excited. She has had quite a week, and I am so very proud of her. Caroline will tell you all about it." Gretchen's eyes moved around Angel's spacious kitchen. "Oh my, how very lovely, and you have so much room and so many cabinets. When I am better, I would like very much to bake some pastries for you."

"In that case, I hope you're much better tomorrow. You don't know it, but I'm the third generation of Meadows men to make their home at Twin Oaks. So this kitchen has seen lots of change from wood-burning stoves to microwaves, and you can thank my little Angel over there for this pretty kitchen. She likes modern things."

Angel winked at her husband. "Yes, and I like Sam too."

"See what I mean, who couldn't love a woman like this?" Sam put his arm around Angel and hugged her to him.

Angel motioned for Gretchen to follow her. "I believe Hattie has prepared the bridal suite for you, Gretchen. We assumed Bella would prefer staying in the room with you. If not, she can always stay in the rose room down the hall."

"You have names for your rooms?" Gretchen's eyes were wide with wonder as she walked slowly down the hallway.

Sam followed with Gretchen's bag. "Well, you see, this little wife of mine is an artist, and the rose room is filled with her paintings of roses she grew right here in her own garden, but the bridal suite has nothing to do with brides. We call it that because everything in the room is ivory-colored. You'll see."

Caroline chimed in. "What that means is the room is probably all decked out for the fall. Angel uses that room like her canvas, and she changes the linens and curtains and accessories as the seasons come and go."

"Mrs. Meadows, having Bella with me is just perfect." Gretchen stepped into the spacious ivory room with its high ceiling and an antique four-poster bed. The breezes gently stirred the white sheer fabric draping several tall, arched windows. The fresh air mingling with a cinnamon spice candle burning on the bedside table smelled the way home should smell. Bronze, burgundy, and deep orange throw pillows gave a warm invitation to nap on the bed or on the window seat. In the corner, atop a white-washed old desk, was a surprise for Bella — a Halloween display of colorful leaves, baby pumpkins, maple candy, coloring books with markers, and a princess costume. Gretchen looked down without moving her head. "I have been told I am a fine seamstress, so maybe someday I can repay you by making you something special for your bridal suite."

"Oh, I'd like that. But what I'd really like is dropping the Mrs. Silva and Mrs. Meadows around here." Angel looked up at Sam and then back to Gretchen. "Sam and I will call you Gretchen, and we'd also like it if you called him Sam and me Angel. What do you say?"

"That would make me happy too, Angel." Gretchen told the truth, but such familiarity did not come easily for one with her humility.

Hattie brought in a pitcher of water and put it on the dresser. "Now, Mrs. Silva, you and that little one of yours, you just need to rest a little while. I heard you say you're a fine seamstress, and I'll tell you I'm a mighty fine cook. And I've cooked up some of my famous chicken and dumplin's for you today. Folks swear they feel better just eatin' them. I figure I've cooked at least two train cars full. And I never allow nobody to pay me for them 'cause how's someone who calls themself a Christian gonna charge somebody who's sick for chicken and dumplin's? The good Lord just blesses me up and down all the time, and I ain't had to make no dumplin's yet without chicken, and I ain't never had to charge nobody for 'em either."

"Your chicken and dumplings sound very delicious, Hattie. May I call you Hattie?"

"Yes, ma'am. Ain't nobody in this town that don't call me Hattie. That's my name."

"I will enjoy your dumplings even more knowing that the hands of such a fine Christian lady made them." She extended her hand to Hattie.

"I don't know nothin' 'bout no shakin' hands. At my house, we don't shake. We hug. And you just remember, the good Lord takes our troubles to heart, and He's gonna take care of you, and what He don't do, I will. Yes ma'am, Hattie's gonna take care o' you and that little angel over there." Hattie wrapped her arms around Gretchen.

Caroline interceded. "Careful Hattie, remember Gretchen's had surgery."

"I know that, Miss Caroline, but they ain't nothin' wrong with the arm that ain't broke." Hattie's laugh was contagious, and before she left the room, even Bella was laughing.

When Caroline had unpacked the bag and left the room, Gretchen sat on the foot of the bed and looked around. She had never spent the night in such a room. She wondered how strangers could be so kind and how her own husband could be so cruel. Even with his cruelty, she hated the thoughts of what would happen to him now.

Caroline returned to the kitchen and joined Sam and Angel at the breakfast table. Angel had the cups and teapot waiting for her. "Sweetie, I cannot tell you how glad we are to see you. This place just isn't the same when you're not around."

Caroline brushed her hair from her face and grabbed her purse. "And I cannot say loud enough how glad I am to be home. I don't care to repeat the last nine days."

"Well, the days are getting shorter, but they've gone slower than Mr. Mosely's old mule around here with you gone." Sam patted Caroline's arm. "But business will pick up now. In fact, it's already picked up."

Caroline reached in her bag for her calendar. "Okay, Judge, I know there's something behind that statement. So, if you don't mind, just come clean."

"Sam Meadows, you could have let her

enjoy her lunch before you start in." Angel lifted the lid on the teapot. "At least let me pour her a cup of tea."

"So, tell me. What's up? Do I need more than tea? Just don't tell me that Ernesto's out of jail."

"No, he's where he belongs. And when Caleb told him about the vans of television equipment parked out on the street and the reporters holding microphones in front of anybody who'd talk, he decided to stay there. Not that he could have posted his bail anyway — a half a million dollars."

Caroline added milk to her tea. "A half a million dollars? That seems huge. They let murderers out on less."

"Not for a wife and child beater in this town, especially after the scene he made at his appearance before the judge. That young judge learned a lot from old Sam. Seems Mr. Silva's an angry, disrespectful man with a drinking and drug problem."

"Drug problem?" Sam got Caroline's raised right eyebrow.

"Yep, not so unusual for truck drivers. Got to stay awake on those long road trips. Word is you can get more than gasoline at truck stops these days."

"Oh, I don't think Gretchen has a clue about drugs. Will that come out in the trial?"

"I'd be as surprised as old Ned was to find that copperhead in the flower bed to hear there's even going to be a trial. If he's smart, Silva will plead guilty and take his punishment like a man."

Angel had been quiet long enough. "Well, he's proven he's not too smart and his manhood is certainly in question. What kind of man kicks his wife nearly to death?"

"I hear that, and I agree. Maybe he'll take what's coming to him like a coward then. Now when Caleb's search produced some drugs, Silva just took on another armload of trouble. I think he'll take a plea bargain. You don't have to be too smart to know you don't have much of a chance before a jury in this town if you're up for drugs *and* assault." Sam sat back and sipped his tea. "Caleb says Silva's had a pretty rough time this week — in jail, no alcohol or drugs. Guess he's detoxing without the cost of rehab facilities. The doctor's been by twice to see him. To tell you the truth, he's probably in bad shape."

Caroline remembered Sam's statement that started this conversation. "So, if Ernesto is locked away in bad shape, what did you mean about business picking up?"

"Sam's talking about the fact that this town is crawling with reporters — television and newspaper. They've been here since yesterday, camped out in front of the jail and parked out in front of the Silvas' house, talking to anybody on the street. Of course, GiGi Nelson made the eleven o'clock news last night. My guess is she saw the news crews, got Gracie to do her hair up, and perched herself where she couldn't be missed."

"Oh, Angel, you wouldn't be jealous, now, would you?" Sam teased.

"Jealous of a hussy who looked like Halloween came a week early? She just doesn't get it. Tangee lipstick and icy blue eye shadow are not in these days. And you tell me, what does that say about reliable reporting when they'll take the word of the town gossip?"

"Just says they don't have much yet, but they're salivating," Sam said.

Angel put her cup down and pushed away from the table. "That story would make you think that they'd just found a child raised by wolves around here!" She got up to look for Hattie. "Hattie, Hat-tie?"

Hattie came from the dining room through the kitchen door. "I ain't deaf yet, Miss Angel. Whatch you need?"

"Not a thing, but I thought I heard you setting the dining table, and I think we should have lunch around the kitchen table. We could eat on the porch, but it's a little cool and breezy. There's plenty of room here for all of us."

Hattie picked up the teapot and moved it to the counter. "Why, I think that's just a fine idea. That way Mrs. Silva and Bella will just think of theirselves as family instead of company. I don't know why I didn't think of that myself. But you do know how I like to get yo' mama's dishes out. I'll just put 'em back in the china cabinet. They'll need washing ag'in before Thanksgiving though."

"Thanksgiving? Something tells me Thanksgiving's going to be mighty fine this year. That is, if we can find somebody who can cook the chicken and dumplings." Sam smiled at Hattie.

"Oh, Mr. Sam, looks like your funny box would be done empty as old as you are. But it ain't. You just keep on makin' them funnies. It's all right though, me and Miss Angel needs a good laugh once in a while." Hattie slung the dishtowel over her shoulder and put the teapot away. "And if I run into somebody that can roll out dumplin's, I'll let her know you're lookin' for her."

Caroline searched her bag for her ringing phone. "Oh, hello, Wyatt . . . just a minute." She waved at Sam, walked out onto the back porch, and closed the door behind her. "There, now I can talk."

He inquired about their trip home and how things were in Moss Point. She gave him the scoop, carefully omitting mention of Ernesto's drug issues. She no longer trusted anyone outside Sam and Angel and Roderick and Sarah. She had not forgotten her suspicions of someone in Dr. Spencer's group leaking the story to the press.

Caroline explained that the town was crawling with reporters and that Newton said the story was going national. Learning that, Wyatt insisted on coming down on Tuesday. She could not convince him otherwise but made sure he understood his day might be spent drinking coffee at Café on the Square. Her piano students were reporting back on Tuesday; she knew it would take her hours to catch up on mail, email, and phone calls, and she had no reason to see Wyatt Spencer.

While Gretchen rested after lunch, Caroline brought Bella to the studio to play the piano. To the sound of Bella's music, Caroline spent the afternoon sorting mail, contacting her piano students, and dodging reporters' phone calls. She called her parents and checked on Betsy and little David.

As she unpacked her bags, she remembered Gretchen's comment about going by her house and picking up some clothes. That was Gretchen's unassuming way of asking, and Caroline knew she wouldn't mention it again. Telling her the house was locked and they were without a key had stalled her on the way in to town. The phone rang as she was on her way to call Sam to ask him to check with Caleb about the keys to the Silva home.

"Hello, Roderick. Are you looking out on the rolling hills of Kentucky?" She liked having a visual image of where he was sitting to call her.

"Actually, I'm going over paperwork at my desk, and I'll reward myself with a walk to the trout stream in just a few minutes. Time to clear my head before I go over for supper."

"Oh, so you're in your office." During her July visit to Rockwater, she was given the run of the house, but she never saw his apartment.

"Yes, and I've hardly been able to work for the squirrels this afternoon, sliding around on this tin roof and jumping from limb to limb. Winter must be on its way because those pesky creatures have been working overtime squirreling away the acorns from this old oak tree. We may have an early snow this year."

"And a white Christmas?" She sat down in her desk chair and curled her legs under her.

"Isn't that what you ordered?"

"I believe I did." She turned around and tried to get Bella's attention. "Can you hear the piano? It's Bella."

"The squirrels are entertaining me and Bella's entertaining you?"

"For the last two hours. She's absolutely amazing. I thought Gretchen needed the rest and Bella wanted to play the piano. How could I refuse?"

"So, you're all settled in, then?"

"Yes, a good trip and of course Sam and Angel and Hattie were standing in the driveway when we got here. Those folks are the only ones I know who could rival you for the host of the year award. They just don't have a trout stream."

"Guess I should practice up before December. I certainly don't want to lose my title. And speaking of December, we need to set a date for that."

"We do need to do that, don't we?" Her calendar was open on her desk. She turned to December.

"While you're looking at dates, I was

198

wondering what you'd think about spending Christmas here at Rockwater. We haven't had a real Christmas here in a few years. Since it's just Sarah and George and me, I usually go to New York to be with friends, and Sarah joins George's family."

"Christmas at Rockwater?" *He won't kiss me, but he's invited me for Christmas.* It was maddening. "That sounds really wonderful, but I don't know about my family and Gretchen and Bella. I've never spent a Christmas away from home."

"Then it's time you should. That would thrill Sarah, and I'd like it too. Just think about it, and we'll talk later. By the way, how are things in Moss Point?"

She told him of the plague of reporters and television coverage and the added complication of Ernesto's drug problem. She detected his silence when he learned that Wyatt Spencer was coming to Moss Point tomorrow.

With the list of items Gretchen wanted from her house and the house keys Caleb delivered, Caroline and Sam drove the few blocks to the Silva home. Nine days gone, and the town looked different. The hardwood trees had fewer leaves, and noticeable progress had been made in clearing the land

199

at the east end of the Twin Oaks property. A new city park would be there by next April due to the goodness of Sam and Angel Meadows and the hard work of Ned and Fred Pendergrass.

She parked the car out front. The yellow police tape still crisscrossed the front door. Gretchen and Bella had walked into her life last spring, but she had never been invited to their home. Ernesto's presence and Gretchen's fear made a fortress and a prison of this frame cottage. She had often wondered what the inside of their house looked like, assuming it would be modest and filled with products of Gretchen's skilled and creative hands.

They walked up the steps to the small stoop. "Give me those keys and let me go in first," Sam barked. He propped his cane next to the door, stripped the tape away, and unlocked the door.

It was late afternoon, and the only light was the natural glow of a sun low in the sky. It seeped through windows and cast shadows around the room. There was light enough for her to see that this room looked nothing like Gretchen lived here. The floor was littered with papers and magazines that shouldn't have been in anyone's home. Beer cans and liquor bottles were scattered on the floor and tabletops. Remains of the last meal Gretchen had served Ernesto were still on a porcelain plate on the table next to the large recliner where Caroline envisioned him sitting to watch television.

They stepped over rubbish to get to the kitchen, which, though small, looked like something out of a magazine showcasing Victorian cottages. This looked as though Gretchen lived here. The wooden floor had been painted white, and the pale blue walls were unblemished. The white muslin curtains, bordered with colorful, hand-embroidered flowers, matched the tablecloth covering a small table for four. The wooden chairs were painted white, and trails of painted ivy and sprays of flowers covered the spindles and the chair seats. A faded bouquet of flowers from Gretchen's garden drooped from a vase similar to the mosaic piece Bella had made for her.

The dining room was a continuation of the kitchen, with framed pieces of needlework lining the sky-blue walls, and the antique china soup tureen and platter Gretchen had told her about. Caroline remembered Gretchen's smile when telling her the story of how Ernesto had given it to her for their first anniversary. She had admired it in the window of an antique shop, commenting it looked like her mother's. Ernesto had remembered and returned to purchase it. So much had changed in the last twenty-eight years.

Caroline followed Sam to the front bedroom where they were to find Gretchen's clothes in an armoire. The bedroom looked as though it belonged in a dollhouse despite its dishevelment. She and Sam stood in the doorway as they perused the room without making a sound or a movement. Caroline gasped at piecing together what must have taken place here — a splintered chair and table, bloodstained bed sheets, curtains pulled off the window, and a shattered lamp. Across the room, dark stains clung to the windowsill, the window where Bella escaped. Apparently, Ernesto had broken it either in anger or in his effort to thwart her getaway, and someone, a neighbor or the police, had boarded it up. Could she ever forgive the man who had overturned furniture and the lives of his wife and granddaughter in this room?

Caroline continued to survey the room like a general looking over a battlefield for casualties. The orange rays of the day's last light reflected on a slender object protruding from just under the bed. She strained to see. She realized what it was and started toward it.

"Careful, Caroline. There's broken glass everywhere." Sam followed her into the room.

She put her hand across her face to smother the smell of desiccated blood. Kneeling, she reached under the bed and took the handle of Gretchen's shattered silver-framed hand mirror. She held it to her chest as she rose from the floor. Sam was there to embrace her as she turned around.

"Look . . . look . . . Sam." Words would not come. In their place flowed tears, tears she had choked for nine days.

"It's okay now. All this is over. All over. Gretchen and Bella are safe, and we're going to take care of them." He held her until the sun was almost down and the room was growing dark. "Okay, little one, we need to get Gretchen's things and get home. We'll take the mirror too. I've already talked to Caleb about it, and I know where we can get it restored."

CHAPTER TWELVE:
ROSES AND DANDELIONS

Late October mornings in Moss Point were almost as promising as April daybreaks, minus the irises. Caroline had slept, really slept, and was ready for the day. She drank her cup of tea from her favorite bench overlooking the waterfall and bog garden. The green spiky stems of the irises, cradling the pond, were curling and turning brown. The foliage was beginning its return to the soil where it would nourish next spring's blossoms.

She was home, home at Twin Oaks, away from the sterile environment of room 602, where doctors and nurses and medical technicians moved around like ants, always busy. But here in her garden retreat, it was quiet and beautiful, and for a few moments she could put away the medicinal smells and her mental pictures of Gretchen's hospital room and the bedroom where Ernesto had done his meanness. Gretchen and Bella were safely asleep about a hundred yards away at the main house, where they would wake to be treated like royalty.

She was looking so forward to the return of her students this afternoon that she had stayed up late to make a batch of fresh peanut butter cookies. Her students' coming and going and the music resonating through her studio would make things seem normal again. The unscheduled morning would give her time to play the piano, work on the *Rockwater Suite,* and perhaps look through her repertoire to find something suitable for a Christmas recital. She had never played a Christmas recital, and she had never spent Christmas away from home.

Her teacup was empty, so she walked the garden path back to the studio terrace, but diverted toward the drive when she heard the familiar rattling and clanking of Ned and Fred's pickup truck.

The sixty-year-old identical twin bachelors were in their overalls and freshly pressed plaid shirts, and they carried hedge clippers and handsaws. When they met her at the corner, off came their John Deere ball caps as though choreographed, exposing graying hair, combed neatly and slicked down to their scalps. The sun had never done to their white foreheads what it had done to their ruddy cheeks. "Why, can it be? Is that really you, Miss Caroline?" asked Ned, the talking twin.

"It most certainly is, and how are you gentlemen this morning?" Caroline greeted them with a smile and a skip in her step.

"We are mighty fine now that you're home. It seems like a whole month o' Sundays since we seen you. And we're so sorry about poor Miss Gretchen and that beautiful little girl o' hers, ain't we, Fred?" He nudged his brother, who rarely uttered a word, especially in the presence of a lady.

Fred nodded.

"We hear they's staying up at Mr. Sam's. Them's the nicest people. Why, Mr. Sam sent us over to Miss Gretchen's house to board up the window to keep ill-intentioned folks and critters out. Ain't nobody wants to go in that house after what happened there. We seen it through the window. Mr. Sam says he wants us to clean it up when the sheriff says it's okay."

Fred nudged Ned with his elbow.

"All right, all right, Fred. I know we's burnin' good daylight and we got work to do. Miss Angel wants these climbing rose bushes cleaned up today, and then we'll go back to working on her park."

"Oh, I noticed the progress as I drove into

town yesterday. It's really looking good. Although I must say I'm going to miss that last little bit of countryside right here in the middle of town." The Meadows' twelve-acre property was adjacent to Twin Oaks, just on the other side of the back fence. River fern covered the ground around tall pines and dogwoods and a few hardwood trees that had grown for centuries. A small stream flowed through the woods and attracted birds and other wildlife. Caroline had enjoyed the best of both worlds — living in town and having her own private forest only a few steps away through the gate.

But the mystery of Caroline's intruder last spring had motivated Sam and Angel to step up their plans to make the land useful to the fine, upstanding residents of Moss Point, not just the teenagers who went there to do their mischief.

Ned looked proud. "Yes, ma'am, we been workin' hard last week. Had to cut down a few trees and still a few more to come. Went home ever' night and apologized to God for cuttin' 'em down. I think He's okay with it though, and I know He'll be smilin' when them little children are squealing and laughing at the ducks. We'll be burnin' the underbrush over there later this week if it don't rain. So if you see smoke, the woods

207

ain't on fire. It'll just be me and Fred, and we gonna take good care o' things."

Fred nudged his brother again.

"Okay, for real this time, Miss Caroline. We's goin' to work afore Fred takes his hedge clippers to my tongue. You have a good one now, and we hope you gonna be playing your piano."

Ned and Fred walked in step over the garden stones to the back rose garden. Caroline entered her studio, her home, her cocoon where her piano was calling her.

"Miss Caroline must be happy today, Fred, she's playin' them happy songs ag'in." Ned bent low, pruning the lowest limbs of the climbing roses. "Why, we must be just about the luckiest men in Moss Point, out here workin' in Miss Angel's garden listenin' to the most beautiful piano playing a man could want to hear."

"Uh-huh," Fred grunted.

Ned stood up to stretch his back and to see how far along his twin was. "Watch out there, Fred, you clippin' them roses mighty close, and you know Miss Angel has one of her fits ever' time you do that."

"Ummph." Fred never stopped clipping.

Ned moved down the fence, pulled out the white handkerchief from his back pocket, and wiped the sweat from his brow before he knelt to prune the Belinda's Dream roses. "Gosh dang it!" Ned loosened his shirt caught on a thorn. "I ain't never figgered out why God had to put thorns on roses. You just think He coulda done better'n that. I mean these women just go ape over roses. Why couldn't they get as crazy 'bout dandelions? Them dandelions'll grow like hair on a sheepdog, and they ain't got no thorns."

"Maybe that's why," Fred mumbled.

"You say something, Fred?"

"Naw."

Ned was quiet for a spell as Caroline's piano music continued to float through the garden. Ned and Fred were contented, good men. Life for them was simple. They had each other. Their parents had left them a small farm on the edge of town and a green pickup truck, and they worked for nice people like Mr. Sam and Miss Angel most days. They hunted and fished when the notion struck them, and at the end of the day, they went home and watched *Magnum P.I.* reruns on their new color television set. Ned did the cooking and laundry, and Fred kept the truck and yard tools in good shape. Housecleaning wasn't addressed. They had more than they needed, and they were grateful.

"I think I finally figgered it out, Fred. I think I really figgered it out."

"What?" Fred growled.

" 'Bout the roses."

"What about the roses? I ain't clippin' too much no more."

"Aint' you heard nothin' I been sayin? I was talkin' 'bout roses and them thorns, and I got the answer. Just think 'bout it. Miss Angel use to be all the time workin' out here in these roses — sprayin', dustin', mulchin', waterin', dead-headin' — always takin' care of 'em, helping 'em grow in spite of them thorns. She don't even see them dadgum thorns. She just sees the beautiful roses. Oh, she knows they got thorns, but havin' a bouquet in her house is worth gettin' pricked sometimes."

"Uh-huh." Fred moved closer to where Ned was pruning.

"Thorns is to remind us that sometimes we gotta bleed a little to get the beautiful things in life. I guess it's God's way of makin' us think about things once in a while. Thorns do that, don't you know?"

"If you say so." Fred kept busy, and bags of rose and hedge clippings continued to grow as the sun headed toward its zenith.

"But you know what, Fred, dandelions can make you think too. I mean, just think about it. They grow ever'where, and they don't need no sprayin' and waterin' or nothin'. You don't even have to plant 'em. The wind just blows the seed and a new one comes up wherever it lands." Ned worked for a moment in uncustomary silence. "Remember, when we was young 'uns and Paw told us to make a wish and it would come to pass if we could blow all that fuzzy stuff off that dandelion stem? You and me, we'd blow so hard — kinda like the north wind through the cracks in the barn. But one or two of them little things was always stuck good to that stem. You remember the day Maw caught us doing that? She come runnin' out the front door with that green-checkered apron flapping in the wind, hollerin' at us to stop before we had a whole front yard full of dandelions."

Ned stopped to spit and chuckle. "You think Maw didn't know the wind would blow them things off if we didn't? It's probably a good thing that folks like Miss Angel grows roses or else all of Moss Point and maybe the whole wide world would be covered in dandelions. Kinda makes you think, don't it?"

"Not much," mumbled Fred.

211

They finished the job, bagged up the last of the clippings, and gathered their tools. Ned sensed his twin's mind was somewhere else. "I didn't know that one piano made more beautiful music than another, but I think this one makes prettier music than Miss Caroline's other piano, don't ya think, Fred?"

"Huh."

"You know what? Miss Caroline tol' me she thought you was the ugliest, meanest man in the whole wide world." Ned checked to see if Fred was really listening.

"Uh-huh." Fred pulled off his gloves and dropped them in the bucket.

"Fred Nathaniel Pendergrass, you ain't heard nothin' I been sayin' all mornin'." Ned knew that hearing his full name would get his twin's attention.

"I did too. You been talkin' about roses and thorns and . . ." Fred stammered.

"I knowed I was right. I just been talkin' to myself. If you had been listenin', you'd know I just said that Miss Caroline says you are ugly."

Fred stood up straight and his faraway look was gone. "Well, you know what that means about you too, Ned Obadiah Pendergrass. You lookin' at me is just like lookin' in the mirror 'cause you and me are two identical peas outta the same pod. So there!"

Ned laughed at his brother, who rarely got a burr under his saddle. "Why, that's more'n you said all mornin' long. And you know, if you'd study it just one minute, you'd know that Miss Caroline ain't said no such a thing. Miss Caroline is a kind lady, and she don't say bad things like that. She sees roses too. She don't see no thorns. Why, I think she even must like dandelions 'cause she's nice to you and me. And I wanna know what's been eatin' at you all day."

Fred put down his bucket. "You right, Ned. We's just dandelions. The world's full of folks like you and me. But that Miss Caroline and Mrs. Silva and that sweet little Bella . . . well they ain't no dandelions. They's roses — like them special roses down yonder in that corner, the ones Miss Angel don't let nobody mess with. Why, that little girl can't talk nor read, and she don't act like other young 'uns her age, but she can make music like nobody's ever heard! Now that's special, Ned."

"Well, I take back what I said." Ned put the last of the clippings in the garbage bag. "You was listenin' to me after all. You're thinkin' rightly, brother. Mrs. Silva and Bella, with that pretty silver hair and them green eyes, they's real unusual all right. And I think it's so nice of Miss Caroline to take 'em in and try to teach that girl. She's got a big job on her little hands."

"Yep, 'cause them roses got some thorns, some sharp ones. And I'm scared that Miss Caroline just might get pricked real good if she ain't mighty careful."

"You said it right 'bout them thorns. We just gotta look out for Miss Caroline 'cause you and me know one of them thorns is named Ernesto Silva."

Caroline lifted both hands high above her head and reached for the ceiling, trying to stretch out the kinks settling in her neck and back from hours at the piano. Manuscript paper, products of frustration, covered the floor around her. She had taken Angel's suggestion years ago and never wadded up the bad ones. Instead, she ripped them off the pad and let them sail to their landing, where she would pick them up later and put them in the box in the attic for who knows what: wallpapering a bathroom, packing paper for when she moved, or for her heirs to fuss over — that is, if she ever had heirs.

The few sheets neatly placed on the piano were keepers — tomorrow's starting point to see if she still liked what she heard. Working on the *Rockwater Suite* was like returning to Kentucky.

She stood, stretched again, and closed the French doors to the terrace before kneeling to pick up the papers. With the last piece of manuscript stacked on the floor, she traced the curve of the massive piano legs with her small hand just as she had done twenty-one years ago when this very piano had been delivered to her parents' living room. She had needed to touch the piano to make certain it was real. Her parents had sold the piano ten years ago, but now it sat in her studio in Moss Point.

Caroline knew the routine. Through the window, she had seen Ned and Fred carry the loads of bags and buckets to their truck, and she knew they'd be knocking on the door at any moment to say their goodbyes. They would have kind and simple words about her music, and they would accept a bag of her homemade cookies with embarrassment and head for home. She was putting the last of the peanut butter cookies in the Ziploc bag when she heard the knock on the door. They never rang the bell.

Caroline laid the cookies on the kitchen counter and headed to the door. There they stood with their ball caps held in their right hands over their chests, just like they had for the last six years.

"Hi, gentlemen, you must be finished for the day."

"Yes, ma'am, we's finished, and we won't be back for a spell. Workin' over here ain't like workin' at all with all that pretty music you make."

"Thank you, Ned."

"Fred thinks so too. Don't you, Fred?"

"Uh-huh."

"And another thing, we do believe this piano makes prettier music than your other one. Can that be?" Ned gave Caroline no time to answer. "You'd figger that one piano was just like any other one, but I guess it ain't. I bet that rich man from Kentucky knowed it too. That's a big job for a man to bring a piano all the way from Kentucky to Georgia."

Fred nudged his brother, but Ned kept talking. "I think that Kentucky feller's tryin' to make you think he's somethin', Miss Caroline."

Fred turned his head toward Ned and held up his hat to cover his mouth, but Caroline could faintly make out what he said. "Shut up, Ned."

"Pianos are a lot like people, Ned. Billions of people in the world, but no two exactly alike. It's the same with pianos. I've played lots of pianos, but never one like this one."

"Well, maybe it's just the right one for you. We best be goin'. Got more work to do at home."

"Wait just a minute. I baked cookies last evening, and they'll make a good snack while you're watching television tonight." Caroline walked back across the room to the kitchen for the cookies.

"Oh naw, Miss Caroline, you don't need to do that. We got four boxes o' Cracker Jacks back at the house."

She saw the interchange between the brothers. Fred nudged Ned and once again positioned his cap to cover his mouth. This time, she could only imagine what he said. She returned with bag in hand. "Well, Cracker Jacks are just fine, but homemade peanut butter cookies are mighty fine." This time she handed them to Fred.

"What in the world is going on here?" Sam walked onto the terrace. "You giving away cookies again?"

"Hey Sam, haven't heard from you and Angel all morning." She walked over and hugged him, nearly stumbling over his cane.

"Well, we've heard from you. We sat on the back porch a while this morning just listening to you play. I was reading, and

217

Angel and Gretchen were sewing buttons on the ends of ribbons. They even got Bella involved. You made such a big to-do over that muumuu Angel made with the ribbon streamers, she's making another one."

"Just be grateful, Sam, it keeps her out of Snook's Pool Hall." She watched Ned and Fred snigger.

"Why, Miss Caroline, you know Miss Angel ain't never even seen no inside of Snook's place! Whatcha mean sayin' somethin' like that?"

"Oh, she's just teasing, Ned. And you're right, Miss Angel's lived over eighty years, and she's never been to a pool hall. Come to think of it, maybe I ought to take her down there one evening," Sam said.

"I don't necessarily think that's a very good idea, Mr. Sam, not for Miss Angel nor them boys at Snooks. Why, if I know her, she'd take one them cue sticks, and she'd have that place cleaned up and cleared out in short order, wouldn't she, Fred?" Ned turned to his twin.

"Uh-huh."

"I think you're right. I'll keep her home and protect the local cue sticks. Did you fellows finish up?" Sam tapped his cane on the terrace's stone floor.

"Yessir, we finished and got ever'thing all

cleaned up just like Miss Angel likes it. We been workin' hard in your park, and we got some things what need doin' this afternoon. Then we'll be back to workin' on the park in the mornin'. We gotta do somethin' with all these croker sacks full o' soda pop cans Fred's been savin'. He says we gonna take 'em to get re-, re- . . . re-somethin'."

"You mean recycled?" Sam winked at Caroline.

"Yep, that's it, ain't it, Fred?"

Fred nodded in agreement.

"Fred reads them magazines 'bout that kind of stuff. He's got so many bags of them cans, I can't even get the tractor outta the barn till we get 'em moved."

"You guys must drink a lot of sodas," Caroline said, noticing the flush in Fred's cheeks.

"No, ma'am, not really. Fred stops the truck ever'time he sees a drink can along the side of the road. Why, I expect him to start goin' through the garbage cans at the fillin' station any day now."

Fred was turning redder.

"So, in the morning, it is," Sam said.

"Maybe we should explain about the shack on the park property." Caroline wanted Ned and Fred to retrieve Gretchen's personal items from the shack before they

219

tore it down.

"Why don't you do the explaining, Caroline? But before you do, I want to sit down," Sam said.

"Sure. Would you all like to come in where it's more comfortable?" Caroline offered.

"Oh, no ma'am, we can't sit down on your pretty furniture," Ned objected. "We too dirty. Can we just sit right out here at the table? There's a chair for ever'body."

Caroline joined them. "I need to explain some things before I tell you about the shack you're going to find on Sam's property over the fence. You know that Bella was the person who was coming through the fence at night to listen to me play the piano."

"We ain't forgot we nearly scared that little girl to death the night she tried to come through the fence and me and Ned was waitin' and watchin' for your snooper. Sure am glad Fred turned over his bucket and scared her off before she came through that fence. We woulda wrestled her to the ground and hog-tied her afore we knowed it was a little girl." Ned fanned his face with his green ball cap.

"Yes, I remember that night too. What I haven't explained is that Bella is a very unusual young girl, a musical savant."

"A what? That don't sound like no word I

ever heard!" Ned said.

"It means that she is a special kind of genius."

"Genius, she's a genius? We ain't never met a genius before." Ned slapped his twin on the back. "We know a genius, Fred."

"It seems that Bella and her grandmother found the old shack in a thicket near the creek bed when they would walk through the woods. They fixed it up and it became their safe place. So if . . ."

"Now, wait just a minute, Miss Caroline. Mrs. Silva is Bella's grandma?"

Caroline saw the wrinkles in Ned's brow, revealing his confusion.

Sam jumped in. "Yes, that's right. You know that Gretchen Silva is Ernesto Silva's wife, don't you?"

"Yessir, Mr. Sam, we knowed that. And that ain't good news."

Sam continued. "You're very right about that, Ned. Ernesto and Gretchen had a daughter named Karina. Bella is Karina's illegitimate child . . ."

The twins' faces flushed simultaneously at hearing the word *illegitimate.*

". . . And she ran away about twelve years ago, right after Bella was born. Ernesto's had nothing to do with Bella except to keep her hidden."

Caroline picked up the story again. "They think of the shack as their safe place, and it's where Gretchen first learned that Bella could play the piano. She kept a small, battery-operated keyboard there. Just wanted you to know so you could gather up their things before you tear it down."

"We done knowed about all this except Mrs. Silva being the grandma. Mr. Sam done tol' us ever'thing else," Ned said.

"My goodness. Why didn't you stop me in the middle of my story?"

" 'Cause it sounds a whole lot better when you tell it. Kinda like music to our ears."

Fred mumbled something to Ned.

"What Fred's talkin' 'bout you already know too. Ernesto Silva didn't just wake up one mornin' mean. His daddy was a mean one, too, and as my maw use to say, 'Apples don't fall very far from the tree.' "

Sam chimed in. "Yep, but he's in jail where he belongs now, so he won't be hurting his wife or granddaughter anymore, and he won't be raising any issues about the park. But I'm not worried about getting his signature for any rezoning issues now."

"That's a good thing come out of all this mess."

"Yes, but if there had been trouble, Angel had a plan. She said we'd just keep it, clear it, and make a twelve-acre rose garden out of it, and invite the whole town to use it." Sam reared back and laughed.

Knowing how much Fred disliked working in the roses, Caroline giggled and watched for his reaction.

"Uh-huh."

Sam got up from the table. Ned and Fred stood up as if on cue. "Well, gentlemen, looks like you've done a good job, and I expect to hear the chain saws humming again tomorrow."

"Yessir, Mr. Sam, you'll hear 'em."

Caroline walked across the terrace and stopped at the door to say goodbye to Ned and Fred. "Thank you, gentlemen, for doing such a good job."

"You welcome, ma'am, and thanky for these cookies. And Miss Caroline, them pansies we just planted in them pots next to the door will bloom again if you'll pull the dead ones off. We'll be seein' you. Bye, ma'am." He paused and looked at Fred. "Fred says bye too."

Sam and Caroline walked across the terrace and into the studio kitchen.

"Are you coming up to the main house for lunch, or do you want Hattie to come down here and get you?" Sam asked.

"I don't think I want Hattie on my case today, but Dr. Spencer came down from the university and he's spent the morning drinking coffee at Café on the Square. I've agreed to have lunch with him. I think he's been talking to news reporters since he arrived." She saw Sam looking at the cookie jar. "But I'll come up to see Gretchen and Bella before I leave, and I'll bring some cookies."

"Good girl. Thought you'd want to know I had a call this morning, and I didn't want to talk about this in front of Gretchen."

"Who called?" Caroline noticed the worry line returned to Sam's brow.

"Sheriff. Caleb says Ernesto wants to talk to his wife."

"What? He wants to talk to Gretchen?" She grabbed the hand towel and started to twist it tightly.

"Says he wants to tell her he's sorry. But he's not too old for his wants not to hurt him, and right now, he deserves hurting," Sam said, passing his judgment.

"We can't let that happen." She slapped the counter with the hand towel and turned to Sam. "Gretchen's not strong enough, and besides, she has such a forgiving heart where he's concerned. What if he tried to talk her out of pressing charges?"

"You don't have to worry about that. Not an option because Bella was involved in the beating, and besides, Caleb says Silva's going to plead guilty."

"Oh, thank God, that means no trial. Doesn't that simplify things?"

Sam reached for a cookie. "For sure, but it still doesn't solve the immediate problem. He wants to see her, and we don't have the right to make that decision for her."

"But where will she see him?"

"Oh, she'll have to visit him in jail, but she'll have full protection."

"Then that solves it. We can postpone it for a few days because she's not physically well enough to make the visit. Won't that work?"

"I think it just might. But one of us is going to have to let her know what's happening." He looked at Caroline questioningly. "Maybe I ought to just walk down to the jailhouse this afternoon and have a chat with Caleb, and I'll give the district attorney a call. He'll tell me what I want to know, and if he hesitates, I'll just tell him that I've been retained as Mrs. Silva's legal counsel."

"That's a fine idea, Sam. Your knee may be creaking, but your brain is in high gear."

"Why, thank you, ma'am. I may just qualify for the oldest practicing attorney in the whole state of Georgia." Sam smiled and strutted toward the door, taking a bite of his cookie.

"I'll be teaching this afternoon, but I'll be up for dinner. Maybe you can walk me back to the studio this evening and fill me in."

"Will do. See you when you bring the rest of the cookies." Sam started up the stone path to the main house.

Caroline straightened up the studio, brushed her hair, and touched up her makeup. She was to meet Wyatt at eleven thirty. She was taking cookies from her grand ma'am's cookie jar when she thought of cutting some roses to take to Gretchen and Angel later.

She grabbed her clippers but left her gloves in the closet. The scent of roses invited her into the garden, her eyes surveying each bush for just the right blossom. It appeared. Standing out above all the rest was a Pristine rose, a perfectly formed blossom with an ivory center, blushing to a sweet pink on the outer petals. It reminded her of Bella, pure, unblemished, and beautiful.

She carefully reached her left hand through the foliage to hold the stem so she could snip it above the five-leaf just like Angel had taught her. When she separated

226

the stem from the bush, a sharp thorn pricked her finger, breaking the skin. Caroline dropped the rose as she quickly brought her finger to her mouth. She cautiously retrieved the stem and brought the blossom to her face, brushed it next to her cheek to feel its softness and to inhale its fragrance. A drop of her blood had fallen and stained the blossom's pearl-like purity. She resolved that claiming a rose this beautiful and fragrant was worth the sacrifice of a drop of blood. But she wanted no marks from her carelessness to stain Bella or her future.

CHAPTER THIRTEEN: UNWANTED VISITORS

Caroline tossed her keys on her desk and looked for Wyatt Spencer's number. "Hi, Wyatt. I'm running late."

"Not a problem. I'm just sitting here, and I'm going nowhere."

She was frustrated. "Actually, I would have been on time, but when I left my driveway, a van and car were parked on the street, and they followed me. I pulled in at the post office to make sure. I gave them time to park, and when I pulled out, they followed me home. They're parked again on the street."

"I'm not surprised. I've already given interviews to three reporters in the last hour and a half. Thought if I talked to them, they'd leave you alone. Do you want me to come there?"

What's worse? Being ambushed by reporters or being alone with Wyatt? "Well, I would say no, but . . . if the reporters are circling like vultures, maybe it's best if you do come here. We can join Bella and Gretchen for lunch up at the main house with Sam and Angel."

"Oh, so it won't be just the two of us?"

"No, but if we need to talk, we can visit here in the studio after lunch." She gave him directions for the walk from Café on the Square.

Caroline didn't like what this media attention was doing to the town. Sam had told her Moss Point hadn't been in the news since the train derailment about eighteen years ago — not even one state-winning championship to make the paper. Folks like Sam, who could handle the reporters, lay low and avoided the attention. Others, like GiGi Nelson, the town gossip who never had a thought that didn't come out of her mouth, were eager to toss in their two cents' worth. Most locals knew little to nothing about Bella, so the information the reporters were getting from the locals would keep the media attention on Ernesto. That could be helpful for Bella's protection, but it would add to Gretchen's grief and embarrassment. Perhaps Wyatt's meetings with them this morning gave them what they wanted, and they would leave.

She called Angel, explained what had happened, and asked if Hattie could set two more plates at the table. Angel agreed and then offered to send down a couple of plates if Caroline preferred having lunch in the studio without them. She didn't prefer it, and lunching with the Meadows would save her from the awkwardness of being alone with Wyatt.

Fifteen minutes later, he was standing at the terrace door in khakis, plaid shirt, and a navy sweater tied around his shoulders. "Come in, Wyatt. I see you found your way."

He stepped into the studio and hugged her politely. "Yes, you gave good directions for the scenic route. And the good news is I wasn't followed."

"Thank goodness." She offered him a chair.

He did not sit; instead, he took a step closer to her. "It's good to see you, Caroline, and to be back in your studio. You look especially lovely, not like a woman who's been through what you've been through the last week." He put his hand on her upper arm and let it slide down to her hand. "I hate to think of you being under such stress."

She moved away and motioned for him to sit. "Oh, if you only knew."

"So, what is it I don't know?" He sat down

and made himself comfortable in her tapestry-covered wingback chair.

Too anxious to sit, she tidied up the area around the piano and got out the materials for her piano lessons later in the afternoon. She sensed him watching her. "Well, let's see. Since I saw you last Friday, I've flown to Ferngrove to be with my best friend for the birth of my godchild, which turned out not to be the girl they were expecting. Instead, they have a son who went home to a pink room. This was on Saturday afternoon after quite an interesting morning with Bella at the Georgia Aquarium. And then came Sunday and the *Atlanta Journal-Constitution* story." She continued her tidying and her nervous chatter. "Then Monday, Gretchen was released from the hospital. We drove home and got settled in. Gretchen needed some of her things, so I went to her house to pick up those items — that's a scene I won't soon forget. And then this morning, I've been told Ernesto wants to see Gretchen, and I've been stalked by two reporters."

"Wow, you have been busy, but I stand by what I said. You're beautiful in spite of it all."

Her face flushed, and she would not look at him. "Thank you."

"Now about being stalked by two reporters. Give them a little credit; they're just doing their jobs. They want the story."

"I know, but it's all so foreign to me, and I just don't like it." She straightened the clock her father made her, the one she kept her eye on while teaching piano lessons.

"No, I don't suppose you would. But you may need to get involved to make certain this story goes the way you want it to."

She stopped what she was doing and sat down. "What story? The story's already out and seems to have a life of its own. And the one thing I learned is it doesn't matter what you say to a reporter, he'll put his own spin on the story — the spin that'll sell papers."

Wyatt crossed his legs and draped his arm across the back of the chair. "That was just an article, but I'm talking about the story — the bigger story that people will remember after the articles and television news segments are long forgotten."

"Television news segments?" She looked at his tan ankles and wondered if he ever wore socks. "Now, I'm certain that we have a better chance of controlling television," she said facetiously, with a raised right eyebrow.

"Actually, we do. Right now, we're just reacting. We're on the defensive. There's

232

only one way to put our spin on this story, and that is to change our game plan. We need to take an offensive approach."

"So how do we go about doing that?" She was becoming more interested in what he had to say.

"Well, we need to come up with a way that gives us more control. Maybe we hold a press conference and introduce Bella to the world. We write the press release. We choose the spokesperson, and we coach that person to answer the questions the way we want them answered."

"Interesting." She wondered how but didn't have to wait to find out.

"We can get the media relations department at the university involved. They're seasoned professionals. My department certainly can host the press conference, and we could ask Dr. Martin to represent the music department. We'll invite the press and give them what we want them to have. We don't have to mention Ernesto's name. This story will be about a beautiful young girl with rare and extraordinary abilities. Isn't that what Gretchen would want?"

"I suppose so, but could we talk about this after lunch? Right now, our hosts are waiting for us at the main house. And if you don't mind, please don't mention this at the table. Gretchen has enough to worry about right now."

He stood, leaving his imprint in the soft cushions of her wing chair. "That's fine. But Caroline, we can't sit on this. We need to move quickly to get control of it."

She started toward the door.

"Wait a minute, where are your keys?"

"I don't need keys. I never lock the door." She turned the doorknob.

"If I were you, I'd lock up just to be on the safe side. The reporters know where you live."

Thoughts of that made her dizzy. She went to her desk for her keys, checked the lock on the French doors, and locked the back door as they left. "I really dislike all this. I just need a bit of time to think and figure out how to talk with Gretchen about it."

"Understood. We'll talk later."

They walked the stone path up to the big house. "You know, Wyatt, it had to be someone on your team who leaked this story. Delia Mullins, the editor of our local paper, said a woman phoned her and gave her a sketchy story, and refused to give her name."

"A woman who refused to give her name?" Wyatt asked.

"Yes. Sounded like this woman teased Delia with the potential for a national story. When Delia naively called Harry Newton at the *Journal-Constitution* to ask about his interest in picking up the story she was about to write . . . well, we know the end of that story."

"I'm sorry to say you're probably right. I handpicked this team, thinking I could trust each of them and their professionalism. I was wrong, and I'm sorry. But Caroline, this was bound to happen. Bella is news. We're talking public appearances, articles in magazines and medical journals, and perhaps books and documentaries."

"All this is beginning to sink in. But right now, I agree with Angel. The story that's been told sounds like a girl was discovered in Moss Point — a girl who's been raised and guarded by a vicious wolf." She stopped to unpluck her skirt from the rose bush, its thorns having ensnared the sheer fabric.

He turned and saw what she was doing. "Exactly my point. We need to take control of the story. Here, let me help you." He knelt down and gently pulled her skirt from its thorny captor.

She stood still. "Thank you."

"Wait, let's make sure there are no thorns left in your skirt." He ran his hand across the fabric along her calf and up her thigh.

Caroline tensed as she felt his hand move almost the length of her leg. She moved. "Oh, not to worry. We'd better hurry. We don't want to keep them waiting."

"Certainly." He stood, facing her on a path that was too narrow for two bodies.

Caroline had not dealt with this kind of male attention in six years. Her face flushed for the second time since his arrival, and she was certain her decision to have lunch at the big house was a good one. She brushed her skirt and walked on with purpose.

Introductions were made, and lunch was served. Hattie was grinning like she won the lottery, finally having opportunity to eat in the dining room. Sam and Angel sat at their mahogany table like they sat in their reserved seats at the local playhouse watching a drama unfold. Their discerning perception would give them plenty to talk about after the lights were out tonight.

Angel noticed how Gretchen, always polite, took opportunity to thank the doctor for spending so much time with Bella while she was in the hospital. She also watched Bella and was amazed that nothing about the child's table manners or her behavior would have given away that she was anything but a normal, well-behaved adolescent girl.

Angel listened to Wyatt carefully, observing how he followed Caroline's lead in the conversation. There was no mention of the media in town or Ernesto. Wyatt came close when he mentioned his walk through town earlier to get to Caroline's studio, but he quickly reeled it in when he asked why the land adjacent to Twin Oaks was being cleared. Angel knew for Sam that question was like asking a fisherman about his new fly rod.

Angel held her breath as Sam answered. She watched for any change in Gretchen's demeanor as her husband told of their gift to the community and the ribbon-cutting ceremony planned for the following April.

Before he left, Wyatt thanked Sam and Angel for their hospitality, expressing his hope to see them again soon. Angel assumed it was the young woman living in the studio he really wanted to see.

"Mrs. Silva, when you're up to it, I would like to return and give you and Caroline a full report from the team who observed and tested Bella." He shook Sam's hand and said his goodbyes from the back porch. He approached Bella and gave her a thumbs-up sign.

As Caroline and Wyatt started down the porch steps, Bella said, "Play the piano. Play the piano." He pivoted to see her. An angelic smile, revealing perfect teeth, spread across her face as she gave him a big thumbs-up. Wyatt returned the smile and the sign.

Angel was happy for the renewed activity in this household and was especially grateful for the first sign of pure delight in Bella. "Come, Bella. I have a jigsaw puzzle for us. Your mammá and I can have fun putting it together with you." She put her arm around Bella and walked toward the library where she already had the card table set up with three chairs. "And guess what it will look like when we finish?"

Bella clapped her hands.

"It's a young girl, like you, playing the piano."

Bella gave Angel the thumbs-up sign, which was almost as good as a hug.

"What lovely people, your Sam and Angel." Wyatt followed Caroline closely.

"Yes, they're salt of the earth kind of people, flavoring and preserving," Caroline said as she stepped stone for stone through the garden.

"You seem like a daughter to them. They don't have any children, do they?"

"No, no children. I guess they look at me as a daughter. They've been family friends since I was a little girl, and when I needed a place to land after college graduation, they offered Angel's studio. And here I am six years later."

Caroline wondered if her piano professor at the university had told him about David's death and how that had charted a new course for Caroline.

"They're lucky to have you around."

"I'm the fortunate one, and I don't know what I'd do without them."

"They're gracious too — I mean giving up that prime land for a city park. What I saw when I was walking to your place was beautiful."

"Yeah, it's something they've been wanting to do for quite a while." She was careful to hold her skirt when she passed by the rose bushes. "I was a bit anxious to see how Gretchen and Bella would take the news."

"Why? What's the park got to do with Bella and Gretchen?"

"Their back yard borders this property a couple of blocks away, and it was through these woods that Bella would creep at night and come to hear me play the piano. She and Gretchen had found an old shack down by the creek bed and fixed it up as their safe place." Caroline explained how Bella played a battery-operated keyboard there because she was not allowed to play at home. "Didn't know how they'd take the news of no more parlor in the woods."

"So, is it still there?"

"As of today, it is. Can't make any promises beyond this afternoon though. The land's being cleared, and the underbrush will be burned later this week. I figure Ned and Fred will tear it down before they do the burning."

"Yeah, you're probably right. Would you take me to the shack to take some pictures?"

Caroline looked at her watch. It was ten after two. "I suppose I could, but we'd have to make it quick because my first piano student arrives at three fifteen and I need a bit of prep time."

"Great. Do you need to change your shoes?"

"My shoes are fine, but I think I'll put on some jeans just in case of poison ivy. Now why is it you need pictures?"

"Caroline, I don't think you understand yet. Bella's going to be the subject of many articles and books and perhaps even some documentaries. Writers will want as much research as possible. We need pictures of this place. It apparently has been an important part of her life as a child."

"Oh, I see."

"And while I'm here, I'll take some pictures of the exterior of their house and of your studio?"

"What are you planning? Your own documentary?" she asked as she unlocked her kitchen door.

"Possibly."

His files on Bella were building, and Dr. Spencer wouldn't miss an opportunity to add to them, especially if it meant an October afternoon walk with Caroline.

He followed her through the kitchen and into the great room where her piano was staged in the bay window.

"I'll just be a minute. Make yourself comfortable."

As Caroline retreated from the room, Wyatt followed her with his eyes. He remembered the curve of her calf. Shaking his head as though returning to reality, he looked at the messages on his phone.

"Okay, better get going." She stood before him.

"That's right. For you, time is money." He pulled the door closed behind them.

"Follow me. This isn't the way I'd normally take, but it's the only way to avoid the chance of being followed." She took him through the shade garden and by the pond toward the rose garden and back fence.

The water, cascading over the rocks into the pond, could be heard before he could see it. "That your garden bench over by the pool?"

"It's Angel's, but I spend early mornings there to prepare myself for the day."

He snapped a picture as he walked by. Now he could think about her in this garden. The roses had been pruned and all the leaves raked. The garden was the kind that could only come from years of planning and planting — mature shrubs, perennials, ornamental grasses — and a thoughtful design that made the pattern undetectable. Wyatt missed nothing, and especially the view of jean pockets in front of him. He would have liked to tarry, but he was following a woman on a mission, and he did want photos of the shack.

The creaking hinges of the garden gate suggested it might have been there for the last century. Through the opening, they entered a virgin forest right in the middle of town, a patch of woods without visible paths or trails. Two-foot-high fronds of river fern covered the ground underneath the trees. Pine straw, summoned by the cool autumn mornings, had begun to fall and draped the ferns and other low-growing plants. This looked much like his East Texas home.

"There it is." Caroline pointed straight ahead. "There's the parlor." She told him she had been there only once, right after Gretchen had told her about it last May.

The wooden shack looked undisturbed, nestled underneath the pine trees at the edge of the creek bank. The unpainted, vertical clapboard structure was less than the size of Sam's one-car garage, with the door on the north wall and a cut-out square for the window on the opposite wall. As they entered, Caroline explained to him how it had been littered with beer cans, cigarette stubs, and leftovers from partying teenagers, and that Gretchen and Bella had cleaned the inside, painted the walls and flat ceiling, and made a curtain for the window. With no money to purchase a rug, Gretchen had covered the floor with one of her handmade quilts. The only piece of furniture was a small table, the kind usually found in a pile of rubbish waiting for the garbage collector. Covered in an embroidered cloth, the table held a scented candle, secured in one of Bella's mosaic pieces.

Caroline walked to the table and picked up the candleholder and handed it to Wyatt.

"Look. Bella made this."

"This is very interesting. How do you know she made it?" He laid the camera on the table and took the piece, turning it in his hands, examining every facet.

"Because she made something like this for me out of a broken teapot. Long story for another time, but it's a treasure." She knelt and pulled out the two large clear-plastic boxes stored under the table. She opened them carefully. One held sewing supplies, a beautiful, unfinished table scarf, and several boxes of matches. In the other box was Bella's battery-operated keyboard. "Guess the boxes protected their things from weather and creatures since there's no covering on the window."

Wyatt put the candle back in the holder, placed it on the table, and pulled out his phone. The afternoon light, stretching its fingers through the lace curtains, brushed Caroline's face. Her almost black hair, loose around her shoulders, became a deep sable brown in the sunlight.

She appeared to be deep in thought as she opened the boxes. He snapped her picture several times before she asked, "What are you doing?"

"I'm preserving your beauty. This moment will never come again, you know." There was something primal about being with her in the silence of this forest in a rustic shack. Like a scene from a movie where lovers take shelter from a thunderstorm. The only things missing were wet clothes and rain. He watched her face flush.

Caroline returned the lids to the boxes and stood up. "Here, let me get out of your way so you can get the pictures you need."

"I have the shots I want." He approached her, slid one arm around her waist, and pulled her closer to him. He outlined her face with his finger. She was perfect in every way, petite but shapely, trim but soft. He studied her face. Bluer eyes had never been closer to his. He was trained to read people, but his desires prevented him from decoding the signals he was getting. He took a chance and leaned to kiss her.

Just as his lips brushed hers, she pushed away.

"What, what is it, Caroline?"

"This . . . this isn't right." She walked to the window.

"What's not right? Surely you must know I'm interested in you, and not just because of Bella." He paused. "I hoped you might feel the same way, and besides, it's time you were over David. Grieving won't bring him back, and you're wasting good years."

When she looked at him now, her signals needed no decoding. The softness had disappeared. He'd never seen her face so steely and resolute.

"How did you know about David? I never told you."

"Annabelle. Annabelle Martin."

"She told you? Why would she tell you?"

He walked toward her again. "Maybe it's because I told her you were the most beautiful woman I've ever seen and that you dance in and out of my thoughts more than any woman in quite a while."

She walked around him to the door. "I'm flattered, Wyatt, and I'm sure you could have your pick of women." She paused and repeated, "It just isn't right."

"Again, I ask you, what's not right?"

"We need to maintain a professional relationship."

"Why? We're both young and single. There's no reason not to explore a relationship." He waited for a response, which didn't come. "It's Adair, isn't it?"

"Why would you say that?"

"I'm the trained mind gamer here, but you're good. You only answer with darn good questions. I say it because I've seen you two together. If that's it, just say it and I'll back off. But if I sense there's even a slight chance for me, I'm telling you straight up, Caroline, I'll be back. So tell me, is it Adair?"

"I can't answer that question."

"Can't or won't?"

"I don't have an answer, and I'd really prefer not having this conversation." She walked back to the table and picked up one of the plastic boxes. "Would you mind taking the other one? Gretchen and Bella might like to have these."

"Sure. But this isn't the end of this conversation." He picked up the container.

She looked at him with that same look. "It is for today, Wyatt." She walked through the door and he followed. After taking a few steps, she stopped, put the box down, went back inside and got the quilt and Bella's sculpture, and put them on top of her box.

They walked in silence back to her studio. She rested the box on the terrace table and unlocked the door. He followed her in and put the box on the counter. She returned from the terrace with the other box. "I really must get ready for my lesson."

He knew this was his exit cue. "Look, I'm sorry if I made you uncomfortable today, Caroline. That would never be my intention. It's just I'm so attracted to you, and you're more difficult to read than *War and*

Peace." He saw something that looked like disappointment in her eyes. "I'm sorry, I shouldn't have said that either."

She said nothing.

"I seem to be apologizing often today. Maybe next time will be better." He walked to the door.

She followed him, but not closely.

"Since you say we need to maintain a professional relationship, would you at least think about what I said — I mean about controlling the story?"

"Yes, Wyatt, I'll think about that. Do you remember how to get back to your car?" She stood at the door.

"Yes, I think I can find it." He looked at her once more. "I truly am sorry, Caroline. I'm just asking for a chance. I'll be in touch."

"Goodbye, Wyatt." She closed the door.

This was a new experience for him. Women usually came on to him, and he couldn't remember one turning down his advances since he was a scrubby-faced fifteen-year-old. He might not have been able to see Caroline, but he heard clearly her goodbye and the door closing.

Clothes changed, Caroline checked the beeping answering machine.

"Hi, Blue Eyes. Sorry I missed you. I'll call again tonight."

Roderick's voice. It calmed her, and at the same time raised more questions. She sat at her desk and put her head down the way she had every day after lunch when she was in the first grade, but she wasn't resting. *I can't answer your question, Wyatt, because I don't have an answer. I wish I did.*

Sam was in his lounger napping, and Gretchen was snoozing on the sofa underneath the window. Bella leaned over the table, picking up the few remaining pieces of the puzzle, turning them over between her fingers. "Flower, flower."

"What about the flower, Bella?" Angel was at the card table reading a newspaper. She gave up trying to help shortly after all the puzzle pieces were turned over to reveal the colored side. Bella was quite capable.

"See the flower." Bella squealed in delight, pointed to the puzzle, and clapped her hands.

"Shh, Bella. Quiet. Sam and your mammá are napping over there." Angel looked at the puzzle. Bella had put in the last piece, the blossom of a red rose in a crystal vase sitting on the piano.

Bella repeated Angel's words. "Shh, Bella.

Be quiet. He will hear you." The expression of delight on Bella's face disappeared.

"No, no, it's okay. You didn't wake them." Angel put the paper away when she recognized fear had kidnapped Bella's smile.

"Do I go to the hiding place? I'll be quiet. I'll be good."

Angel reached across the table to pat Bella's hand. "Stay right here, child. There's no reason to hide. We don't have a hiding place."

Bella rocked in her chair. "Mammá's sleeping. Mr. Sam's sleeping. Miss Angel's not sleeping." Bella shook her head from side to side.

"No, I'm not sleeping."

Bella became very still and looked into Angel's face. "Mammá says angels live in heaven. Do you live in heaven, Miss Angel?"

Angel took her time to respond. "No, my sweet. I live right here at Twin Oaks. But it's a lot like heaven, because the people I love are here — Mr. Sam and Caroline and Hattie, and now you and your mammá. And there's no need for a hiding place."

CHAPTER FOURTEEN:
ADVANTAGES AND DISADVANTAGES

Late afternoon wind whipped across the sand dunes on Myrtle Beach. The southwest edge of a hurricane a couple of hundred miles offshore would bring rain before midnight. Karina had survived a few storms in the last twelve years, and she was glad for late October and the approaching end of the hurricane season. She heard the roar of Skeeter's Harley above the gales and the television as he pulled into the parking space of their beachfront apartment. She changed the channel on the TV, rose slowly from the futon, and opened the sliding glass door to the balcony. As she leaned over the balcony railing, not even the gusts of wind moved her hair — short, spiky, and smudge-pot black with no hint of the silky, platinum strands of her childhood. "Hey, Skeeter, get the mail before you come up, will you?"

"Yeah, yeah. Pop me a cold one." He secured his bike, tucked the helmet under his arm, and walked out of her sight to get the mail.

The wind still whipping, she closed the sliding door. She was drinking the last beer, and the apartment looked like some frat boys might have partied there the night before — beer and cola cans, the smell of leftover pizza in open boxes, dirty dishes covering the counters. She had spent the afternoon on the futon, never imagining he'd be home early. She quickly tried to pick up what she could grab on her way to the kitchen and still hold on to her beer. Hot water from the kitchen faucet was creating suds in the sink when she heard the door slam. She hated it when he slammed the door.

"Looks like you really took the day off on your day off." He chucked the mail on the counter, on top of magazines and news-papers where she'd been clipping coupons Sunday afternoon. "Where's my beer?"

"Here, drink the rest of this." She wiped the soap from her hands, picked up the can, and handed it to him across the counter.

"Guess this is your way of saying you drank the last one." Skeeter snatched the can from her hand, guzzled the last few swallows, and crushed the can in his right hand.

She hated it when he snatched things from her. Her kindergarten teacher always said to her classmates, "Don't snatch. Snatch cats never get fat." She had not understood what snatching had to do with fat cats, but she remembered the jingle. Her mother had explained what it meant.

Skeeter tossed the empty can across the counter, missing the trash can by a foot. She hated it when he did that too. Come to think about it, she hated the sounds he made when he ate, she hated his sweat-stained T-shirts, she hated the way he left his dripping towel on the tub, and she hated the way he slung his arm over her in the middle of the night, startling her out of a deep sleep. But she was accustomed to him, and he wasn't likely to change. Besides, his name was tattooed on her hip.

"You got something from Augusta in the mail today, but you ain't getting it till this mess is cleaned up."

She walked around the kitchen counter. "Give it to me, Skeeter. I would've had the apartment cleaned up before you got home, but you're here early."

"Yeah, finished my job for the day. But you heard what I said. Pick up this mess and you'll get your envelope."

She started to straighten up the place and

253

mumbled under her breath, "And if I don't clean it up, I'll get it too." Her arms still bore the bruises from the last fight they'd had.

"What'd you say?" He approached her, dangling the large brown envelope in front of her.

"I just said I'd get things cleaned up right away." She would comply this time. No need in asking to be his victim again.

He removed his jacket and tossed it on the sofa. "I'm going downstairs to talk to Jerry and see if he has a beer, and this place had better be cleaned up with supper on the table when I get back." He slammed the door again.

Cooking, laundry, and cleaning the apartment were her jobs. Seeing that she did those things was Skeeter's job, but she never understood why. Five mornings a week, she got up at four o'clock to work at a local bakery until noon and waited tables three nights a week at a local bar. She paid half the rent and bought the groceries and managed to put away three thousand four hundred and sixty-nine dollars in case Skeeter didn't come home one night.

He was a mechanic at a garage on the other side of town, the kind of business where they did more than replace mufflers and transmissions. She knew why he was called in the middle of the night to come in and do a rush paint job, but they never talked about it.

She looked under the magazines on the futon for the TV remote. He would be gone at least an hour, and she could hear the last of *Tristan and Isolde* on public television while she cleaned. Listening to opera was something she had done with her mother, but now she did alone. None of her friends had ever heard of the "Tristan chord" or Wagner's use of harmonic suspension. She had taught herself those things. Skeeter and their friends coaxed her to sing karaoke when they were drunk, but none of them knew that she loved the opera. It was her secret, something she kept for herself.

The room smelled like canned mountain breezes, and the clutter had almost disappeared when Isolde began her final aria. Karina's arms filled with Skeeter's jacket, his nasty socks and fishing boots from Sunday, and three days of newspapers, she stopped in front of the TV. This aria and scene were as familiar to her as the smell and feel of the pastry dough her mammá had taught her to make. Her eyes welled with tears at the beauty of the singing, and she felt Isolde's pain as she knelt over the body of her dead lover in this last scene.

Karina dropped what she was holding and scrambled for the remote when she heard Skeeter tromping up the outside stairs. She was barely able to change the channel before he barreled through the door, six-pack in hand.

She knelt to pick up the jacket and boots and piled the papers high enough to hide the emotion in her eyes. "Almost done. Soup's warming and the rolls are rising." She walked down the short hallway to the bedroom they shared.

"Next time you're at the store, get an extra six-pack for Jerry. We owe him one." He changed the channel from news to NASCAR.

Karina answered him from down the hall. "Sure, better put it on the list on the refrigerator."

"You put it on the list. I didn't drink the last beer," he yelled from the futon.

She washed her face and hands and returned to the kitchen. "Where's my letter?"

"Where's my supper?" he growled.

He didn't have to be so cruel. "I told you, the soup's getting warm and the rolls are ready for the oven." She was accustomed to making dough and pastries even on her day off. The rolls had been rising since midmorning. "Give me the letter. I'll read it while the rolls are baking."

He pulled the large brown envelope from under the pillow next to him and handed it to her. His eyes never left the cars zooming around the track.

After the rolls were brushed lightly with butter and in the oven, she pulled a paring knife from the kitchen drawer and ripped open the envelope. It held a section of a newspaper and a scribbled note from Cheryl Hastings.

Cheryl was her childhood friend and the only person from Moss Point who knew where she was. Even after the Hastings moved away after graduation, Cheryl had remained her only connection to her mammá since the day she left home twelve years ago. Karina had written her mammá a few times in the last several years. She'd send the letters to Cheryl, and Cheryl would put them in another envelope and mail them to Gretchen. As a pharmaceutical rep, Cheryl traveled and could easily mail the letters from different cities. Without a return address and different postmarks, the envelopes left Gretchen no trace of how to reach her. Cheryl had kept her promise to Karina all these years.

Karina removed the note paper-clipped to

the newspaper.

Karina,
You need to see this, and you need to think about going home. Your mammá needs you. Here's my card if you need anything. Call me.

Cheryl

Karina folded the note around Cheryl's business card and tucked it in the kitchen drawer underneath the silverware tray. Skeeter knew nothing of her past in Moss Point, and she was determined to keep it that way.

She unfolded the newspaper. Cheryl had drawn an arrow pointing to the headline on the front page of the *Atlanta Journal-Constitution*'s Lifestyle section. "Moss Point Man Imprisons Wife and Gifted Child."

Karina pulled up the bar stool and sat down. She could not take her eyes off the picture of Bella in the hospital hallway, bandage over her right cheek and standing next to a beautiful, nameless young woman noted as Bella's piano teacher. Bella looked exactly as she had when she was twelve — a wisp of a girl, slender and blonde with silvery-green eyes, just like her mammá. Staring at this photo opened a door to a

258

painful past that Karina had so desperately locked away. Between her heart and her gut was a churning of self-loathing for having abandoned her mother and daughter, and anger at her mother for not escaping too.

The article detailed the beating and subsequent hospitalization of the woman and child and the apprehension of Ernesto Silva, now in the Moss Point city jail, awaiting trial. The writer quoted Caleb Mullins, the local sheriff, regarding the assault and crime scene. She was poring over the description of the autistic young Bella and how doctors were observing her to determine the nature of her rare gifts when she realized Skeeter was standing behind her, reading over her shoulder.

He pointed at the picture. "Hey, that girl looks just like you, except for the hair and about fifteen years." He snatched the paper from her hand and turned away from her.

She pounded his broad back with her fists. "Give me that paper, it's mine."

He laughed, stepped away from her, and fanned her face with the newspaper. "Careful, there, you might hurt me." He laughed again.

She hated that laugh. It was mean and condescending.

"Moss Point man imprisons wife and

gifted child?" He chortled.

Karina crumpled to the floor like an accordion fan. Kneeling on the sticky linoleum, she covered her face with her hands. "I hate him. I hate him so much," she mumbled under her breath.

Skeeter, wobbling around like he always did after a few beers, waved the paper in the air. "Hey, do you know these people?"

Her shoulders shook as she sobbed. Her buried past life was now resurrected. "Yeah, I know these people." Black mascara trailed down her face. "These people," she snubbed, "these people are my family."

Gretchen and Bella, accustomed to escaping to their room after dinner to avoid Ernesto's bad humor, retired to their suite shortly after supper. Gretchen climbed into bed and propped her broken arm on a couple of down pillows while Bella sat at the table across the room, pulling out the jigsaw puzzle pieces and replacing them repeatedly. The five-hundred-piece puzzle, still in pieces when the courthouse clock had struck two this afternoon, was now completed. "You finished, Bella. Remember what Angel said. We'll take the board and puzzle out tomorrow. She'll glue it, and when it dries, there will be a beautiful picture of a young girl playing the piano. Angel wants you to have the picture for your room."

Gretchen noticed Bella's agitation now that there were no more puzzle pieces. "Why don't you come lie down, and I'll read to you?"

Bella lay beside her but was fidgety. Just as Gretchen started to read, Bella started to sing, and Gretchen tried to quiet her. "We don't have to read, Bella. Why don't you listen to your music?"

Bella rose, but when her feet hit the floor, she paced. "I can sing. No more Mr. Silva. I want to go to the safe place. Play the piano. Play the piano. Mammá says, 'I'll come for you.' Where's Sarah? No more Mr. Silva. Go to Caroline's. She's playing the piano."

Gretchen got up, found the iPod, and helped Bella adjust the headphones.

"Where's my hat? Where's my hat?" Bella found her hat and pulled it down on her head. Not even the sounds of the whales settled her spirit. "Play piano. Play piano."

Roderick closed the last of the September reports and stacked them in the filing basket on his desk. He removed his reading glasses and rubbed his eyes. The cuckoo clock, one of his mother's purchases in Austria, alerted him it was nine o'clock. As children, he and Sarah had stood in front of the clock waiting for the wooden bird with large white eyes and a red beak to pop out from behind the delicately carved door. As the bird sang his song, another door beneath him opened, and a disk supporting a dancer, dressed in a dirndl, appeared and turned, giving the appearance the girl was dancing. He and Sarah danced in a circle with her.

When he had built his apartment off the courtyard of the main house, he gave the decorator a budget and only two nonnegotiables. The cuckoo clock would hang beside the fireplace, and the fabric for draperies would be the paisley print that reminded him of his father's ties and the sofa in the library.

Roderick rose from his desk, turned on Rachmaninoff, and stepped around to his apartment-sized kitchen for a glass of milk and Lilah's "welcome home" iced pumpkin cookies.

He stood at the window, drinking milk and looking out into the clearest, never-ending sky. The harvest moon he had shared with Caroline only three nights ago was waning.

Returning to his chair and removing his shoes, he got comfortable and propped his feet on his desk. The moon was still visible through the window as he dialed Caroline's number.

"Hello. This is Caroline."

The sound of her voice was like coming home again. "Hi, I was calling Blue Eyes. Is she there?"

"Oh, hello, Roderick. She's here and was just thinking about you."

"I like the sound of that. I hope thinking of me made her smile inside."

"Well, perhaps it did. She was standing in the moonbeams and thinking about sitting poolside with you Saturday evening."

Caroline's boldness took some of his reservation away. "So, I guess we've been looking at the same moon and thinking the same thoughts."

"You're moon gazing tonight too?"

"Yep, standing at my window after two hours of reading September reports. Doesn't get much better than looking out on the night sky here while you're eating Lilah's pumpkin cookies and drinking a glass of ice-cold milk." *Unless you were with me.* "I called you this afternoon."

"I got your message. Wyatt Spencer was here today. This town's crawling with reporters, and several of them spent the morning interviewing Wyatt, and then he joined us for lunch. When you called, we had walked over to take photos of Gretchen's safe place in the woods before they tear it down. Sam's clearing that area for a park. I told you about that."

"Did Wyatt give Gretchen the report from his team?" In his world, Roderick bought out Wyatt Spencers and fired them. The man had better be careful. Spencer was entering Roderick's world.

"No, it's not in its finished form yet. But he did have some ideas about how to get more control over this story. I'm unsettled, so I'd like your opinion. Do you have time to talk about it now?"

Discussing Wyatt's ideas was not why he called Caroline tonight, but how could he refuse? "Certainly. What's he suggesting?" Roderick put his feet on the floor and sat straighter in his chair, the way he did when he was listening to his attorney's counsel during the last stage of a merger.

Caroline described Wyatt's ideas for hosting a press conference at the university and introducing Bella to the public.

As much as Roderick disliked the idea of Wyatt's continued involvement, he knew it was a smart idea. "Well, he's right, Caroline. This strategy would move the focus to Bella and away from her grandfather."

"I thought so, too, but I just needed to hear you say so. But there's a downside. I don't know if we're ready for this much attention on Bella."

"Good question, and there doesn't seem to be a way of judging how much that will be just yet."

"Wyatt says it will be national. He's convinced her gifts are so rare that this is just the beginning. He's talking about articles and books and television segments and documentaries. That's why he wanted the photos he took today."

"If all this is true, and we have no reason or precedent to think that it's not, then I say move forward with the press conference and do it quickly." Roderick was long on strategy and short on patience. In most of his business negotiations, which sometimes took months to get what he wanted, his lack of patience rarely became an issue because he was always working his plan, and often his plan included cooling-off periods when negotiations stopped. He knew when to proceed, when to stay silent, and when to walk away. The media situation surrounding Bella was foreign territory to him, but he looked at it like going into a deal when he didn't know his opponent very well. In those cases, he worked swiftly to flush out the people and potential problems in devising his strategy. "Are you comfortable with Dr. Spencer handling the event and driving the press?"

"I guess." She paused. "I just want to protect Gretchen and Bella."

"What's this uncertainty I hear in your voice?" He practiced a cerebral, nonemotional approach to decision-making, but sometimes he went with his gut. Right now, his gut said something was amiss.

"It's just that someone from Wyatt's team leaked this story, and that's why we're having to deal with this prematurely."

"Well, now. I'd say that gives you some advantage."

"An advantage?"

He twirled a large paper clip through and over his fingers. "Let's look at the playing field. Obviously, Spencer has knowledge that you don't have. He has a professional team of psychologists that you don't have. And he can probably pull together a top-shelf media event at the university to introduce Bella."

"Okay. I get that."

He heard the questioning in her tone. "We know what he has. But do you know what you have?"

"I have butterflies in my stomach like I do

266

just before I walk onto the recital stage."

"Recital? Ah, we'll come back to that in a minute. But first, you must know what you have that Spencer doesn't." He paused, but she didn't respond. "You have the relationship with Bella and Gretchen. Gretchen trusts you. That gives you the power over how to proceed. He'll never have that."

"So, I have something that he doesn't." She paused. "But it balances out because he has something I don't have."

"Yet. He has something that you don't have *yet."*

"Ah, I get it. Perhaps there are other doctors and other institutions that would like access to Bella. That's like a trump card."

She was guileless but quick. He liked that. "Exactly. The University of Georgia is just the first. In business, I'd call that grounds for a bidding war."

"Oh, so now we've moved from navigating through a press conference to a bidding war. I think I'll change my name and move into the witness protection program. I don't like all this."

He laughed. "Witness protection program? But you'd have to change your whole identity, and they'd never let you play the piano again."

"Then maybe I won't. All right, I know

267

what I have and what I could acquire, so what do I do now?"

"You tell Spencer you want the fame-seeking member of his team who leaked this story dismissed. That person is self-serving and cannot be trusted. When that's done, you'll talk with him about a date for the media event. If he's unwilling to do that, threaten him with Sarah. Spencer knows with Sarah's connections at Duke University, he could lose his foothold in a New York minute."

"Sarah. I feel better already. She's to get a copy of their report, and she's such a person of integrity that I'm sure she'd work out some collaboration, giving Wyatt and his team credit for their work if we go with Duke."

"Now you're strategizing." He removed his elbows from his desk, dropped the paper clip, and sat back in his chair and propped his feet up again.

"Excuse me, but did I just get a crash course in Mergers and Acquisitions?"

"Hardly. You just needed a bit of prodding. You figured it out for yourself. Just remember, you have the upper hand here if you don't give it away."

"I'll do my best."

"Enough about that. Now, if I don't do

this, Lilah's going to be on my case in the morning. We must set a date for your holiday recital." He looked out the window again. The moon was inching its way from behind a cloud.

"Then let's set the date. I don't want Lilah serving whole-wheat pancakes and sugar-free syrup in the morning just to punish you. So, tell me what you're thinking."

He put his feet on the floor and sat up straight. He stood and began to pace behind his desk. But he was silent.

"Roderick? Are you there?"

"Yes, I'm here. I was just thinking." *Oh how I wish I could tell you what I'm thinking, but it's too soon.* "Since you don't teach for a couple of weeks during the holidays, what about making a winter vacation of this? I mean, if I must provide snow, you might as well stay and enjoy it. Acer and I will pick you up on Sunday, and you can perform on Tuesday evening."

"And then I could fly to Ferngrove on Friday?"

"You could, but I was hoping you'd stay the week and celebrate Christmas and New Year's here with Sarah and George and me."

"Roderick, you are aware that I am nearly twenty-nine years old and I've never spent a Christmas away from Ferngrove and my family?"

"I know, you've already told me." He longed for that kind of family. "I've met your parents, but most of the conversation was about babies since Betsy was in the delivery room. We talked about your childhood, but now I need to know more about your mom and dad."

"Why do you need to know now?"

"Well, if I'm competing with them for spending Christmas with you, then I need to know my opponents. What is it they have that I don't?"

"Let me see. They have the tree that'll be covered with handmade ornaments. They'll hang the Christmas stockings Grand Ma'am made for each of us when we were three. They'll have my mom's fruitcake and my daddy's eggnog." She paused. "They'll have the Christmas Eve candlelight service in the church where I grew up and Mom's biscuits on Christmas morning when my brothers, James and TJ, bring their families over early for breakfast and the family gift exchange." She sighed. "So, is this the appropriate time to ask you what you might have that they don't?"

"Perfect timing because I'm feeling really good about this. I'll have not one, but multiple Christmas trees and an endless supply of oak wood for the fireplace in the library. Lilah makes a wicked eggnog, and I'll purchase fruitcakes from the monks at the monastery outside of Lexington. We'll go to the early service on Christmas Eve and have a late dinner in front of the fire. Now Christmas morning could get interesting since Lilah won't be here to make biscuits, but I can promise unforgettable gifts."

"Hmm . . . anything else?"

"Yes, one more thing. The potential for a white Christmas is far greater here than in Ferngrove." It was a long shot to pull her away from her family, and he knew it.

Long pause. "Well, I don't know about this fruitcake from a monastery. My mom makes the best. But . . . okay, where do I sign?"

"You mean you're accepting my invitation?"

"I am, but with one request. Please understand, I'll still come even if you say no."

"This wasn't as difficult as I thought it would be if you have only one request. So, tell me."

"Well, I was thinking about Gretchen and Bella. I doubt they even know what a real Christmas is like, and I was planning to take them to Ferngrove with me. Would bringing them to Rockwater be too much to ask?"

Roderick closed his eyes, smiled warmly, and then grimaced, realizing he had missed scoring some points by not thinking of this himself. "Of course, it will be wonderful to have them here. Sarah would love it too. There hasn't been a child in this house since I was young. We'll give Bella the best Christmas ever."

"Thank you, Roderick. I'm not certain they'll come, but I'll do my best to persuade them. This Christmas will be dream-like wonderful."

The last time he heard her voice like this, he had seen tears in her eyes. "You're welcome, and I'll do my best to make it dream-like wonderful. I should be thanking you. It's been a long time since I really anticipated Christmas, but I will this year."

Roderick sat back down in his desk chair. They talked for another hour until the moon was high enough in the sky to no longer be visible through Roderick's window. Comfortable talk about his business and her students. More talk about holding the press conference and how to help Gretchen with her business affairs now that Ernesto was behind bars.

"Hang on, Roderick. There's someone knocking on my back door."

He looked at the cuckoo clock. It was ten forty. The idea of someone knocking on her door so late made him uncomfortable. He heard voices in the background but couldn't make them out or what was being said.

She returned in just a couple of minutes. "I'll need to go now. It was Sam and Bella. Seems Bella can't sleep and kept saying, 'Play piano, play piano.' So I told Sam to leave her with me for the night."

Roderick could already hear Bella at the piano. "Is that Mozart?"

"It is — it's Number 14 in C minor. I played it for her a couple of months ago, and she plays the entire first movement. Strange that she's not bothered by the minor key. That's sometimes more difficult for young pianists. But Bella's not like other young pianists, or any other pianist I know."

"Sounds like you'll be entertained for a while and I need to let you go, although I hate to. I'm flying to Boston for a meeting tomorrow, but it should be a quick turn-around." He sat up in his chair again. "I miss you, Caroline."

"I miss you too." She paused. "Good night, Roderick."

He held the phone for a moment, savoring the goodbye. Leaving the door open as he walked out on the terrace, he needed one more look at the moon this evening.

Bella was into the B section of the Mozart.

Caroline walked around the piano and stood, looking out the twelve-foot-high windows, across the terrace, and into the night sky. The moon had made its way beyond the magnolia tree and was suspended high in the heavens. She replayed her conversation with Roderick. She had known only one man in her life who stirred such feelings.

The piano stool was four steps away. She sat down next to Bella, who was lost in the music and was rocking to the pulse of the allegro. Caroline interrupted by placing her hands on top of Bella's. Her rocking motion stopped along with her piano playing, and Bella sat amazingly still, staring at the keyboard.

"Bella, I want to teach you a new song. Listen to this." Caroline played "Have Yourself a Merry Little Christmas," an arrangement with her own creative embellishments.

The only movement in Bella's body was the slight rise and fall of her chest as she breathed. Her eyes were transfixed upon Caroline's hands.

Caroline repeated the song. "This is a

beautiful Christmas song. I hope you like it, Bella." She removed her hands from the piano and stood up.

Bella said nothing, but before Caroline could take the four steps back to the window, Bella was playing her new song, and Caroline stood, gazing at the moon, imagining as Betsy had told her to do, and singing to Bella's accompaniment, "From now on our troubles will be out of sight."

CHAPTER FIFTEEN: CAPTIVE AND FREE

Life in Moss Point was settling back down the way it always did. Reporters who had filled the tables at Café on the Square with their laptops and cell phones were sitting at other tables in another town chasing another story.

Caroline knew Mabel was glad. She had run the café for years, cooking what she wanted to when she wanted to, leaving time for fishing and short trips in her camper trailer and leaving the locals a sign on the door to say when she'd be back. For the last six days, the doors were open for breakfast, lunch, and supper. Her niece had quickly printed up new menus and jacked up the prices. The reporters didn't know, and the locals weren't bothered either. They knew when the reporters left town, Mabel would be gone for a few days and the old menu and prices would return when she did.

Caroline and the Meadows had established a routine with their houseguests. Hattie was usually up to her elbows in flour and sugar with Gretchen watching from the breakfast table. Gretchen was healing slowly and taking every opportunity to express her gratitude for the Meadows' graciousness. Even with mornings at the piano with Caroline and afternoons with her new iPod, Bella was becoming more verbal.

Roderick's frequent calls had given Caroline something to look forward to each day. She had taken his advice and called Wyatt Spencer to request that he dismiss from his team the person who had leaked the story. When that was done, they could talk about plans for a media event. He had assured her that this dismissal would take place in short order and he'd return to Moss Point for a planning session. Their conversation was kept on a purely professional level.

Sam called before her Friday students arrived. "Caroline, we need to talk."

"I know, it's Friday and you want hamburgers and onion rings from Mabel's."

"Yes, I do. But this is not the kind of talk for the kitchen table. Caleb just called again. Ernesto still wants to see Gretchen."

"I don't know about this. What do you think, Sam?"

"I don't like it, but neither do I feel right

277

about not allowing Gretchen to decide. We've delayed it long enough, and I think it's time to talk to her about it. I've been thinking about it today and I'm about to call Caleb one more time."

"I trust you, Sam. If we must, then let's do it and get it over with. I'll call Mabel and get our Friday night dinner in a paper bag. Be up in a while."

"Thank you, dear. Maybe there'll be opportunity to speak privately after supper."

The early morning sun was sunflower gold, the sky was clear, and the few leaves left on the hardwood trees were clinging to bare limbs for life. Caroline could almost hear her father saying, "If God made a more beautiful morning, then He kept it for Himself." But there was a job to be done this Saturday morning, a job that was like a heavy, gray cloud following her around since yesterday.

She had told Sam after supper last night that she thought Gretchen should come to the studio where Bella could play the piano and she and Gretchen could sit in the garden. They'd had serious chats there before. But after round two of discussions with Sam, they decided that Caroline would come up for breakfast and Sam would be a part of the conversation. Sam could speak to the legal implications of what Ernesto was facing, hopefully addressing Gretchen's questions and fears.

Caroline knew that Sam wanted this over as early in the day as possible. Saturday was the best day for Gretchen to visit Ernesto. Reporters were gone. The town was quiet on Saturday morning, and she could possibly slip in and out without being seen. Caleb had assured Sam the deputies would be on patrol, and he'd be alone at the jail.

After a country morning breakfast, Hattie went home for the weekend, and Angel took Bella to the sunroom to watch a movie. Lucky for everyone that Angel had a collection of musicals. Bella was content for hours to watch and listen.

Caroline poured Gretchen and Sam another cup of coffee and joined them at the table. She interrupted their conversation about some pastry Sam had enjoyed on one of their trips to Switzerland — one that he'd not been able to find anywhere else.

"I know that pastry, and it would bring me great pleasure to have my arm out of this cast and make a gift of sweet treats for you," Gretchen offered. She patted the cast on her left arm.

"Gretchen, Sam and I have something we

279

need to talk to you about this morning."

"Your smile just left the room, my friend. This must be very serious."

"Well, we'd prefer talking about Switzerland and sweets, but this can't really wait." Sam leaned forward with his elbows on the table. "Caleb Mullins, the sheriff, has been staying in contact with me about your husband."

"I see, and I am so sorry that you have to even think about this. Is there something I need to do? Maybe, how do you say it? Bail?"

Sam stirred his coffee. "No, there won't be any need for bail. It seems that Mr. Silva has decided to plead guilty, forgoing the need for a trial. There'll just be sentencing with the judge."

"That is a relief, but it makes me very sad. This means Ernesto will go to prison?"

"Yes, that's what it means." Sam used his most compassionate voice, not the voice he used in the courtroom for forty-three years.

"How long? How long will he be in prison?"

Caroline saw Gretchen's chin quiver. "It will be long enough for you and Bella to start a new life without him."

"For two aggravated assaults, one involving a minor, he'll get at least seven to ten years," Sam answered.

"Oh my, seven to ten years. That is so bad for Ernesto. And what will I do? I have no job and no money. I must find work, but then who will take care of Bella?" Tears filled her eyes.

Caroline said, "You mustn't worry about that now. You just worry about getting well. I'll, no, we'll, help you figure all that out." She looked at Sam.

Curious, Sam asked, "Gretchen, do you know anything about your finances? Like what Ernesto's pay is or anything about bank accounts? Is your house paid for? Things like that."

"Oh, I know nothing. He gave me an allowance in cash every week. This was to buy groceries, and once or twice a year, he gave me extra money for clothes for Bella and me. But I do not know how much he made or where it is, and I do not know anything about the house or the vehicle."

Caroline was not surprised. "When you're feeling better, we'll go to your house and see what we can find. But there is something you must decide today." She paused, not wanting to be the messenger. "Ernesto would like to see you."

"See me? Where?"

Sam pushed away his empty cup. "If you

think you need to do this, Gretchen, I'll take you to the jail myself. But it's best if we go early this morning before the town starts stirring. Do you think you should do this, and are you up to it?"

"Yes, I think I am up to it. But I do not know what to say to him." Her face revealed her fear. "Will I be alone with him?"

Caroline sat quietly. She had done her job. The rest was up to Sam.

"I'll be with you, but when we get to the jail, you'll speak with him privately. He's behind bars, so you don't have to be afraid. Caleb and I will be in the office when you want us."

"But what will I say to him? There are no words this time." She picked up her coffee cup, looked deep into it as though some answer would appear in the dark liquid, and set it back down on the table. "Sometimes, if you go to trial, you are found not guilty, yes?"

"Yes, that's true. With a smart lawyer, sometimes criminals get off."

"Oh, but he is not a criminal. Maybe I should ask him to plead not guilty and go to trial." There was pleading in her voice.

"No, Gretchen, Ernesto has committed a felony. That makes him a criminal. He is guilty, and he is getting a plea bargain to reduce his sentence. If this goes to trial, you and maybe even Bella will have to testify. And I can tell you right now, with all this media, there isn't a group of twelve people in this whole county who wouldn't find him guilty before the judge's gavel called the court to order. Pleading guilty is the best thing he can do for himself."

"But what if I do not press charges?"

Sam sat back in his chair. "Not an option. He struck Bella. You might want to know the first thing he told the sheriff when he sobered up was that someone else broke into the house and he was protecting you and Bella."

Caroline could not contain her disgust. "That's what he told Caleb?"

"As sure as old Rover has ticks, that's what was said. That is until Caleb explained to him the crime scene wouldn't support his story and that he had also found drugs in the house."

Caroline cringed. Sam must have forgotten that Ernesto's drug problem would be a surprise to Gretchen. "That's something else we need to tell you. Apparently, Ernesto has been using drugs on a regular basis. I didn't think you would know about that, only the alcohol problem."

"Drugs? Ernesto uses drugs? I did not

know." She lowered her head and closed her eyes. "Why would he use drugs? Why did I not know?"

"Drugs are easy to get on the road, and he hid it from you with his drinking and with his long trips," Sam said. "He won't be in such great shape when you see him. He's been detoxing in a jail cell. The doc had to go by a couple of times the first week, but he's doing better now."

"Ernesto, Ernesto, what is to come of us?"

Neither Caroline nor Sam could answer that question.

An hour later, Sam and Gretchen were parking the car. "The sheriff told me to park in the alley and take the back entrance. No one will see us, and he's leaving the door open for us." Sam escorted Gretchen into the jail. Sam, with his cane, and Gretchen, with her cast, walked cautiously through the windowless hallway. He tapped on the office door with his cane.

Caleb opened it and led them into the office. He spoke calmly and quietly. "Mrs. Silva, I want you to know you are safe. Ernesto cannot touch you. I'll take you back and give you about half an hour. But you can knock on the door any time you're uncomfortable, and I'll come and get you.

Judge Meadows will be sitting right here when you come out. You'll be safe."

She nodded that she understood, and when she was ready, Sheriff Mullins took her arm and led her through the metal door to the area of the jail cells. The harder she tried to keep from trembling, the worse it was. She feared the sheriff must be aware of her shivering.

She had never seen the inside of a jail before. The walls were of gray-painted cinder block, and the floor was concrete. The opened door revealed the first of five jail cells all in a row. Each chamber had a small window with bars and frosted glass. She wondered what kind of vile things had passed through the open drainpipes in the middle of each cell floor. A commode was in the far-left corner, and a cot was in the far-right corner with a lavatory in between. The beds had thin, bare mattresses with stained ticking, and white sheets, a blanket, and a pillow were stacked at the foot of each empty bed. The area was dank and chilled. She caught whiffs of pine-scented cleaner as she walked through.

They walked slowly past four unoccupied cells. Inside the fifth cell, Ernesto lay on his cot. He was unshaven, wearing a clean white T-shirt and orange pants issued to him by the jailer. Gretchen stood in front of his cell, keeping her distance from the bars while Caleb opened a storage room door at the end of the passageway and retrieved a metal chair. He unfolded it, positioned it in front of the door to Ernesto's cell, and offered it to Gretchen.

"Get up, Ernesto, you have a visitor. You've wanted to see your wife. Well, she's here." He patted Gretchen's shoulder. "Mrs. Silva, when you're done, you just walk right back down this corridor in front of these cells and knock on that door. I'll be right there if you need me." He left her and walked back the way they had come.

Gretchen heard the door close. The metal slamming against metal was louder than usual in these hollow rooms. She sat in guarded stillness.

She watched Ernesto. He moved as though his joints were rusty and perched himself on the side of his bed, elbows on his knees and holding his head in his hands. His face, normally ruddy, looked like it had been painted with the same gray as the walls. He did not speak.

She pulled her jacket closer around her neck, trying to hide the cast on her arm. She waited for him to speak before she finally broke the silence. "Ernesto, Mr.

Meadows explained that you wanted to see me, but I do not know what to say."

Still holding his head in his hands, Ernesto turned his face toward her. "Meadows? What's Meadows got to do with any of this?"

She hesitated. "Bella and I are staying in their home until I am well enough to take care of us."

"You look well enough to me. And you didn't answer my question. What's Judge Meadows sticking his nose in this for?" He stood up and moved toward the window, turning his back to Gretchen. "Oh, I get it. It's that piano lady. She's got her nose in this too. I can read, you know, and I saw the Sunday paper."

It had not occurred to Gretchen that Ernesto could have read the *Journal-Constitution* story. "I am sorry that you had to read that story."

"Oh, no, you're not sorry about that. You're just sorry that I found out about your little secret — you and Bella sneaking off to that piano teacher's house when I was out of town on a run." He turned to face her. "How many times did I tell you not to let her out, that it would be nothing but trouble?"

"Is that why you wanted to see me? To

shame me for trying to do something to help our granddaughter?" She lifted her head, looked him in the eye, and waited for his answer.

He stepped closer to the bars separating them. "I'd say it's a little late for that, wouldn't you? So, no. That's not why I wanted to talk to you. I need you to do something. And you'd better not say no." He grabbed the bars with both hands and moved even closer.

"What is it you need me to do, Ernesto?" His nearness frightened her. She instinctively slid her chair backward until it hit the block wall where he could not reach her.

"You know I'll be behind bars for a while. My attorney's advising me to plead guilty so I'll get less time. He says it could turn out worse if we go to trial. Besides, if this goes to trial, the sheriff's going to use some stuff he found at the house against me."

"Do you mean the drugs, Ernesto?" She caught him by surprise.

"Who told you that?" he snapped. "I ain't talking." His knuckles were white as he gripped the cold bars and shook them as though they might open under the pressure.

She looked at his shaking fists and remembered the icy grip he held on her throat. She coughed. "Does it matter who told me?" Her voice cracked as tears seeped from her eyes. "I do not know why I never thought of drugs. Now I understand, it had to be drugs. Without them, you would never have done the things you have done, Ernesto."

"What do you know?" His voice was so cold. "But if you expect to be able to feed yourself and the little wench while I'm in jail, you'd better do what I tell you. You have nothing, so you'd better listen."

She reached into her jacket pocket for a tissue. "I am listening."

"There's money to take care of you. The house and car are paid for. So, you don't owe nothing — just monthly bills. All the stuff you need, the checkbook, the files on the house and insurance papers, are in that locked filing cabinet in my room. The chain I wore around my neck has two keys on it. One of 'em opens that filing cabinet. You don't need to nose around in anything except the top drawer. It's got what you need in it."

"But Ernesto . . ." Her voice was shaky.

"I don't want to hear no buts. Just do as I tell you. Get the checkbook and the savings account book out of that drawer, lock it back, and hide the key. Everything else had better be just like I left it when I get outta jail. Do you understand? If you watch your pennies, you can feed yourselves out of that money for quite a while."

"Thank you, Ernesto." Her relief in knowing that she could survive momentarily overshadowed her anger for what he had done. Even behind steel bars, he still had the upper hand. "But . . ."

"Didn't you hear me? I said no buts." He dropped his hands, put them in his pockets, and stepped back until he was standing over the drainpipe. "I know people who will do what I tell them to do."

For a moment, she wished he would vanish down the pipe like other loathsome matter. "Where is the key?"

His smirk was sinister. "The sheriff has the key in what they call my personal effects, along with my clothes and watch. Now he can keep that locked up until I get out of jail, or I can sign for you to have them."

"What is it that you want me to do?"

He slithered back to the bars and lowered his voice. "There's a toolbox in the back of my pickup. The key is on the extra set of truck keys in the top, right-hand drawer of my bathroom cabinet. Take the key and unlock the toolbox. Just don't let anybody see you do it. Underneath the tools is a small metal box. Don't open it. You just get it and call Belinda at the office. Tell her that you have the box. She'll pick it up. When I know she's got it, then I'll sign the papers for you to get the key to the filing cabinet. You got all that?"

"Yes, I think so." Her heart was pounding so hard she could almost hear it. *He could be asking me to do the wrong thing, but how else will I be able to take care of Bella if I do not do what he says?* "The box in your toolbox. And the extra keys to your truck are in . . ." She hesitated.

He raised his voice. "In the right-hand drawer of the bathroom cabinet. Just get the box to Belinda. When that's done, you'll get your key and your money. And remember, you leave everything else in that metal filing cabinet alone. What's in the top drawer will take care of your needs. Everything else had better be there if I send someone to check on it. Don't forget. I know some guys who enjoy doing bad things to people."

She closed her eyes, trying to erase this image of Ernesto. She clenched her purse tightly, and her voice cracked. "I under-stand, Ernesto. Is that all?"

"Yeah, just do what I told you, and you'll be taken care of." He sauntered back to his cot and lay down, stretched his arms and folded them underneath his head, crossed his legs at the ankles, and closed his eyes.

She stood up and took three steps before stopping. Without turning to look at him, she said, "Ernesto?"

"What?" he growled.

"Ernesto, are you sorry?"

"Did you hear me say I was sorry?" He paused. "But I'm gonna pay for what happened anyway."

No remorse. No apology. Only cold, calculated orders and threats.

She walked the hollow hallway. When she raised her right hand to knock on the door, it was as if some force kept her from knocking. That moment, with her clenched fist in midair, was a decisive one. She had lived through a rape. She had allowed the embarrassment of her pregnancy to separate her from her family nearly thirty years ago. She had allowed Ernesto to drive her only daughter away. She and Bella had suffered humiliation and physical pain at the hands of this person. For years, she carried guilt for it all.

No one was there to influence her decision at this moment, but it was the clearest moment of her life. She, nor Karina, nor Bella, deserved what had been done to them. When she walked through that door, she was leaving her feelings of guilt and her dependence upon Ernesto in a pile at the door of his jail cell. Her determination to take care of Bella and herself would take their place.

CHAPTER SIXTEEN:
DECISIONS

On Monday morning, daybreak dew covered the pathway as if it had broken out in
a sweat. Another few weeks, and mornings
like this would bring a light frost. In near
darkness, Gretchen walked with caution on
the slippery stones along the path to the
studio. Wearing the cast made her feel off
balance, and opening the wooden gate with
one arm presented another challenge.

Gretchen's mind was made up. She had
calculated her next steps just as carefully as
she measured ingredients for her baking and
added them in the right order. She could
only hope her plans would turn out as well
as her pastries. She knocked on Caroline's
back door.

Caroline answered. "Do you want to come
in or are you ready to go?"

"If you are ready, could we just go?
I would really like to get this over with,"
Gretchen whispered as though someone

might hear.

"Let me get my jacket."

Gretchen stood at the door and waited. The porch lamp spotlighted the burnt orange sedum and the mums pregnant with color. The scent of thyme and rosemary revealed their presence even without morning light.

Caroline bounced out the door, keys in hand. "I'm ready." She extended her arm to Gretchen, and they walked to the driveway where Caroline's car was parked.

"It must really be lovely to live in a garden. I have seen these gardens in the spring, and even in the heat of the summer, and now with the fall colors, and the garden just seems to get more beautiful with each season."

"I think I must be the most fortunate girl around. It's rather like living in an eternal bouquet around here. Angel makes certain something is blooming almost year-round." Caroline guided Gretchen in the darkness. "Look across the street. Mrs. Dickens is at her kitchen window looking at us."

"Perhaps she is just looking out for her neighbors?"

"Perhaps, but for certain it means that the other neighbors will know she saw me leave the studio early this morning. Here, let me open that." She opened the car door for Gretchen. "Oops, I almost forgot. I'll run and get your boxes from the shack in the woods. Remember? I told you I packed up everything from there and brought it to the studio. Now would be a good time to take it to your house."

Gretchen waited for Caroline to return. She dreaded this early morning task and hoped it would not be noticed by anyone.

Caroline drove the few blocks and parked in the driveway of the Silva home. They slowly climbed the front porch steps, unlocked the front door, and went in. The yellow tape left by the police had been removed, and Ned and Fred had gotten everything cleaned up and the window replaced. The air was stale and smelled of bleach.

Cautiously, Gretchen moved through the house as though there might be land mines underneath the carpet. Caroline followed, mostly to assist Gretchen if she stumbled. They stopped at the dining table.

"I'm going back to the car for the boxes. Is it okay to turn on a light?"

"I do not want you to hurt yourself, but I would really rather not turn on the lights. Here, take this flashlight." She pulled it from her pocket.

"That's okay, I can manage with the streetlight."

"If you are sure, then I will get the key while you get the boxes." *The right-hand drawer in my bathroom. That's what he said.* Entering the bathroom, she turned on the flashlight, opened the drawer, and found the keys exactly where Ernesto said they would be. Behaving as an obedient school-girl forced to invade someone's privacy, she touched nothing else.

"Gretchen, where are you?" Caroline returned to the dining room with the boxes. She stacked them on the table.

"I'm coming. I have the keys."

"Good. You found them. So now, the metal box. The truck's in the garage, right?"

"Yes. Ernesto said it was in the back corner of the large toolbox." She handed Caroline the keys. "Just be careful. I am so sorry you have to do this, but this just could not wait until I am well enough to do it."

"It's okay, this is an easy job, but is there a light in the garage?"

"Here, take the flashlight." Gretchen handed her the flashlight and followed her through the kitchen. She opened the door to the garage and stood as Caroline climbed into the back of the black pickup.

The toolbox was underneath the rear window of the cab and ran the width of the truck bed. Caroline knelt and took the padlock in one hand and placed the flashlight on top of the toolbox. She whispered, "Gretchen, can you come and hold the light? I can't see."

Gretchen stepped into the garage, took the flashlight, and directed its beam to the lock.

With both hands free, Caroline opened the padlock and lifted the top, straining to raise the lid.

Gretchen watched as she lifted the tools warily, trying not to make noise.

"I need the light again."

Gretchen directed the beam across the width of the toolbox. "There, in the back corner, there is something wrapped in a heavy-looking canvas underneath the tools."

"I see it." Caroline moved the heavy wrenches, hammers, and saws until she could reach the box. She pulled it out, unwrapped it, and handed it to Gretchen. With the tools replaced and the toolbox padlocked again, she climbed down from the truck and followed Gretchen into the kitchen.

Daylight now seeped through the kitchen window. Gretchen held the box securely under her right arm. "Thank you, Caroline. Now we must go."

"You don't want to open it?"

"It is locked, and I do not have a key."

"Here, let me see." The box was large enough to hold a three- or four-inch stack of letters. It was not heavy, and its contents did not rattle. She lifted the box to look at the lock. "Oh, it has a combination lock. Do you know the combination?"

"I do not know it. Could we leave now?" Gretchen walked out of the kitchen.

"Do you want to look around? Or maybe get some more of your things?"

"You are very kind to offer, but I prefer to leave things as they are. Let us go now. I would like to be back before Bella wakes. Sam did not want us to come alone, and he is probably pacing the floor with worry."

Gretchen led the way to the front door. Her steps slowed, but without turning her head to even look in, she passed the door to her bedroom. The memories of what had last happened in that room were still too vivid, though she had no recollection of being carried out and loaded into an ambulance.

Caroline was locking the door when the phone rang. She looked at Gretchen. "Do you want to go back in and answer it?"

"No. There is no one with whom I wish to speak. Please, let us go."

They got into the car, and Caroline backed out of the drive. "I've never done anything so clandestine before. I think that's how an intruder must feel, going into someone's house in the dark and being so quiet, and leaving before daylight."

Gretchen ran her hand along the edge of the metal box. "I feel like a thief also, taking something that does not belong to me. But I do not think either of us is the thief."

Bella had opened the blinds on all the windows and was sitting in bed with her iPod when her mammá returned. Gretchen put the box on the dresser and removed her jacket. "Good morning, my little songbird. How are you this morning?" She worked hard at being cheerful, forgetting that Bella could not hear her.

She went into the bathroom, washed her face, and patted it dry. "Bella, could you help me with my hair?" No answer. She stepped to the door and called again. "Bella, could you help me?" She raised the hairbrush in her hand.

Bella removed her headphones, hopped out of bed, took the hairbrush, and brushed Gretchen's hair, still damp from the early morning humidity.

"Thank you, my sweet. Now would you please go get dressed for breakfast?"

Gretchen draped one of Angel's hand-knitted shawls across her shoulders and sat in the rocking chair across the room while Bella dressed. All day Sunday, except for mealtimes, she had spent in this rocking chair, thinking and devising what she would say to Sam. She rehearsed it one more time.

Seven thirty and time for breakfast. As she and Bella entered the kitchen, there was a knock at the back door. Hattie wiped her hands on her apron. "Good mawnin', good mawnin', my little white-haired angels. They're comin' from both directions. Let me see who in the world is at the back door this time o' mawnin'. I'll bet it's them Pendergrass twins. They got a habit o' showin' up at mealtimes, you know."

"Good morning to you, Hattie. I think it will be Caroline at the door. She promised to come for breakfast." Gretchen directed Bella to sit at the table.

"Oh, that girl. She does like breakfast. I tell her she eats like a bird, a peck at a time, and a good breeze would still blow her to Mill Valley." Hattie opened the door for Caroline.

Sam and Angel entered the kitchen together, got their morning hugs, and sat down at the table. "Good morning, and what a good morning it is," Sam said. "I just must be the luckiest man in this county, Monday morning breakfast with five beautiful girls."

Hattie looked around the room as though counting females. "Why, Mr. Sam, I ain't been called a girl since my grandpaw died, and I can tell you for sure, I ain't ever been called beautiful. But when it comes out of yo' mouth, I do believe it."

"Believe it, Hattie, and don't you doubt it."

Hattie served her scrambled eggs and biscuits and homemade peach preserves.

Angel passed the butter to Gretchen. "I hope you're feeling better today. You were quiet yesterday. Now when Sam gets that quiet and stays in the library, I know he either has fever or something's on his mind. And I just let him stay in his cave until he feels better or figures something out."

"I did not have a fever, but I did have something on my mind, and I would really like to talk with you about it after breakfast."

"Well, we have all day to talk if that's what you want to do. But for now, would you pass me those preserves? I need something to hold these biscuits on my plate. They're so light, they're about to float off," Sam said.

"Oh, Mr. Sam, you know that sweet talking is cheap. I sure hope you ain't plannin' on it taking the place o' my check this week."

Sam winked at Angel. "No, ma'am, Miss Hattie. Not as long as I get biscuits every morning."

After breakfast, Caroline took Bella to the sunroom and pulled a DVD from the shelf. This time, she tried *Oklahoma*. When the movie came on, Bella stood up and said, "No. *Mary Poppins*. I want *Mary Poppins*."

"You want *Mary Poppins* again?"

"Yes, please. *Mary Poppins,* please." Bella twirled around the room with her imaginary umbrella. *I like Mary Poppins. I like Caroline. I like Sam and Angel. No more Mr. Silva. I can sing. I can play the piano. I like it here. The safe place.*

Sam and Angel sat in their leather lounge chairs in the library. Gretchen and Caroline sat across the room at the oak table where the metal box loomed next to the stack of jigsaw puzzles.

Gretchen fingered the tassels at the end of her shawl. She hoped it covered her shivers. "I must first tell you again how grateful I am for your goodness to me and to my Bella. I thank God every day for the three of you. God just extends His arms to me through you."

Angel, also wrapped in a shawl, responded. "You are so welcome, Gretchen. I know you'd do the same for Sam and me. After all, we're neighbors. And when the park is finished, we'll really be neighbors, and we'll have a beautiful walk from our house to yours."

"Oh, I had not thought of such. But it is true. We are neighbors." A faint smile momentarily dispelled the tension in Gretchen's face.

Sam's voice was loud enough to be heard all the way to the kitchen. "Why, you and that little Bella have brought us a whole heap of joy this last week. It can get real quiet in this big, old house. But you just bring in the sunshine. Of course, now I'm counting on those pastries you promised."

"That will be the first thing I do when this cast is removed. But if it pleases you, I will make them in your kitchen. That fulfills my promise not only to you but also to Hattie. She and I have become such friends."

"You're always welcome in our kitchen," Angel said.

"I am grateful for that invitation." Gretchen had never had such a variety of kitchen gadgets, and baking would be a new experience in Angel's kitchen. She continued to twist the fringe on her shawl. "I apologize for my behavior yesterday. I never meant to cause either of you any worry. My brain was very cluttered with thoughts of Ernesto and our future and the surprising things I have learned about my husband. My thoughts are in order now, and I would like to say them to you."

Gretchen took the next few minutes to describe her meeting with Ernesto. She told them what she had learned about their personal finances, about the keys in Ernesto's personal effects, and what he had asked her to do to get the keys — retrieving the box and calling Belinda.

The report of their early morning visit to her house and Caroline's retrieval of the metal box came next. Grateful that no one had interrupted her, Gretchen breathed deeply.

"Now, I must say something that causes me great pain." Sadness dimmed her eyes.

"I no longer believe Ernesto is the man I married and have thought him to be. He has many secrets, and I think his secrets are of things that have robbed us of a good life.

Life with him will no longer be possible for Bella and me. I do not think it best to be under the control of a man who lives in such darkness."

She stood, slid the metal box to the edge of the table where she could pick it up with her one good hand, and walked across the room to Sam's chair. She handed him the box.

"I cannot do what Ernesto asks of me, even though he might have bad people do bad things to me. I have no idea what could be in this box, but I do not believe that it is good. I do not wish to be a part of whatever it is, even if it means not getting the key to the filing cabinet. I will find another way to take care of Bella. You are so wise, I think you must know what to do, Mr. Meadows."

Sam sat up in his chair and studied the box. "Now, Gretchen, you just go back there and sit down and listen to old Sam for a minute."

Gretchen obeyed Sam's request.

Sam rose from his chair, put the metal box in his seat, and stood in front of the fireplace as though he were about to address the jury. "First of all, your brain is not cluttered. It might have been, but it certainly isn't anymore. You're about the straightest

306

thinking woman I know. You have integrity, and your heart is right, but old Sam needs to straighten your head out on one issue."

The flush in Gretchen's face revealed her embarrassment.

"First of all, Ernesto can threaten all he wants, but I'm not about to let anything happen to you or Bella. And you're probably right about this box. I think there's a whole lot of meanness locked up in there, and I'll help you take care of it. But I don't want you thinking you won't get what's yours. Legally, you're entitled to a portion of whatever Ernesto has, whether it's the house, the car, or money in the bank. And furthermore, you don't have to do anything to get it. There's a crowbar in my tool shed that'll take care of this box and the metal filing cabinet, and I'll tell you — I'd like to use it to take care of Ernesto too. He's lost what smarts he had if he thinks he can manipulate you when you're a friend of Sam Meadows."

Whether from having her rehearsed speech over or finding out that Sam was willing to help, relief spread across Gretchen's face. "Oh, thank you, Sam. There is much I do not understand about what is Ernesto's and what is mine. He has worked to make the money, and he would never allow me to have a job."

Angel pointed her finger at Gretchen. "Well, I've been quiet long enough, and I have something to say. The days of Ernesto telling you what you can or cannot do are over. I mean really over. He's in jail where he belongs, and the only power over you he has left is what you give him. And I'm here to tell you, we just won't allow you to give him any more power."

Gretchen looked shocked at Angel's manner. Perhaps she had never heard a woman speak with such strength and authority. "You are right, Angel. I must determine now what happens to Bella and me. I will not allow Ernesto to control us ever again." She looked Caroline in the eye, and then Angel, and then Sam. "And I am so grateful for three friends who will help me to be strong and to do what is right for my Bella. Ernesto has robbed me of my Karina. And seeing how the two of you love and treat each other shows me I have been robbed of love too." Her eyes welled with tears.

Caroline, who had sat silently through this conversation, said, "I find it most interesting that in this final wicked act, Ernesto has imprisoned himself and freed the very ones he locked away for years."

Angel agreed. "Well said, Caroline. Well said."

Sam took the floor. "I'd say that was about the clearest summation I've heard since Bo Carswell spoke to the jury in the Higgins case in 1983. It may not seem like it today, Gretchen, but there are beautiful days ahead for you and Bella."

"Yes, my heart is sad when I think about the price Ernesto will pay for his choices, but my heart is so happy to think that my Bella's spirit is free. There is no one for her to fear, and she no longer must silence her song. She can now share her music with the rest of the world." If Gretchen had fears about the people Ernesto claimed to know, she voiced none of them.

Sam helped Angel from her chair. Angel embraced Gretchen and said, "I'm going to check on that little songbird who now thinks she can fly around with an umbrella." Angel left the room.

The metal box held Gretchen's future, and Sam knew it. He picked it up from the seat of his chair and looked at the combination lock.

"Gretchen, do you have any idea what combination of four numbers Ernesto might have used to lock this box? Like a birthday or anniversary?"

"No, Sam. I do not, but I can give you numbers and dates that have significance for me." She gave him Ernesto's birthday, their anniversary, digits in his Social Security number, phone numbers, every number she could think of. None of them worked their magic to open the metal box.

"That's okay. The box may be destroyed to get it open, but what's in this box could buy your future."

"Buy my future? I do not understand."

"What's in this box could become the leverage you need to get rid of Ernesto for good and to do it peacefully. Ladies, I'm going to excuse myself and take a little trip down to the park with this box. I've already heard Ned and Fred's chain saw humming this morning. They'll have the tools, and they'll help me get this box open. Now, I don't want you to worry about what's in the box or what I'm going to do with it. I won't even let Ned and Fred see what's inside. You stay right here until I get back. Then we'll open it together and decide what to do with it."

Sam excused himself and left Gretchen and Caroline sitting in the morning light in the library. He took his jacket and cane from the rack at the kitchen door and started his walk through the garden to find Ned and Fred. A rescue mission had a way of putting a skip in his step. He'd seen a trainload of meanness in his time, and not all the mean ones were locked up. But for now, Ernesto was out of the way, and Gretchen and Bella had a chance for a new start. He hoped the contents of the metal box would secure that chance without complicating matters.

CHAPTER SEVENTEEN:
A KEY TO THE
PAST AND FUTURE

Sam returned within half an hour. Even with his curiosity at peak levels, he stood by his word and did not open the box. Ned and Fred had taken care not to reveal its contents even when using a claw hammer.

"I'm back." Sam hung up his jacket and headed for the library where Caroline and Gretchen were seated at the table awaiting his return. This time he did not stop at his leather lounger but went straight to the oak table where he placed the box. "Well, it took a bit of elbow grease and a whole lot of prying, but Fred broke the lock."

"What's inside?" Caroline's voice quavered.

"Don't know. Gretchen, this box is under your control now. Would you like to open it?"

"I wish my hands had never touched this box, so I would be pleased if you opened it."

He propped his cane against the brick hearth and stood at the table with Caroline and Gretchen seated on each side of him. "Okay, ladies, let's see why this is so important to Mr. Silva." He opened the lid.

Gretchen and Caroline leaned over the table for a closer look.

Sam pulled out four plastic bags, one holding several ounces of crushed, dried brown weed and three smaller bags containing white powder. Underneath was money, lots of money.

"What is all this?" asked Caroline.

"Well, I'd say this is more jail time. Add on drug possession to aggravated assault. Looks like with this amount of drugs, we're talking another felony." Sam flipped through the stack of bills secured with a rubber band. "Might have been doing some dealing on the side too."

Caroline took the stack of money and started to sort the bills.

The color had drained from Gretchen's face. "Why? Why would Ernesto get involved in this? He is not a teenager experimenting with drugs and alcohol. He is an adult."

Sam tried not to pour fuel on the fire that had just been lit. "Well, this could have started fairly innocently. Maybe he just was taking something to keep him awake while

313

he drove those long runs. Then he needed something to help him sleep, and one thing led to another."

"But where would he get drugs?"

"Not hard at truck stops. Dealers hang around. Maybe another driver. Who knows? But he got them. He's been using them. And I got a feeling he's been selling to support his own habit." Sam imagined other sordid things, but he thought that he had said enough.

Gretchen rose from her seat and looked out the window. "I just do not understand." She looked back at Sam. "What should I do now?"

"Not hard to figure that one out. We only have one option. We must turn this over to the sheriff."

"The sheriff? But Ernesto will know what I did, and then what will he do?"

"More time. That's what he'll do. And besides, we can't keep Ernesto from knowing that you have the box."

Caroline stopped counting the bills. "Sam's right, Gretchen. He will know."

"I do not understand how he will know. He can just think I never found the box."

"You're forgetting something," Caroline said. "Ernesto told you to give the box to Belinda. That means she's expecting it.

Eighteen thousand dollars here, and I'm not finished. I don't think Belinda and Ernesto will just quietly forget about that kind of money."

Sam piped up. "She's right. If she doesn't get the box, somebody will be around looking for it. That's a lot of money, and that's not even counting the street value of these drugs. We're talking big money here, and possibly some kind of organized operation that includes this Belinda."

"But that means more trouble for Ernesto, and it will be my fault."

Caroline stopped counting again. "Gretchen, none of this is your fault. These are the results of Ernesto's choices, not yours. You had no knowledge of any of this two days ago. But now you do, and sometimes your choices are just taken away from you. Like right now — your only choice is to do what's right to protect yourself and Bella, and forget about Ernesto."

"Caroline's right again. You and Bella wouldn't be safe possessing this box. I'll get it to Caleb, explain the situation, and let him handle it. And more than likely, it's going to involve some other folks."

Gretchen sat down. "You are right. There is but one thing to do, and that is to give it to the sheriff. I will go with you. I cannot

315

allow you to do this alone."

Sam shook his head. "You're a courageous woman, Gretchen, but I'll handle this because there's something else you have to do. We have to get into that metal filing cabinet. There's a reason Ernesto didn't want you looking in that filing cabinet. You must find out what's in it."

"But when?"

"No better time than right now. Ernesto's probably been sweating all weekend about this little box. I'll call Caleb to make sure he's in. Then you and Caroline need to go to your house. I'll send Ned and Fred over there with you. Go through that filing cabinet, and let's see if Ernesto has any more secrets." Sam passed by the phone next to his lounger and left the room to make his call.

Gretchen paced in front of the fireplace. Caroline finished counting the money, leaving it in neat stacks of like bills. "Twenty-two thousand four hundred and sixty dollars. That's a lot of money to be hauling around in a toolbox."

In less than five minutes, Sam was back with his jacket in his hand. "Okay, Caleb's in. Caroline, put everything back in the box." He put on his jacket. "How much?"

Caroline told him.

"Here's the plan, ladies. I'm leaving now with the box. We've decided not to drag Ned and Fred into this. I'm sure they'd love to help, but no need in tangling up this web any more than it already is. Caleb's sending over a deputy to meet you. Probably Jess. He'll be there in ten minutes. Now if you get there before he does, then just drive around the block until you see the squad car."

"Why the deputy?" Gretchen asked.

"He's bringing the key to the filing cabinet from Ernesto's personal effects, and he's there to protect you until I get there. We can't take a chance that someone's watching the house. Caleb said that Ernesto had made a couple of phone calls yesterday, and he didn't phone here. I'm guessing Belinda got a call over the weekend, and she's expecting the delivery of a metal box."

Twelve minutes before ten, Caroline pulled into the Silvas' driveway. The squad car was parked out front, and the deputy was coming from the side yard. "Hi, Jess."

"Good morning, Caroline. I was just looking around. Everything here looks clear." Jess was a local high school football hero from the past decade. His time in the military police as a Marine made law enforcement a natural for him when he returned to Moss Point three years ago, plus he had integrity and little fear. He was a mountain of a man with biceps larger than his head, but he was smart and committed to serving the public. His daddy brought him up to respect and protect females, and the Marines taught him how best to do it. He had found a seat next to Caroline a few times at church functions, but she had not encouraged him. He was engaged to a girl from Baxley now.

They climbed the steps to the porch. Gretchen handed him the house key. He opened the door and asked them to step inside and stay at the door until he was certain things were clear.

Caroline could only hear when he opened and closed doors. Even as big as Jess was, no one could have heard him walking through the house. Years of deer hunting had made him light on his feet. "All clear. Come on in. Here are the keys Sheriff Mullins asked me to give you. Would you like me to open the filing cabinet?"

"Yes, please. I would be very grateful."

Caroline's palms were clammy, and she saw the tremor in Gretchen's hands.

Jess moved the keys around the long chain

318

and unlocked the cabinet on the first try. "Here, ladies." He opened the top drawer. "I'll leave the key right here in the lock. I guess these are your husband's dog tags from the service, and I don't know what the other key is for." He stepped aside. "I'm going back to the front, and I'll lock you inside. I'll be standing guard right here on the front porch. I think Judge Meadows will be here within half an hour. But you ladies are not to worry about a thing." He walked away.

Silently, they looked into the top drawer. Large brown envelopes and manila file folders were neatly arranged and labeled. Not what Caroline expected from what she knew of Ernesto. Realizing the cast on Gretchen's arm would make things difficult for her, Caroline suggested, "Would you like to sit at the dining table, and I'll bring the files to you?"

"Yes, thank you." Gretchen left the room.

Caroline pulled things from the file drawer. A checkbook. A savings register. Files with bank statements and deposit slips. Income tax files from the last ten years. A life insurance policy. A file with the papers on the house and property. *Ernesto's a neat, organized scoundrel. Gretchen can be grateful for that.* She took a stack into the dining

319

room and put it on the table.

"I do not know where to start." Gretchen shook her head. "I know nothing of any of this."

Caroline sat down beside her. "Let's see. Let's start with what's most important. You need to know what money is available to you, so why don't you look at the checkbook and savings account book? And while you do that, I'll go look in the other two drawers." She wanted to give Gretchen privacy in her financial matters.

"Oh, but you must not look there. Ernesto said not to . . ."

"It doesn't matter what Ernesto said, remember? He's in jail and he will never control you again."

"Oh, I am sorry. It is just that I went from being a child in my parents' home to being the wife of a very controlling man. Making decisions on my own is new, and it will take some time to change my thinking."

"Of course it will." Caroline was on her way back to Ernesto's bedroom when she heard the key in the lock.

"Caroline, Mrs. Silva, it's Jess. Judge Meadows and I are coming in." Sam walked through the door, and Jess locked it and stepped back outside.

320

"I am in the dining room, Sam."

Sam joined Gretchen. "Where's Caroline?"

"She is in Ernesto's room looking in the filing cabinet. I am trying to understand this checkbook. Would you take a look?"

Sam reached in his pocket for a different pair of glasses. "Let's see. He banks here in town. That's good. Now when was the last entry?" He turned the pages. "October sixteenth, so this is fairly current. Looks like he's got about eleven thousand in this checking account."

"Eleven thousand dollars? But he always told me we were poor and to make every penny count."

"You're not poor, Gretchen." He handed her the checkbook, pointed to the balance, and then picked up the savings account book. "No, and you're not destitute either. Gretchen, there's over three hundred thousand dollars in this savings account."

She gasped. "Three hundred thousand dollars? How could he have so much money?"

Caroline could hear voices. "Sam, is that

you? Can you come here?" The second
drawer held more files. Nothing that looked
incriminating at first glance. But as she
opened them, she realized they were documentation of Ernesto's driving assignments
for the last several years. Other files with
lists of names, addresses, and numbers with
some sort of alphabet code. More files. She
opened the bottom drawer. A neat stack of
porno magazines in the front and another
metal box. She pulled the box from the back
of the cabinet. "Sam, are you coming?"

Sam walked through the door as she put
the box atop the filing cabinet. "I'm here.
So, looks like we have another metal box,
bigger than the other one. Let's see." Sam
picked up the box. "Heavy too." He put it
back down.

Caroline acted on a hunch and pulled the
key from the filing cabinet lock and moved
Ernesto's dog tags around the chain to get
to the other key. It fit the lock. She opened
the box. Another stack of bills and a small
revolver.

"What have we here?" Sam took his pen
from his shirt pocket and slipped it through
the metal ring guarding the trigger and held
the gun up.

"Careful, Sam, what are you doing?" She
backed away. Even growing up around guns

with her father and brothers had never softened her fear of them.

"It's all right. I was just checking, and I really didn't want my fingerprints on this pistol. Caleb will have to run a check to see if Silva has a license for this." He looked at the stack of bills. "Must be at least another fifty thousand there. My guess is that Ernesto's been hauling more than refrigerated food products, and he's getting paid in cash."

"So, what happens to all this money?"

"Well, Caleb has the money we found in the box this morning. Don't know what will happen to this pile. Lots of folks keep cash at home, though not usually this much. But if there's no proof of something illegal here, then it's Gretchen's. But it'll take time to decipher all of this. Meantime, the three hundred thousand dollars in the bank means you can stop worrying about finances. She's going to survive and do well." He looked up at Caroline standing behind him.

"That's good news. But why am I thinking we've opened up more than a metal box?"

"Probably because we have. But the good news is we're done with the boxes. We're turning all this over to Caleb, and he'll take care of it."

When she got back to the studio after lunch, Caroline had a message to call Wyatt Spencer. She dreaded it, but she did have an hour before her first student. Her mom had taught her never to put off bad jobs. Get those over with first, then the dread would be over. This was another thing her mom was right about.

She sat down in front of her computer and called him back. She clicked through emails waiting for him to answer. "Hello, Wyatt, this is Caroline Carlyle."

"Oh, hi, Caroline. Thanks for getting back to me so soon."

"You're welcome. I had a rather busy morning, but I have a few minutes before I start teaching."

"I just wanted to update you. I did some checking, and Dr. Elena Daniels is no longer on my team. It was a wise requirement you made of me to get rid of the leak on the team."

"That's quick progress."

"It was necessary and necessarily quick. We need to get moving on this press conference. I emailed you a detailed memo this morning."

"I'm looking at it now."

"Good. I've met with members of the university's communications department, and they're putting together the press release and the logistics for the event. They want to schedule it for a Thursday, maybe even a week from this Thursday. Seems Thursday's typically a slow news day, and they think the media response will be better then. Reporters looking for stories for weekend editions, I suppose. Do you think Mrs. Silva's up to it?"

"Yes, I think so. I'll read your memo and go over it with Gretchen and Sarah." This event was something else she was dreading, so getting it over so soon was almost as good as finishing a root canal.

"Oh, I've met with Dr. Martin. She's on board to speak to the issue of Bella's musical abilities. She had another rather captivating idea. You can read about it in my memo. My team's putting the finishing touches on our report, and I'll be sending a copy to Dr. McCollum at her request."

"That's good. I know Sarah's very anxious to read it. She has a stockpile of notes herself." She would not play the Sarah trump card until it was necessary, but for now Wyatt was being compliant.

"After you've read the memo, maybe we

can talk again tomorrow and discuss what role you'd like to play. I know you're not so comfortable in this arena, so the communications staff is available to prep you."

"Thanks. Let me think about all this and I'll call you tomorrow. I really need to go now." Knots in her stomach grew tighter as she stood and paced the room. She wanted off the line before the conversation took a personal turn and before her voice betrayed her panic.

"I'll be waiting for your call. Ciao, Caroline."

Next Thursday. That's soon, eleven days. Need to talk to Roderick and Sarah and Gretchen and Dr. Martin. How will Bella react to this? She's changing. More verbal and her musical repertoire is expanding. Cancel lessons for next Thursday. Get this event over. What then?

Karina opened the kitchen drawer and lifted the tray of silverware. Cheryl's note and business card were where she left them. It had been almost a week since she received Cheryl's package. The picture of Bella standing in the hospital hallway haunted her waking thoughts and visited her dreams. Standing at the counter, she turned the card over and over. No more hesitation. She picked up her cell phone and dialed Cheryl's number. *Please be there. Please answer.*

"Good afternoon, this is Cheryl." Her voice was professional and cheerful.

Karina hesitated.

"This is Cheryl," she repeated.

Sheepishly, Karina said, "Hi, Cheryl, it's . . . it's Karina. I got your package."

"Oh, Karina, I was hoping you'd call. It's been a while since I've heard anything from you. Are you doing all right?"

"Yeah, I'm all right, I guess."

"I hope that means yes. I've really been worried about you, and I wasn't even sure you were still at the same place."

"You know I promised to let you know if anything changed."

"I know, but it's just been so long."

Karina picked up the egg timer. "I've been sort of busy working two jobs and keeping up with Skeeter."

"You're still with him? Are you married?"

"Yeah, I mean I'm still with him, but no, we're not married." There had been no mention of marriage in a very long time. She was surprised Skeeter was still coming home.

"Good. Karina, I know we haven't been close in a long time, but I know you. And you can do better than Skeeter." She emphasized his name.

Karina had given up that thought years ago. "You don't even know him, Cheryl. Anyway, I didn't call to talk about that. I read the article, but I haven't been able to find out much of anything else. I did some searches on the internet. Found several stories, but they all say about the same thing. Have you heard anything from Moss Point?" She turned the egg timer over and watched the sand pour through the hourglass.

"I talked to my aunt over the weekend. Your mammá and Bella are back in Moss Point, and your mammá has been on the prayer list at church. The report is that they're both doing better, and they're staying over at Judge Meadows' house."

"Judge Meadows? Is that the old man who owns Twin Oaks?"

"Yes, and you remembered."

"So, he's in jail." She always referred to Ernesto as a nameless third person. "So why didn't Mammá just go home?"

"Maybe she wasn't well enough to go home, and besides, that piano teacher lives in the Meadows' studio apartment. I think she's a good friend to your mammá and Bella."

"The one whose picture was in the paper?"

"Yeah, I think so. I don't know her or anything. I've just heard her play the piano at church when I'm in Moss Point to visit my relatives." She paused. "So, Karina, don't you think it's time you went home? It's been twelve years."

"I am home, Cheryl. This is home." She shook the egg timer, trying to speed up the sand.

"You know what I mean. Home to see your mammá."

"I don't know. Skeeter doesn't know very much about my past or my family, that is until he saw the newspaper article."

"Does he know you have a daughter?"

"I never told him. He has this thing about kids. He hates kids."

"Maybe that's good, and besides none of that has anything to do with your going home. Just pack a bag and tell him you're going to see about your mammá. You say he read the article, so he knows your family has problems."

"Oh, he wouldn't like that."

"So? Nothing in your voice tells me that you really give a rip. Go home, Karina. It's time to go home." Silence. "Will you at least think about it? The part about going home?"

"Yeah, I'll think about it. I'm getting another call. I'll call you again sometime. Bye, Cheryl."

Karina hit the button on her phone. "Hello?"

"Why didn't you answer the phone?" Skeeter barked.

"I did answer the phone. We're talking, or at least that's what I think we're doing." She opened the kitchen drawer and put Cheryl's card back under the silverware tray.

"Late night tonight. Can you bring me some supper?"

"You want me to cook and drive thirty minutes across town to bring your supper? Can't you just order some pizza or something?" She didn't want to go to the garage, and she knew that the next thing he'd say was to bring enough for the rest of the crew. Her money, her time, her cooking, for what?

"If I wanted pizza, I would have ordered it. You're not working tonight, so get your butt over here with something to eat, and bring enough for the rest of the guys."

"I'm tired, Skeeter. I've been up since four this morning."

"You're always tired lately. Just forget it."

She could hear the guys' voices in the background. She didn't want to know what kind of job they were doing tonight. "Wake

330

me up when you get home. I want to talk to you about something."

"You don't want to bring my supper, but you want to talk about something?"

She hated his tone of voice. "No, maybe I don't need to talk to you about it after all." She slammed the kitchen drawer shut. "I've already made up my mind."

CHAPTER EIGHTEEN: THOUGHTS OF THINGS MISSED

Caroline turned on the kettle and went to the china cabinet for two cups and saucers. She and Gretchen would visit over tea. Bella would be drawn to the piano like a moth drawn to a flame, giving them time to talk about the press conference.

The kitchen window provided a frame through which she viewed Gretchen and Bella, walking hand in hand, stopping to pick up a few of the golden sycamore leaves and to look at the mums and sedum. Only two weeks ago, Gretchen was regaining consciousness after surgery, but the last several days had been packed tighter than Aunt Maggie's vacations — unpacking in a different place every day.

Caroline went out to open the gate for them. "Good morning, ladies." Bella, still wearing her straw hat, came into her arms for a hug. Along with increased verbalization, natural hugs were new, and they brought a smile to Caroline. "Let's go make some music."

"Play the piano." Bella clapped her hands and ran in ahead of them.

"Good morning, Gretchen. I hope you slept well last night. I know you had so much on your mind."

Gretchen took Caroline's arm and they went inside. "I must say I have slept better. It seems there is this bottomless bucket of new things I learn every day."

"I can only imagine, and I have something else to put in that bucket this morning." She led Gretchen around to the bistro table in the kitchen. Bella was already playing the piano.

"The kettle's on. Darjeeling?" She reached into the tea box.

"That would be lovely. It seems like a long time since we shared a cup of tea at this table." Gretchen removed her shawl, folded it, and put it on the back of her chair.

"You and I were having the same thoughts this morning. How are you doing with everything?" She put the teacups on the table with the honey.

"It is all so new. My life is changing, and I am not so certain I can keep up, but my heart is hopeful."

"There is great reason to have hope." She

leaned over the counter separating the kitchen from the great room. "Bella, would you like your hot chocolate now or later?"

There was no answer or acknowledgment. After all these months, Caroline knew that look. Bella, like a homing pigeon roosting on the piano bench, had moved into her world, a musical kaleidoscope of sounds and colors, where her head and hands were connected. Caroline imagined that outside this magical, musical place, almost everything else was gray for Bella.

"We'll just let her play. We need to talk about this press conference at the university. I had a call and a memo from Dr. Spencer yesterday." Caroline went to her desk and retrieved the copy of the memo.

Gretchen thumbed through the three pages. "It seems he is serious about moving forward. My mind has been so busy with other thoughts. What do you think about this?" She put the memo on the table and pushed it to one side.

Caroline poured hot water into the teapot and brought it to the table and sat down. "It's like handing over the metal box to the sheriff yesterday. You didn't have a choice. And if you want Bella to be all she can be and you want to share her with others who would appreciate her gifts, then this is where we start. Dr. Spencer was very convincing, but I didn't just take his word for it. I called Sarah and Roderick."

"Tell me, my friend. What are we to do?"

Caroline saw the hope and joy returning to Gretchen's countenance. "Well, we just show up in Athens for Bella's big coming-out party at the university. The press will be our guests, Bella will wow them at the piano, and Dr. Spencer's team will educate the press about savant syndrome and Bella's rare abilities. And guess who else is coming?"

"Maybe someone from Kentucky?" Gretchen smiled.

"So much for guessing. You're right. Roderick will pick up Sarah in Raleigh, and they're flying into Athens just for the day." Caroline checked the tea and filled their teacups. "And I'm hoping Sam and Angel will go with us."

"You do not think that Roderick and Sarah are only coming for the press conference, do you?"

"He has to leave Athens and fly to the West Coast, but I'm trying to get Sarah to come back with us to Moss Point and stay a few days and then head back to Raleigh." Bella was playing Saint-Saëns, and Caroline's fingers played right along with her on the breakfast table.

"It makes me so happy that Bella is loved. Karina never had a chance to love her, and Ernesto did not know how. But you and Roderick and Sarah, and now the Meadows, all of you love her. And perhaps she is not the only one experiencing new love." Gretchen reached across the table to pat Caroline's arm.

"New love, me? Oh, I can't allow myself to think about that." Caroline had thoughts of her future with Roderick, but her fears and insecurities kept her from believing in the possibilities she was beginning to imagine.

"But you would like to?"

"Maybe."

"I remember being young and in love with Peter. It was gradual, but oh so powerful. Falling in love is like baking. One must have proper ingredients, measure them accurately, put them together in the correct order, and bake at the appropriate temperature for the right amount of time. Then you have something wonderful and sweet. I think you and Roderick have the right ingredients, and both of you are putting them together in the right order, and someday soon perhaps something lasting and sweet will come of what you are making now."

"Interesting you should say that. I don't even remember the last time I thought of this, but it's something Angel said to me a few months after David was killed. We were sitting in her sunroom, and she said, 'Caroline, I don't think God set a timer on David's life like I set the timer on my automatic oven, and the time's up when the buzzer goes off.' "

Gretchen laughed. "I am sorry not to be serious about what you just said. I believe Angel to be wise in her thinking, but I look at life differently because of who I am and what I do. I am like Angel. We are cooks and bakers. But you? You and Bella are musicians. You relate life to music and musical terms."

"How did you get to be so wise, my friend?" Caroline sipped her tea.

"Living, I suppose. And one needs no wisdom to see the brightness in your face when you speak of Roderick. I hear how much you are enjoying your conversations with him in the evenings. It is good to close your day together by talking about how you spend your time and getting to know each other's thoughts. That is something Ernesto and I never did."

Caroline watched sadness hover over Gretchen's countenance like a dense, morning fog. "You've been talking about my future this morning — one that is very uncertain and most unlikely. But what about yours? Are you planning to stay married to Ernesto?"

Gretchen looked down and toyed with her teaspoon. "In twenty-nine years of marriage, I never questioned that I would be married to Ernesto until I die. Oh, I often wished things were different, and it made me very heavy of heart sometimes, but I never considered not being married to him, never in all those years." She bit her lip. "But he is a different man than I thought he was, and perhaps we were never truly married in the spiritual sense." She never looked up.

Caroline thought that was the saddest thing she had ever heard. Nearly thirty years of Gretchen's life never to be recaptured. But she didn't want the same to be said of her ten years from now. *"Poor girl, never married, living like a widow all these years." That's what people would say.*

"Have you thought about . . . ?" Caroline hesitated to use the word. "Have you thought about divorce?"

Gretchen looked up. "Sam spoke with me about that last evening, and it shames me to say that I am thinking of divorce. Even though Ernesto will be in prison, I fear he will still have control over my life if I am legally married to him. If I give up my freedom to him, I would be giving up Bella's freedom also. So, I am thinking about it. Sam offered to handle the legal side of things, and he thinks it would take only a few weeks before things were settled."

"Well, that's good news. Then we can daydream and imagine together about the future."

"There is another thing — adopting Bella."

Caroline put down her teacup. "I never thought about that. I guess I assumed you and Ernesto adopted Bella when Karina left."

"No. We did not. This trip to the hospital caused me to think of things differently. I have no legal right to give the doctors permission to help her. I tried many times to speak with Ernesto about adopting her, but he would not hear of it."

"Did you talk to Sam about that too?"

"Yes. He promised to help. Legally, Bella has been abandoned and I am next of kin. Sam thinks that it will be a matter of for . . . forma . . ."

"Formality."

"Yes, that's the word. Formality. I must remember that word. Can you explain what it means?"

"It means that you are just making legal what is already your relationship to Bella. There's something I've never asked you, Gretchen. Does Bella think of you as her mother?"

"I think so. There is no reason for her to think anything else. She was just an infant when Karina ran away, and I could not bear to tell her that her mother was gone. I thought it was unnecessary to tell her, and I do not know if she would understand. If I adopt her, then I am legally her mother, and it's really no difference to her."

When the music from the piano stopped, so did this conversation. Caroline could see Bella from where she was sitting.

Bella removed her straw hat and began to play again. This time it was the new song Caroline had taught her. Then she began to sing. For Caroline, it was like opening a door and being surprised by your unknown identical twin staring you in the face. Bella's voice was pure and bell-like and sounded amazingly like her own.

Gretchen turned around in her chair, never having heard this song before. She stood up, looked at Bella who was quite engaged, and then looked at Caroline. "She sounds just like you, my friend. Did you teach her this new song?"

"Well, yes and no. I mean I played and sang it for her the other night when she stayed with me, but I don't think she has to be taught. She just absorbs the music and it becomes a part of her."

"Christmas. The music of Christmas was always so beautiful when I was growing up. My mother filled the house with smells of cookies and pastries, and Grandmammá filled our rooms with music."

Caroline observed Gretchen drifting back to another place and time. "Then there was the Christmas when Peter could not go to church with me to hear the music. That night changed the lives of so many people I have loved. That was the Christmas that changed Christmas for me."

"I'm so sorry, but surely you've had happy Christmases since then."

"No. Ernesto always took jobs driving during the holidays because the pay was double. So Karina and I had quiet Christmases when she was at home. I baked, and we had a small tree and our handmade gifts. And then when she left, Bella just took her place."

Caroline stood as though making an announcement. "Well then, I have news for you. This is going to be the Christmas to remember. You and Bella and I are spending Christmas in Kentucky."

Gretchen looked up at her. "Christmas in Kentucky? With Roderick?"

She claimed the moment. "Yes, Christmas with Roderick at Rockwater. I had planned to invite you to spend Christmas with my family in Ferngrove, but Roderick has invited me to do a Christmas recital and spend Christmas and New Year's with him and Sarah and George. And . . . he's invited you and Bella. I was going to wait to tell you, but I just couldn't wait any longer. You and I, we need a different kind of Christmas this year. Will you go with me?"

Gretchen stood and walked around the table to Caroline. No hesitation. "Yes, my friend, we will go with you." They hugged. "Christmas in Kentucky."

"Yes, Roderick has promised snow and Christmas trees and eggnog, and I can't wait for you to see Rockwater." She held Gretchen's shoulders and looked into her eyes with a promise. "This, my friend, is going to be a Christmas to remember."

Tom Ellison's office was in the Greystone Tower, a five-story historic building on the square. Even with a stiff knee and a cane, Sam refused to take the elevator. He liked the feel of the solid, smoothly worn banisters against his hand as he climbed the stairs, giving him time to view the historic photos lining the stairway wall and to remember his return to Moss Point with a law degree and a young bride sixty years ago. At the time, cars were scarce and so were lawyers. His steps echoed through the hallways of preserved wood floors and plastered walls.

Tom's name was etched in the glass panel of the door. Sam tapped lightly on the doorframe with his cane and entered. The wooden floor from the hallway carried into the office reception area with coordinated Persian rugs placed appropriately. Brown leather chairs and a plaid sofa provided clients and guests a comfortable place to sit. Prints of ducks and bird dogs lined the teal grass cloth–covered walls, and deep red curtains framed the window overlooking the town square.

Midafternoon sun streamed through the glass panes of the office windows as Sam entered the door. A young woman, who looked maybe sixteen, rose from the large desk that surrounded her. "Good afternoon, Judge Meadows. How nice to see you."

Sam removed his hat. "Well, thank you

343

very much. It's nice to be seen, and when you're as old as I am, you'll know what that means." He approached her desk.

"Yes, sir. I just hope I make it that long." Red crept from her neck to her cheeks. "Ah, what I meant to say was . . ."

Sam realized her embarrassment. "Oh, it's all right, whatever you said or were going to say. I hope you make it this long too. Life's good and you don't want to waste a day of it. Is Tom in?"

"Yes, sir. He's expecting you. In fact, when you phoned he asked me to clear his calendar for the afternoon. He's anxious to spend some time with you. Could I get you a cup of coffee?"

"Is it good coffee? I don't waste my time on second-rate coffee or bourbon these days."

"Yes, sir, it is. I'll make a fresh pot just for you and Mr. Ellison."

"Well then, that'll just be fine. Could you take me in now and worry about the coffee later?"

"Yes, sir." She led him to a door at the end of a short hallway, knocked softly, and peeped in. "Mr. Ellison, Judge Meadows is here to see you."

"Well, you just bring the judge right on in here."

The two men shook hands and moved to a small conference table in the corner next to the windows. Sam looked him over. Tom Ellison was a tall man like him, but thirty years younger. He had a head full of wavy hair the color of ashy embers. When Tom sat down with pad and pencil, there was no hint of bulge in his crisply starched white shirt. The brass buckle of his alligator belt was clearly in sight. The gray, cuffed trousers hid most of his argyle socks. Tom did not practice casual days, and neither did his staff.

Sam put his hat on the table and sat down. "Thank you, Tom, for seeing me this afternoon. You know, these days, I don't plan too far ahead anyway, but this is some business that's come up on short notice, sort of like Henry's sudden announcement he's running for mayor. It needs tending to in short order, and I knew I could count on you."

"Sam, you and I've been through some short notices and short orders before. I've heard the Silva woman is staying with you and Angel, so I'm assuming it's related to her husband's case. Tell me, what do you need?"

"Well, you're right, but it's not his case that's on my mind. I hear he's pleading guilty, and there's good reason for him to plead out, and I'll explain later. But I'm mainly here because we have to protect Mrs. Silva and this child, and I have definite ideas about how to do that."

"Nobody in this town would be surprised to hear that Sam Meadows has definite ideas." Tom wiggled the knot in his tie.

Sam smelled the fresh coffee the young receptionist brought in. "Now you wouldn't think of serving this coffee without real cream and sugar, would you?"

"No, sir. It's right here. Anything else?"

"No, Vicky. And thank you." Tom nodded his head.

"You've heard of child labor laws, haven't you? She's got to be all of fifteen, maybe sixteen."

Tom chuckled. "Sam, we're just getting old. Vicky has three children with one in high school. Here, have some cream and let's get down to business."

Amid sips of coffee, Sam told Tom the story, starting with Bella's birth and how Karina, Bella's mother, had run away out of fear of her father. He described the history of physical and mental abuse, ending with the brutal beating just over two weeks ago. Details of what the sheriff had found at the crime scene, Gretchen's Saturday morning visit with Ernesto, and then the retrieval of the metal boxes on Monday followed in Sam's explanations, along with his suspicions about Ernesto's illegal activities, which were synonymous with leverage in Sam's way of thinking.

"Tom, she's got grounds for divorce, multiple grounds, I'd say. Ernesto's had a good job with honest pay, and there's plenty of money in the bank with the house and car paid for. As best I can tell, there are no debts outside of monthly living expenses. I want her to have the car, the house, and sixty-five percent of the cash. Can we have her divorced from this rascal within four to six weeks?"

Tom was taking notes. "Sounds reasonable."

"Nothing about this is reasonable. If I had my way, she'd get it all because she's earned it, but she won't have it. She says he's worked for the money and half of it is his. I had a job on my hands just to get her to agree to the sixty-five percent for the sake of the child."

"I understand. Anything else?"

"You've been around long enough to know that nothing's usually that simple. A couple more things. There's eleven thousand in the checking account and about three hundred thousand in a savings account. Oh, then there's cash that was found in the metal box at home, about fifty-six thousand dollars. To my way of thinking, legally, there's no way to prove that money was ill-gotten, and there's nobody around this town who's wanting to press it. So, as far as I'm concerned, all that cash should belong to her. We'll just call it the Christmas Club account they kept at home. But it's a potential gnat in the lemonade, and we don't want it popping up later."

"Got it. And I agree with you about the cash, but I'll have to check it out and get that taken care of." He paused. "But I see some problems here, Judge. It's one thing to use the drug charges as leverage to get Silva's cooperation and his guilty plea. But somebody else knows about that money, and maybe that somebody's not going to be so easy to get along with."

"I hear you, Tom. Already thought of that myself, which leads me to the next matter."

Tom sat straighter in his chair. "And what is that?"

"Adoption. Gretchen Silva has raised this child single-handedly with a few dollars tossed her way weekly to buy groceries. The girl's never been to school because Ernesto didn't want her in public, and some first-grade teacher told Gretchen six years ago they couldn't handle Bella. So, with her mother gone and no other living relative that's not in jail, we need to get legal custody of this child for Mrs. Silva."

"I understand all that. But what's that got to do with somebody else being in on the drug deals and knowing about the money?"

Sam noticed the puzzled look on Tom's face. "You don't think Old Sam's losing it, do you, Tom?" He leaned forward, arms propped on his walking cane. "Adoption's got plenty to do with this money thing. People get hurt over a lot less money than we're talking about here, and this woman could be in danger. If Mrs. Silva has legal custody, then she can get passports for herself and the girl and get out of the country for a while. She's wanting to go back to Austria to see if she can find her family."

"Oh, I see. Well, it shouldn't be a problem, that is, unless a parent shows up."

"Well, Karina hasn't shown up in twelve years. What makes you think she'll show up now?"

"Don't know that she will, but she could, and the child does have a father."

Sam tapped his cane on the floor. "You mean an opportunistic sperm donor. He

349

abandoned Karina and his child and has never offered either of them anything but his backside when he walked out the door twelve years ago."

"Now Sam, you've been around the block. You know that money changes things. People read, even those who haven't shown their faces for a while, and the article in the *Journal-Constitution* a couple of weeks ago might not help our case here."

Sam pulled off his glasses and rubbed his eyes. "Yeah, I thought of that, and I didn't like it any better when I thought of it than I did when you just said it. And to top it off, there's going to be a big press conference at the university next week. So, we need to get a move on."

"Now, you know we can't move that fast. We have to follow certain procedures."

"I know. So that's why we get started today. Gretchen is the only relative who has that child's best interest in mind, and she must have legal custody, do you understand?" Sam stood and picked up his hat.

"I got it, Sam. I'll start drawing up the papers. It doesn't sound like Ernesto's in any position to contest any of this. You use your clout with the judge, and we'll get this done as quickly as possible. I'll need to see some documentation of their finances and assets."

"I'll see that you have all that tomorrow. Got to get this done before something or someone else jumps out of the bushes."

"I'll start this evening, and just so you know, I'm getting eighty-five percent of that money for Mrs. Silva. What does he need money for in jail? And besides, she has the responsibility of the child."

"I like it."

Tom walked Sam to the door. Vicky had already gone home and locked up.

Sam strolled the few blocks down to Twin Oaks. The sycamores and the crepe myrtles were so vibrant with color in the late afternoon November light that he felt, like Moses, he was on holy ground. It was good to feel alive and that what he was doing could change somebody's life.

CHAPTER NINETEEN:
ON STAGE

Wondering at how quickly this day had arrived and wishing it were over, Caroline looked at her watch. It was quarter to eleven. Alison, the communications director for the University of Georgia, handed her a folder with the revisions to the press conference agenda. "Take a look at this please, and just be prepared for Plan B as we discussed yesterday." Alison opened the door and peeked through the crack. "Looks like we're having an amazing turnout for a Thursday morning press conference, even reporters from national cable channels. Where's Bella?"

Caroline pointed to where Gretchen and Bella were standing backstage. Alison approached, adjusted Bella's hair, and made certain she was wearing the pale blue dress. Gretchen had wanted white for Bella but conceded because blue was good for television. If any mortal twelve-year-old girl could be mistaken for an angel, it was Bella. Her silky platinum hair fell in relaxed curls inches below her shoulders over the softly draped bodice of her dress. Gretchen stood beside her, their hands clasped.

Caroline thought back to yesterday. They had arrived in Athens on Wednesday afternoon to give Bella an opportunity to play the piano in Ramsey Concert Hall. This hall, seating only three hundred and sixty, would be more intimate than the larger Hodgson Hall. Alison explained that Ramsey Hall would look full with certain invited professors and graduate students and the media in attendance. She explained to Caroline how this would affect the energy in the room.

Caroline listened dutifully, never telling Alison that she had played two recitals in this hall and understood not only the dynamics, but the acoustics of a full auditorium.

Arriving a day early gave the video team time to shoot footage of Bella walking around campus and interacting with Dr. Spencer. Edited overnight, a DVD would be provided to all the television and internet media as B-roll for their broadcasts.

Caroline was antsy herself and trying to keep Bella calm. "Oh, this is going to be

such fun, Bella. You get to play the piano."
The video team had returned to Ramsey
Hall to complete their shot list with scenes
of Bella at the piano. *Bella has no idea this
is her dress rehearsal on a debut that will
change her life forever.*

Caroline escorted her to the piano and
removed her straw hat, and thirty minutes
later, it was the promise of the return of the
straw hat that moved Bella from the piano
bench. Her playing had only been briefly
interrupted at the end of each selection
when she robotically stood up to announce
the name of the next piece and its composer.
Over the last week, Caroline had worked
with her to learn the names of the pieces
and their composers, with no indication that
the words meant anything to her, more like
adding another two measures of music to
the beginning of each piece.

Caroline soaked it in, so proud of Bella.
She performed artfully for the cameras
without even knowing she was the focus of
their attention. She had simply entered her
world where only music existed, where common time indicated by the composer in the
time signature became anything but common for those who experienced her music.

Before they parted Wednesday afternoon,
Alison discussed options for Caroline's

intervention in the press conference if Bella, for some reason, became frightened or refused to play. Caroline assured Alison that this scenario could be moved to the bottom of her list of things to worry about.

Caroline slept very little, like the nights before every recital she ever played. And she was more than anxious about seeing Roderick again. She thought the sun would never rise, but once it did, Thursday morning marched by quickly, the minutes and seconds steadily ticking away like the metronome on her piano. Her adrenaline was pumping. She could hear her own heart beating, and her palms were sweaty, just as they had been before she walked onto this stage for her own recitals. But this was not her day. It was the day that could start a new movement in the lives of Bella and Gretchen, and it was too late to turn back now.

Roderick, Sarah, Hattie, and the Meadows came backstage briefly before Alison asked them to take their reserved seats in the auditorium, but it was long enough for Caroline to learn that Sarah accepted the invitation to return to Moss Point with them. Roderick would pick her up on Sunday. *Another chance to see Roderick.*

"Five minutes, everyone." Alison paced,

putting check marks on her clipboard, lining up the participants, and double-checking to make certain everyone was present. The concert grand was center stage with the press conference podium stage right. "Remember, when the screen comes down and the video starts, take your places on the stage."

Even amid the rumble of conversation of the reporters and guests in the auditorium and the mechanical sound of the screen being lowered, Caroline looked at Bella, smiled at Gretchen, and retreated to her quiet place. She never had imagined that into her humdrum life of near solitude would walk one so exceptional. Over the last several months, Bella had become such a part of her everyday, walking-around life that she had forgotten how truly rare Bella was.

"Let's go, people." The university president followed Alison onto the stage. Dr. Wyatt Spencer led his team and Dr. Annabelle Martin to their seats around the podium.

Roderick removed his reading glasses and put away the press kit. His eyes followed Caroline as she took her seat next to Bella. He watched her eyes search the auditorium until they met his. What he felt was reminiscent of the night Caroline played her summer night's recital at Rockwater.

His spell was broken when Alison stepped to the podium to welcome the press and other invited guests. She explained the contents of their press packets and teased them with the news they would be the first audience to witness the giftedness of a newly discovered musical savant. There was a low rumble of discontent when she explained that neither Bella nor Mrs. Silva would be giving interviews today.

Alison turned and pointed to the giant screen. "Ladies and gentlemen, here's why you are here today." The video opened with shots of Moss Point, of the Silvas' home, of Caroline in Bella's safe place in the woods, and of Caroline's studio. It continued with footage of Bella, Gretchen, Caroline, and Dr. Spencer walking around campus and shots of the department's team working with Bella in an unnamed clinical setting. The video ended with Bella playing the piano on the very stage they were on now. The holy hush that had enshrouded the audience now lifted as people turned to each other, no doubt expressing their amazement at what they had seen.

Roderick observed Bella's growing agitation as she saw herself on the big screen. At times, her enthusiasm erupted into applause. Just four weeks ago, her face was swollen and bruised, with bandages concealing wounds. And here she sat in the middle of a concert stage. As pleased as he was with the video, his face twitched at the thought of Wyatt Spencer taking such pictures of Caroline.

At the end of the video, Alison stepped to the podium again to introduce the president of the university, who gave his own words of welcome before introducing Dr. Wyatt Spencer. Roderick listened closely to Dr. Spencer's layman's-terms explanation of savant syndrome and what was being done in the study of this phenomenon. Not only was he gaining information from Spencer, he was sizing up his opponent. He smiled on the inside at the thought of Sarah's spending the next couple of days in Moss Point and of the surprise offer she would be making on behalf of Duke University.

When Dr. Spencer finished his presentation of the mental and psychological issues related to savant syndrome, he invited Dr. Annabelle Martin to the podium. Dr. Martin described her first encounter with Bella when she was brought to her studio by the talented pianist Caroline Carlyle. She went on to describe Bella's abilities from the musical perspective and how they were still in the process of determining if Bella was a prodigious savant — that is, was she only a human tape recorder or did she have creative abilities of her own?

Alison returned to the podium, acknowledged the remaining members of Dr. Martin's team, and recognized Gretchen and Caroline. She turned to Bella. "And now, ladies and gentlemen, I present to you the remarkable Bella Silva."

Roderick watched Caroline assist Bella to the piano bench and then take her own seat, attempting to hide in the chair on the back side of the piano. Bella froze. She looked at the audience and then at the keyboard. Her hands remained perfectly still in her lap. The air was tense with silence. Roderick leaned again to Sarah. "What if she won't play?"

"Don't worry. She'll play. Her muse is beside her."

He watched Caroline slip to Bella's side and wondered what she whispered in Bella's ear. It was as though Caroline had delicately touched the wires of Bella's brain to the nerves in her fingers, and Bella began to play. Her eyes closed as her nimble fingers danced on the keyboard, playing the notes as her brain had recorded them, caressing those that were to be caressed, giving nuances and decrescendos just as she had memorized them. Applause filled the room as she finished. She stood as Caroline had taught her, oblivious to her listeners' response, and spoke words that no one could hear above the clapping. She sat down and started to play again. This went on for the next half hour with the audience now silent between pieces, eager to hear the voice of the gifted one.

Roderick's eyes were on Bella, but he could only hear Caroline's music. He wondered what the next few months might bring if Gretchen decided to take Sarah's offer. What would it mean for Caroline?

He reached for his glasses in his jacket pocket, put them on, and glanced at the program. This was Bella's last piece. As she struck the final chord, the entire audience rose as if on cue. The room resonated with enthusiastic applause and the crescendo of people expressing their awe and amazement.

Bella stood, unmoved by the attention, and turned to Caroline. Then she sat down again and started to play. The crowd, puzzled, returned to their seats.

Roderick smiled at the familiar melody that would have no meaning to anyone else

in the room except Caroline. Bella was playing Rockwater Suite, the piece Caroline
composed after her visit to Kentucky in the
summer. He had only heard Caroline play
the first movement, a musical painting of
the summer evening's thunderstorm, which
had been the recital's backdrop through the
picture window.

Bella smiled and nodded when Caroline
slipped to the bench beside her and whispered in her ear. *I play the piano. Mammá
likes music.*

Bella began the second movement. *Storm's
over. No more thunder.* Her left hand forced
the current of melody while her right-hand
fingers trickled down the keys like water rip-
pling over rocks. *Music like water in Caroline's garden.* The brooding look on Bella's
face during the first movement dissolved
into a playful smile. *Mammá likes the garden
with Caroline. I play the piano. They talk in
the garden. Hear the water.*

A steady ritard of higher-pitched cascading sounds and a subtle key change brought
rich, lush harmonies and the sound of still,
deep water. Then above the full, dark chords
floated a lyrical melody, appearing like a
budding water lily just breaking the surface.

No longer Caroline's composition but a new melody, Bella's own. *The sea canary likes to sing. I play music for the sea canary.*

Her hands still at the keyboard playing her new melody, Bella turned to Caroline and smiled. *I play for Caroline. She likes song of the sea canary. Pretty song. Sea canary. I sing with the sea canary.*

Bella's voice, as clear as crystal, rose above the sounds of the piano and reverberated through the auditorium. The purest vowel sounds, unintelligible to the human ear. *Sea canary words. Water words. I like water music.*

Roderick observed the darting looks and stares between Wyatt, Alison, and Gretchen. Gretchen slipped from the stage, returning with Bella's straw hat. Alison took it to Caroline. At the end of the second movement, Caroline went back to the piano bench, grasped Bella's shoulder to show her pleasure, whispered something in Bella's ear, and handed her the hat. Bella took it, pulled it low across her brow until it touched her ears, stood up, and took a bow.

The crowd responded by rising to their feet again. Roderick looked around the room and then back to the stage where Caroline stood demurely behind Bella, who remained perfectly still at the piano.

Caroline breathed deeply, relieved that Bella had charmed the audience with her playing and with her surprising creation of the sea canary music. She glanced at Gretchen, standing erect with tears flowing. The lines that oppression etched in her face over time were gone. Not one astute, fact-seeking reporter would have any reason to think Gretchen had suffered such indignities and loss in her life. Instead, her face radiated pride and hope for her Bella.

Caroline's eyes moved to the front row where Roderick stood between Sarah and Angel, all still clapping. And there next to Angel was Sam. Though leaning upon his cane, he did so with an air of confidence. The past couple of weeks had energized him. She knew he was feeling useful again and engaged, knowing that what he was doing was changing the future for this gifted one. And then Hattie, grinning from ear to ear, dabbing at her eyes with a borrowed handkerchief. Would that life came with more moments like these.

Dr. Spencer rose and stepped to the podium. It was only when he spoke that the applause subsided. Caroline took Bella's arm and they returned to their seats behind the podium. Dr. Spencer gave his summation much like an attorney would at the end of a trial and then opened the floor for questions. Even with Dr. Spencer's reminder of the background information in their press packets and his suggestions for their line of inquiries, Caroline still held her breath, hoping the reporters would stick to questions about Bella's gifts and not about her home life.

For the next half hour, Dr. Spencer, Dr. Martin, and a couple of professors from Spencer's team fielded questions. Dr. Spencer recognized a news reporter. "I'd like to know the name of the last selection Bella played for us. It was not in the program, and I don't recall hearing it before."

Wyatt Spencer looked at Caroline. "Perhaps Miss Carlyle could answer that question for you." He motioned for Caroline to approach the microphone. This was a violation of the agreement they had. Caroline had not wanted to speak, but now she had no choice. She released Bella's hand and walked to the podium.

"Sir, the name of the last selection is *Rockwater Suite.*"

She had already taken two steps toward her seat when the same reporter asked,

"And please tell us, who is the composer?"

This was worse than her anticipation of Bella's performance. She played the piano and composed for the love of music, not for applause, and situations like this one made her uncomfortable. Reluctantly, she stepped back to the microphone and gave Wyatt Spencer her raised right eyebrow. "Sir, I am the composer of *Rockwater Suite.* Bella's playing of it this morning was just as much a surprise to me as its unfamiliarity is to you. However, the final portion that she played this morning was music of her own creation, and she sang a song of her own composition. It has been previously determined that Bella is a prodigious musical savant, as you have witnessed for yourselves this morning. So perhaps in the future, we will all hear more music of her own creation." She nodded to Wyatt and moved away from the podium.

Another reporter was recognized. "Since Miss Carlyle discovered Bella, I'd really like to hear more from her."

Her mind buzzed, not about what she should say but more about what she should leave unsaid, knowing that telling the whole story would be embarrassing for Gretchen. She approached the podium once again, took a deep breath, and began. She edited the story discreetly, only telling of Gretchen's request for piano lessons for Bella and her invitation for them to attend her students' spring recital, and how that resulted in Bella's ability to play the entire recital program with only one hearing. She described how Bella's unique gifts were obvious, and that she had asked for Dr. Martin's assistance in evaluating her.

She paused and then finished. "Bella and Gretchen entered my life as strangers, and now they are family. I have been called Bella's teacher, but I must correct that statement. I have become the student, not only to Bella but also to Gretchen. Never have I seen a human being with more devotion and more tenacity than Gretchen Silva. Even when teachers told her that they could not help Bella, even when financial resources limited Bella's opportunities, Gretchen stimulated Bella's creativity and exposed her to good music. She focused not on Bella's limitations, but on her tremendous and rare abilities. I hope you recognize that you are in the presence of greatness today, not just with Bella's amazing gifts but with Gretchen's total devotion and relentless love and patience. Thank you." Caroline left the podium this time with determination to reach her seat.

"And with that, ladies and gentlemen, I think it has all been said. Thank you for coming." Dr. Spencer motioned for his team to stand and leave the stage. Before they could leave through the side door, a flood of reporters rushed the front of the stage, attempting to reach Bella. Cameras flashed and reporters called to Bella and Gretchen and Caroline.

Alison told the reporters she would return momentarily, and then led Caroline, Gretchen, and Bella through the side door and called for her assistant to take them to the designated room. Caroline, previously annoyed with Alison's drill-sergeant attitude, was now grateful for her intervention. It was Alison's job to go back through that door to answer questions and deal with any further requests for personal interviews or invitations.

They moved with haste behind Alison's assistant. Only when they were safely inside the room did Caroline turn to Gretchen and Bella. "Bella, never have you played more beautifully." She removed the hat long enough to give her a hug. Bella, seemingly unbothered by all the attention, reached for her hat again and walked toward her bag, which was in a chair across the room. Caroline knew she was headed for her iPod and that the hat would come off only long enough to put on her earphones and start her music.

"Gretchen, it's only a matter of time now." Caroline beamed.

"Time?"

"Yes, only a matter of time before hundreds of thousands of people will know about Bella and her music. Today was the beginning of realizing your dreams for her."

"I do suppose you are correct, but about one thing, I must correct you. Today is not the beginning as you say."

"Oh?"

"That day began when Bella played for you, the day she sat at your piano and played 'David's Song' and you were so shocked you dropped your favorite teapot."

"How I remember that day! I had the same feeling today when she played *Rockwater Suite.* Just glad I wasn't holding a teapot. I can't even remember playing it for her." She looked across the room at Bella, now sitting happily listening to her iPod. "She truly is amazing, isn't she?"

"Yes, my friend, she is."

"But neither of us could have imagined this November morning on that April afternoon." She looked at the cast on Gretchen's arm. "In an odd sort of way, Ernesto played a part in this."

"Yes. It is amazing about our choices. We have spoken of this before — the choices we make and their outcomes that we never intended."

"Ah, I call it the ripple rule. Just can't control the ripples once you toss the pebble into the pool. Little did Ernesto know that his very efforts to control Bella with a beating would propel her to a concert stage. Life's strange that way."

They turned to see Roderick, Sarah, Hattie, and the Meadows enter the room. Caroline approached Roderick and Sarah. "Sarah, I didn't get to tell you earlier, but we're so glad you're going home with us for the weekend. We promise you'll be glad you did."

"We're already glad, aren't we, little brother?"

"I'd be more glad if I didn't have to leave in fifteen minutes. Acer has the plane ready, and the driver's waiting outside, but I'll see you both in Moss Point early Sunday afternoon. Maybe in time for lunch if Hattie's cooking." Roderick spoke loudly enough to get Hattie's attention.

"I heard that over there, Mr. Adair, and you don't know up from under if you think I'd miss cooking Sunday lunch for you. I'll

369

be in charge of the chicken and dumplin's, but I may get Gretchen to do dessert. She's been teaching me about pastry and cream, and we're thinking we may start a business." Hattie laughed loudly, the kind of laugh that made her middle jiggle.

"Why, that sounds like a fabulous idea. If you need underwriting, you just let me know. With you two ladies, I know my investment would be successful."

"We ain't looking for no partner unless you're wanting to put on an apron."

Caroline took Roderick's arm and looked up at him. "Actually, he makes a fairly decent omelet, and he's not bad with rainbow trout either."

"Why, thank you very much, Miss Carlyle, and I must tell you, you were quite eloquent this morning. And had I closed my eyes, I would have assumed it was you playing the *Rockwater Suite.* Have you finished it yet?" Roderick was curious.

"I recall asking you to trust me. Two movements completed and one to go. I'll finish it in time." Her words were confident for one who had not a clue about the third movement.

"Perhaps in time for your Christmas recital?" He looked at his watch.

"Perhaps, but only perhaps. I hope you

have just a moment to speak with Gretchen and Bella."

"Of course." They walked together across the room.

Roderick hugged Bella and kissed her on the cheek. She smiled and did not resist his hug. "Well, my lady," he said as he held both of Bella's hands. "You were really quite something this morning. I'm so very proud of you. And I can hardly wait for you to come to Rockwater for Christmas."

"I play my Christmas song. My Christmas song." Bella clapped her hands.

"Oh, you know a Christmas song?" His eyes questioned Caroline.

"Yes, she knows a Christmas song, and she'll play it for you."

"Play the piano. Play the Christmas song. Bella plays the piano now." She walked toward the door.

Caroline stopped her. "Not now, Bella. Let's make it a surprise for Roderick and Sarah at Christmas, okay?"

"Okay. A surprise for Roderick and Sarah at Christmas." Bella clapped again.

Roderick was applauding inside. "It's going to be a wonderful Christmas."

"Wonderful Christmas," Bella repeated.

"A truly wonderful Christmas," Caroline echoed. "Best get you in the air before Acer leaves without you. We'll take care of Sarah, and just call us with your schedule."

"I will. Are you leaving Athens this afternoon?"

"Yes, after a quick lunch and a follow-up conversation with Alison."

He said his goodbyes to Sam and Angel and Sarah, and then walked with Caroline to the door. She liked the feel of her hand in his large and muscular hand. They stopped at the door, and he was leaning down to her when Alison barreled through the door, bumping Roderick's shoulder.

"Oh, excuse me, I'm sorry, but Miss Carlyle, I need to speak with you and Mrs. Silva." Her drill-sergeant tone returned.

"All right, just a moment." Caroline turned back to Roderick.

Alison was persistent. "I really need to speak with you now."

Caroline's right eyebrow went up as Roderick squeezed her hand just before releasing it.

"See you Sunday."

"I'll call," he said as he slipped through the door.

Caroline followed Alison across the room to where Gretchen and Sarah were seated.

"I need to tell you this press conference was hugely successful. Bella will make the weekend publications in a very significant way. CNN will be doing a big story on Sunday morning."

"Oh my," Gretchen said in disbelief.

"And there'll be other television coverage as well. But this is only the beginning. We're already receiving inquiries about personal appearances. I think it's time you thought about hiring a publicist or a manager, Mrs. Silva."

"A manager? A publicist?" Gretchen repeated. "I do not know about such things."

Caroline started to explain, and Sarah interrupted. "Thank you for this information. I'm certain Mrs. Silva is thrilled with the success of this event. But she'll need the weekend to process all this, which is very new to her."

"I understand." Alison stood, reached into the pocket of her navy suit, pulled out a card, and wrote something on the back. "Here's my card if you need me over the weekend, and my cell number is on the back." She handed the card to Gretchen.

"Thank you, Alison." Gretchen stood.

"I'm sure you know how to reach Dr. Spencer, and I know he wants to speak with you, but he'll be tied up with the press for another hour. Could you wait?"

Caroline was about to speak when she saw Sarah shake her head discreetly. "You know, Alison, this has been a long morning. We're hungry, and we need to get back to Moss Point."

"You can't wait just another hour?"

"No, we'll be leaving as soon as we gather our things. But thank you for all your help."

"No problem. I'll email you about the television coverage as soon as we know channels, stations, and times." Alison marched off like a woman on a mission.

Sarah took Caroline's arm. "Thanks for reading my mind," she whispered.

"Your mind? Your eyes and that head shake would have been hard to miss."

"I just don't want you or Gretchen to make any commitments until you hear what I have to offer."

"I'll explain later, too, but Bella proved this morning she's more than just a human tape recorder."

They gathered their things and left through the side entrance. "Here, Sarah, take the keys. My car's parked next to Sam's. I need to say goodbye to Dr. Martin." Caroline reentered the building, spoke to Dr. Martin, and was on her way down the hall when she was abruptly approached by Dr. Elena Daniels.

"Congratulations on round one, Miss Carlyle, but the match has just begun. There's more to this story, and I intend to uncover it." She retreated as abruptly as she had charged in.

CHAPTER TWENTY:
CONFIDENTIAL CONVERSATION

"You'd better get in here; the evening news is coming on." Sam plumped down in his leather chair and turned the volume up.

"We're right here, Sam. Alison just called and said to watch the Athens station at six and again at eleven. She'll let us know about CNN, but she's still thinking Sunday on that." Caroline pointed to the seats at the oak table, careful to preserve the other lounge chair for Angel. "Here, Bella, you sit here. You're going to be on television."

"Mary Poppins." Bella inched to the edge of her seat.

Caroline knelt in front of Bella's chair. "No, Bella. Not *Mary Poppins.* You're going to be on TV. You know how you were on the screen at the university this morning?"

Bella clapped her hands. "I play piano."

"Yes, you played the piano. All of North Georgia will see you on the television tonight. You and your mammá can watch

Mary Poppins later. Let's watch Bella right now."

Caroline left Bella rocking on the edge of her seat and joined Gretchen and Sarah.

Sam hit the mute button during the commercial. "Where's Hattie?"

"We helped Hattie clean up the kitchen so she could get home and watch the news with her family." Angel shifted in her chair and rubbed her arms. "Sam, throw me my happy serape, would you?"

"I'll do better than that. I'll bring it to you and stoke the fire to get it going."

"Thank you, my love. You take such good care of me."

He draped the shawl around her shoulders. "Got to take care of you so you'll be around to take care of me."

"See girls, there's always a catch with these menfolk." Angel chuckled and pulled the shawl around her arms. "Everybody got your cup of cider? There's more simmering in the kitchen."

"Yep, there must have been a sale on cinnamon and cloves. Hattie's got the whole house smelling like November." Sam pulled the screen across the fireplace to protect the Persian rug from the fire's sparks. Angel had purchased the rug to cover the scorched planks, which held stories of other winter nights in former generations.

Caroline, contented with friends and a cup of cider, soaked in the scene. It could have been the cover of the *Saturday Evening Post* in a bygone era. A cozy room with an amber warmth, walls lined with books, knitting needles and yarn stuffed in several baskets, a flickering fire, a quite contented elderly couple, an eager adolescent girl, and three other women drinking apple cider and waiting for the news broadcast. A surprising sadness enveloped her — sorrow for the nights like this that Gretchen had missed. Such a tender spirit and a rare faithfulness, and no man could have hoped for a finer wife. But Ernesto had been her husband, and he had robbed her of so much.

And then Sarah, the psychologist and professor's wife, sitting by the window on the periphery of the scene. Caroline had only a brief time in Rockwater with Sarah and George, but long enough to note how they related in affectionate and intimate ways in spite of the formality accompanying wealth, scholarship, and academia. They looked at each other when they talked. They held hands at the table. She curled up next to him on the sofa and played with the thinning, graying curls edging his collar.

Did Sarah learn this tenderness from her

mother? Would Roderick be so familiar? The scene, the cider, or perhaps the flames took her to the library at Rockwater. She was summoned to return when Sam hit the volume button on the remote control. "Here it is ladies, what we've been waiting for. There's our Bella."

The newscaster led with the morning's press conference before picking up on the background story of the beating that had brought Bella to Atlanta, where a team of doctors had been able to study her. Caroline quickly looked at Gretchen and Sarah for answers. Should Bella be taken from the room? There was no indication from either of them. Bella sat mesmerized seeing the video of herself and the still photos of today's events. The segment ended with clips of the standing ovation.

Everyone in the room laughed with the last clip of Bella putting her hat on and walking offstage. Bella rocked and applauded. Sam hit the mute button at the end of the segment when a local exterminator began explaining the dangers of termites and how he could rid your home of the pests.

"Now, *Mary Poppins. Mary Poppins,* please." Bella walked over and tugged at Caroline.

"Can you believe such a selfless ego? What do you make of that, Dr. McCollum?" Caroline succumbed to Bella's pleading and rose from her chair.

"I'd say the world would be a better place if there were more Bellas and fewer people overfed on self-centeredness." Sarah pushed away from the game table and stood. "Could I get anyone else another cup of cider?"

"Not for me. I'll be setting up *Mary Poppins* in the sunroom for the only one in the room who was totally unimpressed by being on television, then I'll be back."

Later that night, Sarah tied the belt to her robe as she entered the great room in Caroline's studio. "That was quite an evening. A bowl of soup the likes I haven't had in a while and enjoyable conversation." She sat down on the sofa and pulled up her socks. "A chilly evening for mid-November."

"Sure is, and the firewood is wet. Here, take this. It's one of Angel's hand-knitted happy serapes."

"Thanks." Sarah wrapped the shawl around her shoulders.

Caroline turned up the thermostat and joined Sarah on the sofa, sitting at the opposite end. She spread a quilt over their legs. "When Sam built this for Angel, he'd come down and start the fire for her. They have very distinct roles in case you didn't notice."

"I did notice. It certainly seems to work for them. Of course, I guess most any assignment of roles will work if you really love someone."

"You're right about that. Look at Gretchen and Ernesto. Defined roles and scripts, and it's been a tragedy from the get-go. Speaking of Gretchen, now that we have time to talk, tell me about this offer from Duke."

"Well, I certainly don't want to burden Gretchen, or you for that matter, by adding to the heap of confusion that's already building, but I did speak with a few decision makers at Duke and told them Bella's story."

"And of the University of Georgia's involvement?"

"Of course, full disclosure, but that was fairly inconsequential to them."

"And they have interest?"

"Yes. They're offering housing and food on campus, an education for Bella, and a piano instructor if she needs one. And Gretchen doesn't need to hire anyone to represent Bella, especially not a publicist. Sam will look out for her legally, and Duke will do the rest. Do you think Gretchen would be interested?"

"If I've learned anything in my life, it's not to guess what someone else thinks. But you do need to know about some of the developments since we returned to Moss Point." Caroline told Sarah about Gretchen's meeting with Ernesto at the jail and about the metal boxes with cash and about the surprising amount of assets that Ernesto had kept secret from Gretchen. "Finding out that Ernesto has money has relieved her of some of her financial pressure, but I don't know what bearing this would have on her decision."

"But she's still interested in what's best for Bella, isn't she?"

"Oh, I don't think that'll ever change, and Sam's helping her get a divorce and legal custody of Bella."

"That's progress and could simplify things. What about her house?"

"Debt free, so Gretchen could have well over three hundred thousand dollars plus the house when all's said and done. That's a fortune for a woman who's only been getting grocery money from her husband for the last thirty years."

"Will the divorce be simple?"

"Sam thinks so. Ernesto's going to prison,

and with this drug thing hanging over him, he's in no position to contest anything. Gretchen only wanted the house and was prepared to get a job, but Sam finally persuaded her to take sixty-five percent of the liquid assets if only to provide for Bella, but the attorney is asking for eighty-five percent."

"That was a good argument, but what about the custody issue? I can foresee a bit more trouble there. I mean, Bella does have birth parents."

"Yeah, but Karina left when Bella was only about three months old and has never returned. And the father left town when he found out Karina was pregnant. So I don't think there's a judge or jury in this part of the country who'd consider giving custody to either of them, even if Gretchen had a terminal illness."

"You're probably right, but it doesn't mean that neither of them would cause trouble."

"I guess we just have to hope for the best. Just for talking purposes, let's assume Gretchen's divorced and has legal custody of Bella. So, given Duke's offer, they'd be moving to Raleigh?"

"Yes, they'd have to move and agree to certain testing and observation of Bella while she is there."

These were completely new thoughts to Caroline. She'd always assumed she'd be the one moving if Dr. Martin's offer for a teaching position still remained at the University of Georgia next fall. It never occurred to her that Bella could be the one moving.

"Wow, I've worried about leaving them here next year if I move to Athens." Caroline twirled the fringed ends of the blanket between her fingers.

"So, do you think you'll make the move?"

"If the offer is still available. I've already told Gretchen and my family. They all agree it's time I make a change in my life. Not much of a future here in Moss Point. I guess it's time to make the plunge if there's an opportunity."

"I agree. I can't see you here a year from now."

"Do you think the University of Georgia would make the same offer to Gretchen, especially if I'm going to be there?"

"They'd be missing a world-class opportunity not to. Either way, seems like Bella will have the chance she deserves whether at Duke or the University of Georgia."

"Let's see. Tomorrow's Friday. Maybe

Sam'll have news from Tom Ellison, the attorney, and we can talk to Gretchen about your offer."

"Sounds good. But if you'd put on the teakettle, then I'd like to talk with you about something else."

Caroline removed the quilt and slipped her feet into her house shoes. "Oh, I'm not short on teapots, teacups, or tea around here. I was eating peanut butter and jelly sandwiches and sipping tea while Grand Ma'am ate her cucumber slices with cream cheese on homemade bread. She taught me the love of tea."

"Your grand ma'am?"

"She was my grandmother, and I was her only granddaughter. What can I say? You want me to make a pot or do you want me to bring the tea chest?"

"I'll join you in the kitchen and see what you have." Sarah followed Caroline around the counter to the kitchen, surveying the layout of the room as she went. "Wow, Sam did a fabulous job in designing this studio. It's almost like loft-living in the city. It's so spacious and functional. And your piano, perfectly framed in that window. Can't wait to see the garden in the daylight."

Caroline opened the tea chest and filled the teakettle. "It won't be easy leaving this place. It's been like this warm cocoon for the last six and a half years. And the acoustics for the piano and the view of the garden while I play. Where will I ever find something so perfect for me?"

"Well, that's what I want to talk to you about." Sarah walked to the built-in china cabinet in the breakfast room. Perfectly displayed teacups and teapots filled the glass shelves.

Caroline, intrigued by the notion of where this conversation might be headed, watched Sarah. "Choose one."

"Choose one? One what?"

"A teacup."

"My choice of any of these?"

"Of course."

Sarah opened the glass door, made her choice, and brought it to the kitchen counter.

"Lovely. That was Grand Ma'am's favorite. I'm glad you chose it."

"My father was a fanatic about tea too. He and Mother shared a cup whenever he was home in the afternoons."

"I remember. Roderick said your mother loved everything French and your father loved everything English." She checked the teakettle.

"That's true. But they both enjoyed English tea and French wines."

Sarah wandered around the great room looking at the photographs, the clock made by Caroline's father, and the accessories that made this room Caroline's. Caroline answered her questions about the clock, the photos, and other objects. "Water's ready, and I don't see a teabag in your cup."

"I didn't hear the teakettle whistle."

"Never. That would mean the water's boiling and the tea's ruined."

"You do know your tea." Sarah thumbed through the tea sachets in the chest and held one up. "This one good?"

"Quite lovely, but not good for sleeping."

"I'll have it anyway."

Caroline surmised their conversation could be a long one. "Guess I'll join you then. Wouldn't want you up talking to yourself for the next few hours." She poured the water into the cups.

Sarah laughed. "Thanks. But I saw chamomile. We can have that later."

Not since Betsy had Caroline been so comfortable with another woman other than her mother or Gretchen or Angel. "Sounds good. Would you like a cookie? I always have homemade cookies for my students, and I confess I never met a cookie I didn't like. The cookie jar's on the counter under the window."

Teacups and cookies in hand, Caroline and Sarah returned to the sofa and wrapped the quilt around their legs like two schoolgirls determined to stay up all night at a sleepover. "So now, what else is this you want to talk to me about?" Caroline took a big bite out of her snickerdoodle.

Sarah claimed this moment to speak honestly with Caroline. "I might as well speak directly. I want to talk with you about my brother."

"Your brother?" Caroline choked on cookie crumbs and took a sip of her tea. "Well, that's an interesting subject."

"That's an understatement. Roderick's smitten with you, you know. And I just want to say I couldn't be happier about anything."

Caroline sat in silence.

Sarah saw the dismay in her face. Ordinarily with a client, she'd wait until there was a response before she spoke again, but Caroline was not a client. "Well, aren't you going to say something?"

"I'm not sure what to say." Caroline held the teacup just under her chin and inhaled the steam.

"Well, you could start with telling me how you feel about him. And I hope you feel the same way, otherwise I'll go to bed very sad this evening."

"Oh my." Caroline paused and took another swallow of her tea. "My thoughts and feelings about your brother are very muddled. I haven't had these kinds of feelings since David, and to be honest, I'm so unsure of myself."

"I know. I know." Rod had told her the story of David's death. "Your understanding of love has been seasoned by your grief. But so has Roderick's. Rod never got over Mother's death, and then that fiasco of an engagement he had, so he just went to work. Adair Enterprises became his passion and has been for the last fifteen years."

"I understand that too. This studio and all my students have been mine. Like I said earlier, this studio has been my cocoon."

But you've already broken the fibers of the cocoon and you're stretching your wings.

"What if I put on my professional hat? That would mean I'm bound by confidentiality." Sarah set her teacup on the coffee table.

"Not even your brother would know?"

"Not even my only brother, whom I adore." She sat back with the intent of analyzing the movement of every facial muscle and every word.

"Well, let's see. It started when I heard his voice. It hooked me in our very first telephone conversation. I suppose that's why I accepted his invitation to do the recital at Rockwater."

This whole thing of their meeting is too mystical to be chance. There has to be a design here. "I think he was hooked when he saw your picture and found out you were a pianist. That's why he invited you. Proof again that men fall in love with what they see, and women fall in love with what they hear."

"Interesting. I can tell you I was so anxious about making the trip. It was quite a bold step for me, but I wasn't disappointed."

Sarah could barely contain her grin. Caroline hadn't resisted the "falling in love" phrase. "I can only imagine. Leaving the safety of your studio and Moss Point . . . but it was time."

"I think I knew that. But when I met Roderick, I was like the dancer on top of the pink satin jewelry box Grand Ma'am gave me when I turned seven. I turned the key and the ballerina twirled round and round en pointe to a Chopin waltz." Caroline paused. "But sometimes in my dreams, the dancer would leap off the chest and dance around my room, with movements like a fairy, so glad to be free of the fixed position atop the jewelry box." She suspended her words like the dancer atop the chest.

Sarah noted the pensive look in her eyes. "So, you leapt from atop the box and went to Kentucky?"

"That's not what I meant. I meant, when I got there, and I was so comfortable with Roderick, and we talked and walked and fished and laughed — that's when I came off pointe and moved my own arms and legs again. I was doing more than going through the motions."

"So that was there, but what about when you returned home? Did your feelings change?"

"I'm not sure. I don't think my feelings changed, but I did get my head back on straight. The trip was like the dancer in my dream. But when the dream is over and the sun comes up, she climbs back on the chest and stays."

"And why is that?"

"Because she knows it's only a dream. How can a man like Roderick, a brilliant businessman, sophisticated and wise to the world, ever be interested in me?" Caroline finally looked straight into Sarah's face. "Our lives and our experiences are so different. And I'm most certain he could have his pick of beautiful women who come from his world."

"True, and there have been many who would have done anything to be his choice, but Caroline, you underestimate yourself. You're real. You're beautiful, educated, and extremely talented, and you have the kindest heart."

Caroline's chin dropped.

"I thought we were talking about Roderick." She set her cup on the table beside Sarah's.

"I am. I'm talking about the qualities you have that would be attractive to my brother. Rod told me about meeting your family when you flew home for the birth of your godchild. Because you grew up the way you did, you're grounded. You have faith and humility. You know who you are, and you don't parade yourself as anyone else. You're so real. Why do you find it difficult to believe that Rod would find those qualities appealing? He's not some spoiled rich guy who never grew up. He's real, too, and he's committed to those he loves."

"Oh, Sarah, I've never thought he was spoiled or shallow. I'm just afraid, afraid to let go."

"Let go of what?" Sarah pressed. "I think

you're afraid of letting go of your grief. You're used to it, and you've decided it suits you."

Caroline looked up. "Maybe I have. But Sarah, I don't want it to suit me anymore. Betsy told me that I must imagine what my future could be like, to imagine my life as I would like it."

Sarah smiled. "I think I like your friend Betsy even though I've never met her. You should really listen to her."

"I did."

"And?" She waited. "And what do you imagine?"

Caroline removed the quilt, stood up, and walked to the picture window. "I dare not imagine anything yet. But I can tell you this. I wake up and I wonder where Roderick is and what he's doing. The phone rings and my palms get sweaty, and I hope it's his voice. I play the piano, and I dream of sitting in front of the picture window at Rockwater. I look out at my garden, and I think of your mother's daylilies. I feed my goldfish, and I think of sitting beside Roderick on the big rock at Blue Hole."

Ah, the dancer is off pointe and doing pirouettes around the room. Sarah moved slowly to the edge of the sofa, careful not to break Caroline's soliloquy.

"I see something beautiful or wondrous and I want him to see it too. I hear music that stirs my soul, and I want to squeeze his hand. And late at night, when it's quiet and aloneness is my companion, I want to hear his voice. And . . ." Caroline started to cry. "And . . ."

Sarah joined her at the window and hugged her. "You don't need to say anymore. Your secrets are safe with me, and I'm going to bed happy, very happy." *And you're going to make my little brother very happy too, Caroline.*

CHAPTER TWENTY-ONE: PHONE CALLS

Dr. Elena Daniels shuffled through the notes on her desk until she found the picture. A week ago, she simply typed "Karina Silva" into her search engine, and this photo of a spiky-haired brunette with a rock band appeared after just a few clicks. Her hair might have been different, but the eyes, the delicate features, and the bone structure were the same. One call, a two-thousand-dollar retainer, a private investigator, and her plan had been set in motion. Now a week later, she had an address and a phone number, and she had no doubts Karina was Bella's mother. The retainer and expenses were an investment in what could be a lucrative career.

She picked up the phone and dialed the number and waited. Her part of the conversation had already been well rehearsed.

"Hello."

"Hello. This is Dr. Elena Daniels. Is this

Karina Silva?"

"Yes, but how did you . . ."

"I know. You don't know me, and you must be wondering why I'm calling, but please don't hang up. I have information that you will find extremely interesting." She waited and there was no response. "Karina, I am a professor at the University of Georgia, and I have been working with your daughter, Bella."

"You must be mistaken. I don't have a daughter."

"Wait. Please wait, Karina. I know that Bella is your daughter, and it wasn't difficult at all to find you. I'm just glad I got to you before anyone else did."

"What is it you want?"

"I just want to help you and your daughter. There are some very unsavory folks who intend to exploit your mother and your daughter, and thus rob you of what is rightfully yours." Elena sneered, just imagining what Karina was thinking right now. "Your daughter is a very rare and gifted person. Are you aware of that?"

There was hesitation on the other side of the line. "Yeah, I know something about that."

"Well, there are some people here in Athens and in Moss Point who stand to make a lot of money using Bella's gifts, and they may not have her best interests at heart. And I was just thinking that if the two of us work together, then you would be able to control what happens to Bella and who has access to her."

"Yeah? You and me?"

From what she knew about Karina, Elena imagined she was adding this up quickly. "Can we talk about that and what it would mean?"

"Maybe, but I have to get to work right now, and I need time to think about this."

Trying to exercise patience and build rapport, Elena agreed. "Of course, you need time to think about this. Here's my number. Will you take it down?"

"Sure. What is it, and what did you say your name was?"

"My name is Dr. Elena Daniels, and the number I'm giving you is my private cell number." She called out the numbers very distinctly. "And Karina, I don't want to press you, but time is really important here with Bella. If you and I cooperate, you'll likely not have to go to work ever again. Do you understand?"

"Yeah. I got it. Now I have to go."

Elena heard the click of Karina's receiver. She'd give her the weekend, and she'd call again on Monday.

Caroline said goodbye to Jay, her last student for the week. The phone rang as she locked the door. She figured it was Sam. It was Friday, the day for ordering hamburgers and onion rings, and he always called about this time. She answered the phone. "Okay, Sam, let me guess, the burgers and onion rings will be coming out of their brown bags by the time I can get there."

"I beg your pardon?" A familiar, unfriendly female voice asked, "Is this the home of Caroline Carlyle?"

"Yes, I'm so sorry. I was expecting another caller. This is Caroline."

"Hello, Miss Carlyle, this is Liz, Roderick Adair's executive assistant."

Caroline noticed she had given herself a new title. "Oh, hello, Liz. How are you?"

"I'm quite fine. I'm calling with a message from Roderick. He is in flight to Hong Kong as we speak, an emergency business trip, and wanted me to let Sarah know that he'll not be coming to Moss Point as planned. However, Acer will still pick her up Sunday afternoon and get her back to North Carolina."

"I see. Is he all right?"

"Can you please see that Sarah gets the

message?"

"Yes, of course. I'll tell her right away." She tried to hide her disappointment.

"Good evening, Miss Carlyle."

The abrupt sound as Liz slammed her phone to its cradle startled Caroline. Liz was territorial when it came to Roderick, and Caroline had invaded her turf when she visited Rockwater. She still remembered Liz's red dress, the gold jewelry, and her crimson claws on the night of the recital. She had to wonder if that was the only message Roderick had instructed Liz to give, but one thing was for sure; it was the only one she was getting.

She dialed the Meadows' number while the phone was still in her hand. She knew Sam would answer. "Are we still on for cheeseburgers and onion rings tonight?"

"Is it Friday?" Sam retorted.

"Only judges get by with answering a question with another question, but it was the answer I was hoping for. Do I need to pick them up?"

"No, Mabel's sending her nephew as usual. Just come on up. He should be here any minute. Angel and Bella are in the kitchen making root beer floats."

"I can hear a commotion in the background. Everything okay?"

"Yeah, Gretchen and Sarah just joined them for the fun."

"Sam, while it's just us, did you speak with Tom Ellison today? Any report?" Caroline was concerned about the legal custody and adoption issues after what Sarah said last night.

"Yeah, the old boy's making progress. I figured it was best if I waited until you were here to give the report. I don't suppose Gretchen would mind if Sarah hears too."

"No, I'm sure that'll be fine. In fact, she has some things she wants to speak with Gretchen about. An offer for them to move to Raleigh and live on the Duke campus. Now that's a twist."

"Yep. This saga has more twists and turns than Abner's Creek. Just get yourself on up here."

Sam hung up the phone. No goodbye. Just click. Caroline turned on the lamp on the counter, grabbed her keys, and headed up to the main house.

Friday night dinner with friends. Cheeseburgers that caused sleeves to be rolled up. Crispy fried onion rings out of a brown bag, root beer floats, and more ice cream for dessert. Enjoyable small talk at the table.

Caroline scraped the bottom of her mug for the last bite of ice cream and elbowed

Bella. "I don't know who likes the floats best, you or Sam."

Bella looked at Sam and back at Caroline, a big ice cream mustache covering her top lip. Her smile said it all.

"Tell me, Bella, what are you watching tonight? Is it *Mary Poppins* again?"

Bella put her mug on the table. "No *Mary Poppins. August Rush. August Rush.*"

She stood and took Caroline's hand, pulling her to a standing position.

"Is that the one about the musical prodigy?" Caroline looked around the table.

Sarah responded, "Yes. We all took a ride with Sam this afternoon. He was showing me around town, and we stopped at the movie rental place. I thought Bella might enjoy the movie."

"I take it she has already seen it."

Gretchen blotted her lips with her napkin. "Once, and then we had to stop it halfway through the second time when the hamburgers arrived."

Bella tugged at Sarah. "Okay, okay, Miss Bella Rush. I'll go turn it on for you. But you know what? I think I need to teach you to run the DVD player." Sarah followed Bella into the sunroom, started the movie, and hurried back to the kitchen.

Sam said, "Gretchen, I have news from

401

Tom Ellison. Would you like to hear this privately, or do you mind if Caroline and Sarah are present?"

"Oh, so soon? That is good, I suppose. And I would like it if we all heard it together. You wonderful people are like my family now."

"And you to us. Well then, ladies, do you mind if we just sit right here around the table? And I'll tell you what I know from Tom." He turned to Sarah. "Tom's a friend and local attorney. He's handling Gretchen's affairs for her."

"There is no finer place to sit in all of Moss Point than here around your family table. But I'll clear the food away." Sarah rose and began gathering the paper bags they had used as plates.

Gretchen reached for the mugs. "Here, let me help you. One more arm will make things go quicker."

"Forgive me for not helping, ladies, but Mabel's cheeseburger and the ice cream have anchored me to this chair." Angel giggled. "Sam, we could get real used to having these young folks around here. But we'd be so spoiled."

"Okay, ladies, while Bella's entertained, I want to tell you what Tom said." Sam began his report. Tom had already filed the divorce papers and had paid Ernesto a visit. No contest. Ernesto agreed to everything, the division of the assets and the fast track for the divorce. Ernesto's sentencing and the final divorce decree would probably be pronounced around the tenth of December. All that was necessary was Gretchen's five-minute appearance before the judge, and she would be divorced. Tom was handling the changing of the titles on the house and car and the bank accounts.

Gretchen said, "That is so much for him to do. It is all happening so fast."

"In this case, fast is good, Gretchen." Caroline got up to pour the coffee. "What about the adoption proceedings?"

"He's started those too. They're not quite as simple, but Ernesto has nothing to do with the process since he has no legal ties to Bella. Basically, the court would consider that Bella had been abandoned and that you're the nearest of kin, Gretchen."

"So, there are no hitches?" Caroline served the coffee and put the cream and sugar on the table.

"Don't think so, but a legal ad announcing Gretchen's intentions will have to run in the paper for a few weeks, and if no one comes forward to contest it, Tom will file the final papers, and the adoption is done too." Sam used his courtroom voice as though he were rendering an opinion.

"And who might contest this?" Angel asked.

"Probably no one, but the only ones who would matter would be blood relatives. Bella's birth parents or the other set of grandparents."

The worry lines reappeared on Gretchen's face. Caroline jumped in for another rescue. "But that's not likely, right? I mean, Gretchen has raised Bella."

"Now ladies, I have to tell the truth here. If this had happened six months ago, I'd be sleeping like a baby tonight without a thought of anyone contesting this adoption. But Bella's picture was in every paper in Georgia today, and she'll be on national television Sunday morning. Now that kind of attention causes certain folks to come out of the woodpile."

Sarah sat quietly observing. Angel sipped her coffee, but Caroline could not let this go. "Gretchen, what about Karina? Isn't she the only one who could contest this?"

"Karina left when Bella was only three months old, and I have heard nothing from Karina for over three years. For the first few years, a friend of hers delivered letters to me. But now, I do not know if she is even alive, and if she is, I have no knowledge of where she is. And the young man who fathered Bella left town the day after Karina told him she was pregnant."

"Do the other grandparents live in Moss Point?" Sarah pursued.

"The young man was older than Karina and did not go to school. I know very little of him and nothing of his parents. I only know he became very afraid of Ernesto, and he ran."

"Do you think Karina ran away to join him?" Sam joined Sarah's inquisition.

"Oh, I do not think so, but I cannot be certain. He broke my Karina's heart and spirit, and for months, she said over and over how much she hated him." Gretchen's voice quivered. "But I know only too well that frightened, desperate young girls often make choices that a wiser person would not make."

"That's the story of the ages. So now we wait and hope," Sam summed it up. "Gretchen, I think you're in good shape. The legal matters will be over within about forty-five days, and your finances are in great shape. I have a friend who is a financial planner, and he'd be a good choice to help you invest your money."

"Thank you, Sam. For years I prayed, and

I wondered if God was listening. He was, and you are part of the answer to my prayers. God brought Caroline and Sarah to help with Bella, and He brought you and Angel to rescue us and give us a safe place for a time. I thank God every night for you." Gretchen wiped a tear from her cheek, and so did Angel.

Caroline smiled, thinking of how Sam had stepped up to help. And then how Sarah and Roderick appeared at just the right time. She was beginning to sense God's hand in weaving together the frayed threads of so many lives. Peace, if only for a few moments, settled around her.

"And He brought you and Bella to us too. You wouldn't want to know how we spent our Friday nights before now." Caroline chuckled to lighten the moment. "Anybody want a warm-up for your coffee?" They shook their heads. She knew Sarah was biding her time for the right moment to mention Duke's offer.

Sarah cleared her throat. "I suppose now is as good a time as any to bring up another serious subject." She looked at Caroline. "I explained this to Caroline last night, and I'll just keep it as simple as I can, and you must realize that details will be worked out later if you are interested."

The room was so quiet that the movie's soundtrack could be heard playing from the sunroom. She turned to Gretchen and began. "Duke University is inviting you and Bella to come to the school. They are prepared to provide your housing and food, education, and music study for Bella."

Caroline watched Gretchen's face again for her response. What she read was surprise.

"An education and musical training for Bella?" Gretchen said. "They would give her that?"

Sarah responded, "Yes, they'll provide the best they have to offer for Bella. But they are requiring some commitment on your part. They are requiring periodic testing of Bella and some public appearances. But those details are yet to be spelled out, and please know that I will help design that in Bella's best interest."

"Oh my, it seems that every day, my life with Bella changes. For so many years, my days marched forward like a parade of identical wooden soldiers. The last month it has been a hospital, a jail, Twin Oaks, a press conference, and now a university. No more wooden soldiers."

Caroline said, "You're right, Gretchen, the wooden soldiers are all in a pile, but you have the complete freedom to make your own choices, and the really good news is you don't have to make them tonight. Sarah and Sam and I will be there to help prop the wooden soldiers back up if that's what you want."

Gretchen stood. "Now I must say something. I have not English words or any other words to say my gratitude to you, but I think it is time Bella and I go home to our house. You have cared for both of us when I could not even care for myself. I must not impose upon you any longer. So, tomorrow, if I could ask one more thing of you, Caroline, I would be grateful if you would help us to get settled back in our home."

Angel jumped in before anyone else could respond. "Oh Gretchen, do you have to go? Hattie and I won't know what to do around here without you."

"Oh, then I will come every day for a visit. But I must not be a bother any longer."

Caroline understood Gretchen's need to be at home, in familiar surroundings to think and make decisions and to get accustomed to the changes in her life. "I'll be happy to help you. But might I suggest that tomorrow we go over and get things ready, and then make the move on Monday? That way you won't miss any time with Sarah while she's here."

"Oh, I am so sorry, Sarah. That is a fine idea, Caroline. And I know Bella will be happy to spend time with Sarah also."

A storm blew through late Friday night and took the last leaves off the trees, leaving an early morning fog that hovered until nearly midday and smothered the naked limbs. Roderick's call from Hong Kong had awakened Caroline at seven thirty. The white painted pine floor was cold to her bare feet as she crossed the great room to get the phone. Hoping she caught the call before it woke Sarah back in the bedroom, she tiptoed quickly back to the sofa and pulled the quilt and blanket around her for her chat with Roderick. She blurted out the latest news, basically the report Sam had given about Tom's work, seeing Bella on the news, and the fun she was having with Sarah around. Her last night's conversation with Sarah about Roderick was skillfully edited out of the report.

Sarah sauntered into the room. Caroline sat up at the end of the sofa, pointed to the phone, and whispered without halting the conversation, "It's Roderick in Hong Kong."

"Lovely. Thank him for the wake-up call.

I'm headed to the kitchen to make the coffee."

"That was Sarah. She's up and in the kitchen making coffee." Banging doors echoed around the room. "At least she's moving around in there looking for coffee. Maybe I should go and help her." She looked over the counter to see that Sarah had found the mugs. "Come here, Sarah. Talk to your brother. I'll make the coffee."

"That's okay. I found everything. I'll come join you till it brews." Sarah took the other end of the sofa and pulled the covers around her.

Caroline handed her the phone. "Here, he wants to say good morning."

"Good morning, Rod. How's Hong Kong?"

While Roderick and Sarah talked, Caroline replayed her own chat and realized it had been quite one-sided. She'd not asked one question of him, and she wanted to know everything.

Sarah continued, "Yes, I've really enjoyed myself, and I wish you were joining us tomorrow." Pause. "I know. Business. We understand." Another pause. "I think we'll be in for the morning, trying to stay warm. Storm blew in last night and left us the shivers." Pause. "Yes. And then I think we're going over to Gretchen's house. She and Bella will be going home on Monday, and we'll be getting things ready." Pause. "Here she is." Sarah handed Caroline the phone and headed for the kitchen.

"Okay. We're glad you called." She couldn't help herself, even at the risk of tattling on Liz. "After Liz called with the message for Sarah, I wasn't sure I'd hear from you. But I'm really glad to hear your voice."

"Yes, I'm afraid Liz isn't fond of you, and I'm sorry about that. I'll be back in the States on Wednesday, I think."

"That much business?"

"Not quite, but I do have a secret assignment that I must complete before I leave."

"Nothing to do with the FBI or the CIA or any of those agencies that are only known by acronyms, I hope."

"Oh, no. Nothing like that. It's personal."

Her curiosity was rising like the steam on the cup of coffee Sarah handed her. "Then I suppose I shouldn't ask."

"And I suppose you'd be correct about that. You girls enjoy yourselves today. Take care of my sis. She's the only sister I have."

"Will do."

"Good night, Caroline."

"Good morning, Roderick."

Still in their nightclothes and on the sofa,

they passed the morning with more conversation — what-ifs for Gretchen's plans, realistic hopes for Bella, and the potential fallout from the media attention. When she listened to Sarah, she realized Sarah's investment in Bella and Gretchen was a sincere interest and a commitment to help.

Caroline fidgeted. "Gretchen asked me to tell you something that would help you understand. She knows you're investing yourself into this situation, and she doesn't want you to be surprised. And I think now is a good time to tell you."

Sarah sat quietly without interrupting Caroline's recounting of Gretchen's story about her life in Austria, her engagement, and the rape that forced her to leave her home and family. "Nicolai raped her after a Christmas service at her church, so I can imagine Christmas is not necessarily a time of peace and joy for her with those memories and then living with Ernesto for the last thirty years."

"Well, let's see what we can do to change that." They batted around ideas for the recital, for Christmas, and for a New Year's celebration like sorority sisters planning a gala.

The clock her dad made struck eleven. "Can you believe it's eleven o'clock and we haven't dressed or had breakfast?"

"Yes, but we've solved several problems, and had a pot of coffee and at least a pound of your snickerdoodles. We'll call them breakfast."

"What do you say we get dressed and I'll call Angel and tell her I'm taking you to Mill Valley for lunch? There's a lovely tearoom there I think you'd like. And we'll be back to pick up Gretchen around two thirty."

"Sounds fine." She looked out the picture window. "Fog's lifting, but it's still kind of icky out there. We'd better get a move on."

Gretchen woke from her after-lunch nap and looked at the bedside clock. Ten until two. Caroline would be by to get her shortly.

Sam was still snoozing by the fire in the library. A movie was playing in the sunroom with Bella sitting cross-legged on the floor only a few feet from the television screen. From her sewing cabinet Angel had pulled a skein of the finest mohair yarn, one she'd been saving for a special project, and she sat in the sunroom, knitting and purling through rows of a happy serape for Bella.

Gretchen entered the room and sat in the wicker rocker next to Angel. "I see Bella is watching the movie again."

"I'm enjoying it myself, and her enjoyment of it doubles mine. How was your rest?"

"Rest is always sweet in your home, Angel." She rocked gently, the rocker creaking across the wooden floor.

"Well, if it's so sweet, I can't figure why you want to leave so soon. Sam and I kind of like it with you and Bella around here."

"Oh, not so much as we like it here, but it is time we get on with our lives and you and Sam can get back to yours."

Angel's bamboo knitting needles never faltered or slowed. "Why don't you leave Bella here this afternoon? She'll be just fine."

Thoughts of Bella's reaction to going home and Ernesto's obvious disappearance had troubled Gretchen. "Do you think it unwise to take her back home today?" She talked as if Bella were not in the room, because she wasn't. Bella was lost in the music and in the story of a young musical prodigy.

"Oh no. I just like having her around. But now that I think of it, maybe it'd be better if she didn't go. You can get things ready, and then she can go on Monday; that is, if we can't change your mind."

Gretchen whispered, "Angel, she has

never asked about Ernesto. She only says sometimes, 'No more Mr. Silva, no more Mr. Silva.' "

"Then she understands all she needs to understand right now. You just don't worry about it and let things happen naturally."

Caroline and Sarah entered unexpectedly. "Sorry if we startled you. We knocked on the back door, and no one answered. And what's this that's going to happen naturally?"

"Whatever is supposed to. That's what." Angel chuckled and pointed her knitting needles at Bella.

Sarah laughed. "Well, that's a relief."

"Bella's staying here with me while you all take your little trip down the street. We'll be right here when you get back." Angel pulled a long stretch of yarn from the skein.

"I'll have my cell phone in case you need us. I don't think we'll be long." Caroline led the way down the hall and through the kitchen.

Sunshine would have allowed them a stroll through the soon-to-be park now that Gretchen was better, but the cold drizzle forced them to take the car the few blocks to the Silvas' house. Caroline parked as close as possible to the front door.

Gretchen, one arm still in a cast, pulled

the key from her sweater pocket and unlocked the deadbolt. She opened the door,
stepped in slowly, almost reluctantly, and
found the light switch. "Come in, please."
They stepped through the entrance, and
Gretchen closed the door. "I had hoped to
open the windows and let fresh air blow the
staleness out, but I think that is not wise on
such a dreary day."

They walked the hallway, which divided
the house down the middle with the living
room, dining room, and kitchen on the right
side, and three bedrooms and a bath in a
line on the left. "I know Rockwater must be
grand, and my eyes long to see it. But this
is home for Bella and me, and I long to see
it again too. We will be returning to a happy
home."

Gretchen turned on the heat to get rid of
the dampness. She checked the refrigerator
and the garbage cans. The window had been
replaced in her bedroom and the crime
scene tape had been removed. "The men
Sam sent to take care of the house did an
excellent job. There is little to do here. I
will check the bed linens and laundry basket."

"I think Ned and Fred got the big stuff
done, but Hattie came over to do the things
that would never cross a man's mind,"

Caroline said.

"Oh, I did not know. I must thank Hattie in the morning." She checked the garage door in the kitchen and looked around the dining room. "I think there is nothing to do here. Shall we go?"

Sarah and Caroline followed Gretchen. She stopped at the door to her bedroom. She went in and stood next to the bed. She surveyed the room in silence, still not remembering much about her last night in this house. Caroline and Sarah stood at the door.

"I think it is time to go." She was reaching for the light switch when the phone rang. The only phone in the house was in the living room next to Ernesto's chair. Gretchen looked at Caroline. "Maybe I should answer that, although Caroline is the only one who calls for me."

"Maybe not. It could be some of Ernesto's friends or someone who saw us come into the house," Caroline said.

Gretchen started toward the ringing phone, ignoring Caroline's suggestion. "I must not avoid these things. I will answer."

"Maybe Caroline is right. Maybe it's not a good idea right now. Could even be a reporter," Sarah chimed in.

The phone rang for the eighth time. "I

must learn to deal with whatever happens now." She picked up the receiver. "Hello."

No response.

"Hello." Still no response. "Is someone there?" She could hear noise in the background. "Hello, please answer."

Sarah and Caroline stood at the living room door exchanging questioning glances.

"Hello, who is this?"

A weak, hesitant voice responded. "Mammá?" Pause. "Mammá? It's Karina, Mammá."

Gretchen sat down in Ernesto's chair as the blood drained from her face. "Karina? My Karina, is it really you?"

"Yes, Mammá. I want to come home."

CHAPTER TWENTY-TWO:
LOOKING IN THE MIRROR

Karina rinsed her toothbrush and stuck it and the toothpaste in the plastic bag.

Skeeter, in his underwear, stood in the bathroom doorway while she got ready for work and packed the last of her things. He never got up at four o'clock before to see her off. "So, you're taking the toothpaste too?"

"Yes, Skeeter, I'm taking the toothpaste, but there's a new tube in the drawer."

"What time you leavin'?"

She moved around him as though he were a bathroom fixture and went to the bedroom where her half-filled suitcase was on the floor. "I already told you. I'm leaving as soon as my shift at the bakery's over. I want to get to Moss Point by dark."

"I still don't get it. You ain't been home in twelve years, and you see your kid on television, and now you're busting a gut to get there?"

419

"I told you, Skeeter, and I'm not explaining it again. It's Thanksgiving, and I want to see my family." She had not told Skeeter about the call from Elena Daniels. Her instincts kept her stalling a meeting or any kind of alliance with Dr. Daniels. She wanted to weigh all her options for herself.

He sat on the edge of the bed and ran his fingers through his hair. "I know you said she's your daughter and all, but you better not bring the brat back here. We don't need no *ree-tard* around here to take care of."

She put the last stack of neatly folded clothing into the suitcase and zipped it shut. "Do not call her a 'ree-tard' ever again. Do you hear me? You saw the news. Any of your talented friends play the piano like she does?" She picked up the bag and walked down the hall.

Skeeter followed. "You heard what I said. There's no room for a kid around here. I don't care if she can play the piano."

Karina put on her jacket and grabbed her purse. "You really don't get it, do you?" She got right in his face. "My daughter is going to be a star. A star, do you hear?"

"Sure, she is. Just like her mother." His voice became louder. "You just remember what I said."

"I'm out of here." Just before she slammed

the door, she said, "Happy Thanksgiving, Skeeter."

Gretchen leaned over the dining table, putting finishing touches on the centerpiece, a basket with tiny pumpkins, dried corn, pinecones, and a smaller basket of gold mums. With her arm now out of the cast, she took pleasure in straightening the candles and smoothing the tablecloth. "Bella. Bella? Are you dressed?"

Bella appeared in green corduroy pants and a yellow sweater. "Karina's coming. Karina's coming, Mammá."

"Yes, she is, and we will have a lovely time."

"A lovely time. I look pretty?"

"Yes, my Bella, you look very pretty." Gretchen's eyes surveyed the room to make certain everything was in place. She walked to the front door and turned on the front porch light. "Where is the gift you made for Karina?"

"Gift for Karina."

"Go get your gift. It is in the bag, remember?" Gretchen rounded the corner to the kitchen and lifted the lid from the pot and stirred the beef. The smell of burgundy in the rich sauce competed with the yeasty aroma of homemade rolls rising next to the warm oven. Beef stroganoff had been Karina's favorite meal growing up, and there was apple streusel for dessert.

She looked at the clock. Six fifteen. Caroline would be arriving any minute. Having a guest for Karina's arrival was not her first choice, but Caroline was headed to Ferngrove for Thanksgiving, and this would be her only opportunity to meet Karina. Besides, Karina might as well know that Caroline and Sam and Angel were practically family now. They had been present when family was needed the most.

The phone rang. Gretchen walked to the den, hoping that it wasn't Karina calling to say she wouldn't be coming after all. She answered, "Hello." Silence. "Hello." More silence. "Hello, Karina, is this you?" She heard the click. It was the second call like this today.

Bella reentered the room, bag in hand. "I made a gift for Karina."

"Just put it at the end of the table." The phone call had distracted her.

"At the end of the table. Mr. Silva's chair?"

Gretchen brushed the last roll with melted butter, washed her hands, and went into the dining room. "Come here, Bella." Bella complied. "Listen to me, my sweet. Mr.

Silva is not coming. Mr. Silva is not ever coming back to the table." She never seemed to know quite what to tell Bella about Ernesto. "Why don't you and I move the chairs around? And no one will sit at the end of the table." Gretchen slid the side chair down and moved the armchair from the end of the table beside it. "Can you do the same thing on that side? That way, you and I can sit across from Caroline and Karina. I think that will be nice."

"Nice. Karina is family."

"Yes, Karina is family, and she has been away for a long time. She will see you all grown up." Gretchen was pleased with Bella's improving verbal skills.

There was a knock at the door. "Answer the door, please. Caroline is here."

Bella opened the door. "Mammá." Her voice rose in pitch and desperation. "Mammá?"

Gretchen stepped from the kitchen into the hallway and walked toward the front door, taking her eyes off Bella just long enough for a glimpse of Karina. She saw Bella standing next to the open door, her body still as a stopped clock, staring into a face that looked like hers, but a face of which Gretchen knew she could have no memory. Edging beside and facing her was a girl only a couple of inches taller than Bella. She was slim, with very short black hair, the kind of smutty black that looked like it might stain a towel. But the silvery-green eyes and the ivory skin were the same even with the garish eye makeup and the scarred punctures that piercings make. In jeans and a sweater revealing a slightly fuller figure than Bella's, Karina stood with her jacket in one hand and a small suitcase in the other.

"Karina?" Gretchen walked toward the door, extending both arms as she had many times in her dreams over the last twelve years; but this time, the morning light would not wake her. Karina was home.

Bella's feet were planted as Gretchen moved beyond her through the door to reach Karina. "Oh, my Karina, you are finally home."

Karina held on to her suitcase and her jacket as her mother wrapped both arms around her. "Yes, Mammá, I'm here."

"I can only believe what my hands can feel. Let me see you." Gretchen said nothing of the hair color as she held her at arm's length. "You still look so beautiful. And look at Bella. She is now a beautiful young lady too." She stepped aside and took Bella's hand, pulling her into the doorway. "Look,

Karina is home."

Bella clapped her hands. "Mammá is happy. Karina is home. Karina is family."

Never knowing if Karina would ever appear again and unsure of what Bella could understand, Gretchen had never told Bella that Karina was her mother. She wasn't even sure if Bella understood the concept or if she would only be parroting the words the way she reproduced a Bach prelude.

"Come in. Let me take your bag."

"No, Mammá, I can carry it." She stepped into the room, and Gretchen closed the door. She looked around. "The place is still the same. Not much has changed."

"We will take your bags to your room. Do you still remember?" She understood Karina's reticence. This had been her home many years ago, but time and the unknown made this an awkward encounter rather than a joyful homecoming. She would be patient and not rush her.

"Of course, Mammá. I remember." She followed Gretchen to the middle bedroom.

"You can put your bag here." Gretchen pointed to beside the bed. "Let me have your jacket." She opened the closet door and pulled out a hanger.

"See, I saved some of your clothes, and look on the shelf." She pointed to a wooden shelf in the top of the closet. "Some of your stuffed animals are still here. Bella has worn some of your clothes, but I saved these for when you would come home again."

"That's nice, Mammá." Karina handed her jacket to her mother. "How did you know I'd come home?"

"Your mammá knows these things. I knew you would return."

Karina put her purse down and looked around the room. She went to the dresser and lifted the lid of the small crystal box. The hairpins and pearl barrette from her childhood were still there. Silver strands of hair clung to the barrette as she lifted it from the box — silver threads to her past.

The doorbell rang. "Bella, please answer the door. It must be Caroline this time."

Bella left the room, and Gretchen moved to Karina's side. Karina returned the barrette to the box, replaced the lid, and turned to Gretchen. "Who is Caroline?"

"You will love Caroline. She is our friend, and she is Bella's teacher, her piano teacher."

Karina turned slowly, still surveying the room. "Why is she here tonight?"

Gretchen noted the change in Karina's demeanor. "She is here because I wanted her to meet you. She will be leaving Moss

426

Point tomorrow to spend Thanksgiving with her family, and this is the only time we could all be together."

"Oh. Does she know about me?" Karina tugged on her earring that dangled nearly to her shoulder.

"Oh, yes."

"All about me?"

Gretchen's excitement was beginning to fade under Karina's inquisition. "She knows that you are my beloved daughter and that . . ."

Karina interrupted her. "And that Bella's my daughter?"

"Yes, she knows." She watched the muscles in Karina's face tighten. "But she understands why you had to leave."

"I'm sure she does." Karina turned from her mother and looked into the mirror above the dresser. She ran her fingers through her spiky hair.

Karina's insolence bothered Gretchen. "Oh, my Karina, I am sorry if this is not the homecoming you wanted, but I so wanted Caroline to meet you."

"Because you're so proud of me, right?"

"Because you are my daughter and I am so glad you came home. Caroline will be a part of our lives, and so will the Meadows." Gretchen could see Karina's reflection in the mirror.

"You don't really think I came back to this house to stay, do you?"

Gretchen moved away from Karina and sat on the edge of the bed. "But you said you wanted to come home when you called."

"Wanted to come home for Thanksgiving and see Bella. Didn't you get that part?" She reached for her purse in the chair. "Just go see to your guest. I'll be out in a minute. I need to call someone."

Gretchen, wounded but still hopeful, rose from the edge of the bed and walked to the door, pausing before she left the room. "Karina, this is your home for as long as you would like it to be. I must tell you that Bella only knows you are family. I could never bring myself to tell her you are her mother."

Karina threw the phone on the bed. "Oh, so you can tell a stranger that I ran out on my daughter, but you can't tell my daughter she has a mother."

Familiar feelings of being put down and wanting to cower in the corner hovered over Gretchen like thick brown smog. "Karina, there is much that you do not understand. Shall we have a nice dinner and speak of this later, when there is no guest and Bella is asleep?"

"Sure. Later." Karina picked up her phone.

Gretchen delivered their plates to the table, and Karina remembered beef stroganoff was her favorite meal even before her mammá reminded her. Bella ate quietly, and Caroline made small talk answering Gretchen's questions about how she and her family would celebrate Thanksgiving.

While they ate, Karina added little to the conversation and spent her time staring at Bella, wondering why she rocked back and forth and repeated what others said. She saw herself in this chair at the table when she was Bella's age, always sitting erectly, eating in silence, only responding when her father asked a question. Memories of those meals had all but erased the memories of happier times when her father was on a driving job.

"Karina?" Gretchen touched her arm.

She turned to her mammá. "Yes. I'm sorry. I was thinking."

"Caroline asked what it is that you do."

"Oh, I work in a bakery." She deftly omitted that she waited tables at a bar on the weekends. "Pastries and cake decorating are my specialties."

"Cake decorating? Now that's an art and exactly why I only bake cookies." Caroline took her last bite of streusel. "I guess baking runs in the family."

"Yeah, I guess."

"Gretchen told me you loved to sing when you were a little girl. Do you still sing?"

Karina did not tell her she watched opera every Saturday afternoon and knew the libretto to most of the soprano arias in many operas. "Only in the shower. No one wants to hear me sing."

"Oh, that's a shame, but you must hear Bella sing."

"That would be nice, Karina. Bella sings like you did as a child," Gretchen added.

"Yeah, that'll be nice." Karina toyed with the pastry on her plate and never made eye contact with Caroline or Bella.

Caroline sipped her tea. "Maybe you all could come over in the morning before I leave for Ferngrove." She turned to Bella. "Would you like to come to my studio in the morning and play the piano for Karina?"

"Play the piano. Yes. Play the piano for Karina." Bella put down her spoon and began to sway and clap her hands.

Karina stared at Bella's unfamiliar movements and watched her mother's response.

Gretchen touched Bella's hands. "Yes, we

will go in the morning, but we must not stay long because Caroline is going home for Thanksgiving."

"Going home for Thanksgiving." Bella waved at Caroline.

"And speaking of going, I think I should get home and finish my packing." Caroline pushed away from the table. "Thank you so much for the meal. The beef stroganoff was a delicious change. It'll be turkey and dressing around here until the New Year."

"Oh, please do not go so soon. A pot of chamomile tea might find its way to the table if you will stay."

"Sounds good, but I can't go to sleep yet. Things to do, and you and Karina need time to catch up." Caroline stood up, hugged Bella, and started to the door.

"Thank you for coming and sharing our supper. Now you have met my Karina."

"Yes, I have, and she's just as beautiful as you said." She turned to Karina. "You've made Gretchen very happy by coming home."

Karina toyed with her earring and looked away. "Thanks. Guess it doesn't take much to make her happy."

Gretchen followed Caroline to the door and stood on the porch until she drove away.

431

The sky was clear, and the moon was almost full. She looked across the street at the two unfamiliar cars in Mrs. Marsh's driveway. Usually at this time of night, only a faint light coming from Mrs. Marsh's kitchen indicated any life in the place. But tonight, it appeared every light in the house was on. Since her husband died, Mrs. Marsh lived alone, but her driveway was always full on holidays, and her solitude was invaded by lots of grandchildren. Silhouettes of her grown children and their spouses dotted the windows, and their laughter could be heard across the street. They were home for Thanksgiving, and they would all return for Christmas. Gretchen imagined they were playing dominoes or Scrabble and drinking coffee and eating snacks. Their conversations would be quite different from the one she was about to have with Karina.

She prayed silently for wisdom and patience before she entered the house again, closing the door and turning off the porch light.

Karina was already clearing the table, and Bella remained in her seat. "Mammá, movie time, movie time."

"Yes, it is movie time." Gretchen had gone shopping after learning she was not a pauper. Bella had new clothes and art supplies and a television for her room and half a dozen movies. Never had she spent more than fifty or sixty dollars at one time, and that was for groceries. Even with her freedom and independence, her old conservative ways kept her frugality intact. A piano was the only thing left on her wish list, but it would only come after she had made her decision about the future. "You get ready for bed, my sweet, and we will turn on the movie." Gretchen went to the kitchen.

Karina rinsed the dishes. "I've been gone twelve years, and little has changed. You're still washing dishes. Don't you know they make dishwashers?"

Karina's sarcastic words pained Gretchen. "Oh, Karina, I will wash the dishes. Let us go sit and talk for a while. The kitchen can wait."

"Well, at least that's a change. We can actually leave the kitchen before the dishes are done. Not like I remember."

"It is not like that anymore." She reached for the teakettle. "Would you like a cup of tea?"

"No, no tea. I've had enough." She walked out of the kitchen and into the living room and sat down on the sofa.

Gretchen followed. "Let me check on Bella. She likes me to brush her hair before she goes to sleep."

"She's nearly thirteen. Can't she brush her own hair?"

"No." She paused. "Would you like to go in and spend some time with her and maybe brush her hair?"

"I don't think so. I'll see her in the morning."

Karina's stomach churned either from memories of other nights in this room or from the conversation she was about to have. Was Pappá at home or working? Was he drunk? Would Mammá be able to protect her if he was? Was Skeeter coming home? Was he drunk this time? Was there enough money to pay the bills? *And now, sitting here in this room, I still don't know what to expect. What will Mammá ask? And what will I tell her?*

Gretchen returned shortly and sat in her rocking chair across the room from Karina. "Is there anything I can get for you? A glass of water or milk? Or maybe you would prefer coffee?"

"Nothing." She looked at her watch.

"You must be tired from the drive." Gretchen picked up her knitting from the basket beside her chair. "You never told me where you are living. Was it a very long drive?"

"Not too long. About four hours, I think."

434

She twisted the bracelet on her arm. "I see you've taken up knitting."

"Only recently. When I was released from the hospital, Bella and I stayed with Sam and Angel Meadows for a few days. Angel taught me to knit. It is much easier now that the cast is off my arm."

"The Meadows? You're talking about the old judge who lives through the woods over there?"

"Yes. But by spring, the woods will be a park with flowers and walking paths and even a gazebo down by the creek. The Meadows are giving it to the town." Gretchen told her how Bella slipped through those woods late at night to Caroline's studio to hear her play the piano. She described how they fixed up an old shack in those woods, calling it their safe place and going there so Bella could play her keyboard.

Karina remembered the old cabin and slipping out through the same window in the middle of the night to meet Gil Grayson in those woods. At first, it was just to talk and to be together, and then holding hands and a kiss good night weren't enough. Then came the night that Gil grabbed an old tarp from the trunk of his car and spread it on the splintered floor. That was the night Bella was conceived, conceived in the very shack that became Bella's safe place years later. And now it was gone, torn down and replaced by a garden.

"Karina?"

"What? Oh, I was just thinking." She abruptly changed the subject. "Tell me about Bella."

"I cannot believe you are sitting here with me and we are talking. I have prayed every night since you left that you would be safe and find happiness. I understood why you wanted to leave, but I have missed you so much, and I am so grateful to you for the gift of Bella."

"Tell me about her."

"I want to hear about your life first." Gretchen kept up her knitting, slowly and deliberately.

Karina pulled her legs up under her on the sofa. "Not much to tell."

"But it has been over twelve years. That is nearly half your life. Please tell me. I want to know."

"Well, when I left home, I went to Atlanta to find Gil. That's where he went when I told him I was pregnant. He was scared Pappá would kill him." She paused. "I found him, and we were together for a while. But his parents talked him into coming to live with them after they moved away from Moss Point, and he left again. So, I moved in with some girls I knew. I was just working, but I got my GED while I was in Atlanta. My boss talked me into it. She thought I was really smart."

"Oh, I am so glad you finished school."

"Yeah. I was thinking about college, but then I met this guy who was in a band. He thought I could sing pretty good, so I traveled with the band for a while. But I got tired of that." Shame kept her from telling the parts of the story that included drugs and a short stint in a local jail in Beaufort, South Carolina, and the broken promises of too many men. "Anyway, I quit the band and settled down about three years ago and got a job at this bakery in Myrtle Beach."

"Do you like it in Myrtle Beach?"

"I guess so. I mean I have a job and an apartment, and there's Skeeter."

"Skeeter?"

"Yeah, he really wanted to come with me to meet you and Bella, but I wouldn't let him. I mean, this is the first time I've been home in a long time. I thought it would be better if I came alone."

"I would really like to meet this Skeeter. Maybe he can come the next time you come to visit Bella and me."

Karina shifted her position on the sofa, put her feet on the floor, and sat up with her elbows on her knees. "Mammá, you don't understand."

"Oh, I understand. You're not coming home to live. You have a life and someone you love in Myrtle Beach, but you can still come home to visit us, and Skeeter can meet Bella."

"No need for him to visit Moss Point to meet Bella. I came home to get my daughter."

CHAPTER TWENTY-THREE: A LETTER FOR KARINA

Caroline cherished November mornings almost as much as April mornings, crisp and promising. Morning light streamed into her bedroom through Palladian windows. The air was clear, and the sky was bright blue, with only an occasional rogue cloud dotting the horizon. No driving in the rain today. She hummed Rachmaninoff's *Rhapsody on a Theme of Paganini* as she put the last of her toiletries into her tote bag.

The basket of yellow irises Polly had delivered from Roderick yesterday put a smile on her face as she passed by them on the dresser. Moss Point tongues would be flapping again after Polly retold the story of the overnight delivery she received from England. Roderick had called and told her to expect it and gave instructions to deliver its contents in a basket of irises to Caroline. No doubt he made it worth her while. Polly tapped out her creativity to please Roderick

439

and staged the porcelain pumpkin carriage, horses and all, on gold foil right in the middle of the basket.

When she delivered it, she insisted on bringing it into Caroline's studio herself. Polly removed the porcelain piece from the basket and set it down on the counter. When she opened the carriage door, revealing Cinderella with one bare foot, *Rhapsody on a Theme of Paganini* began to play. Caroline had listened patiently as Polly told her about Roderick's instructions and then retold the story of Cinderella. She had no heart to tell Polly the music was a classical piece written by a Russian composer, not the theme from a romantic movie.

Caroline hummed the quixotic melody this morning as she pressed hard to get her favorite red sweater in the suitcase and zipped it shut. Gretchen and the girls would be ringing the bell in about half an hour, giving her enough time to run up to the main house to see Sam and Angel before she left. She grabbed her tote bag, rolled the suitcase to the door, and was thumbing through CDs to choose music for her drive home when the phone rang. She pulled a couple of CDs from the stack and answered the phone.

"Good morning, Caroline. It is Gretchen."

"Oh, hi, Gretchen. Are you on your way?"

"That is why I am calling. We will not be coming. I have some important business to attend to." Gretchen's peaceful voice was shaky.

"What's going on?"

"Karina told me last night that she came home to get Bella, so I must deal with her this morning. We went to bed last evening without settling this."

Caroline quickly added up trouble. "To get Bella? She can't just waltz in here and take Bella. Do we need to wonder any longer why she would come home now after twelve years?"

"I think we know why she came now, but she has not said. She is my daughter, and I feel I owe her things I never had the opportunity to give her, but I will never allow her to take Bella."

"Of course not. What are you going to do?" Caroline tossed the CDs in her tote bag.

"The night was long, but it gave me time to think and pray and write a letter to my child. A letter that will explain many things to her. We will first have a talk. She does not know that I am divorcing Ernesto and

441

adopting Bella." Gretchen cleared her throat. "Do you suppose the Meadows would allow me to bring Bella over for a time this morning while Karina and I talk? I do not wish Bella to hear this conversation."

"I'm sure they'd love to see Bella. Just bring a movie. You know, Gretchen, this could get complicated. Do you need Sam to talk with her?"

"Let me speak with her first. I think I can solve the problem. I must learn to do these things myself. It is not right for my problems to intrude in so many other lives."

"I'm so sorry. I'll tell Sam. I was headed up there to see them before I leave."

"Thank you. Please ask Angel to call me if I may bring Bella over. Now, you go to your family, and we will talk when you return."

"Okay, but I'll give you a call when I get to Ferngrove. I'll be anxious to hear what happens." She really hated to leave Gretchen at such a critical time. "Remember, Sam and Angel and I think of you as family now, and you really don't have to do this alone."

"I know and I am so grateful, but you go and have a blessed Thanksgiving. I will call you if anything significant happens."

"I'll expect it, and I pray your Thanksgiving is all you wanted it to be. Goodbye, my friend." Caroline hung up the phone and headed straight up the path to the main house. Joy and anticipation could turn so quickly.

The smell of buttery corn bread baking and caramelized onions met Caroline at the kitchen door. "Good morning. I was just about to tell Sam to get off the phone so I could call you." Angel handed Caroline a burgundy organza bag tied with gold ribbon. "Here, before I forget, this is for your mother."

"Wine for Thanksgiving?" Caroline had not seen this impish expression on Angel's face in a while.

"Hardly. It's her Christmas present, but I really didn't want to take the chance of shipping it, if you know what I mean." Angel gently tapped the top of the bottle, holding it from the bottom.

"Is this the good stuff?" Caroline took the bag and held it securely.

"If you classify the peach brandy I made with the July peaches and the family recipe as the good stuff, then yes. I know how Martha loves it over ice cream, and I knew you'd be making your Christmas fruitcakes Friday, so tell her to go ahead and open it.

There's a small jar of the brandied peaches too. Tell her to throw a cupful in the fruitcake."

"Oooh, Lawdy, I'm going to Ferngrove for fruitcake." Hattie lifted the lid on the turnip greens. "And tell Miss Martha the brandy has to last a whole year or maybe longer if the peaches are lost next year."

"I'll tell her."

Sam came in from the hallway. "Who are you telling what?" He went straight for the coffeepot and grabbed a mug.

"You, that's who, and it's not good news." Caroline had no time for her normal reservation this morning. "Gretchen just called and said that Karina's home to get Bella."

Sam froze with the coffeepot in midair. Hattie dropped the lid to the turnip pot. Angel jumped at the sound of clashing stainless steel, and then sat down at the breakfast table. "Well, that's just not going to happen. Who does she think she is, appearing after twelve years like the orchestra just played the fanfare and somebody opened the stage curtains?" She slapped the table with her hand. "Karina can't just come in here and take Bella." She turned around to Sam. "Can she?"

Sam poured his coffee and joined them at the table. "I had a feeling something like this might happen. I've been on the phone this morning talking to Tom. He's got the adoption papers ready, and he's bringing them by in about half an hour for me to take a look at them. But we need to get them to Gretchen."

"That won't be a problem. When she called, she wanted me to ask you if she could bring Bella over here for a while this morning. She doesn't want Bella to be around when she has this talk with Karina. Will that be okay?"

"Sure, it's okay," Angel said.

"Would you give her a call and let her know?"

"I'll call her right now, and then I'll get dressed." Angel, still in her bathrobe and slippers, shuffled to the phone and called Gretchen.

Still holding the gift bag, Caroline said, "I hate leaving town with things in such an uproar, but I really need to get on the road."

"Of course you do, honey. Don't you worry about a thing. Ol' Sam'll take care of Bella, and she'll be right here when you get back Saturday."

She hugged Sam, opened the oven door for one last whiff of corn bread, waved at Hattie and Angel, and walked out onto the porch.

Angel hung up the phone quickly and followed. "You be careful with the liquid gold and give your folks our love."

Karina stood in the hallway and watched her mammá seal the envelope and put it on the dining table before she started toward the kitchen. She would see how things developed this morning. If they didn't go well, she wouldn't prolong the visit and would leave today.

After delivering her purpose for coming home last evening, she had abandoned her mother much like she had left Moss Point after delivering Bella twelve years ago. No talking, no pleading, she just stood up and left. She had gotten up twice during the night and had seen the light on and Gretchen sitting at the dining table.

Karina's own nights of waiting for a man to come home had brought thoughts of how she left home without a word, and she wondered how many days and nights her mammá stood at the door waiting. Her conscience had calloused over as the years passed, and compassionate thoughts were now strangers.

She had settled for a life that paid the bills and kept her from being alone. But she knew there had to be more, even more than her parents had. She wanted it, whatever more was, and it appeared Bella was her ticket. She didn't have it all figured out yet, but she had seen the television segments and had read the online articles. An autistic, prodigious musical savant was extremely rare, and people would pay for access to her. Those payments would provide for an education and a start in a legitimate singing career.

"Oh, I heard your beautiful singing as you showered this morning. You still remember the aria from *La bohème*?"

"Yeah. Got any coffee?" She ran her fingers through her short, wet hair.

"Yes, and I made your favorite coffee cake." Gretchen reached for the yellow mug, turned to Karina, and brushed her face with her fingers. "I remember kissing the sugared glaze from your sweet cheeks when you were small."

"I make about twenty of those every morning at five o'clock, and they're usually out the bakery door by eight. Took me a while to figure out the recipe." She saw the twinge in her mammá's face and wished she could recall her words.

"Oh, I am sorry. I did not know. What would you like for breakfast?"

"Just coffee."

"Okay, have a seat, and I will bring your coffee." Gretchen paused. "Karina, I do not know how you like your coffee. You left home before you started drinking it."

"Just black." She saw the envelope with her name on it on the table.

"I will heat a roll. I think they do not have homemade peach preserves in Myrtle Beach. You will like them." She opened the refrigerator. "Do you still love opera?"

"Yeah. I listen once in a while." Karina sat silently. Her mammá was still serving, trying to make everyone happy, even when she just got slapped in the face. "Where's Bella?"

"She is in her room listening to her iPod, waiting for you to get up."

"Well, maybe we could talk before she comes in." She dreaded this conversation as much as she dreaded the one she'd have with Skeeter when she got home. But she had enough money now to get her own apartment, and she would have Bella.

"Yes, we do need to talk." Gretchen brought Karina's coffee and roll to the table. "I have spoken with Caroline and with Mrs. Meadows this morning."

"Oh, so what did you tell them?" she asked sarcastically.

"I told Caroline we would not be coming

to the studio, and I asked Mrs. Meadows if she would watch Bella for a few hours this morning while you and I get to know each other again."

"Get to know each other again? Like anything has changed? What's to get to know?" She pushed the plate with the roll and preserves to the side of the table.

"Karina, you have become a woman since I saw you last. There is so much that I do not know about you."

"I told you last night what you need to know. You just need to accept that I'm Bella's mother, and I want her with me." She stared out the dining room window into the cottage garden where she played as a child while her mammá worked in the flowers. Looking her mammá in the face was too hard.

"There are many things you do not know, my daughter. Things about me, and about Bella, and about your father. I wrote a letter for you, and it would please me if you would read it while I take Bella over to the Meadows'." She picked up the envelope and moved it near Karina's hand. "Would you do that?"

"Yeah, I'll do that."

"Thank you, Karina. Now, I will get Bella."

Karina stared out the window while she waited. The envelope would remain sealed until she was alone.

"Karina's home. Karina's home." The sound of Bella's voice was musical as they entered the room.

"Yes, my sweet, Karina's home. Would you like to give her a good morning hug?"

"A good morning hug. A good morning hug for Karina." Bella walked to the dining table where Karina was seated and stretched her arms out in a stiff, robotic fashion.

Karina embraced Bella, expecting the kind of warm, cuddly hug she was accustomed to from Beth, her boss's daughter. Instead, it was a stilted, uncomfortable meeting of two foreign bodies. "Good morning, Bella."

Bella moved away. "Good morning, Bella. Karina said, 'Good morning, Bella.'"

"Yes, she said, 'Good morning.' Now get your jacket. We are going to see Angel. She is waiting for you and wants to watch a movie." Gretchen took Bella's shoulders and turned her toward the door. "Get your jacket." She said to Karina, "I will be home in about half an hour. It takes a bit longer to walk since we cannot take the shortcut through the woods."

"Why don't you just drive?"

Gretchen chuckled. "I am afraid that

would take much longer. I do not know how to drive, but Caroline has promised to teach me. We were waiting for the cast to be removed from my arm."

"I'll drive you."

Gretchen put on her coat. "No, no. That is not necessary. Bella and I like the walk. She likes to tiptoe through the acorns on the sidewalk. Since I told her acorns are squirrel food, she will not step on one, and she likes to stop to pick up the red and yellow sycamore leaves." Gretchen followed Bella onto the porch.

"Suit yourself," Karina said as the door closed. She could hear Bella whistling like a canary as they walked away. She picked up the envelope and twirled it in her fingers before she opened it. It was several pages of her mammá's handwriting. She freshened her coffee and sat down at the table to read.

My dearest daughter,
    I have much to say to you from the deepest places in my heart, but I cannot find the words to express my heart so easily. I express my heart language in my mother tongue even after all these years. So that I could say to you what I want you to hear, I write my thoughts and hope you can understand.

There are things I can tell you now that I could not tell you before. You were just a child, but now you are a young woman and your understanding of life is grown up like you are. When you left, words cannot say the grief that strangled me and the worry that overtook me at times. In the place that mothers know things beyond all reason, I knew you were alive. Sometimes that made more pain because I could not come to you when you were hurting or when you were sad. But when you left, you gave me a beautiful and precious gift. When you named your little girl Isabella Gretchen, it made me so happy. "Bella" means beautiful. Do you remember?

I cared for Bella and protected her just as I cared for and tried to protect you, but you had dreams and the notions that come to a young girl's mind. You left to make them become real. But you left without knowing about me and how I came to have the life I was living. I know I told you happy stories about your grandparents and how I grew up in Austria, but there were some stories I never told you. You were just too young to understand. This is the story I must tell you now.

Karina read each shocking word.

When I was nineteen, when I could no longer hide that I was carrying a child, I ran. I ran away just like you, Karina. I took a train to Germany, and it was there I met Ernesto Silva.

It has been almost thirty years since I left my family. I could not bear the pain that my situation would have brought them and Peter's family. I left Peter, my parents, my grandmammá, and my younger sister without saying goodbye. They do not know that I am alive or where I am to this day, and I know not if they are still living.

Karina, you are Nicolai's child. Although you were not conceived in love, you were born in my heart and into my arms, and I could not have loved you more. You are my child, my child alone. Nicolai has no knowledge that he fathered you. I am sorrowful that I had not the means or the strength to give you all that you needed when you were with me. I was in a foreign country, married to a man who became a stranger to me. I had no education or skills to make it on my own, so I settled for life with Ernesto. I thought I could make it up to you, but I could not.

When you became pregnant, I could see the story unfolding again. I lived under such oppression that I had not the strength to help you then. And when you ran away, I breathed only pain and spoke only tears at the thought of never seeing you again. I feared our life stories could end up the same. Only you left Bella with me. I had a second chance at being a mother. I have loved her. I protected her. I taught her what I could when the teachers at school could not help her. I hid things from Ernesto to give her what I could.

God answered so many of my prayers. He brought Caroline into our lives. She has been God's instrument to help Bella. And then God brought you home, and I am praying we can be family again. Judge Meadows is helping me do and learn the things I need to know to live my life and take care of Bella.

Karina, Ernesto is going to prison for a long time, and we will be divorced before Christmas. All these years, he has taken care of us, providing for our needs. He will no longer be doing that. I must make it on my own and provide for Bella. Before you contacted me the first time, Judge Meadows was helping me with adoption proceedings. I want to be Bella's parent legally and take care of her. I beg of you to allow me to adopt her. I know not what Bella thinks. I am not even certain she really understands the relationship between a parent and a child, but I have been the one who has taken care of her and the one who has learned to reach her. Nothing would make me happier than if you came back to be family with us and let me take care of both of you.

There will be changes in our lives in the next few months. Through Caroline, we have come to know Dr. Sarah McCollum. Sarah is a child psychologist at Duke University. She has made a very generous offer for Bella and me to move to Raleigh-Durham. The university will provide housing and an education for Bella. They recognize how rare she is, and they want to help. There may be a similar offer from the University of Georgia. I am praying and listening to the counsel of my friends to help me make this decision. I am willing to do whatever is best for Bella.

Before I can begin a new life, I know in my heart there are some matters I must settle. I plan to return to Austria to find my family. My hope is that you will go with me. When that is done, then I can make the decision about Bella's future and what is best for her.

Karina, I do not want you to settle as I thought I must do. I am prepared now to provide you with something I could not provide before. I could hear in your words last night how you wanted to finish your college education. Here is a check for twenty thousand dollars to help you do that. How happy I would be if you were with Bella and me and could get your education with us.

My dearest daughter, life has been unkind to you. I know you had young girl dreams, and it is not too late for you to make them come true. Do not settle for less, I beg of you. God has answered my prayers in protecting you and bringing you home. I look at you, and my heart aches for the years we have been apart, but my eyes see a beautiful life for you. I know so little about your last twelve years, but I know that no matter what you have experienced, even now there is a little girl with very big dreams inside you. You still have a song, a beautiful song, and I so want to be there to hear you sing it.

With love always,
Mammá

Karina sobbed as she read the last words. She read the letter a second time. A beautiful life? A beautiful song? Not possible. Not enough beauty in the world to cover up all the ugly. She folded the letter, returned it to the envelope, and walked to the window. The side garden was relatively unchanged. The old-fashioned roses she remembered as a child were shedding their last blooms before winter. She was there again as a five-year-old, singing with her mammá while gathering the roses. Gretchen would cut them, rid them of their thorny stems, and hand the blossoms to her. She sat on the grass and tore the blossoms apart petal by petal, dropping them in the basket. When the basket was full, Mammá told her to stand up, close her eyes, and twirl around slowly and sing the rose song. As she spun, Mammá showered her in rose petals. They laughed and sang, dancing in the late-afternoon sunlight. She could see it all now and even smell the fragrant petals, but the tight grip of sorrow in her throat kept her from humming the song.

Karina went to her room, dressed quickly,

and packed her bag. She made the bed hurriedly and left the room neat and in order as her mammá would like. On her way out, she picked up the check from the dining room table but left the letter. Turning one last time to survey the room, she opened the front door.

Silvery-green eyes, having seen too much pain, stared back at her own silvery-green eyes. "Mammá?"

Holding the brown envelope in her hand, Gretchen stared at the suitcase Karina clutched. She stepped through the doorway and realized that if she had arrived sixty seconds later, it would have been to an empty house. Karina was leaving again.

"No. No." Gretchen folded her arms around the envelope and swayed, teetering on the verge of collapse. Years of consoling Bella when she was frustrated and rocking back and forth had become natural to Gretchen in her own despair. Tears left their salty path down her cheeks. "Please, Karina, I beg of you, do not go." She bowed her head and gripped the envelope.

"Don't do this, Mammá. Just don't do it." Karina stood motionless.

"I know not what to do. I have opened my heart and my life to you. Will you not stay and talk with me?" She lifted her head and looked into Karina's cold eyes.

"What do you want me to say? That I understand and I forgive you for living a lie?" Her jaw was clenched and her grip on the suitcase was tight. "What can I say, Mammá?"

"You may hold on to your words, but would you sit with me and listen?" She reached for Karina's arm. "There are no words to tell you how sorry I am. How I wish I could have done better for you, my sweet daughter." She pulled a tissue from her sweater pocket and wiped her face.

Karina put her purse and suitcase down, closed the door, and took off her jacket. "Okay, Mammá, I'm listening."

"Could we go and sit? I will brew us a cup of tea." She took Karina's arm and led her to the dining room table.

"Mammá, a cup of tea won't fix this. It never did, and it won't do it now." She sat down at the table.

"No tea. No tea. We will just talk." As she pulled out her chair, Gretchen put the brown envelope down on the table next to the open envelope with the letter inside. "Did you read my letter?"

"Yes. I know I'm a bastard child and that I ruined your life."

"Oh, no. It is not like that. You were the only good thing in my life, Karina. You were the reason I smiled for so many years, and when you left, I thought my joy was forever gone."

Karina sat rigid in her chair. "Sure. But if I'd never been born, you could have married that Peter guy, and there would have been no Ernesto. You'd still be living with your real family in Austria."

"It is not like that, Karina. Life is about choices. Nicolai made a bad choice, and yes, his choice changed lives. But I made a choice too. I chose you, and I chose what I thought was the easiest way for my family and for Peter's. I was young and afraid, and perhaps I should have chosen to stay and tell the truth. Peter would have married me and raised you as his own. But I did not choose that way."

"Yeah and look what you got. You live your life in a dump with a lousy husband, and you got an even lousier daughter. And what did I bring you but more grief?"

Gretchen stood up. "Karina, in nearly twenty-nine years, I have never raised my voice nor my hand to you, but you are sitting in my house, and you will not speak like that again." Surprised at her own strength, she swallowed and tried to regain her composure. "I will not lie, when you left home, I grieved. But the sweetness and the joy you brought will always be what I remember. And think of Bella. The chain of choices we each made brought Bella to the world. Do you not understand what a gift she is?" Gretchen sat back down.

Karina said nothing.

"Do you remember when you were a little girl and you imagined being a fairy princess? I made you a little pink costume, and we made your fairy princess wand with the star on the end, and you waved it and waved it. I know in your young heart, you wanted it to change things, but it did not. There is no magic wand or a way to bring back the past and make it better, but we have the future, Karina. Your future. Bella's future."

"Future? What kind of future?" She sat with her arms folded.

"That is your choice. You are angry, and you want to punish me for my choices and maybe for some of your own. Leaving again would do that, but you would be punishing yourself and Bella too. I can help you make a better future for yourself. And now, we have the help we need for Bella. She is a gift to the world, and I know you do not understand that now, but she is."

"Oh, I understand. I understand more

than you know." Her tone was angrier.

Gretchen took the brown envelope and pulled the papers out. "Here is how you can help Bella. If you sign these adoption papers, I will be legally responsible for Bella. I promise to take care of her and provide for her the best life possible." She turned to the fourth page where there was a line for Karina's signature.

"So that's what this is all about? You just want Bella. You want the book deals and all the money you can get because of her."

Gretchen's face showed her shock. "You think I want to exploit Bella?"

"Looks like it to me. You write me a check for twenty thousand dollars so I'll sign my rights away. You must be planning to make a whole lot more than that."

"Surely, you cannot believe what you just said. And who, my daughter, who taught you to think like that? You did not learn that from living in this house." She straightened the pages of the document and replaced it inside the brown envelope. "I will not be angry with you, for I think you are unhappy enough with yourself. What could erase all you were taught in this house? Do not allow your pain to bury the goodness, daughter."

"Pain and goodness." Karina stood up and pushed her chair back. "Guess you know all about that." She took the brown envelope and walked toward the front door. "I'm taking the check."

Gretchen followed her down the hallway. "But Karina, how will I reach you, and how will I explain to Bella that you are gone?"

"You don't need to reach me. I'll be in touch when I'm ready." She grabbed her bag and jacket and slammed the door.

Gretchen leaned against the doorframe as she watched Karina pull out of the driveway and head down the street without ever looking back. She backed into the room, closed the door, and walked down the hallway to Karina's room. The bed was made, and the curtains were open. There was no visible sign that anyone had been in the room. It was as though Karina had not been there at all, but she had. She had the full story now, and the adoption papers were in her possession. Not wanting to think of the alternatives, Gretchen trusted that Karina would sift all these thoughts and she would make the choice that would be best. She had to believe that.

The phone rang. As if on autopilot, Gretchen walked to the front of the house where the only phone was, next to the new chair she had purchased to replace Ernesto's. When she decided to divorce him, she

463

disposed of his chair, which though stained and stinking of him, had loomed as his seat of power for years. It reigned now somewhere on a garbage heap out in the country. She sat in her new chair and answered the phone. "Hello." No sound, only her knowledge that someone was there. "Hello, who is this?"

A raspy tone of someone obviously trying to disguise his voice responded. "I'm the one who knows you have my money. My money. Do you understand?"

Gretchen slammed the phone down. Her hands trembled as she pressed them against her face to catch her tears.

CHAPTER TWENTY-FOUR:
THANKSGIVING

A heavy fog blanketed Ferngrove, the kind of fog that made deer hunters unhappy. But Caroline heard the voices of the Carlyle men and knew a bit of weather wasn't keeping them from their Thanksgiving morning ritual of crawling into a deer stand. This year, three generations of Carlyles would be hunting together. Last night, her eight-year-old nephew proudly showed her the rifle he had received for his birthday and sat quietly for a couple of hours as all the men told hunting and fishing stories of epic proportions.

Caroline smiled, but stayed snuggled in bed until she heard her mother moving around in the house. It felt wonderful to spend the morning in the kitchen with her mother, catching up on all the news, and explaining about her Christmas plans.

Thanksgiving was as it had always been ever since she could remember — far too much food, ample laughter and storytelling, and a sweetness that started with the love her parents had for each other and the family. Midafternoon afforded her a short visit with Betsy and Josefina and her new godson, David, before she returned home for the late afternoon tradition of cutting up the fruit and nuts for the fruitcakes, which her mother would bake tomorrow.

"I'll turn on the coffee for dessert. Glad Lilah had pity on us and sent you here to Partridge Manor with one of her homemade pumpkin pies. Are you sorry you didn't stay at Rockwater and have Lilah bake a turkey?" Sarah cleared the plates from the table and stacked them on the counter.

"Who'd trade broiled, pepper-encrusted, beef tenderloin with a rich burgundy sauce for a stuffed turkey and cranberry sauce?" Roderick teased his sister.

"Oh, I think I know someone who would if that turkey was going to be served at a table where a certain young woman was eating." Sarah returned with cream and sugar and stood next to her husband's chair as she waited for her brother to respond. He said nothing, but his face did.

Sarah served the pie and coffee and got an update on her brother's philanthropic endeavors and Christmas plans while they ate. With the last crumb gone and a second cup of coffee in hand, George excused himself to the study to work on a journal article.

Roderick moaned. "Guess I should get back to Rockwater." He pointed to the window. "Those clouds look like snowfall to me."

"You don't want to stay for dinner?" Sarah inquired.

"You have fed me sumptuously, sis. I may not eat again until Christmas, but if I get hungry this evening, Lilah left something in the fridge for me."

"Well, I'm glad you came into Lexington to eat with us."

"Wouldn't have missed it. Besides, you came from Raleigh, and I haven't been here in months. I took after our Francophile mother and live in her chateau, and you got Father's Anglophile genes and took the manor house. So, this afternoon, you'll be reading in a mahogany paneled study while I'm roaming the forest at Rockwater to mark the Christmas trees we'll cut in a couple of weeks. I'd say that's a fair trade."

"We have sweet memories of holidays in both houses. Mother and Father made certain of that — but I do remember more celebrations at Rockwater."

"Yes, we have lots of wonderful memories and a few painful ones, but no one to tell them to. We're it, sis. Our family's gone. No uncles or aunts or cousins, except for Mother's eccentric aunt, and we haven't heard from her since Mother died."

"Sounds rather sad, doesn't it? And no children. What's to become of our family, Rod?" Sarah would not miss the opportunity for this conversation with her brother. "So, tell me about Christmas."

Rod sat up in his chair and propped his elbows on the dining table. "Lilah's making plans for the perfect Christmas. She started her list-making when I told her Caroline was coming for a Christmas recital. And then when plans developed for Gretchen and Bella to join her and spend the entire holiday season with us, Lilah's gone through two legal-sized notepads."

"Doesn't sound like either of you need my help."

"Just put it like this, you haven't seen Rockwater this festive in the last twenty years — Christmas trees all over the house, lights, fudge, presents, nothing will be left out. You and George are coming for several days, aren't you?"

She watched his face beam as it did at

Christmastime when they were children. "We'll be there for the recital, and then we'll come back into Lexington until Christmas Eve. If there's room, we'll plan to spend the night and stay for Christmas Day. We'll come back here for a few days before returning to Raleigh. George's department at the university is having a New Year's Eve party. Command performance, you understand."

"Sure. Been to a few of those myself." He looked out the dining room window again. "I need your opinion about something."

"Like Mother, I don't think I'll run out of those anytime soon." She snapped her fingers. "What is it you need to know?"

"Caroline's concerned about Sam and Angel."

"I was just there, and they were fine."

"I mean about Christmas. She mentioned that usually they go to Ferngrove with her, but they're not doing that this year. With Caroline, Gretchen, and Bella away, they'll be alone for Christmas and New Year's. I was thinking about inviting them to Rockwater as a surprise for Caroline."

She reached over and patted him on the back. "Well . . . my brother, next to George, you're the most thoughtful man alive. Of course, you should invite them. It'll be like having a real family with three generations. The more the merrier."

"Good. Then I'll make the call over the weekend. They're good at keeping secrets." Roderick sipped the last of his coffee and stood to go.

"Wait, you needed my opinion, but I'd like some information."

He sat back down at the table. "You're not running out of opinions, and I'm full of information."

"I wonder if there'll be anything special under the tree for Caroline?" She watched for any visible sign from Roderick.

"Of course. I had something made for her when I was in Hong Kong."

"See, what did I tell you? You're a thoughtful man." She leaned forward and whispered. "What is this gift you had made for her in Hong Kong?"

He grinned. "Just because I have information doesn't mean that I'll impart it all to you." He got up to leave again. "Tell George goodbye for me. I don't want to disturb him, and I need to get on the road."

She followed him to the front door. "Wait, I have another question."

He grabbed his coat from the hall tree and put it on, removing his scarf and gloves from his coat pocket. "I'm listening. Go ahead."

He wrapped the plaid wool scarf around his neck.

"Rod, you're really crazy about Caroline, aren't you?"

"If living to make her smile or not being able to think of my life without her means I'm crazy about her, then the answer is yes. Is that all?" He took his gloves and tapped her lightly on top of her head.

"Don't do that. I'm serious. You're crazy about her. She's crazy about you, and yet, you sidestep around each other like you're rehearsing for some dance competition and you're afraid of making a misstep. Stop it. Just tell her how you feel and see what happens."

"Is that my sister or the psychologist giving advice?"

She stepped closer to him and adjusted his scarf. "Both."

"Then I guess I'd better listen."

"I've never seen you this way about a woman. Usually, it's dinner a few times and then you send your proverbial goodbye flowers. But don't you think it strange that Caroline's spent a week at Rockwater for a summer recital, you spent days with her when Gretchen and Bella were in the hospital and flew home with her when her godson was born, and now she and most of the folks she loves are coming for Christmas, and you've never even asked her out for a romantic evening? You must admit, Rod, that's not the usual way of doing things."

"That is true, and maybe by the time I get around to asking her for a real date, she'll say yes."

"Yes to what? Dinner at Luciano's or an engagement or what?"

"Something she'll be comfortable enough to say yes to." He turned toward the door.

"If you ask me, she's getting uncomfortable at why you don't ask. You're this distant man who flies in and out of her life, yet you're there when she needs you. You send flowers. You gave her a piano, and I'll bet you haven't even kissed her, have you?"

He hugged Sarah, kissed her on the forehead, and headed out the front door. "Love you, sis. Hey look, it's snowing." He turned and waved. "See you at Christmas, and by the way, I only loaned her the piano."

She closed the door and walked to the library. *Christmas it is, little brother. I have my own plans for your Christmas.*

It was midafternoon, and the embers in the fireplace were those of a fire that had been burning since early morning. The library at Twin Oaks was toasty. Sam read in his lounge chair. Gretchen and Angel sat in the plaid chenille chairs near the window, knitting and talking.

Bella sat with crossed legs in the chair next to Sam. Angel had given her some yarn and knitting needles earlier and taught her a beginning stitch. "Knit and purl. Knit and purl." She wrapped the yarn over the needle again. "Knit one. Purl one. Knit one. Purl one."

"It's nearly four o'clock and I still feel like a stuffed turkey." Angel took off her glasses and rubbed her eyes. "I knew it when I reached for seconds."

Gretchen kept knitting. "I fear we all ate more than our bodies require, but how do you stop when it tastes so good? Now I know what a Thanksgiving meal should be like."

Puzzled, Angel responded, "Well, it stands to reason you didn't celebrate Thanksgiving in Austria, so how would you know what a Thanksgiving in Georgia would taste like?" Angel was curious.

"I learned from television and the two Thanksgivings we spent with Ernesto's stepmother in our early years. But your table looked like a picture in a magazine, and the food was so fine."

"See there. Who in the world would have

bragged on the sweet potatoes if you and Bella hadn't joined us?" She put her glasses back on and started knitting again.

"Our Thanksgiving did not turn out as the scene in my wishes. It would have been quite lonely without you and Sam."

"I'm so sorry. I could just make Karina sit in the corner for a while for the way she disappointed you." Angel had to explain what sitting in the corner meant.

"I am so worried. She took the money and the adoption papers, and I do not know how to contact her or when or even if I will hear from her."

"Oh, you'll hear from her. Just think about how far you've come in such a short time. Things will work out. It just may take a little longer."

"But without the proper papers, I cannot get a passport for Bella, and we cannot go to Austria to find my family. All these years, I never thought my eyes would see my family again. And just when I have hope, it disappears. I worry for my family."

"Stop worrying. Sam'll fix things. He always does."

Sam cleared his throat and put his book in his lap. "Did I hear my name?"

Angel retorted, "You most certainly did. I'd hate to have to call Ned and Fred to drive in to town to put another log on the fire."

"Does that mean you want me to get up and go out in the cold damp air to get another chunk of firewood?" He pushed down the lever on his lounge chair and sat up straight and stretched.

"Yes, it does."

"Guess it's a good thing we're clearing that patch of forest to make a park and Ned and Fred are stacking oak along the back fence. It's just November, and we're burning firewood like there's no January." He stoked the fire. "Miss Bella, you've been knittin' and purlin' a while. You want to go with me to get another log?"

Bella did not respond. "Knit one. Purl one. Knitting is fun. Knit one . . ."

"Guess not. Okay, you just sit there and knit and purl, little songbird." He stopped before he reached the door and tapped his cane near Gretchen's foot. "And by the way, stop worrying. You're just robbing yourself of today's joys and pleasures. Angel's right. Ol' Sam'll take care of things."

She stopped her knitting. "My friend, you are so wise, and I will do what you say. I will stop worrying right this minute." She looked through the window's lacy sheers at the gray, wintry skies. "Maybe it would be good if Bella and I followed you out. We really should be going home before the weather gets worse and it gets dark."

Angel said, "I'll not hear of that. You must stay for supper. We have enough leftovers to feed the local Boy Scout troop. Sam'll drive you home after supper."

"Sure, I'll drive you home." Sam walked out the door and down the hall. He called back to Gretchen. "And next week, I'll help you trade in that overgrown pickup truck for a fine little car, and you're going to learn to drive. Then you can chauffeur me around."

Gretchen's smile erased the worry lines in her face. "Learning to drive. Flying to Kentucky. My world is spinning so fast, Angel. I hope I can keep up."

After supper, Sam made good on his promise to drive Gretchen and Bella home. Bella sat in the back seat listening to her iPod until they pulled into Gretchen's driveway. "Well, it's been a mighty fine day at Twin Oaks, ladies. I'm so glad you could join us."

"It was indeed a fine day. We are so grateful to have been included at your Thanksgiving table." Gretchen reached to open the car door.

"But I'd sure sleep a whole lot better if I knew what's troubling you besides the adoption. You know I'll take care of that. You hid it pretty good all day long, but Old Sam's just got a sense about these things. So why don't you just tell me what's on your mind?"

Gretchen looked to see that Bella was still occupied with her music before she told Sam about the phone calls she had been getting, the ones where no one spoke, and then yesterday's caller who mentioned the money, his money.

This came as no surprise to Sam. He never figured whoever was dealing with Ernesto would just walk quietly away from this much money, but the sheriff still needed time and some more evidence to put this case together. Sam was unable to persuade her to return to Twin Oaks for the night, but he reassured her that her phone would be tapped tomorrow and the deputy would drive by several times during the night.

They said their good nights, but Sam wouldn't pull away until Gretchen and Bella were securely inside and the outside lights were on. He called them once he got back to Twin Oaks to verify they were safe. Having his Thanksgiving end on this note riled him but also gave him new ideas about how to get this whole case solved once and for all.

■ ■ ■ ■

It was dusk and the wind was picking up in Myrtle Beach, bringing a damp chill in through the unsealed glass doors. The apartment was still and quiet except for Brahms's *Requiem* coming from the CD player. Skeeter had gone with Chub to Hilton Head and wouldn't be back until Saturday. Karina's half-eaten bowl of canned tomato soup and part of a cold grilled cheese sandwich were still on her plate on the coffee table, along with the contents from her purse, which she had dumped onto the table.

She picked up the check. News that Ernesto was not her biological father brought relief more than anything. Through her childhood, she had wondered about her mammá's past, and the answers her mammá gave were never quite enough to complete the picture. Her ninth-grade biology lessons initiated questions of her parentage when she learned that dark eyes and dark hair are usually dominant in offspring. She had nothing of Ernesto's black wavy hair or his large, black eyes or his deeply tanned skin. She was her mammá's child as though she had sprung from her head like Minerva

478

sprang from the forehead of Zeus.

The question of why Gretchen had stayed with him hit too close to home for her to ask. Skeeter was no better. Thank God, she had never married him. That made things simpler if she decided to leave. And he had made it clear he wanted no part of having Bella around.

Bella, her daughter, her rare progeny and a gift to the world, so Mammá said. Some gift. Almost a teenager and couldn't dress herself without help. An autistic savant requiring round-the-clock care for her lifetime. So much for the child genius she was expecting to make her life easier. This reality was like taking the diamond ring Chuck had given her to the pawnshop. She had wanted to get married, so he bought her an engagement ring, took a road job with a band, left three weeks later, and never came back. When it was apparent Chuck was history, a trip to the pawnshop revealed the ring was about as worthless as Chuck. Just glass. Nobody and no money to ensure her future. It was happening again.

She ran her fingers across her mammá's signature on the check. Twenty thousand and possibly more where that came from. She picked up the stack of adoption papers on the table and turned to the fourth page where there was a blank line for her signature. If the signature of Gretchen Silva was good for twenty thousand on this check, Karina wondered how much her own signature on the adoption papers was worth.

She sat silently listening to Brahms, lost in her thoughts. As the soprano began the fifth movement, Karina's crystal clear, natural voice soared with the recording.

"Look upon me:
I suffered for a little time;
toil and labor were mine,
and I have found, at last, comfort."

CHAPTER TWENTY-FIVE: GETTING READY

Smells of gingerbread and sounds of Bella's repetitive playing filled the studio. Caroline stepped back from the window and checked the garland. With three red velvet bows, a hot glue gun, and a few seedpods from the magnolia tree, her piano would be perfectly framed in the bay window. The oven's buzzer alerted her that in less than thirty seconds her gingersnaps would be charred, and no amount of white chocolate would cover the taste of burn.

Gretchen had volunteered to do most of the baking for her students' Christmas recital, and after Angel's lecture that it was time to allow Gretchen to return some favors, Caroline had accepted the offer. Gretchen's excitement proved that Angel was right yet again.

Caroline grabbed her Santa Claus oven mitts and went for the cookies before she turned off the buzzer. The phone rang as she slid the cookies onto a rack to cool. "Hello. This is Caroline." She held the phone to her shoulder as she removed the quilted red mitts from her hands.

"Merry Christmas, Caroline. It's Hank. Just thought you'd want to know your programs for your Christmas recital are done. Hope you don't mind, but I noel-ed 'em up a bit with some clip art and printed 'em on green paper."

Caroline cringed, but Hank would never know it. "Oh, thank you, Hank. I'm certain it will be just fine. I'll pick them up during lunch." She moved closer to the kitchen door so that she could hear him. Bella had been completely unbothered by the buzzer or the telephone ring and continued to play with gusto.

"Rotary Club meets today, so I'm closin' up for a spell. I'll leave 'em in a brown bag next to the front door."

"In that case, I'll get there before lunch, and how much do I owe you?"

"Oh, don't hurry, it's not rainin' and nobody'll bother these programs. Who around here's gonna have a Christmas recital but Caroline Carlyle?"

"I suppose you're right, but I still need to bring a check."

"Well, I've been thinkin' about that. I see

where this savant girl is playin' on the program. What would you say if we just trade? I'll give you the printin' if you'll give me and my little wife two seats to hear your students at Christmas."

She didn't tell him that Bella was playing her heart out right this minute. She imagined Hank was trying to get rid of Christmas green paper. "That's certainly fair, but I'll give you the seats and pay you for the printing."

"I wasn't exactly finished. The only other thing we'd really like is if you'd sing something for us. Just some pretty Christmas song you think we'd like. My wife's been ailing a bit lately, and I think it'd make her smile if I bought her a Christmas dress and took her to something fancy like your Christmas recital."

"Your wife's blessed to have you as her husband. You're a thoughtful man, Hank, and you'll be treated as honored guests at my Christmas recital. I'll pick up the programs around midday." She hung up the phone and tried to imagine the dress he would choose for Maureen, whose shape was somewhere between a wine barrel and an okra hamper.

Sam had accompanied Gretchen for her appearance before the judge today, and

Caroline offered to keep Bella. She would pick up the programs after Gretchen returned for Bella.

With the recital programs in hand, her December checklist would be almost complete. Studio decorated. Ned and Fred on board to pick up and arrange the folding chairs. Polly delivering the poinsettias. Gretchen catering. Caroline couldn't tell if her mother had been hurt or relieved not to have to cater the recital this Christmas, so she had called her several times to ask for advice and to get a cookie recipe.

On another page in her calendar, another list was almost completed. Her Christmas shopping was done, and after a quick Saturday trip to Ferngrove, her simply wrapped presents would be scattered among the artfully wrapped gift boxes under her mother's Christmas tree. The blue velvet dress she had chosen for the Rockwater recital was hanging in her closet. Some new wool slacks and a couple of holiday sweaters rounded out the shopping for her Kentucky trip. Watching Gretchen shop had been the best shopping experience ever.

A solo Christmas recital had motivated her to learn a few seasonal selections to add to her program, but a few of her own arrangements had lessened the memorization process. Her hours of practice were over, and her program was polished with two weeks left before the performance.

Ned hummed along with the Bing Crosby Christmas recording coming from inside the sunroom at Twin Oaks. He balanced himself on the ladder outside the window. "Fred, pick up that nail I just dropped."

"Why don't you keep some extra nails in your pocket like Pa told you to do?" Fred had fussed all morning as he untangled the strings of Christmas lights.

"I have some in my pocket, but it'd take a lot less time for you to just hand me the nail so I don't have to take off my gloves and this heavy jacket." He harmonized with Bing.

Fred hung the untangled string of Christmas lights on the wooden porch rocker, walked over to the ladder, and picked up the nail. "If I hand you this nail, will you please just shut up and let Bing sing all by hisself?"

"What I want to know is, did you eat razor blades for breakfast when I wasn't lookin'? You been sharp-tongued all mornin', and it's Christmas."

"Christmas. Yeah, it's Christmas, and we been stringin' and unstringin' these lights

485

for Miss Angel for how many years? And how many times have I told you to put 'em up right so they don't come out lookin' like my kite twine the rooster got into?"

"Well, I'll trade jobs with you, Fred." He started singing again.

Fred walked off mumbling. "Trade jobs. Huh . . . you know I don't like ladders."

They finished their job. Icicle lights hung from the eaves of the porch that surrounded the house, and the cedar bushes on each side of the steps were covered in a net of tiny bulbs. "Well, it's done one more time. Let's check 'em out." With the plug in his hand, Ned walked to the electrical outlet next to the front door.

"You just slow your mules, brother. You done that last year. It's my turn to plug 'em in this year." Fred took the cord from his twin's hand.

"Well, just plug 'em in, and maybe it'll give you a little Christmas spirit." Ned held his breath, knowing if the lights didn't come on, they'd spend the afternoon checking one bulb at a time until they found the culprit.

Every light came on, and within thirty seconds, the lights covering the cedar bushes began to twinkle. "Hallelujah and Merry Christmas. Well, ain't that just beautiful?" Ned said as Bing sang "It's Beginning to Look a Lot Like Christmas."

"It's beautiful iffen you like white lights. But what I can't understand is why don't she get some of them all-colored lights?" Fred fussed.

"I suppose 'cause Miss Angel likes white lights." He walked up the porch steps and grabbed a couple of boxes. "Here, take these, and I'll go tell Miss Angel we're ready for the garland and bows that go on the brick wall out front. And when we finish that job, we'll go see if Mabel's serving meat loaf and mashed potatoes today." He checked to see if his twin was smiling.

He was.

"I think that's enough, don't you?" Angel stood in the doorway to the living room where Hattie was draping silver icicles on the tree. She had learned years ago to watch Hattie carefully with the Christmas decorations after it took her until May to scrape the last sprayed-on snowflakes off the lead glass windows across the front of the house.

"Well, I suppose any Christmas decorations is enough for somebody who ain't even gonna be home for Christmas." Hattie picked up the last icicles on the floor and tossed them on the tree.

"We had to decorate or else I'd be dealing

with Caroline, and I certainly don't want to spoil Mr. Adair's surprise."

"Ooo-eeee. You and Mr. Sam flyin' up there on that private plane to surprise Caroline for her recital. Now that's somethin'. That Mr. Adair done thought o' ever'thing, didn't he?"

"I can't exactly tell what all Mr. Adair's thinking these days, but whatever it is, I'm certain it's tasteful and lovely." Angel, dressed in the red sweats she had worn for years when she decorated the house for Christmas, waddled across the living room and moved a couple of the Christmas ornaments.

Hattie yanked on Angel's shirt sleeve. "What you got all over the sleeve of that red sweatshirt? You done ruined your red sweats with pink paint?"

Angel looked. "It appears that I did. I got up early this morning, trying to finish my project. I'm going to make some spiced tea. Would you like some, Hattie?"

"Sure would, and I'd like to sit a spell while I drink it. But before I do, I gotta confess. I peeked in the bedroom upstairs to see your project a couple of weeks ago. It's mighty beautiful. I just can't wait to see it finished."

"I knew you'd been in there just like I

knew you'd confess." She winked at Hattie, took her arm, and walked arm in arm to the kitchen. "Now you sit while I make the tea."

The jingling on the porch door announced Sam's arrival. "Well, it appears from the lights on the porch that Christmas is coming." He took off his hat and coat and hung them on the hall tree next to the kitchen door.

"Sure is, and you're in time for a cup of spiced tea. Care for some?" Angel held the teakettle under the cold-water tap.

"I think I would, and we'll begin the season this morning. After all, we have something to celebrate." He sat down at his place at the breakfast table next to Hattie.

"In that case, Hattie, would you get the Christmas teapot from the dining room?"

"Is tea strong enough for the celebration or should I get the eggnog?" She chuckled.

"A little early for eggnog." Angel reached for the tea canister. "So, tell us, how did things go before the judge?"

"Just like they should have gone. Gretchen is now divorced. The decree is signed and sealed, and the judge told us that Ernesto's residence is now in a cellblock in the Metro State Prison in Dekalb County as of Tuesday."

"And Gretchen, how is she?"

"Just fine. She drove me to the courthouse and parallel parked. That's quite a feat for somebody who's just learning to drive."

"I've already heard enough about her driving for the last week. I'm just a bit more interested in what the judge had to say." Angel pushed up the sleeves of her red sweatshirt.

"Well, before he signed the decree, the judge went through the formalities of the questions. Then it took him all of about thirty seconds to pronounce it was done after her answers. And she took the news of Ernesto's incarceration in stride. She's going to be just fine."

"Praise the Lord." Hattie ran warm water and rinsed out the teapot.

"Oh yes, this week has given us great cause to celebrate. Ernesto's guilty plea and sentencing. Gretchen's divorced and learning to drive — that makes for a free woman. That's a significant week in anyone's life." Angel heard Sam, but the tension in his face didn't match his words.

"For sure. Miss Gretchen's a free woman, a free woman indeed." Hattie smiled.

Angel clapped her hands, hoping to change Sam's mood. "Now, if we can just get the adoption settled, then she'll be a truly happy, free woman." Angel watched the wrinkles grow deeper in Sam's brow. She knew Sam never worried unless there was good cause.

"Your marriage to Ernesto is over?" Caroline sat at her kitchen table while Gretchen gave her report over gingersnaps.

"Yes. My marriage is over. And talking to the judge was not so painful. He asked me three questions, I answered, he signed the paper, and said that it was done. My mind was puzzled when I tried to imagine what it would be like, and it was so different, so . . ." Gretchen struggled for words.

"So businesslike? So cold? So unemotional?" Such a contrast to Bella's beautiful piano playing in the other room.

"Yes. It was all those things, and now I feel a strangeness. How does one erase thirty years of two lives with three questions and a signature? And without tears and without ceremony?" Gretchen turned to look out the kitchen window over the sink.

"Guess you're right. We pay for huge weddings and we celebrate. And a divorce is like a funeral, but there's no formal closure."

"Like a death, but I must learn not to carry the corpse around with me." Gretchen wiped a tear from her cheek. "It is over and buried."

Caroline saw beyond Gretchen's serene outward show. "Why don't you just cry or scream or do something to let all this out?"

Gretchen turned to her. "I must not. That behavior would be so upsetting to Bella. I will be fine."

"But take time for yourself. I'll keep Bella, and you can just go home and cry for a while or take a walk or listen to some music. She'll be fine here with me."

"You are so wonderful, my friend. But I will take Bella with me, and we will do something together. She loves the Christmas movies, and she busies herself with wrapping presents and tying ribbons. She wants to wrap everything in sight, and then she wants to unwrap it and wrap it again." A smile visited her face.

"I trust you. You know what's best for you. But I'm just glad it's settled and over. Now you can really begin to think about the future." Caroline pulled a plastic container from the cabinet.

"I can after one more issue is reconciled — Bella's adoption."

"Still no word from Karina?" Caroline began to put the cooled gingersnaps into the storage container.

"No word. Sam did explain something this

morning. He could do a search for her. She did say that she lived in Myrtle Beach, but I do not know if she is always a truth teller."

"But it's a place to start."

"If only I had gotten the tag number from her car, they could locate her."

Caroline closed the lid on the container and moved it to the countertop. "That's true, but it's still no guarantee she'll sign the papers once you locate her. Maybe it's better not to find her. That way they can run the announcement in the paper, and if she doesn't come back, then you automatically adopt Bella."

"That is exactly what Sam says. As much as I want Karina to be a part of our lives, I know it must be so only if she wants it that way. I miss her and long for her to return to us and to how she was taught, but I have grown accustomed to waiting. I will wait always for her, but I will not wait on the adoption."

"That's right. You need passports so the two of you can make your trip to Austria."

"Yes. I would so like to go in the spring, or I will wait until summer if you will go with us."

Caroline saw the smile return to Gretchen's face with her thoughts of her homeland and of seeing her family again. "That sounds perfectly lovely, but could we get through this recital and our Christmas in Rockwater before we make those plans?"

Gretchen embraced Caroline. "Yes, my little friend. Let us enjoy a perfectly lovely Christmas, and then we will make our plans."

Wyatt Spencer never hesitated to start or finish a conversation about anything with anyone. But with Caroline, he was different. Since his early November visit to Moss Point and revealing his personal interest in her, he now walked a tightrope in talking even about business. But he needed to speak with her. He took a deep breath and dialed her number.

Caroline was standing at the door watching Gretchen cautiously back out of the driveway when the phone rang. She answered. "Oh, hello, Wyatt."

"Hi, Caroline. We haven't spoken since before Thanksgiving, and I wanted to see how things are progressing in Moss Point." His pre-Thanksgiving call had yielded scarce information. Caroline cut the call very short after telling him about her unpleasant encounter with Dr. Elena Daniels in the hallway after the press conference. "I hope your Thanksgiving was an enjoyable one with family." *I hope it didn't include Roderick Adair.*

"It was lovely. Thanks for asking. Actually, you just missed Gretchen and Bella."

"Oh, I'm sorry. I trust they're doing well?"

"I think they are. Gretchen appeared before the judge this morning. She was granted her divorce. Finally, one thing is settled."

"That's good. Check that one off." He needed to report before he posed the big question. "Just wanted you to know I've made some progress on this end of things too." He paused.

"Progress?"

"Yes. I've had a conversation with Dr. Daniels. Your report of her conduct in the hallway after the press conference was very disturbing to me. And when I spoke with her, I was even more disturbed."

"Can't imagine you disturbed."

He was glad she couldn't see the puzzled look on his face. What did she mean? "I don't usually allow too much to disturb me, but I really made a mistake by putting Elena on my team."

"Yes, but you dismissed her before the press conference."

"I did. At least I got her off the team, but it didn't keep her from following through

495

with her own plans. She's very resourceful. Elena did her own research and hired someone to find Bella's mother."

"Dr. Daniels found Karina?"

"Seems she knows where Karina is and apparently has contacted her, but I don't think they've met."

"Well that explains some things. Karina showed up in Moss Point for Thanksgiving, intending to take Bella back to South Carolina with her."

"Did she?"

Wyatt made notes as Caroline explained what happened during Karina's visit and about the twenty thousand dollars Gretchen gave her daughter.

"I'm so sorry. I think Dr. Daniels may have instigated this in some way, but I don't want you worrying about it." He now had enough information to threaten Elena with ethics violations that would take care of her for good.

"I don't really worry about Karina taking Bella or even some court giving Bella to her, but all this unnecessary drama really stresses Gretchen."

"Well, you remind Gretchen that I will personally take responsibility for her and Bella when they get to Athens." He hesitated. "We'll see to it that Bella gets the best this institution has to offer, and that Gretchen will be pleased and compensated. And since you'll be here, too, you can make certain we honor our commitment."

"I'm sorry, Wyatt, but I really do need to go now."

Wyatt was puzzled. This was new territory. No other woman bailed on him. "Certainly. We can talk about all this later. Just know that I'll take care of Dr. Daniels, and don't give her another thought. Give my best to Gretchen and Bella, and tell them I hope to see them during the Christmas holidays."

"I will tell them, and goodbye, Wyatt."

"Bye." He heard the click of her phone in the middle of his "bye." He gained no knowledge of Caroline's plans and no crack in her armor where he was concerned. Gretchen's divorce would free her to make a decision, and he didn't need Elena Daniels negatively influencing that decision. He had a job to do, and he would enjoy ensuring Elena Daniels's exit.

Gretchen had locked the door of their house earlier that morning as Ernesto's wife, but when she returned, she crossed the threshold of her house as a single woman. Her new blue chair sat in the place of Ernesto's

497

ragged lounge chair. Choices and decisions were now hers, and no permission was needed. "Bella, I have an idea. The sun is shining, and I would like to go for a nice, long walk before lunch. Or maybe we'll just walk by the drugstore and have a chocolate soda for lunch. Would you like that?"

In step with the music on her iPod, Bella was already halfway to her room and did not respond.

The ringing of the phone quenched Gretchen's lighthearted spirit. Even though there had only been two or three suspicious calls in the last week, the piercing ring still set her on edge. She laid her keys on the sofa table and sat in her chair to answer. "Hello."

"You're home."

The gruff voice was unmistakable. "Yes, Ernesto, I am home."

"Well, ain't that nice. You're home, and I'm standing in a hallway making my weekly phone call."

She was silent.

"Are you there? You'd better answer me, woman."

"I am here. Why are you calling?"

"My lawyer called today and said we're divorced. You got everything you wanted, but you didn't do what I told you to do."

"Yes, we are divorced, and I have nothing more to say to you." She rolled the phone cord in her sweaty palm, working up the courage to hang up.

"Then you'd better listen. I warned you. There are some people still expecting a delivery from you. You got one more chance." His voice grew louder. "Do you hear me? You know what to do, and if you don't . . ."

Gretchen calmly laid the receiver back in its cradle. Weak-kneed, she checked on Bella before phoning Sam with the report of Ernesto's threat.

CHAPTER TWENTY-SIX:
ROCKWATER WAITS

Across the courtyard from the main house, Roderick sat at the desk in his office. The home contained so much life when he was a child, yet was tomb-like after the death of his mother. He could not bring himself to live in the main house, but neither did he have any interest in selling it. It was home.

He was quite comfortable in the cottage and office he had built just twenty yards from the kitchen door. It was nestled in the shadow of his boyhood tree house in the oak tree that shaded the courtyard. The cottage was where he lived and worked. Liz, his assistant, had her office in a transformed mudroom right next to the kitchen in the main house.

Roderick picked up the package Liz had left on his desk earlier. He knew she'd give the designer dress she purchased for his Christmas party to know what was in the box that had arrived from Hong Kong. He noted her curiosity when she asked, "Did you leave something like your cufflinks in the Hong Kong hotel on your last trip?"

He muffled his grin. "Articles forgotten in a hotel don't usually arrive in a box with a jeweler's return address."

She left a trail of indignation when she swooshed in front of his desk and out the door.

He would open the package later and check to see if it was to his liking before he'd ask Lilah to wrap it. He trusted her with everything, all his secrets and his sufferings, and with all the details related to this Christmas.

He knew the gardener and the stable hand had been retrieving boxes of decorations from the attic since mid-November so that Lilah could take inventory and determine what was needed. Some of the items had been stored so long they were no longer usable, and Lilah suggested calling in a professional.

Wanting this to be the perfect Christmas, Roderick took her advice and called Mary Ann Rhodes, a decorator who had been his mother's friend.

Lilah was pleased. "You did the right thing, Roderick. Ms. Rhodes said she knew exactly how to restore the grandeur of

Christmas at Rockwater. In fact, I think she learned a thing or two from your mother's direction. Now, I'd be truly happy if Liz would break out with a case of untreatable hairy red warts and be confined to home until January. I don't know why you put up with that woman."

He wondered that himself sometimes. From the picture window in his office, he watched the activity all morning — Lilah's silhouette passing across the loggia, delivery trucks coming in the back gate, and men hauling large boxes going in and out of the house. By tomorrow the greening of Rockwater would be complete and all that would be left to do was dressing it with ribbons and ornaments and fresh flowers. He had requested red roses and white irises. Mrs. Rhodes agreed and suggested several crystal bowls with paperwhites and fresh holly, delivered so the blossoms and the berries would be at their peak for the recital.

After making a couple of phone calls and returning a few emails, he picked up the small package from Hong Kong again. The clock struck noon. Lilah would have his lunch ready. He laid the package back down on his desk, got up to close the glass doors to the fireplace, and opted out of getting his jacket for the short walk across the court-yard.

He opened the back door of the main house to a box-filled kitchen with no Lilah in sight and no sign of lunch. Quietly, he made grilled cheese sandwiches and heated the leftover chili from last night. He was putting two plates and two soup bowls on the breakfast table when Lilah almost exploded into the kitchen.

"Slow down, slow down. Lunch is ready. What would you like to drink?" Roderick asked.

"Lord, have mercy, don't you ask me that question right now, Roderick Adair. I might just tell you to get the bottle from the cabinet above the refrigerator. I cannot believe the morning's gone and I've been busier than the beavers that dammed up your creek last spring. I just plumb forgot about your lunch."

"Well, have a seat, and tell me what you've been doing while I get you a glass of ice water. With all these boxes, bringing out anything but water would be unwise." He smiled at the thought of Lilah taking a nip at lunchtime.

"You, for certain, have spoken the truth. I'm not going home till these boxes are emptied and back in the barn and the seven

Christmas trees are standing tall and proud where they're supposed to be." She spread the paper napkin in her lap and picked up her spoon.

"Lilah, you cannot possibly decorate seven Christmas trees this afternoon." He delivered the grilled cheese sandwiches from the griddle.

"Truth again. Mrs. Rhodes is taking care of that with some of her help, but I have to boss those men around to get the trees put up and the boxes out of the way and get the artificial garland hung. I didn't know it was so much work bossing folks around."

Roderick brought the two bowls of chili to the table and sat down. "Do you need Liz's help?"

"For what? You just keep her busy in her office and outta my hair. I wouldn't want her to chip a fingernail." She took a bite of her sandwich and pinched the stringy cheese with her fingers, her eyes widening as Liz walked in from her office next to the kitchen and poured herself a cup of coffee.

"What was that about a chipped fingernail?" She added cream to her coffee and stirred.

Roderick looked at Lilah. He wanted to see how she'd get out of this one.

"Nothing. You didn't hear right. I was just

504

telling Roderick we need to be careful with the small nails to hang the mistletoe in the doorframes. We don't want them chipping the paint. And with Caroline Carlyle here for ten days, we're hanging mistletoe in every doorframe of this whole house — even the bathrooms and closets."

Roderick grinned as Liz's nostrils flared and Lilah's eyes bulged.

"Well, if you'll excuse me . . ." Liz strutted out of the kitchen.

"You're certainly excused." When Liz was out of sight, Lilah added, "And you're certainly one big excuse for . . ."

Roderick laughed out loud, partly out of amusement but mostly out of covering what Lilah was about to say. He had no interest in refereeing a catfight on a cold December afternoon.

"She's been quizzing me up and down about that little box that arrived special delivery from Hong Kong this morning." She winked at Roderick. "You'd better hide that box."

The afternoon passed with a continued flurry of movement in and around the big house, and he had the ringside seat at his desk. He assumed Liz had sulked in her office all afternoon, for she only put two calls through, and she hadn't come by before she left for the day. Lilah had enjoyed herself and was probably still patting herself on the back for the big lob she slammed Liz with at lunch.

The sun had long slipped beneath the horizon, and the night was perfectly clear, cold, and still. Roderick paced between the picture window, where the night sky looked like black velvet dotted with diamonds, and the fireplace with its embers of slow-burning oak giving the room a burnt sienna hue. He had never spent so much time or so much pacing over a business call, but this one had to be just right. He took the last sip of the aged brandy and put his glass down. He picked up the phone and held it tightly, dialing slowly and deliberately.

A welcoming male voice answered. "Hello."

"Hello, Mr. Carlyle. This is Roderick Adair. I hope you're well."

"Well, we're just fine and many thanks for asking, Roderick. I'd be better though if you'd just call me Jay. It's good to hear from you, and how are you, young man?"

Roderick could hear orchestral music in the background. "I'm also very well, thank you."

Before Roderick could say another word,

Jay commented, "So, I hear my little girl is spending Christmas in Kentucky this year. Oh, we'll miss her, but this is the first time we've seen her so excited in a spell."

Roderick's grip on the phone relaxed. "I'm so glad to hear you say that. I wasn't quite sure if you'd even answer my phone call. Caroline has told me that this will be the first Christmas she's ever spent away from home."

"Yes, that's true, and it won't be the same without her, but we're planning a bit of an early Christmas gathering around here this weekend. She's coming home, and her brothers and their families will be here."

"I know it will be an enjoyable time for your family." Roderick was ready to get down to business. "I don't want to take up too much of your time, and I suppose it's rather bold of me to ask another favor of you."

"Ask away. Sometimes we get things we don't ask for, but not usually."

Caroline had told Roderick of her father's humor and witticisms. He already liked J. Rogers Carlyle. "You're right, and I don't want to take the chance. Actually, I have two requests." Roderick picked up the brandy glass and twirled it in his fingers. "I'd like you and Mrs. Carlyle to come to

Rockwater for Caroline's recital. I'll pick you up on Tuesday and fly you back home the next day. I'd really appreciate it if you'd come, and I know it would be a great surprise for Caroline."

"Well, my goodness, here all this time I thought you were such a smart fellow, and now I find out you don't know the difference between asking someone for a favor and offering them the best present that parents of a gifted young pianist could receive this Christmas."

Roderick could hear Jay's muffled laughter and his calling out to his wife. "Martha, scrape the cookie dough off your hands, and come in here. We have something to talk about." Then he said to Roderick, "Could you give us just a minute? My wife's in the kitchen and we need to have a family meeting right quick like."

"Of course. Would you like me to call back a little later?"

"No need for that. You don't know my Martha. I can assure you this will take about thirty seconds to get a decision."

Roderick heard the explanation Jay gave Martha, and in short order, Jay was back on the phone.

"Roderick? You still there?" he asked.

"Yes sir, right here."

"Martha and I would be so pleased to accept your invitation, but Martha needs to get back home that evening if it's not too much trouble. She has something she has to do early the next morning to get ready for Christmas here."

"That will be fine, although there is a lovely room for you right here at Rockwater." Roderick explained that he had invited the Meadows to come for Christmas and they'd be flying to Kentucky together on Tuesday. "I'll make all the arrangements and give you a call, and of course we won't let Caroline know about this. It would spoil our pleasure at seeing her face when you walk through the door." He hesitated. "There's just one other thing. I know how much Caroline loves her mother's fruitcake. Do you suppose it would be too much to ask if Mrs. Carlyle would bring one for Caroline's Christmas?"

Jay laughed out loud. "Just a minute."

Roderick could hear Martha's voice in the background. "You tell Roderick that I'll hand deliver it and cut the first slice for him."

His mission accomplished, Roderick stoked the fire and watched the sparks rise and disappear. He imagined Caroline at her piano in her studio practicing this evening, and then he pictured her at the piano in his loggia, against the windows framing another black velvet sky, only she'd replace the sparkling stars as she brought her gift of music. He smiled. *Caroline Carlyle, this will be a Christmas to remember.*

"Thirty thousand dollars? You sent Karina thirty thousand dollars?" Caroline shouted into her phone. She had never used this tone of voice with Gretchen.

"Yes. I did. But she promised to sign the adoption papers." Gretchen was calm.

"But that's like blackmail or extortion or something illegal. She can't do that."

"How can it be illegal to pay for your daughter's education?"

"It wouldn't be, but that's not exactly what this is." She sat at her desk as she talked.

"I am giving Karina fifty thousand to pay for her college education . . ."

Caroline interrupted her. "Wait a minute, you just said thirty thousand. Now what's this with fifty?"

"When she was here at Thanksgiving, I gave her twenty thousand. And now that the attorney has found her, I am giving her thirty thousand more, and hopefully she will give us the gift of Bella's legal adoption."

"That's just wrong, just plain wrong, Gretchen."

"I am sorry that you do not agree, but it is money that will help Karina get an education, something I could not provide for her before."

Caroline walked a fine line. She never wanted to offend Gretchen by speaking ill of her daughter, but she couldn't allow Gretchen's goodness and naivete to cost her so much. "But that's a lot of money, and you have to think about yourself and Bella." The doorbell rang. It was too early for her last afternoon of piano students before Saturday afternoon's recital. "Hang on just a second, Gretchen, someone's ringing the bell."

Smiling, Polly stood at the terrace door behind a glass bowl filled with white irises and holly. Caroline was white-glove polite but quickly explained she was on an important call. Polly was still smiling when she waved goodbye and walked around the corner to her van.

"I'm sorry, Gretchen. I'm back."

"If you need to go, we can talk later."

"No, everything's fine. Polly just delivered some flowers. Probably from the parents of one of my students. I think they get together and take turns sending flowers just before a recital."

"Oh, the student recital. I am almost done with the baking. Bella and I will bring everything over tomorrow morning."

"Thank you, Gretchen, but let's finish the conversation about the money you're shoveling into Karina's bank account." She pulled a tissue from the box and wiped up the droplets of water around the base of the bowl of flowers.

"Until she decides to come home, she has money for her education."

Caroline thought of how Karina might use the money, but, somehow, she couldn't imagine that Gretchen would be pleased if she knew. "But —"

"Let us not speak of this again. It is done, and I will trust and pray that Karina will do what is right. If she does not, then I have done what I think is good and fair. Please, Caroline, trust me and trust in that part of Karina that is good."

She had no choice. "Only because you ask me. We won't talk about this anymore, but what about telling Sam?"

"Sam knows." Gretchen paused. "There is something else that Sam knows, and I have not told you." She calmly told Caroline of the suspicious calls and of the threats from

Ernesto and the man trying to disguise his voice.

Feeling like someone had punched her in the gut, Caroline sat at her desk to listen. "Why didn't you tell me?"

"Because there was nothing you could do, and I did not want you to worry. I tell you now because I do not like keeping secrets from you, and there is no need to worry. Sam and the sheriff are taking care of things."

"What do you mean taking care of things?"

"You know about the box and the money. The sheriff is gathering all the evidence to prosecute the others involved in the selling of these drugs."

"I'm so sorry I didn't know you were dealing with all this on top of everything else. And you feel safe, and Sam thinks you're safe too?"

"Yes, I am safe, and we have things to do. I have cookies to bake. I am sorry I did not tell you these things sooner, my friend. I just did not want you to worry. Everything will be fine. Let us not speak of these things again."

"I know. I know. Thanks, Gretchen. See you tomorrow." She held the phone in her hand.

Her suspicion of Karina's intentions paled when she thought about threatening phone calls. *Karina appears only days after Bella is introduced to the world with national news coverage in television and print. Coincidence? Not even someone as naive as I am would gamble on those odds.*

The receiver never touched the phone before she dialed Sam's number. No polite conversation, just a direct question. "Sam, Gretchen just told me about what's going on. Are you certain that she and Bella are really safe?"

Sam answered, "Well, good afternoon to you too. Sounds like you got your knickers in a twist. When did you ever know ol' Sam not to take care of business? Gretchen and Bella are safe. Caleb has the officers patrolling the area day and night. He's got a tap on her phone, and he's about to close this investigation. They're all going to jail."

"Okay, so she's safe, but this whole thing about giving money to Karina is not likely to come to any good end."

"Took care of that as well. How do you think Karina would fare in court if it ever came to that? No judge is going to award her custody. She abandoned her daughter. She's been gone for twelve years, and she's taken fifty thousand dollars. Don't you worry. Gretchen will get custody of Bella, and there'll be no more money handed over to Karina. All we can do now is to wait and see if she keeps her end of the bargain. And if she doesn't, I still remember how to write a letter that'll scare her into next August."

Caroline's fears were calmed, but Karina held the keys to Gretchen's return to Austria. Without legal adoption, there would be no passport for Bella and no trip to the homeland. Caroline knew how much this trip meant to Gretchen, and she knew that revisiting one's past was like crawling into a shadowy cave with skeletons poking out of dark crevices. She hoped that Gretchen would find a buried treasure instead of hidden bones.

The holly pricked her finger as she reached for the card protruding from the iris stems. Reaching for the damp tissue she had used to wipe the water droplets off the vase, she wiped her finger and opened the card. "Twelve of your favorite blossoms, one for each day before your arrival at Rockwater. But who's counting? Awaiting, Roderick."

At the reading of the card, the tautness in her face dissolved into softness again, like watercolors making contact with wet paper.

Tuesday afternoon brought Polly to Caroline's door again, smiling through another arrangement of white irises with stems of holly, only the card read eleven days this time. Wednesday brought Gretchen's baked treats for the recital, and yet another visit from Polly with ten irises. Roderick was marking off the days like Caroline's mother marked off Advent with the pocketed fabric calendar she made. Each of the twenty-five pockets held three treats, one each for her and James and TJ, and each day, they untied the ribbon and reached in for things like peppermint candy or a coupon good for an extra cookie. When all the ribbons were untied, it was time for the real celebration.

The following days passed quickly. Phone calls to her parents and Betsy in Ferngrove. Nightly conversations with Roderick. The daily crystal containers of white irises arrived, always with one less than the day before. Another Christmas student recital. Her Sunday replacement at the church was secured. All the gifts were wrapped. Her packing was done. Another shopping trip to Atlanta with Gretchen, who hadn't even owned a suitcase before, and now she had filled four with new clothes for their trip to Rockwater.

Saturday morning arrived. Before Caroline could dress and head up to the main house for breakfast and slip Christmas presents under Sam and Angel's tree, the doorbell rang. This time, Polly's broad, isn't-this-something smile was not peeping through irises. Instead, she handed Caroline one long-stemmed red rose, no vase, no ribbon, only a card that read, "No longer waiting. Tomorrow, you'll walk through the doors of Rockwater again. Anticipating, Roderick."

With eyes closed, she inhaled the rose's fragrance and imagined just like Betsy told her to do. Yes, she would miss Christmas at Ferngrove, her family and Betsy and the babies, but if this Christmas was anything like she imagined, it would certainly be one to remember.

Chapter Twenty-Seven: Music Returns to Rockwater at Christmas

Sunday morning was cold and clear without a cloud in the sky, a perfect day for a flight to Kentucky. Sam and Angel delivered Caroline, Gretchen, and Bella to the local airport with Ned and Fred Pendergrass following, the back of their pea-green pickup loaded with suitcases and boxes. Sam knew going to the airport would be the most excitement Ned and Fred would have during Christmas, so he suggested to Caroline that she ask the twins to handle all the luggage and Christmas packages headed to Rockwater.

The Moss Point delegation lined the fence like magpies, awaiting the arrival of Roderick's plane. Nervously, Ned and Fred, in their overalls and red plaid flannel shirts, stood behind the group. Sam knew Fred loved anything with a motor, and as stoic as Fred was, Sam watched him fight to contain his excitement over seeing his first private jet.

When Sam spotted the plane in the distance, he pointed it out to Bella. Bella's face lit up, and she clapped her hands. Ned and Fred joined her. A few moments after touching down, Acer opened the door of the plane and lowered the steps with the assistance of a one-man ground crew.

The Pendergrass twins waited to see Roderick come through the door of the plane before retrieving the bags from their truck. Sam knew that Ned and Fred had been wary of Caroline flying off with some Kentucky gentleman back in July, and now they would see their fears were unfounded.

Roderick, dressed in a green sweater and a Santa hat, descended the steps and made his way across the tarmac to the fence, where he hugged everyone in the receiving line. Ned and Fred stood still, holding their John Deere caps across their chests, until Sam introduced them to Roderick. Only then did they put on their caps and haul the suitcases and boxes of Christmas presents across the tarmac to planeside, where the crewman loaded them into the belly of the plane.

Before Fred had time to examine the jet, the ladies had disappeared up the stairs into the plane, Sam and Angel had waved goodbye, and the door was shut. They stood on the tarmac and watched the jet take off. Fred said, "Ain't she a beauty?"

"Well, ain't you talkative this morning? And yeah, I'll bet that plane ain't never had so many beauties in it, all dressed up and just a smilin'."

"I wuzn't talkin' about the ladies, brother. Would you look at that plane?"

Sam watched Fred, standing like a statue, never taking his eyes off the jet.

"Something's wrong with you, Fred."

Sam chuckled.

Roderick made hot chocolate for his guests to enjoy on the hour-and-fifteen-minute plane ride to Lexington. Before he took the copilot's seat, he showed Bella the screen where she could watch their course and where they were flying. Between that and her iPod full of Christmas tunes, she was mesmerized for the entire flight.

After a smooth landing in Lexington and a private conversation with Acer about their Tuesday flight plan, Roderick loaded his vehicle and began the drive to Rockwater. "You'd better enjoy the beautiful weather today because I've ordered snow for Christmas."

"Snow. I've never seen a white Christmas,"

Caroline said.

"Oh, I dream of the snow-covered Christmases we had back in Austria. My village was so very beautiful." Gretchen sat in the back seat holding Bella's hand.

"Let it snow, let it snow, let it snow," Bella sang.

"That's right, we're going to let it snow," Roderick said. He pointed out landmarks and horse farms along the drive. "And here we are, the entrance to Rockwater. Sorry, Caroline. We've already had a freeze and one snow, so these grass-covered hills that usually look like green velvet are already brown."

"Brown, but still beautiful. What about your mother's roses?"

"Not to worry, we'll have roses." He slowed as they approached the covered bridge. "Now this is the stream that winds around the property. I took Caroline fishing upstream last summer, and my father built this bridge for my mother."

"He built a bridge for your mother?" Gretchen was wide-eyed.

"He did. The stream narrows in enough places that she could get across, but he built it as shelter from the afternoon showers when she was out riding her horse."

"Caroline told me you have horses."

"And when you come back in the spring, you and Bella can ride, but I have something else in mind this trip." Roderick smiled at Caroline, who had been sitting quietly in the passenger's seat.

"I can see you riding every day across these hills. You must feel so free," Gretchen said.

Roderick's tone changed. "Actually, I don't ride."

"You do not ride?"

"No. I leave that pleasure for others. I haven't ridden in many years." He stopped the vehicle and pointed in the opposite direction. "There's Rockwater, made from the stones gathered from the stream we just crossed. If you look, you can see the house briefly before we round this next curve."

Bella clapped her hands. "Rockwater. Rockwater." She began to hum *Rockwater Suite.*

Caroline joined her humming. "That's right, Bella. It was this place that inspired me to write *Rockwater Suite* back in the summer. Wonder what we'll be inspired to do this visit?"

They drove along the winding road to the front door of the rock mansion. Lilah met them at the front door and welcomed them while Chip, the stable hand, took care of the luggage. They entered through the huge curved wooden door into the foyer.

"Lilah's the one in charge of dressing Rockwater for Christmas, and you'll see she's been very busy," Roderick said.

Lilah hugged Caroline like she was a long-lost daughter. "Oooh, there'll be music in this house again." She stepped back. "And you brought your friends. This must be Mrs. Silva."

"Oh, please call me Gretchen." Gretchen attempted to shake her hand politely before Lilah engulfed her in a hug.

"Gretchen it is, and this must be the beautiful Bella." She moved closer to Bella. "Now Miss Bella, I'm Lilah, and I'll be your best friend around here because I'm also in charge of candy and cookies and Christmas presents. I know we don't know each other very well yet, but it sure would make me happy to give you a hug."

Bella stepped up and silently wrapped her arms tight around Lilah's thick waist.

Roderick noticed the tear rolling from Lilah's eye and down her brown cheek. "Bella gives good hugs, and Lilah's not far behind."

"Bella gives good hugs." Her arms went around Roderick, and she buried her face into his soft cashmere sweater. "Bella gives good hugs."

"Yes, you do, my little canary." Roderick smoothed Bella's hair as her head lay against his chest. He smiled at Caroline. "Now, let me show you to your rooms before lunch. If I know Lilah, she has one of her famous pots of soup for this cold day."

Roderick led them to the grand piano sitting in the loggia, pointing out the parlor to the left and the dining room to the right. He pointed down the hallway to the right where the kitchen, breakfast room, and morning room were in the west wing of the house. Then they passed the library where windows welcomed the sunshine from the east every morning. The U-shaped house was built around a courtyard with flagstone paths, raised flower beds, large urns, and bird feeders disguised as garden art.

Roderick led them through the loggia, past the library, and to the next room. The door, which had remained closed during Caroline's July visit, Roderick now opened with the announcement that this had been his parents' suite and it would be Caroline's during this visit. She had already told him how much she was looking forward to her upstairs, sunshine-yellow and cornflower-blue suite with an outside balcony to the courtyard, but he had other plans.

Creamy, buttery yellow washed the walls of this bedroom suite, which was larger than her entire studio apartment at Twin Oaks. Double French doors on the east side opened to a walled garden, complete with cushioned chairs, a cascade of water coming from the rock wall into a small pond below, and an iron gate leading to the side yard.

Opposite the wall of French doors was a stone fireplace flanked by two large dark green chairs with ottomans and red and yellow throw pillows. Above the rustic mantel was a large, heavily framed portrait of a man and woman. The gentleman stood in the foreground, back turned and faceless to the viewer as he gazed upon the woman on her knees in the garden. She had turned to greet him, her smiling face vibrant as her gloved hand brushed the long curly wisps from her face. "Those are my parents. My father commissioned this painting because that's how he saw her. She lived in her gardens. Father said 'she lived in beauty,' and he was right."

Roderick noted that neither Caroline nor Gretchen uttered a sound as he showed them the room, perhaps out of their sheer dismay or reverence. Floor-length drapes of a Provençal pattern with primary colors framed the windows. The large four-poster bed was covered with a lush deep-red comforter that floated pillows made of fabrics tying the entire room together. An antique French armoire, dresser, and writing desk lined the walls, and original oil paintings of vibrantly colored flowers in an old-world style filled every available inch of wall space.

Near the French doors opening to the garden was another door. Through it, Roderick led Caroline into a luxurious bathroom with travertine floors and shower, white marble countertops, and a large marble tub sitting in the window overlooking the walled garden. A chandelier of hand-blown glass blossoms in red and yellow was suspended above the tub. Potted ferns of various sizes in carefully chosen and aged pots were tucked away in several places in the room. Plush red towels hung on brass towel rods. A tufted red satin chair was positioned in front of a vanity that had been designed for Roderick's mother. A large brass tray held a collection of crystal perfume bottles, and next to it was a large porcelain vase filled with fresh red roses and white irises.

"Are you certain I should stay in this suite?" Caroline asked.

"As certain as I am that Gretchen and

Bella will stay in your suite upstairs." He didn't want to give away any of his secrets. "George and Sarah are coming, and they'll be in the green suite down the hall."

"But wouldn't they prefer your parents' room?"

Caroline's sensitivity was one of the many things he adored about her. "I think not. Your bags are already here, so why don't you unpack and get settled in." He opened the armoire. "I'll knock on your door when lunch is ready."

He led Gretchen and Bella up the stairs to a balcony hallway that looked down into the first-floor loggia. Pointing out his father's office, he led them to their suite — dressed in white, bright yellow, and blue. Covered in a lush white comforter, the four-poster bed was so tall it required a set of wooden steps on each side. Yellow and blue floral pillows rested on the bed. There were more paintings of flowers, a chaise lounge next to the fireplace, and French doors opening to a balcony with stone steps to the terrace. A large bouquet of white roses greeted them on the dresser, and a six-foot Christmas tree decorated in ornaments of brass and glass musical instruments sat next to the hearth. Their bags were already on luggage racks in the walk-in closet.

Roderick knew this was a very long way from their humble house on Third Street in Moss Point, but he had every intention of making this a fairytale Christmas for Gretchen and Bella.

Sunday afternoon was spent exploring the house and grounds. Caroline made a game out of going from room to room, counting the manger scenes, Christmas trees, and candles. Bella repeated the numbers as Caroline counted. The stairs fascinated the adolescent. They climbed them together — eight steps to the landing before turning and climbing eight more to the top, and then back down.

Uncertainty of how Bella would react to a new environment had set Gretchen and Caroline on edge. But now, their fears evaporated.

"Rockwater, my beautiful castle. Rockwater, my beautiful castle." Bella repeated the phrases off and on all afternoon, almost making a song of them. Her midafternoon piano playing brought Lilah to tears again and reminded Caroline of how special Bella was — this angelic girl who lived in a world that was hers and hers alone. And yet, when she played the piano, a part of her musical world vibrated heartstrings and resonated with listeners in their deepest places. Her limitations magnified her rare gifts.

Sunday evening was spent in the library with a roaring fire and a selection from the movies Roderick had purchased for the occasion. Roderick sat in his chair by the window and the fire, and Gretchen and Bella on the sofa. Caroline pondered. *It's too comfortable — so comfortable it's frightening. I wish we could stay here forever, but we can't.*

The sun shone again on Monday, inviting them for a jaunt to the stable to see the horses and an afternoon walk down to Blue Hole. Between activities, they read, watched more movies, and Caroline played through her program with Bella at her side. They took turns playing and singing.

The early morning sun burst through the windows on Tuesday. It was recital day. Caroline had been here before on such a day and knew it'd be as busy as the mall on Christmas Eve. Lilah and the caterer would spend the day preparing. A smorgasbord of finger foods and desserts would be placed on silver trays, chairs in theater fashion would be set up in the loggia, an acre of fresh flowers would adorn tables, and Christmas lights would twinkle throughout the house.

Caroline found a note under her door. "Good morning, Blue Eyes. I have to make a trip into Lexington this morning, but I'll return by midafternoon. Enjoy your day, and get ready to shine again this evening. You will be a lovely Christmas gift to my friends and family. Always, Roderick."

And that was Roderick, always thinking of everything. Shaking her head, Caroline tucked the note into her pocket. He had entertained them all day yesterday and yet he still felt guilty for taking a business trip.

Caroline had not told Roderick or Gretchen that she was including Bella on the program. Not certain about Bella's secret-keeping ability, she had not even told her. Caroline's plan was to simply call Bella to the piano at the appropriate time in the program. She couldn't wait to see how the guests would respond.

Sarah and George arrived midmorning and kept them busy through lunch. Caroline and Gretchen filled Sarah in on the divorce, Ernesto's incarceration, and the impending adoption while George and Bella watched a Christmas movie.

When they went to check on the movie watchers, Sarah nudged Caroline's arm and smiled. "Look at them. You know that brainy professor over there is no child magnet. But they look like two peas in a pod."

They returned to the kitchen, and Sarah inquired about Gretchen's decision to accept or reject Duke's offer. Gretchen explained no decision could be made until the adoption was legal, and she was waiting until Caroline made her own decision about accepting a position at the University of Georgia.

Caroline informed Sarah about Gretchen's obvious omission of Karina's holding the adoption plans hostage until Gretchen wired thirty thousand dollars. They discussed Bella's opportunities at Duke as opposed to Georgia and the impact Gretchen's decision would have on Caroline's life. They agreed it was best to get through the holidays and then talk about decision-making.

Everyone rested after lunch, even Bella. Caroline set her clock for two just in case she fell asleep. After a nap, she joined Lilah in the kitchen for a cup of tea before she ran through an abbreviated version of her evening's program.

She was in the middle of her carol medley with Bella and Gretchen as her only audience when Roderick entered the front door. "Ho, ho, ho, and Merry Christmas." He stood aside, and coming from behind him in single file were Caroline's mother, carrying something wrapped in tin foil, and her dad, followed by Sam and Angel.

"Am I to believe my eyes or did Lilah spike my tea?" She rose from the piano and rushed to the door to embrace her parents and Sam and Angel.

"You weren't gone on business!" Caroline nudged Roderick, but he shrugged and grinned like he'd opened the best Christmas present ever.

"Never said I was on business."

Roderick truly was a man who thought of everything.

The noise alerted Lilah and others in the house that Roderick had returned with his surprise. They converged in the foyer, meeting, hugging, and laughing, sounding like the gaggle of geese in "The Twelve Days of Christmas."

Martha Carlyle proudly handed over her six-pound fruitcake to Lilah. It came with tales of Angel's brandied peaches and brandy-soaked cheesecloth and with instructions it was not to be unwrapped until Christmas Eve.

When sounds of happy folks quieted, Roderick explained his surprise. "Acer and I flew to Moss Point and Ferngrove this morning to pick up this precious cargo. Sam and Angel will be with us for Christmas, but I'm sorry, Caroline, I couldn't persuade your parents to stay. Acer will fly them back home after the recital this evening. Seems your mother has some Christmas chores to attend to in the morning."

Recital guests were to arrive at six thirty and the recital would start at seven thirty. Without one minute alone with Roderick to thank him for the wonderful surprise, she withdrew from the group at five to get ready for the evening. She ran the oversized tub nearly full of water for a relaxing soak. The Christmas music playing throughout the house could not compare with the music resonating in her mind. She felt like the Cinderella in Roderick's pumpkin carriage music box he gave her at Thanksgiving. She could only hope the clock would never strike twelve.

Her mother and dad came in later to change clothes and freshen up. Martha slipped into the bathroom while Caroline was seated at the vanity finishing her makeup and hair. She put down the hair spray and turned to her mother. Caroline's long dark hair was piled loosely on top of her head and fell elegantly in unruly curls.

"So, what do you think?"

"I think you must be about the luckiest girl in Georgia, and I think Roderick Adair is quite smitten with you. That's what I think."

"I meant about my hair."

"It's lovely as usual, but if you tell me you're wearing a navy-blue suit, I'll disown you. Your turn, what do you think?" Martha unzipped her own garment bag to reveal a deep burgundy jacket and long skirt.

"I think you won't disown me. Look on the door behind your bag." She pointed to a deep blue velvet gown with spaghetti straps and a beaded bodice.

"That's lovely, too, but we seem to have trouble staying on point. I meant, what do you think about Roderick? Are you as smitten as he is?"

Caroline picked out her silver sandals and reached for the gown. "I don't know that he's so smitten. I just know that what I feel is growing more frightening. His life is so different from mine." She stretched her arms out and slowly turned. "Just look around. I could put my entire apartment in this suite."

"You just remember this. Roderick Adair could have chosen anyone to be in this room tonight, but you're the one who's here. So,

I don't want to hear any more talk about being afraid."

"But I am afraid. Anything could happen, and this could disappear as quickly as it materialized."

"Yes, anything could happen." She paused. "But you mean like it happened to David?" Martha looked at her daughter's face. "Tell me. If you had known what was going to happen to David, would you have shielded yourself from loving him?" She paused again. "The answer to that question will tell you whether or not you should keep yourself walled in where it's safe."

Caroline slipped on her dress and backed up to her mother for zipping. When zipped, she turned around and said, "What would I ever do without you, Mother?" She kissed her mother's cheek.

"Now go and play pretty. Wait, you forgot your pearls."

"Thanks, and I love you." Caroline fastened the pearls and walked through the bathroom door into the bedroom where her father sat next to the fireplace. She gave her father a hug and walked into the loggia.

The ringing phone echoed through the loggia as Roderick checked the lighting for the piano. He heard Lilah's excited "hallelujah" all the way from the kitchen. They met in the hallway. "From the sound of your voice and the look on your face, may I assume you just won the lottery?"

"Nope. Next best thing. Liz just called, and she's not feeling very well and sends her apologies for missing the party."

"Well, that's too bad. It's going to be the loveliest event of the season."

"Guess she won't get to paint that red dress on herself after all." Lilah winked and returned to the kitchen.

Roderick knew Liz was accustomed to owning a room when she entered it. He surmised she had no interest in standing in Caroline's shadow this evening.

Roderick returned to the loggia and was lighting candles at the piano when she appeared. He had missed her July entrance down the stairs in that pink cloud of a dress, but he was determined to be the only one in the audience for her entrance tonight. She was stunning. The indigo velvet was somewhere between the color of her eyes and the early evening blue sky. Long wispy curls brushed bare shoulders, which he had never seen. The pearls encircling her neck were almost the color of her soft flesh. If he'd known she was wearing blue, he would have searched the safe for his mother's sapphires. But not even the sapphires could have added to Caroline's simple beauty.

Before he could begin to tell her how lovely she looked, she thanked him for bringing her parents and Sam and Angel to Rockwater. He tried to listen, but he longed to kiss her gently in the soft curve of her neck as she spoke. And then he lost the opportunity. As though their conversation had summoned everyone, doors around the gallery began to open and close. George, Sarah, Gretchen, and Bella descended the stairs. Sam, cane in hand, escorted Angel from their suite, and Caroline's parents joined the Meadows in the hallway. He was happy that Rockwater was filled with guests, people who were important to Caroline. But he longed for a quiet moment with her.

Sounds of Christmas created festive background sounds for the guests as they arrived, filled their plates, and toasted the season. Roderick and Sarah made certain everyone was introduced. The only time Roderick left Caroline's side was when she was deep in conversation with Mrs. Carson, a patron of the arts, who had expressed interest in Caroline's idea of starting a Guatemalan children's choir. She was following up to see if Caroline had made any progress since their meeting back in July.

Caroline agreed with Sarah that Bella should be kept out of the crowd until the recital started. So Bella was with Gretchen in the library.

On the grandfather clock's chiming of the seven-thirty hour, Lilah and Sarah began to corral the guests into the seating area in the loggia where Roderick stood at the piano next to Caroline. He held her hand tightly as he formally introduced Gretchen and Bella, the Meadows, and Caroline's parents. After introducing Caroline, he kissed her cheek, released her hand, and took his seat on the front row next to Bella.

The moment between when Caroline sat down and when her fingers stroked the keys was timeless and electrically charged with memories of her summer recital in this very room. The thunderstorm. The surprise finale and her performance of "David's Song." For months, she had not given herself permission to dream about another evening in this room, and yet here she was, one more magical evening in Roderick's presence.

After a rousing fanfare of sounds of Christmas bells and "Joy to the World," Caroline played familiar holiday tunes she had arranged, leading the audience to sing along at times. Midway through the program, she stood and asked Bella to come to the piano. The puzzled looks on Gretchen's and Roderick's faces revealed their surprise. Caroline extended her hand to Bella, who was seated just feet away on the front row.

Bella, in a winter white sweater with seed pearls and a white velvet skirt, took her seat on the piano stool. Caroline pulled her long, silvery blonde hair away from her face and over her shoulder to reveal her cameo-like silhouette to the audience. She whispered into Bella's ear, "Hark! How the bells, sweet silver bells . . ." That's all it took, and Bella's fingers danced over the keys in Caroline's arrangement of "Carol of the Bells." Caroline slipped away from the piano and took Bella's seat next to Roderick. She held Gretchen's hand as Bella played.

Having no knowledge Bella was a savant, Roderick's guests were ecstatic to hear the child play so proficiently and rewarded her with applause. Bella stood at the piano, smiled, and clapped with them.

Caroline returned to the piano for the rest of her program, and she invited Bella back to accompany her. Bella played while Caroline stood in the curve of the piano and sang "Have Yourself a Merry Little Christmas" just as they had done weeks ago in Caroline's studio. Originally Caroline had planned to play it until she realized Bella had heard her and could play it as well. Applause once again resounded through the halls of Rockwater, all calling for an encore.

Caroline slipped to the piano once again and sang softly into Bella's ear, "O holy night, the stars were brightly shining." Caroline smiled and began to play while Bella sang. At the chorus, Caroline joined her in singing. The two soprano voices, clear as bells and in harmony, sang, "Fall on your knees! O hear the angels' voices. O night divine, O night when Christ was born." The crowd was on its feet again by the last "O night divine."

Halls and hearts were filled with Christmas music, joyous Christmas music, transporting people to the place where happy Christmas memories are stored, but all agreed they'd never heard the music of the season as they heard it tonight.

Even though her parents had to leave right after the recital, Caroline was so grateful to share this evening with her parents and with Sam and Angel. It was a night more beautiful than she had imagined, playing and singing the music of Christmas against the backdrop of a Kentucky December night sky.

CHAPTER TWENTY-EIGHT: CHRISTMAS PRESENTS AND ONE EMPTY BUT FULL BOX

"Right on cue. Just like I ordered." Roderick opened the plantation shutters in the library. "It's snowing, everybody. Come take a look."

They joined him, crowding around the windows as excited as school-weary children on a snow day. Caroline hugged Bella. "Look, Bella. Snow. You've never seen snow." She took her hand. "Let's go. Put on your jeans and your warmest clothes. We must go see."

Roderick inquired, "Now? You're going out there now? You don't want to wait until it accumulates?"

"Do I look like I want to wait?" Caroline was halfway out the door. Gretchen followed to help Bella with her coat.

"Okay, the lady speaks and the gentleman hears. Let's go." Roderick grabbed his heavy jacket.

Gretchen and the others declined and

stayed by the fire while Roderick, Caroline, and Bella caught snowflakes only to see them melt shortly after they were touched. The wonder of snow flurries put a sparkle in Bella's green eyes, and the chill put a rosiness in her cheeks. Even though it was only three o'clock, the sky was a thick, bluish-gray and getting darker.

Later, Roderick announced, "Lilah has prepared an early Christmas Eve dinner of fruit salad, French onion soup, and baked ham sandwiches on croissants, the same meal our family used to share every Christmas Eve. She's joining her own family celebration. After our dinner, we're off to church."

When he could take his eyes off Caroline, he watched Bella. She could hardly eat for staring out the window at dancing snowflakes in the courtyard.

All dressed warmly after dinner, loaded into two cars, and drove down the road to Christ's Church for the seven o'clock candlelight service. The service was simple and elegant as Scriptures were read, songs were sung, and candles were lit to tell the Christmas story. The purest sounds of his mother's soprano voice echoed in his memories, shrouding him for a few moments until he realized it was Caroline's voice he was hearing. Without her presence, the sadness would have overtaken him. Neither Roderick nor Sarah had been here on Christmas Eve since her death. It had been too painful for his father to attend.

Driving home over the icy roads after the service, Roderick missed the clear skies dotted with stars and a full moon. But thick, gray clouds piling on top of each other assured him there'd be a mantle of white covering Kentucky bluegrass on Christmas morning, just like he had imagined and just like he'd promised Caroline.

They shed their warm jackets, scarves, and gloves and settled in the library. Sarah, Gretchen, and Caroline dashed to make coffee and hot chocolate. When beverages were ready, Caroline called everyone to the kitchen for her family tradition of the cutting of the fruitcake. They formed a circle around the island in the kitchen. Sarah handed them each a Christmas mug filled with their choice beverage.

Caroline removed the layers of tin foil and finally reached the cheesecloth. She invited everyone to enjoy the aroma of Angel's homemade brandy saturating the cheesecloth and fruitcake. "Now let me tell you about this cake's history. Every Thanksgiving, as soon as lunch is over, my dad and brothers all watch the ballgames. And all the females spend the afternoon in Mother Martha's kitchen, cutting up candied fruit and chopping pecans. Early on Friday morning, my mother mixes the spicy batter, and we add the fruit and nuts. I'm here to tell you, there isn't a wooden spoon in all of Ferngrove that will stand up to that stiff, sticky, fruit-filled cake batter. We have to work the batter with our hands and feet."

An impish grin spread across her face.

"If Mother Martha were here, I'd ask her to verify this." Sam stepped forward. "Since she's not here and I'm the judge, I'd like to swear you in before you finish this testimony."

Everyone laughed. "Okay, okay, so I'm getting a little carried away. We kept our shoes on, but we mixed this batter with our hands and pushed, shoved, and packed it into the cake pans and then baked them in a slow oven for three hours."

"That's better. Somehow I couldn't see that lovely mother of yours with her shoes off and her toes in cake batter." Sam laughed again.

Caroline nodded at him. "And when the cakes were cool, Mother soaked layers of cheesecloth in Angel's fine brandy and wrapped the cakes. Oh, and she might have stubbed her shoeless toe and spilled some brandy on the cakes before she covered them in foil."

Roderick said, "And then? Come on, everybody." He encouraged them with his waving arm. They all joined in. "And then?"

"And then she tucked them away in the darkest corner of her cabinet."

Roderick led them again. "And then?"

"And then on Christmas Eve, Mother Martha gets on her knees on the kitchen floor and drags out the Christmas fruit-cakes."

"And then?"

"And then, she does exactly what I'm doing. She slowly unwraps each layer of foil and brandy-soaked cloth, and then she cuts one slice." She pressed the knife firmly through the dense cake. "And then she chooses the one family member who gets the very first slice. She's not here, so I get to choose." She looked each person in the face one at a time. "And this year, I choose Roderick."

Everyone clapped, and Roderick stepped forward.

She broke one bite off the slice of fruitcake and fed it to him. He savored the morsel, but not as much as he savored Caroline's nearness in this moment and the taste of her delicate fingertips.

"Best fruitcake ever! Let's all have some." He kissed Caroline on the cheek and took the knife from her. He sliced. She plated and encouraged everyone to gather back in the library around the fire.

A while later when they were all gathered, Roderick slid the antique porcelain manger scene from underneath the tree and placed it on the hearth in front of the glowing embers, pulled a Bible off the shelf, and asked Sam, "Sam, I know we've already been to church this evening, but would you honor us with a reading of the Christmas story?"

Sam took the Bible and turned to the second chapter of Luke. "It would be my honor to read this wonderful story to you." Sam began reading, not in the voice he used on the judge's bench, not even in the King James English voice he used when he prayed, but in the voice of a loving grandfather.

As Sam read with the carols playing in the background, Roderick looked out the window. It was still snowing. Then he surveyed the room, brushed with the warm colors of the fire and lamplight and smelling of pine and cinnamon. Sam sat in the wingchair next to the fireplace with Angel facing him in the matching chair.

Next to Angel was Gretchen in the rocking chair with Bella on the floor in front of her, her right arm laid across Gretchen's lap. Rhythmically, Gretchen stroked Bella's hair as they rocked in sync. Holding her coffee mug in both hands, Sarah curled her legs up under her and cuddled next to George on the sofa.

Caroline was seated in his mother's chair at her writing desk near the Christmas tree. He stood behind her and rested his hand on the back of her chair, watching the tree lights dance in her hair. His was the best view in the room, the best vantage point to see faces, faces that had been washed in tears this year.

Roderick thought of George and Sarah's move to North Carolina and of their longing for a child. He remembered the scare of Angel's heart attack and the severe beating Gretchen and Bella had taken only weeks ago. And then came Caroline, the one who brought a smile back to him, the one who returned the music and life back to this house, and the one he thought of in the middle of doing business. This night was perfect. They were here and not one face showed the crevices of pain, only the presence of serenity. He could only hope that everyone was experiencing what he was feeling — the purest of joy and gratitude.

Sam finished the reading, and as he closed the Book, Caroline led them in joining the music resonating through the house. "Sleep in heavenly peace. Sleep in heavenly peace."

"A Norman Rockwell Christmas, hey, little brother?" Sarah adjusted the tie belt on her Christmas robe before plugging in the coffee and lining up the Christmas mugs.

"If Rockwell Christmases are perfect, then yes, it is." He balanced the breakfast casserole on his way to the oven. Before retiring for the evening last night, all had agreed on a seven thirty breakfast followed by checking out the gifts underneath the Christmas tree.

"Merry Christmas, you two." Caroline entered the kitchen in her red Christmas robe. She hugged Sarah and then Roderick, looking into his eyes longer than usual.

He looked at his watch. Six forty-five. "Well, you're up early," Roderick said. "Breakfast isn't for another forty-five minutes."

"Couldn't wait. I heard Santa and his reindeer early this morning, around four, I think. I guess he was delivering monogrammed Christmas robes. Looks like you both got one too."

"Oh, he was trying to be quiet. Sorry he woke you." Roderick winked at her.

"I suppose I'm not the only one excited about Christmas. Okay, give me an assignment."

Sarah peeked under the foil to see the scones. "Get out the jelly and jam. The Christmas bowls are over there."

The three worked for the next half hour before they were joined in the kitchen by everyone dressed in red monogrammed Christmas robes. Cards had instructed them to wear the robes to breakfast, all compliments of George and Sarah disguised as St. Nick.

All around the table, eight people in matching scarlet robes passed butter, dabbed jam from the corners of their mouths, sipped hot coffee, and chattered about last evening and the gift-giving after breakfast. Roderick could hear in their voices more excitement about the gifts they had chosen to give than the ones they hoped to receive. "Perhaps it is a Rockwell Christmas," Roderick whispered to Sarah.

Gretchen remembered Christmases around her mother's table when her grandmammá and grandpappá were alive, Grandmammá's stollen and wassail, and the music in the cathedral. They were lovely memories. But the good things were nearly swallowed by the last thirty Christmases and thoughts of what had been stolen in a dark alley. Christmas has been silent for so long, with nothing to replace Gretchen's sad memories with happier ones.

And though she was angry with him for what he'd stolen from Bella, sadness pulled at Gretchen that Ernesto would never know the warmth of family and friends at Christmas. *What is his Christmas Day like in prison? And Karina, where is she? Is she celebrating?* She pushed those thoughts from her mind, determined not to let the questions rob her of the joy of this Christmas.

She followed the others as they left the breakfast table, went to the library, and took their seats from last night.

Roderick stood in front of the fire, a grin playing on his lips as he pronounced, "It is my understanding that the one who was chosen to eat the first bite of Mother Martha's fruitcake also has the honor of being Santa. Is that right?"

Everyone riotously agreed. Bella clapped and began to sing, "Here comes Santa Claus. Here comes Santa Claus." They joined her while Roderick made his way to the Christmas tree.

"I don't remember all these gifts. Just tell me, did it look like this last night?" He pointed to the area underneath the tree.

Everyone said, "Noooo."

"See, there truly is a Santa Claus," Sam said.

There was a sound of a singing canary. Everyone looked at Bella. Gretchen caressed Bella and smiled, remembering their 3 a.m. visit down the stairs and into the library to put their presents underneath the tree. Others must have done the same thing.

Beautifully wrapped presents, big ones, little ones, boxes with velvet bows, and organza gift bags were passed around the room. Soon the floor was knee deep in paper and empty boxes.

Carefully chosen for Roderick because he was a Kentucky gentleman, Sam and Angel gave him a first edition copy of Drape's *The Life of Daniel Boone.*

Even though Gretchen had seen an earlier version of the painting, she was stunned along with everyone else when Caroline opened the large, flat box containing Angel's portrait of her dressed in her pink gown, playing the piano at Rockwater. Then their holy hush was followed by a gasp at its beauty. Caroline cried. "But I thought you stopped painting."

Angel replied, "I had until I saw you in that pink dress. So, Roderick assisted me with some photos, and here you are."

"How can I thank you? This is such a treasure, but you two will just have to wait until you get home for your gifts. On the sly, I put them under your tree before I left because I had no idea you'd be here with me."

Next came the boxes Gretchen and Bella brought. Gretchen's face brightened as her new friends opened them. Bella had made one of her mosaic and plaster pieces for each one of them: a small replica of Twin Oaks for Sam and Angel, a whale for Roderick, and a Mary Poppins umbrella for Sarah and George.

Gretchen held the box for Caroline. "This is for you, my precious friend. There would be no Christmas like this for any of us if you were not a part of our lives. Bella and I love you dearly." She handed the box to Caroline.

Caroline opened it carefully. "A teapot." She examined it more closely. "A teapot with pansies, like the one I dropped when I first heard Bella play." Her eyes welled with tears.

"Yes, my precious one. Pansies, the symbol

of our friendship that will forever be."

There were boxes and bags with movies and recordings and new clothes for Bella. Then Roderick reached from behind the tree and pulled out something large covered in a dark green cloth. "This is for you, Bella. I'm not certain how long he'll keep quiet."

Bella slowly pulled the green cloth from what appeared to be a large box. It was a white wicker cage housing a bright yellow canary that began to sing immediately as if joining the festivities.

"Look, Bella, a singing canary. Now you have someone to sing with you all the time." Gretchen's face said everything that needed to be said to Roderick, and Bella's delight was audible as she joined the canary's song.

"I'll teach you how to take care of the canary. It's a boy, so you'll have to name him. You must be careful when you let him out of the cage because his wings have not been clipped. The vet told me he'll be very social and sing off and on all day, but he won't sing when you put the cover over the cage," Roderick said as he knelt next to Bella.

Gretchen saw Bella's joy. "We'll never put the cover on or clip his wings. Canaries are created to fly and sing, just like Bella."

"That's why I gave her the canary." Then

Roderick handed a small box to Caroline. "And look, a little something for our other songbird."

Caroline pulled the velvet ribbon and lifted the lid. Two silver combs adorned with delicate flowers made from pearls and tiny rubies, sapphires, emeralds, and diamonds lay on the dark velvet lining of the box. "They're so beautiful. Where on earth did you find them?"

"Find them? I couldn't give you something I could find. Then someone else might find ones just like them. I designed them and had them made when I was in Hong Kong. But I had to pray they'd get here in time for Christmas."

She removed one comb and brushed back the hair from her temple and inserted it into the sable curls.

"Just like I knew it would be. Beautiful in your hair," he said.

"Thank you so much, but I . . ." She paused. She reached into the pocket of her robe and pulled out a square envelope. "This is for you."

Roderick tore the flap from the envelope. Inside were a CD and a parchment note handwritten in calligraphy.

You are invited as the honored guest for
the debut performance of
Rockwater Suite.
A moment in time where life, spirit, and
music flow freely.
Composed and performed by
Caroline Carlyle, pianist
Hodgson Hall on the University of
Georgia Campus
February 13, 2009, at 8:00 p.m.

"You finished? You finished the suite?" He
looked at the CD.

"I did, that is, with Bella's help. I told you
to trust me, that I'd finish it someday."

"I can't wait to hear it."

"This is a recording I made in the university studios with a synthesizer, but there'll
be a full symphony orchestra when I play in
February. So, I guess I designed something
for you too." They hugged each other —
she clutching the comb left in its box, and
he clutching the CD.

Gretchen sighed in utter satisfaction. The
blush on Caroline's cheeks and the look in
Roderick's eye were the picture of love.
These two were deeply in love, and everyone knew it but them. If only they knew
what a gift from God that kind of love is,
they'd not waste another minute being so

cautious. She watched Sam and Angel beaming over the scene before he reached into his pocket and stood up.

"Well, this one was too big for even Roderick's plane, so we just brought a drawing of it." He handed Gretchen an envelope.

"Oh my, something for me?" It had been a very long time since anyone handed her a gift, whether in a box or an envelope. She opened it and savored it just for a moment before she revealed its contents, a penciled sketch of "Gretchen and Bella's Gazebo" in the new park in Moss Point.

"I fear I know not what to say."

Angel raised her arms with her red sleeves flowing. "Just say that Bella will play lots and lots of concerts from your gazebo in the park."

"Oh, she will. I will see to it."

Sam chimed in. "We figured since we destroyed your little parlor in the woods, we would replace it with a gazebo with your name on it. Now everyone will know whose it is."

"Thank you so very much. Look, Bella. Our very own gazebo."

Caroline rose. "Wait, there's one more thing." She slid the box from underneath her chair and took it across the room to Gretchen. "This is my gift to you." She stood in front of Gretchen while Gretchen peeled back the beautiful wrapping and opened the box.

Underneath layer upon layer of tissue paper was a silver framed mirror. Gretchen lifted it from the box, her chin quivering. "A hand mirror."

Caroline corrected her. "No. It's not *a* hand mirror. It's *your* hand mirror. I had it restored."

"I truly have no words." She remembered her laments to Caroline about using her hand mirror, the last genteel thing in her life, to protect Bella and herself from Ernesto.

"You don't need to say anything. I know how much that mirror meant to you, and I remember what you said when you handed me my teapot. Bella had made something beautiful of its shards, and you told me that even broken teapots could be restored and made useful again. I want you to have your mirror to remind you of your roots and to look into to see how truly beautiful you are." She knelt next to Bella and embraced a sobbing Gretchen.

The silence was interrupted only when the canary began to sing. Gretchen laughed, wiping the tears from her cheeks. How could anyone be sad when a lovely bird sang its beautiful song?

Sam stood up again and pulled a large envelope from behind his chair and a pen from the pocket of the white dress shirt he wore underneath his Christmas robe. "If there are no other gifts to be given, here's the last one, and I think it'll make us all happy."

He walked to where Gretchen sat and handed her the pen. "When Tom Ellison received this and tried to deliver it to you, he called me. I promised him I would hand deliver it. So here it is." He opened the envelope and removed a document and turned to page four. "Gretchen, if you'd be ever so kind as to sign your name right here on this line, Bella is now and forever officially your child."

Gretchen's tear-filled eyes could hardly focus on the blank line and the line next to it with the signature of Karina Anna Silva. Gretchen trailed her fingers across her daughter's name, wishing Karina were here and not just her signature. Gretchen's hand was almost too shaky to hold the pen, but she gratefully signed. Her prayers had been answered. The adoption would be final, and she could move forward with her plans.

Sam announced, "And the only thing to say after all this is 'Merry Christmas.'" The room reverberated with "Merry Christmases" and "Thank yous" and hugs.

Overtaken with so much gratitude, Gretchen slipped from the room, taking with her the lavender-scented envelope that had been paper-clipped to the document. Before she could open the letter, Sam slipped to her side in the loggia. "Gretchen, I didn't want to bring this up in front of the group, but I wanted you to know the sheriff called late last night to tell me you won't be getting any more threatening phone calls. The culprits are in custody, and you don't have anything to worry about."

"You mean it is all solved?"

"Not quite. Ernesto's business partners are in jail, and Caleb has the evidence he needs to put them away for a long time." He pointed to the papers in Gretchen's hand. "Now with the adoption complete, you'll be able to take your trip to Austria. And by the time you get back, the trial will be over, and all of this will just seem like a bad dream."

"Oh, thank you, Sam. Thank you so very much."

He kissed her forehead gently. "I'd best get back to the party and let you read your letter."

She stood in the loggia as the snow continued to fall and opened the sealed envelope and read these words:

Dear Mammá,

Forgive me. Forgive me for running away years ago, and please forgive me for listening to a stranger who wanted me to take Bella from you. Here are the adoption papers and a money order for the $30,000, which I am returning to you. I could no more keep that money than I could keep Bella from you after everything you have done for her. Forgive me, Mammá. I didn't understand. I'm glad I came home, and you were right. There is still inside me a little girl with dreams, and I'm going to do it. I'm enrolling in college in January. I can sing, and I want to be a music teacher. I'll be using the money you gave me for my education. Be patient with me. And I don't know how, because there are some things I still must straighten out in my own life, but I want to be a part of your life and Bella's. I'm finding my way home again, Mammá.

With love from your first daughter,
Karina

Gretchen's tears fell like the silent snow.

Not only would the adoption be complete, but somehow her daughter had reached way down deep inside herself and taken hold of some goodness and had done the right thing. This truly was the most splendid Christmas, making up for all the sad ones. Lives had been restored, and the future held such promise. She heard the canary singing in the library — or was it Bella?

Caroline stood at the loggia window waving at Bella and Gretchen and the Meadows in the sleigh, all huddled together like baby birds. Roderick covered them with extra blankets and took the driver's seat. He was taking them on a horse-drawn sleigh ride around the property. When they were out of sight, she went to the library and curled up on the sofa with a Christmas book. The pages and illustrations were no more pictur-esque than the images lingering in her mind from the recital, Christmas Eve, and the gathering around the tree this morning. She was grateful for the silence and the solitude and a few moments to herself.

In a little while, she saw Sarah and George walking down the hallway. "Hey, you two. Get your warmest gear together. We're next for the sleigh ride."

Sarah stopped, and George kept walking.

"Not sure we're going on the ride. We need to get on over to Lexington and check on the Manor House. Everything should be fine, but we'd like to get home before too late."

"When you return next week, perhaps. Roderick may be too cold to go another round when he gets back anyway." Caroline got up from her seat, slipped on her loafers, and joined Sarah in the hall.

"George is getting our things to the car." She paused. "Listen, Caroline. It's been an incredible few days. I can tell you it's been too many years since this house has heard this much laughter and music. Thanks for coming, but there's one other thing." She paused and turned her head as though listening to something. "Sounds like they're back. It'll wait."

The noise was coming closer. The sleigh riders were home. As the Meadows were pulling off their coats and gloves, Sam said, "We're headed for a nice warm shower. That's all that'll thaw us out and get these old joints moving again, but it was worth it."

Angel added, "I've heard of 'Moon Over Miami,' but Caroline, you need to write a song about the 'Christmas Moon Over Kentucky.' I can hear it now."

Gretchen and Bella were close behind. Bella was singing and clapping her hands. "I guess you can tell from Bella we had a great time."

Caroline responded, "Sounds like it, but where's your driver?"

Gretchen said, "In the kitchen getting something warm to drink."

George came back in, and they said their goodbyes to the Meadows and Gretchen and Bella, who were headed to warm showers and soaking tubs.

"Come on Bella, would you like to go first? I will run the water, and you can put in the bubbles." Gretchen walked from their bedroom suite into the spacious bathroom. "You can have a nice, warm soak, and then we will have dinner and another lovely evening in the library." Gretchen knelt at the tub and turned on the hot water.

"Mammá, Bel Canto is lonely. Bel Canto will not sing if he's lonely."

Gretchen turned to see her holding the wicker cage where the yellow canary was perched. Bella had shocked them all earlier this morning by naming the bird Bel Canto. At first, they were all puzzled by where she could have come up with such a name, then Gretchen remembered Caroline had told

Bella months ago that her name sounded like an Italian musical term, *bel canto,* and it meant beautiful singing, just like Bella's.

Bella's ability to remember and associate was encouraging and made the decision about her education more eminent.

"Mammá, Bel Canto is lonely. He is not singing. Bel Canto is lonely."

"Bring him here." She took the cage from Bella and set it on the vanity in front of the mirrored wall. "Oh look, Bella, Bel Canto will see himself, and he will think he has a new friend."

Bella leaned and looked closely at herself in the mirror. "I see Bella. I have a new friend."

Gretchen smiled. "Yes, you do, my sweet. Always remember to be your own very best friend." She helped Bella with her clothes and her hair, and when Bella was submerged in bubbles and singing, Gretchen almost waltzed into the bedroom and over to the French doors.

The day had been so full she'd had no time to absorb it. She stood at the French doors looking across the moonlit hills. *Ah, today makes up for all the days I had no smile. My Karina is finding her way home, and my precious friend Caroline is finding her way back to her own heart. And my Bella, sitting in soft bubbles up to her neck, singing a song we have sung together hundreds of times. Before, the words only voiced a wish. Now, they are real, really real.*

Gretchen went to the dresser and picked up the restored silver-framed mirror of her youth. Looking at herself, she smiled as she listened to Bel Canto's trills harmonizing with Bella's pure, bell-like voice . . .

"Not a tear, not a fear, only joy in my
      song.
Like the lark in the breeze who sings for
      the dawn.
The cage now opened, I can sing with
      glee,
And my song is from a heart that's free."

Caroline called to Sarah, "You'd better come and say goodbye to your brother. We're in the kitchen."

"Be there shortly."

Roderick and Caroline were stirring hot chocolate in Christmas mugs when Sarah walked into the kitchen alone with a gold foil-wrapped box in one hand and Caroline's jacket, scarf, and gloves in the other. It was a painstakingly wrapped box, topped with a huge silver bow. To see its contents, the recipient only needed to lift the lid and the wrapping was not destroyed. She put it in the middle of the breakfast table.

"What, more presents, sis? I can assure you my red robe was enough," Roderick teased.

"I saved the best for last — my gift to the both of you." She motioned for the two of them to join her. "Here, Caroline, you sit here. And Rod, you sit over there." She seated them at opposite ends of the table, and she stood in between.

"Little brother, you know I'm crazy about you even when you're making me crazy." She turned then to Caroline. "And Caroline, over these last few months, I have become very fond of you, sort of like the sister I always wanted."

Caroline's eyes followed the gift box as Sarah pushed it into the middle of the table. "Now what I am about to do is against all ethical standards and practices of my profession, but since neither of you is my client, I have weighed the options and decided to proceed."

Caroline felt a fluttering in her stomach the way she did just before a recital. She watched the more serious lines drawn in Sarah's face.

"Since your visit here in July, Caroline, nothing has been quite the same. Things

566

changed in a good way. Now I've spent time with each of you over the last few weeks, and I've spoken with you about your feelings for each other."

George, smiling as if he knew a secret, entered the room and stood at his wife's side. Sarah continued. "Each of you has divulged information to me that I've only told George. I keep nothing from him." Caroline saw how Sarah looked up at George with a look known only by lovers and soul mates.

"This box symbolizes all the things you've told me about your hopes, your fears, and your feelings for each other. I can tell you they are all good and positive things upon which to build a lasting relationship. So, here sits this beautiful box, with even more beautiful and treasured contents inside, but neither of you will lift the lid."

Sarah leaned across the table and removed the top of the box. "There. My Christmas present to you. I have opened the box. It only looks empty, but it's full. I've lifted the lid to the conversations you need to have. No more wasting time. Now it's up to the two of you to speak the truth to each other, the truth you've spoken to me." She put her arm around George and they walked out the kitchen door. She turned before closing the door and said, "Merry perfect Christmas, Rod and Caroline."

They sat stunned at the table as Sarah left. Caroline, though reluctant, spoke first. "Roderick . . ."

"Wait, I have an idea. Sarah brought in your jacket and scarf. What do you say we take a sleigh ride down to the stream and talk in the moonlight?"

"Great idea." They put on their jackets and headed out toward the back entrance. As Roderick opened the door, the crisp, winter air greeted them like a breathy kiss on the cheek. An indigo sky hovered over a blanket of unblemished snow, and the moon and stars lit up the rolling hills. He pulled Caroline to his side as they paused in the doorway.

She sensed his nearness and his arm around her. He had been almost this near the summer evening after her first performance at Rockwater when he had asked for permission to kiss her. But her yearning and caution churned deep inside then, and her caution had risen to the top. She said he could kiss her when he felt he didn't need to ask.

She lingered in the threshold and looked across the wide sky to the full moon. "Isn't it just like God to provide such light on a night like tonight?"

Roderick pulled Caroline closer to him and turned to face her. As one arm went around her waist, he looked up and pointed toward the berries and glossy foliage hanging overhead. "Do you think He provided the mistletoe as well?"

Quite breathless from his closeness, she whispered, "Perhaps He did." A flutter, almost like a new melody, rose inside her. Now encircled in his arms, Caroline smiled, rose on her tiptoes, and searched his warm brown eyes as her hands caressed his neck as naturally as they caressed the piano.

No more waiting. No more wondering. He didn't ask. He kissed her just the way she had imagined. She longed to hold the hands of time so that this perfect moment on this perfect evening and this perfect kiss would last forever.

ACKNOWLEDGMENTS

As always, I begin by acknowledging you. Without you as a reader, I'd have no reason to write and no place where my stories come to life. If you have read *Return of the Song,* I hope you enjoyed returning to Moss Point and Rockwater and to these lovable characters who are plain and peculiar people. And if this was your first time spent with the characters, I hope you'll read the first book and begin to see the thread of faith woven throughout.

Thank you, Catherine DeVries, Janyre Tromp, and Cheryl Molin for putting the spit shine on this book and for allowing me to write my story.

When Bella appeared in my imagination and I began to see her as a significant character in this series, I sensed it was a priority to depict this musical savant with sensitivity and authenticity. I'll always be grateful to Dr. Darold Treffert, world-renowned expert in this field, for making certain that I did depict Bella accurately. And to Dr. David Shacklett, a dear Christian gentleman, friend, and ophthalmologist, I owe gratitude for always being there when I needed medical information and answers to technical questions.

I'm so grateful for friends and family who encourage me . . . understanding when I'm not available yet quick to ask, "How's the writing coming?" when I come up for air.

There'd never have been a book with my name on it without my Bill. He's my champion, my cheerleader, my teacher, the one who stirs my pot of ideas, and the one who gives me freedom to do what I do. He's such a gift to me.

And there is my heavenly Father, the source of my music and the one who gives freedom to my song. I am humbly grateful.

ABOUT THE AUTHOR

Phyllis Clark Nichols grew up in the deep shade of magnolia trees in Georgia and weaves her Southern culture into character-driven stories that explore profound human questions. She is a classically trained musician and enjoys art, books, nature, cooking, travel, and ordinary people. After retiring as a cable network executive, Phyllis began leading mission teams to orphanages in Guatemala and now serves on three non-profit boards, where she works with others who are equally passionate about bringing hope and light to those who need it most. Phyllis and her husband live in the Texas Hill Country.

The employees of Thorndike Press hope you have enjoyed this Large Print book. All our Thorndike, Wheeler, and Kennebec Large Print titles are designed for easy reading, and all our books are made to last. Other Thorndike Press Large Print books are available at your library, through selected bookstores, or directly from us.

For information about titles, please call:
   (800) 223-1244

or visit our website at:
   gale.com/thorndike

To share your comments, please write:
   Publisher
   Thorndike Press
   10 Water St., Suite 310
   Waterville, ME 04901